The Doughnut Tree

CATHERINE L. KNOWLES

ISBN: 1503135756
ISBN 13: 9781503135758
Library of Congress Control Number: 2014920082
CreateSpace Independent Publishing Platform
North Charleston, South Carolina

DEDICATION

I would like to dedicate *The Doughnut Tree* to Herman Deeley. Mr. Deeley was the last black man hanged in Madison County, Alabama. Reading about his hanging less than a mile from my house started me on my journey to study the history of this area and may have in a small way caused me to write the book. Not much is known about Herman's life, but to me he was the Music Man.

Catherine L. Knowles

TABLE OF CONTENTS

ACKNOWLEDGMENTS

First and foremost I give full credit to my Creator for the success of this novel. Thank you for guiding Dr. Vernon Reynolds, Dr. Ruth Yates, and Lilian Geldmeier in saving my life and allowing me the opportunity to author this work so close to my heart.

Next on my grateful list is Forest, my husband, best friend, and reluctant frontline editing coordinator. When my computer skills let me down, he propped me up, and he is astonishingly more patient than any human I know. His kindness, tireless effort, and nudging pushed this project to the finish line. My newest friend, John Rankin, gave me the gift of confidence. His guidance and enthusiasm during my research in the Madison County Records Center at the Huntsville Main Library encouraged me to do the best I could and to think big—not to mention the fact that he gave me the secret knowledge that our history is found in the old court records and newspapers. Ancel and Jeanie Hodges persuaded me to write the story down on paper...yes, paper! Dixie Robbins, Jamie Hinds, Randy and Carolyn Keefer had the courage to read my first draft. The Studio's Dawn Chenault and Jenny Freeman and their Pilates Reformer classes have kept me healthy and fit while I've been able to bounce ideas off the other clients. Bob Baudendistel shared his historical research on Taylorsville. Last, but just as important, I love my dear friends Carolyn, Dixie, Gail, Jamie, Lynn, Shelly, and Tom for believing in me during my journey. Oh, and then there's Sugar...eighty pounds of unconditional love under my feet that helps me breathe.

INTRODUCTION

Welcome to Alabama's colorful, perhaps as lawless as Louisiana's, early 1900s era. Percy Taylor, prominent northern Alabama former attorney and judge, stepped outside for a break from the wedding reception. He had always loved the sound of waves breaking on the sandy beach and the smell of the Gulf of Mexico. The full moon revealed the unusually wide, white beach at low tide. The receding waves left behind a scattering of seashells, starfish, jellyfish, and seaweed. His lovely bride was upstairs changing before the wedding guests would send them off on their honeymoon. Events in his life had been anything but "normal"—especially for the South...or were they more unusual than even he realized?

Percy had put wads of folding money into the hands of the headwaiter and the bartending captain. Word about the large gratuity had spread quickly among the staff. It was the grand war-free year of 1920. The big event at the Grand Hotel would be the talk of the area for years. After all, there was drinking of alcohol with blacks in and at a white wedding of a known madam to a filthy-rich bootlegger, with a dog as "best friend" and a homosexual male bridesmaid...all during Prohibition!

Percy took a sip of his Bacardi rum and Coke as he looked up at the summer night sky and reflected on the previous twenty years and the small north Alabama town called Taylorsville.

Section I

1900–1910

The twentieth century in America had begun with great optimism during a time of prosperity and materialism. To an extent never before in human history, a middle class had begun to emerge because of the great successes of capitalism. America was the land of promise to any self-made man with dreams of rags to riches—even blacks—but the path to success was riddled with roadblocks for men and women of color. Discrimination based on both race and sex permeated general society across the nation. Soldiers were home from the Spanish-American War. President William McKinley won a hard-fought, very expensive reelection, only to be assassinated four months later. Theodore Roosevelt was sworn in as his successor. Henry Ford, the Wright brothers, and many others were about to change the world paradigm.

Some would say the South was sleeping and not in step with the rapidly changing events of the era, but that was not so. The great state of Alabama had an image problem, one that persists even to this day. Some aspects of it were accurate, but mostly it was undeserved. With a few more Percy Taylors, who knows what Alabama would have become? Henry Ford almost moved his automobile production to Muscle Shoals, Alabama. Muscle Shoals could well have become the Detroit of the South. Vanderbilt, Carnegie, Rockefeller, and many other movers of the time had eyes on the South. Every state and area of the country had its own little idiosyncrasies, problems, and secrets. Such was the "state of the union" at the turn of the century. Now, welcome to Alabama of the very early 1900s.

ONE

JUDGE PERCY TAYLOR

Percy Taylor's father, Christopher Columbus "C. C." Taylor, was a private during the Civil War. Wounded and captured at Gettysburg, he was sent to Rock Island prison in Illinois. Released in 1865 as part of the war exchange effort, he married a woman in 1872 from the Hobbs family, for which Hobbs Island in the Tennessee River at Taylorsville, Alabama, was named.

Although the river makes a large S curve or "Great Bend," putting Taylorsville on the east side of the river at the foot of Wallace Mountain thirteen miles from downtown Huntsville, many locals call Wallace Mountain Green Mountain and consider Taylorsville on the north bank of the river, forgetting that the river flows directly north at this location. Named in honor of Percy's daddy, Taylorsville was the hub on the Whitesburg and New Hope Trail. It had a train depot, three general stores, a post office, a feed-and-seed store, and the Taylor homes and farm, which included a bed-and-breakfast.

Taylorsville was the end of the line for the railroad...sort of. Yes, the train—a steam locomotive and cars—could turn around at the Y in Taylorsville's depot or travel another mile to the river, where there was a ramp down to the water. When the water was high in those days before the Tennessee Valley Authority built dams along the river, the locomotives could then load the cars onto barges for a twenty-one-mile steamboat ferry ride to Gunter's Landing in Guntersville. At Gunter's Landing, another locomotive would pick the cars up and head to Gadsden, where their cargo would be loaded onto boats for a water route to Mobile, on the Gulf of Mexico.

As one of the busiest depot stops, Taylorsville had a huge amount of passenger travel and freight shipments. The Taylor family had a widely known reputation for being hospitable to travelers. During the journey to and from Gunter's Landing, passengers boarded the paddle-wheeled steamer and enjoyed the scenic beauty of traveling on the water.

Percy Taylor was proud to be a graduate of the University of Alabama at Tuscaloosa. He later attended law school at Vanderbilt University in Nashville, where he met Vernon Reynolds, who in later years became a close friend and business partner. Business, however, would have to wait. Immediately, after receiving his law degree, Percy joined the military to see the world. While in the army, he served during the Spanish-American War directly under former Confederate general Joe Wheeler. The war involved Cuba, Guam, the Philippines, and Puerto Rico, but Percy's troop, part of the Tenth US Cavalry, was in Havana and Santiago, including San Juan Hill.

While serving in Cuba, Percy met Emilio Bacardi, whose family was in the rum business. Emilio had been jailed several times, fighting for Cuba's freedom from Spain. During the attack in the famous charge up San Juan Hill, Percy was hit in the back by friendly fire. While Percy was in the hospital recovering, Emilio visited his American friend often, and the two men, based on a handshake, decided to set up a rum distribution system to the United States. During this time, Emilio was elected by his Cuban friends to be mayor of Santiago de Cuba.

When Percy had recovered sufficiently from his wound, Emilio took him on a tour of his rum distillery before Percy left for home in Alabama. Emilio showed Percy the reason behind the bat logo on the bottle that later became the mark of Bacardi rum: fruit bats hung in the rafters of the distillery. According to Cuban lore and Emilio, the bat represented "good health, good fortune, and family unity." There was a coco palm tree near the door of the facility. According to Emilio, "As long as El Coco has living roots, the distillery will thrive." American soldiers of course welcomed the local availability of rum in Santiago and celebrated a free Cuba in neighborhood taverns with a new drink called Cuba Libre.

After Percy returned in 1900 from the short war in Cuba at age twenty-three, he practiced law in Huntsville for a few years. An open judgeship in Madison County became available, and he was encouraged to run. A war hero to many, known and respected throughout the county, he was elected without opposition. He was honest and fair in his rulings, and he despised crooked politicians who used their positions to hide illegal or immoral activities. This character value would later lead him to resign his judgeship to retain his business relationship with Emilio. The two had set up their distribution system for rum from Cuba. Although it was legal at the time they set it up, Judge Taylor resigned when Alabama went "bone dry" rather than be a hypocrite against his own values.

Percy had one daughter, Shasta, whom he had raised alone. Shasta was educated in Huntsville's finest female finishing school, then at the New Orleans Female School, and finally at the Paris Learning for Women College in Paris, France. She had Percy's personality...always on top of current events, an absolute fanatic about current news in the world and locally. Like her father, she despised crooked politicians.

Percy had business and close personal friends and acquaintances in New York City, Chicago, Washington, DC, New Orleans, and Mobile. He was involved in civic groups such as the Twickenham Men's Club, the Elks Theater Board, and the Rotary Club, and was a lodge member of the Masonic Fraternal Order. He had an ever-changing, sometimes crazy, band of friends, followers, visitors, and entourage. His lifelong best friend and companion was Hugh Freeman. They studied law together by correspondence while at different colleges, and Hugh enlisted to serve in the army alongside Percy.

Although Hugh was a lawyer by trade, he became Percy's personal driver and silent business partner on many ventures. Percy purchased the finest, largest cars and didn't think he needed a driver, but Hugh would say, "Percy, you never know when one of your seizures could come on, and besides...after the 1901 Alabama Constitution, I don't believe I could be a lawyer and always be looking down." Percy just nodded. He didn't know what to say. It would be hard to practice law and swear to uphold a constitution when its very premise disenfranchises you because of your skin color…Hugh was Negro.

Percy's father, C. C., died in 1910. After his father's passing, Percy, depressed from losing his best supporter and strongest counselor, was prone to drinking himself into a stupor under an old cherrybark oak tree, all alone. Lily, a hardworking Negro woman, often made fried doughnuts with a melted sugar glaze to bring as a means of Percy's grief counseling whenever she saw him sitting under the tree. She would challenge Percy to eat all ten deep-fried sugary delights before he had anything to drink, because his stomach would then be buffered from the alcohol, too full and bloated for him to get drunk or even to drink for a while afterward.

Lily became Percy's good friend…his "go-to" person during emotional events in his life. He was always good to her in return. She was one of only a few Negro women to own property in Madison County at the time. Besides the house Percy helped her buy, she had her own Model T Ford, although she was usually too afraid to drive it. Lily started off to go somewhere many times and then returned home to either walk or take the horse and carriage. Her worst problem was Earl King, her husband and frequent physical abuser.

Yes, Lily was Percy's coach in life matters, and "the doughnut lady." The two often met under the tree house built in that huge southern cherrybark oak tree on the riverbank close to the Taylorsville Arena. Percy allowed the folks of Taylorsville to use the arena for community meetings, and the Taylor family used it for picnics. At times, members of the circus used it to practice their show. Shaped like an amphitheater, the naturally depressed bowl with seating on the slopes made for a functional gathering place. While there, Lily would stuff him with doughnuts, even when he wasn't depressed.

Percy's mother, Laura Ann Hobbs (Taylor) died in 1905 at age sixty-three, and so did his wife, Linda Gail, at age twenty-six. Percy had asked Linda Gail Strong for her hand in marriage under the old oak tree. Linda Gail was from Shadow Hollow, near Fayetteville, Tennessee. Her brothers were in the liquor business. The cause of her death remained a mystery.

Percy's younger brother, Chase, attended Auburn University and became an architect with an office on the courthouse square, overlooking the Big Spring in downtown Huntsville. Chase designed buildings locally as well as in many other southern cities.

Percy also had a younger sister, Grace, a rebellious child who eventually became a preacher's wife, although the firecracker side of her sometimes resurfaced. She loved and admired Percy and would do anything, even risk burning in hell, to protect him or other family members. However, for the most part she played the role of a model preacher's wife.

Percy's health suffered throughout the rest of his life from the war wound to his lower spine…the friendly-fire bullet from the battle at San Juan Hill remained embedded in his body. Fear of paralysis prevented him from having the bullet removed. The leaking, poisonous lead caused Percy to have seizures, but with legally available over-the-counter cocaine in those days, he was able to maintain a degree of control.

TWO

THE BEAUTIFUL YOUNG MOLLY TEAL

In 1905, Molly Teal was a striking young girl. Her elegant body was long and lean, and she held her shoulders back naturally to complement her long, slender legs and narrow hips. She was fourteen years younger than Percy Taylor...about his sister's age. He thought his sister had a very smart, beautiful girl as a close friend. Molly loved Percy's sister, Grace. Grace seemed to Molly to be living a perfect life, with fairy-tale parents. She dreamed of having a family like Grace's.

Molly had already lived a life of hell on earth. At eight years old she had been kidnapped by her uncle David Overton. Uncle David had committed his sister and Molly's mother, Annie Teal, to the Cedar Craft Sanatorium near Nashville. His good buddy Judge W. T. Lawler had all the paperwork drawn up, signed and legal. Overton was the police chief in Huntsville. He was abnormally attracted to his eight-year-old niece and didn't want anyone else to have her. Uncle David wanted to keep her to himself. He could not restrain himself as she developed breasts and hips much earlier than other girls her age.

Yes, David Overton was married. He encouraged his wife to drink heavily, always pouring her whisky doubles while he eagerly waited for her to pass out. That was when Molly's nightmares began. Every night he would enter her bedroom, even when the door was locked, and turn on the electrical lights. Uncle David would make sure Molly was wide awake before he began his ritual. He would have the lights on bright, slowly removing his clothing while she just lay there and watched, all sleepy eyed and childlike. Every night started off the same: "Molly, do you want to tell Uncle David what can happen to your mommy if you tell anybody about our secret tonight?"

The young girl would recite, "My mommy will hurt and die if I cry or tell anyone about my uncle David and his secret." By age twelve, she had to repeatedly tell him she loved him while he had sex with her. Whenever she didn't adequately pretend that she had enjoyed herself with Uncle David, he would finish raping her and then slap her hard across the mouth, careful not to leave any marks that would arouse the suspicions of his drunken wife. As Molly continued to mature, she desperately searched for an escape plan, even saying to herself, *Jump on a train, Molly, to anywhere, Molly!*

Three

Run Molly Run

Molly had run away before, but she was now nearly fourteen. She had begged Uncle David's wife, Aunt Loretta, to protect her and make them stop. Loretta would say only, "Young girls should be more appreciative of their families taking them into their home and should never make up lies." Molly knew she had been kidnapped by her uncle. She never kept quiet about the abuse, but it seemed those she told simply joined in rather than helping her. Her aunt and uncle would give their consent and bring various men to her jail of a bedroom.

Although Molly was exceptionally good at arithmetic, especially for a girl in an era that did not encourage women to be good at math, she stopped attending school because she was often badly bruised when she was hit and beaten for not fully complying with her uncle's cohorts. She hated her life as a sex slave and devised a plan. Fighting off the men stopped. She just let them have their way, and after they went to sleep, passed out or otherwise distracted, she would rummage through their trousers for money. When she first started taking the money, she took only small amounts, so it would not be noticed. This practice was soon replaced with the "full amount in the pocket" approach. She figured the worst that could happen was that they would start the beatings again. *So what,* she thought to herself; she had the money safely hidden away.

While no one was home, she would read all of Uncle David's books in his office. She especially liked law books. She plowed through the books on politics, farming, and banking. Then she found a book on travel, and that's when Molly's plans started to ripen. She wanted to see the cities in America: New Orleans, Denver, San Francisco. They all appealed to her.

In a matter of a few months, she managed to lift fifty-six dollars between the six men. She planned her escape for July 10, her fourteenth birthday, two days away. Her plan was to go to New Orleans by train. On July 8 she went over her departure plans once again. She shuffled through, one last time, Uncle David's locked files and came across a folder with her name on it. Her eyes nearly bled as she read the document: Adoption of Molly Teal Overton. Parents named David and Loretta Overton. The other papers in the folder were about her mother being treated for hysterical conditions. Her mother had been permanently transferred to Bryce Hospital for the insane in Tuscaloosa from Cedar Craft Sanatorium near Nashville. Other papers declared Mrs. Annie Teal an unfit parent and incapable of child rearing. "Not true!" Molly cried out.

More medical papers. Some had Aunt Loretta's name on them. One doctor's paper used the word *infertile*. Molly concluded that this was why she had been taken from her mother...so that mean Aunt Loretta would have her own child. Molly held this information to herself for the next two days. She had been kidnapped, her mother had been forced into a mental hospital, and she had never gotten a complete explanation for any of these things.

July 10..."Happy birthday to me!" Molly said out loud. Today was the big day. She couldn't have been happier. While she ate breakfast with Uncle David and Aunt Loretta, she waited for some acknowledgment of today being her birthday. That did not happen.

She noticed new jewelry on Aunt Loretta's hand: a gold ring with a large ruby, Molly's birthstone. Loretta bragged and rubbed it in to Molly. "Molly, when you're a good wife, you receive gifts for no reason at all from a wonderful husband." They did live elaborately on a police chief's salary. After breakfast, Uncle David went to work.

Molly left a note on Uncle David's desk saying she was old enough to live on her own and that she was leaving. Aunt Loretta was in the bathtub when Molly walked by her bedroom for the very last time, and right there on the dresser, she saw the big red ruby ring. She slipped it on her finger, admired it, and thought, *Maybe it should be mine. Why not?* The ring made a great parting birthday gift to herself from her wicked aunt Loretta and cruel uncle David. She told herself she was not a thief, took off the ring, and laid it back down.

Next to the big ruby ring was Loretta's purse. *Why not? They stole my childhood. A little missing cash is not going to break them,* she thought. Her find was unbelievable. Molly found more money than she had ever seen in her life, including the amount she had accumulated on her own. *There's more than a hundred dollars here. Who keeps that kind of cash on them?* Molly took only a hundred dollars.

Also in the purse were keys to their pretty new motorcar, a 1904 American Populaire Tonneau. *Another gift?* The car had a twelve-horse-power output with a top speed of thirty miles an hour. Under the front seat was a six-gallon gasoline tank. It had three forward speeds and a reverse gear. The ignition was jump-start. Also in the purse were red lip stain and a pair of white gloves. To be on the safe side she had taken a revolver and ammunition. She tied the gun to her thigh under her dress.

Out the front door on Echols Hill, Molly went with a suitcase, a purse, a gun, and $156.00. "I *am* a thief," she said out loud, and then she ran back in and swiped up the keys and the ring. She would sell them if she needed the cash. As she went back out, the brand-new screen door slammed behind her. *Forget about taking a train: I'm driving to find my mother.* This decision forever changed her destiny.

Her first stop was the filling station for gasoline and service. Molly dressed like a lady and was noticed by all the male employees. All the service station workmen tended to Molly's car by cleaning the window, checking the oil and coolant water, and filling it up with gasoline. Meanwhile, she carefully studied the map of the state on the wall, writing down the directions to Tuscaloosa. When she looked up, her best friend Grace Taylor's older brother stood staring at her. Percy Taylor could not believe the difference between his sister's and Molly's appearances.

Molly's face wore a more mature look, but she also noticeably displayed something else: extreme determination.

Percy struck up a conversation with her, and unlike with most men, she felt at ease around him. As they chatted, she revealed that she was leaving town. Her life was much too difficult for anyone to understand. She looked at him and said, "I know you won't tell anyone, but this is a secret. I'm going to go find my mama. We will start our lives over somewhere else." Percy was very drawn to Molly, not because she was so strikingly beautiful as much as because she chose to be trusting and straightforward in communicating with him. He advised her how dangerous it would be to travel alone.

She signed the papers to have the gasoline put on her uncle's credit bill. Percy told her he and his wife were traveling to Mobile. They could follow behind her as far as Birmingham. She took a big swig from a brown-colored bottle of cold Coca-Cola and said, "Okay." She didn't want Percy to realize what an inexperienced driver she really was and said, "I'll follow behind you." Her hands were shaking. She was really leaving. Her mouth was dry. She took another big swig of Coca-Cola. Embarrassing as it was, she had to ask the attendant to crank the car. Her mind had gone completely blank, and she had just forgotten how to crank it.

Meanwhile, Percy brought his wife, Linda Gail, over to Molly's side of the car and introduced them to each other. As they were ready to drive off, Percy said, "Molly, the best way to Birmingham is to go down Whitesburg Pike to the Tennessee River. At Ditto's Landing we'll take a ferry across to Lacey's Spring, and then we'll go on south down to Birmingham. However, before we cross the river on the ferry, I need to stop in Taylorsville. Grace may be at the farmhouse, and you can talk and tell her good-bye." Molly agreed to this plan.

Percy took a few minutes to pay for his gasoline. Molly overheard him mention to the attendant that he was going to let Molly follow him until she was on the road to Nashville. Molly started to yell out to correct him, but her mind was on how to drive the car. Percy and Linda Gail hopped into their Ford Model F touring car, and off they went down Jefferson Street, glad to get away from downtown and the crazy new tenant in their guesthouse. Molly caused the car to jump and lurch forward as it almost choked out before she left the filling station lot. Finally, she got a grip on her emotions and remembered how to use the clutch and accelerator simultaneously to operate the car smoothly.

She stayed right on the bumper of the Taylors' horseless carriage. Percy had to pull over twice before they reached the river to tell her to stay at least a train car's distance from his automobile's rear end. About the time she was getting the hang of driving on the all-weather gravel road of Whitesburg Pike, they came upon the beautiful Tennessee River. As Whitesburg Pike ended, either you could take a ferry across the river or you had to turn left on Ditto's Landing Road over a one-lane steel bridge.

Percy crossed the bridge as soon as the oncoming car cleared. He looked behind and noticed that although Molly was at the threshold of the bridge, she was stopped. He got out and motioned for her to come forward. She shook her head dramatically left and right with both hands clamped down on the steering wheel. She leaned out behind the windshield, red faced with embarrassment and breathing deeply as she said, "This bridge is not wide enough for me to drive across."

Percy said, "Yes, it is, Molly. You saw my car go over, and we had two people in it."

"It's not strong enough," she yelled back.

By this time, Linda Gail had walked over to Molly's door to see if she could lend a hand. Others were backing up on both sides of the bridge now. Molly had pulled the front two wheels onto the bridge and shouted over the sound of the engine, "The bridge will fall into the water when I drive across."

Percy, like his father, had to get all technical and explain the engineering of the bridge and how it had been built by US Steel by a fellow named Andrew Carnegie. "This fellow Carnegie combined his big US Steel company with Federal Steel and National Steel, which made the world's first billion-dollar company. When they make bridges out of steel, they'll last more than a hundred years. It won't fall down.

"Molly, dear, steel is how I made a ton of money. I knew Judge Moore. He was a fellow at National Steel Company. I knew him when I was in the war. He told me I might need to own all the steel stock I could afford and to buy it up. So I did. When the Carnegie fellow sold his part for gold, so did I…Thought he might know something. My daddy always said, 'Get paid in gold, son.'"

By this time, Linda Gail had squeezed up beside Molly. With Linda Gail's foot on the brake, Molly slid to the passenger side and out the door. Linda Gail put the car in gear and drove across the bridge. Molly walked across. The people waiting in the other automobiles or in horse-drawn buggies began to clap as she reached the other side. Linda Gail stayed at the wheel, telling her, "Molly, there will be another smaller bridge at Heidi Burrow Road, and not far after that will be Taylorsville."

Molly confessed she hadn't spent much time behind the wheel and then asked, "What was Percy going on and on about a steel man from a war?"

"Percy's heart is made of pure gold. That is his way of trying to help calm your nerves and distract you with a war story. It always seems to work," Linda Gail explained.

Linda Gail was excited about getting home to see her little girl, Shasta. Shasta was thrilled about the family trip to the shores on the Gulf of Mexico. Not too far from Mobile were the beaches, where the family owned several cabins. Molly had daydreamed about beaches while she looked through Uncle David's travel books.

They made it across the second bridge by Molly closing her eyes and ducking her head below the dashboard. Linda Gail thought Molly might have quit breathing too! She quickly thought to tell Molly the story of Shasta's name, to distract her.

Percy and Linda Gail had been on their way back from their honeymoon in San Francisco when they arranged to stop at Shasta Springs, a healing resort for many people, in the upper Sacramento River canyon. Train passengers loved stopping there to drink and bathe in the natural spring water. Shasta water reputedly had beneficial results when used as a remedial agent. For five cents, an incline railway would take passengers to the main resort high above the gift shop and depot. The main resort had a large bathhouse.

Rotary plows had to clear the tracks of heavy snowfall in the winter months. The Southern Pacific train between San Francisco and Portland stopped for luxury lodging and world-class meals. Many loved the fishing for rainbow trout and salmon. Mineral water was loaded in glass-lined train cars to deliver to local bottling companies.

The newlyweds loved the place so much and felt so well and healthy drinking and bathing in the mineral water that they stayed for a full week. On their last morning at the resort, Linda Gail told Percy that she thought she might be pregnant. She had morning sickness. Percy was beside himself with excitement. He told everyone who would listen that if it was a girl, he would name his child Shasta. Before he got on the train the next day, he had purchased a bottling-rights partnership from the owner as a gift to his wife. She was now carrying his child, Shasta. He thought one day they could make soda pop out of this healthful mineral water. Throughout Shasta's life, Percy loved to tell the story of the place where she had been conceived. Shasta cherished the story and always listened to the love her parents shared and how she had come about.

FOUR

The two cars arrived in Taylorsville around nine o'clock in the morning. Molly slowly got out of her car at the Taylors' farm and took in all the scenery. She looked up to the top of Wallace Mountain and the southern tip of Green Mountain to her left and noticed how Wallace Mountain gently sloped down to kiss the Tennessee River's edge. Far off in a field, she could see dozens of horses and stables, all surrounded by white fences. Much farther away she saw what looked like hundreds of cows within another fence, but she wasn't sure. Directly around her were three houses. All were two stories high and had lots of windows looking out over large front porches, upper and lower. All three were painted white. A fourth house close by was under construction. Across the road and the train tracks were the town's businesses.

First, there was a train depot with a large covered platform area for passengers to get on and off the train out of the weather. Molly noticed how different this train depot looked compared with the ones in downtown Huntsville. This depot seemed freshly painted, and there was no trash lying around on the grounds. Shrubs, flower beds, and hanging flowerpots decorated the area. Thick layers of pebble stones covered the parking area, and small gravel was around the train tracks...like someone's home. Everything looked neat and well kept.

Behind the depot was another set of tracks and more cars to be used to transport goods from the large storage warehouses. Next door was a train maintenance building. Right up next to the tracks, for convenience, was a large feed-and-seed store with a huge area for loading and unloading. She noticed numerous cats near the feed and seed. All around were flowering shade trees that seemed to have a sweet smell. A café had a large glass window so that the customers could see the trains arriving. Lefty's, a saloon, was next to that with no windows and swinging front doors. The barkeeper's right hand had been shot off while breaking up a Saturday night brawl. There was a ten-room hotel, a five-room bed-and-breakfast, a delivery stable, a motorcar garage, a tire repair store, and three general merchandise stores.

It seemed kind of odd, but another building stood alone...Lily's Bakery, where there was a line of customers out the front door and into the yard. The passersby were enjoying the aroma of freshly made doughnuts.

Behind the Taylors' three homes, and up closer to the mountain's edge, was a large spring under the shade of a tall, wide sycamore tree whose leaves made music in the wind. The spring fed into a rock basin, which built up to four feet of water before it fell over a bluff down into a stream that led between the Taylors' homes, under the railroad tracks and down to the river. The way the sunlight lit the water, it appeared to be moving silver as it sparkled and shimmered. Looking back north, Molly realized she had missed the fields coming into Taylorsville. There was row after row, too many to count, of different fruit and nut trees: apple, pear, plum, peach, pecan, walnut, and cherry. In a field up closer to the rocky area were grapevines, with enough grapes for a whole city, Molly thought.

A truck loaded with goats passed them by. Linda Gail broke Molly out of the trance. "Molly, let's go inside. I need to check on Shasta." Molly followed her up small steps to the large front porch.

Like an explosion, out came Grandpa Taylor and little beauty Shasta. They were playing cops and robbers, using their fingers as guns. Linda Gail grabbed up her little girl and squeezed her, and then turned around and introduced her to Molly. "Nice to meet you, Miss Molly," said Shasta, and she curtsied like she had practiced many times in front of the hall mirror near the front door.

Grandpa introduced himself and added, "Word is, young lady, you can't drive worth a damn, so before you leave, I'll give you a lesson on how to properly drive your automobile. I've taught everyone up and down this trail from Whitesburg to New Hope how to drive and deliver 'shine."

Molly was confused. "Deliver 'shine?" she asked.

"I'll 'splain it to you later," said Grandpa.

Next came Big Mama Ruth, the house mammy. She opened her arms and pulled Molly close into her big bosom. "I's a-makin' you a birfday cake for tonight's supper, baby."

About that time, Percy walked in with Molly's heavy suitcase. "Molly, I told you a little fib. We're not leaving for Mobile until the morning. Linda Gail and I didn't think it was safe for you to travel alone. I heard you tell the filling station attendant that today is your birthday. So, while we were waiting at Ditto's Landing and Linda Gail was driving your car across the bridge, I called home and asked Big Mama to start baking a cake for our guest's birthday. Then Daddy got on the phone and told me someone called from Ditto's Landing about you being in need of some driving lessons. Linda Gail and I don't want you to go. Please stay at our home tonight. Enjoy the farm today. Have a big dinner and a good night's sleep. We can get up early and leave for Birmingham at dawn." Molly agreed to stay.

Grandpa and Shasta took Molly for a driving lesson. They went round and round the track that was used for horse racing. He then had her turn around and go in the opposite direction, and do stops, turns, slow circles, and fast takeoffs. Grandpa Taylor had trained all the bootleggers from Gurley to Cloud's Cove how to drive and outrun the sheriff. Molly truly was learning from the best around. Grandpa admitted while Shasta was sitting in his lap, "You're the only girl other than Shasta that I have taught to drive, and she's only five. Grace wants nothing to do with learning about motorcars." Molly caught on real quick to all the driving maneuvers. "Molly, think of the backseat full of bottles clanking around. You don't want to break any of them, but you don't want to go to jail 'cause of them either."

Next they had lunch with Percy's mother, Laura Ann Taylor, who at age sixty-three was known by almost everyone around town as Grandma Taylor. She was the absolutely most loved woman in the small town, and everyone was proud to know her and be part of her community. Grandma was the biggest reason Grandpa Taylor and her two sons, Percy and Chase, put everything on hold and, along with all the other menfolk around, built a church house, which was also used as a school.

Lunch was BLTs: mounds of bacon topped with fresh-from-the-garden, right-off-the-vine, ripe, juicy tomatoes and lettuce with mayonnaise on top of freshly sliced homemade bread. There were tall glasses of lemonade with thin slices of lemons floating in the pitcher, and another pitcher of the sweetest iced tea you've ever put in your mouth. Dessert was a slice of chocolate brownie pie from Miss Lily's bakery down the street.

Percy had the stable hands saddle enough horses for everyone to enjoy a trail ride. By this time, Percy's younger sister, Grace, had returned home from a Bible study at Mount Zion Church in Owens Crossroads. Her mother had made Grace go after she and Grace had had a "come to Jesus" meeting about smart mouthing, talking back, and thinking only about the boys and not studying her Bible. After a long, difficult morning with ministers and church elders, Grace was delighted to have Molly for companionship that afternoon and evening. Right behind the stables was the start of the trail which S-curved underneath a canopy of trees up the side of Wallace Mountain. Molly had never been on a horse before. She was terrified but had the biggest smile on her face at the same time. Grace enjoyed Molly's happiness after seeing her so sad at school.

The trail came out on top of the ridge. If you got close to the clearing of trees and looked down, you could see all of Taylorsville and gently flowing water as far as you could see north and south along the river until it turned west again. The view was one of those places that just stuck in your mind, like a postcard picture.

"Look, Percy, I've never noticed your tree house from up here," Grandma Taylor said. "Have you added on to it again? Maybe having it will help bring me more grandchildren." She smiled and winked at Linda Gail.

Percy explained that he had bought up all the land he could after he sold his steel stocks for gold. He and his family had big dreams for Taylorsville one day.

Grandma told them that much of the land they were looking at had belonged to her father, Isham Hobbs. "Our family also owns and farms the island out there in the middle of the river. The island is two and a half miles long. An old Indian couple still lives there. His name is Standing Bear and she is White Dove. They stay to honor and protect their ancestors' ancient burial grounds on the south end of the island. Rumor has it there is a small Indian girl on the island too. I have never seen her, though."

Grandma Taylor took her sketch pad out and started to sketch a picture of Molly on her horse. She couldn't help but stare at Molly. "Molly Overton," she blurted out, "you are so beautiful. You remind me of a friend from long ago."

"Maybe you knew my mother," Molly said as she opened the locket with her mother's picture. "Aunt Loretta is not my mother," she added indignantly.

"I know, sweetheart," Grandma replied as she looked at the picture in the locket.

The horses stayed on the plateau of the mountaintop. At times there were steep dips followed by steep inclines as they passed through burrows and hollows. The trail extended all the way to the foot of Green Mountain in the Bailey family's cove.

They turned back toward home by going down to the bottom of the mountain to the railroad tracks and followed them, the horses in single file, all the way back. Everyone was so hot when they returned, they went for a swim in the cool springs. Percy's brother, Chase, was also with them. He was home from Auburn University to work for the summer. He was studying engineering and hoping to change his major to architecture when the new architecture program rumored to be offered soon at Auburn was launched.

When they arrived back at the house after the swim, the backyard was a buzz of activity. Men were unloading wood for a big bonfire.

Another bunch was standing around cooking pits slowly turning whole chickens over hickory wood. Railroad Bob assisted while telling the latest stories of daily life on the rails. The ladies were directing a few unfortunate bystanders into putting up the latest tent Percy had made of canvas, like the ones in the circus. They were tying ropes to the trees and stakes in the ground, and it was accomplished in no time. Tables and benches were brought from the warehouse. Ladies draped the tables with cloth, and the food delivery line began: large bowls of green beans, mashed potatoes with gravy, sliced tomatoes, onions, cucumbers, fried okra, corn bread, butter beans, and poke salad made with eggs and onions.

Linda Gail gave Molly a brand-new dress from a department store, with a tag still on it. It was royal blue and too small for Linda Gail to wear. Molly felt really special in it that night. Many people showed up. They introduced themselves to Molly as they arrived, wishing her "Happy birthday, Molly!" Most gave her some kind of small gift: a jar of grape jelly from one, goat cheese from another, baskets of ripe fruits and vegetables. Grandma headed off any gifts of moonshine.

Just as everyone was finishing up with the feast, out the back door came Big Mama with the biggest yellow cake with warm chocolate frosting. The top of the cake looked like it was on fire with huge candles off the dining room table candelabra.

Herman Deeley and a couple of local musicians got the crowd started with "Happy birthday, dear Molly." Molly became all choked up, and her cheeks turned bright red. This was the happiest she had been in a long time. She knew exactly how long: she had just turned eight when her aunt and uncle from Huntsville had come to Nashville for a visit. Six long years ago was the last time Molly had felt joy.

The fiddlers with Herman had most folks up dancing while others had more cake and homemade ice cream. After things were cleaned up and put back to order like Grandma wanted, the Taylors went indoors to the living room for family time. This was time to be grateful and share with others. The couches and chairs were covered with bodies, and the last in the room sat on the floor, Indian-style. Molly was amazed by how much the members of this family loved one another. They all seemed to feel blessed to be a part of each other's lives. One at a time, they named something they were grateful for that day. Linda Gail, Grace, and Shasta all said they were grateful Molly had come into their lives. Grandma agreed.

Before everyone had gone to sleep for the night, Linda Gail and Grandma had Molly in the kitchen alone. "Molly, we're both very worried about you traveling by yourself," Grandma blurted out. "Stay with Grandpa and me. You can go to the beach with us and come back and live in Taylorsville for a while. I'll carry you to see your mother." Molly just stared at Grandma Taylor. That was the most loving thing anyone, except her mother, had ever said to her. Tearing up, Molly blurted out, "I can't...I want to but I can't. My mama needs me and Taylorsville is too close to Uncle David." Her happiness earlier turned into rivers of tears as she slowly told the two women about the horrors of her life, starting with the kidnapping. All the men, every single night. "I'm just a kid," she kept saying through all the sobs and crying.

She eventually got around to how she had discovered her mother's location. "I'm heading to Bryce Hospital to reunite with my mother tomorrow," she said. The two women held Molly until she stopped shaking. They came up with a plan. They would travel as far as Birmingham with Molly. Then she would go to Tuscaloosa to save her mother. Afterward, she could meet up with them in Gulf Shores at the family cabins on the beach.

There wasn't time for the Taylors to go to Tuscaloosa with Molly. Percy had a meeting in Mobile with Dr. Reynolds of Vanderbilt University, his partner in a new business...importing bananas. Once there, they would meet Captain Keefer, steamship captain of the partnership's newly acquired SS *Americos* of Brazil. The captain would be in port for only two days.

At daybreak, Molly was the first one up, and she got in her car, ready to go. The car was sitting under a huge tree on the riverbank, and when she noticed the tree house up above, she decided to take a peek. She lit a leftover birthday cake candle and held it in her mouth as she climbed the newly-made ladder. The inside had a secret, magical feel. It was large enough for a bed that was level with the windows for viewing. She looked out and watched the low-lying clouds riding on top of the water flowing down the foggy river.

After she climbed back down, without startling her, a skinny little Negro woman came up to her side of the car. "You must be Miss Molly. I'm Lillian, the doughnut lady, Big Mama's baby sister. Everyone just calls me Lily. I want you to have the first batch of the day. Doughnuts for your birthday," she said as she handed Molly a paper sack. "I sell them at Lily's Bakery right over there, and we send some to a bakery downtown." Then Lily leaned over and kissed Molly's forehead. "Bless you," she said. It was as if they had some connection. Molly didn't know it then, but Lily had an abusive husband. For a reason Lily did not know, people felt comfortable telling her almost anything. The two talked for a short time and finished with Lily saying a prayer out loud on her new friend's behalf. "Amen," they said together.

The caravan of cars left Taylorsville right at sunrise. Molly drove over both small bridges without any fear. However, she was scared to death driving onto the ferry at Whitesburg. She could feel the movement of the water as all the motorcars and horse carts and buggies loaded. "Knock, knock!" Grace was walking alongside Molly's car. "I talked Mama and Linda Gail into letting me ride with you, Molly," she said, sounding excited. "Daddy told them you could drive real well now that he had taught you. Linda Gail didn't think you should be alone right now, and we'll be in the car right behind them."

As soon as Grace got into the car, she said, "I've got to confess. Molly, I listened to the entire conversation last night in the kitchen. I am so sad that that happened to you. When you go get your mama and meet us at the beach, we'll help you get better, and you can forget all that. Leave it all behind. I'm still real curious about men, though—about their bodies and about sex."

Molly was terribly embarrassed. She was not the expert to be answering any questions about sex. "Grace, as far back as I can remember, sex has been like a large knife being shoved up into places you didn't know things should go. Then the knife would be twisted and turned to cause great pain." Grace was horrified as Molly continued. "After they finish moaning, they put all their weight on your body, and it feels like every one of your bones will just be crushed." Molly did not notice, but Grace was twisting and grimacing the more she spoke. "Their faces stink of alcohol or cigars, and rough and scratchy beards rub your skin raw as they try to kiss you. It is just awful." Molly didn't know it at the time, but she had a profound effect on Grace's curiosity about boys.

The caravan stopped several times for "Mother Nature calls" in the woods off the side of the road. They arrived in Birmingham by midafternoon. The entire Taylor family tried everything they could think of to have Molly stay the night with them. "I am just too close to my mother to not continue on the road to rescue her," she said. "I have money. If they don't let her go, I'll sneak her out, and we'll see you at the beach. You've written down all the directions for me, Percy. Grandpa, you made me into a better driver. Big Mama made fried chicken and biscuits. I have enough to last a few days. Plus, I have doughnuts Miss Lillian gave me."

Percy and Chase checked Molly's car one last time. They all felt awful about letting her go alone.

FIVE

THE INSANE ASYLUM

M olly's heart was pounding as she pulled into the parking area of a large hospital that evening. She slowly walked toward the Italianate-style building, stopped at the front door, and took a deep breath.

It was eight o'clock according to the wall clock when Molly went to the front desk to inquire about her mother and her release. The staff acted confused and kept talking quietly out of Molly's hearing range. The head nurse asked Molly to have a seat and said they would have to locate their supervisor. It was late, and things could take a while. Molly found a ladies' restroom down the hall. She splashed water on her face to refresh herself. After six long years, she was so excited. Tonight she and her mother would reunite and start their lives all over again.

She walked toward the front desk and chairs, where she was asked to wait. As Molly walked past a closed door marked "Private," a woman came out, quickly took Molly's hand, and pulled her into the room. Her eyes were kind and her smile was warm, compassionate, and trusting. She wore a nurse's uniform. Later, Molly was unable to remember her name, because at this point her life became a blur.

The kind nurse explained to Molly, "You don't have much time. They're looking for you. The sheriff's department was here. I recognized you from an old picture Annie had in her room at her bedside."

The woman was her mother's night nurse, and they had become friends. "Your mother knew she didn't have anything wrong with her, and she stopped taking all the hyoscine the doctors use to keep the insane hypnotic or sedated. We stayed up nights talking. She told me about that night when they took you away from her. The trial by her crooked brother and his awful judge friend. His wife wanted a child and couldn't have any. They took you and put her here."

Molly kept repeating, "Where is she? Please take me to her. Where is she?"

The nurse tried to keep Molly quiet. "Your aunt came looking for you yesterday. She had the sheriff and his deputies with her. Told them you were a runaway and that they needed to lock you up. Your mama was a thirty-two-year-old woman with nothing wrong with her. They had her locked up in here anyways. Your aunt stayed with her alone for a good while yesterday. She was asleep when I came on shift at three o'clock. Molly, your mama never woke up. They declared her dead of natural causes last night at ten o'clock."

Molly was in shock. She and the nurse wept in each other's arms. Her knees began to buckle underneath her as the nurse held her up. "You can't stay here. It's not safe. The sheriff's deputy has come by twice today already, looking to see if you showed up. He's supposed to take you to jail for stealing a car."

"I need to see her," Molly begged.

The nurse shook her head. "She's in the morgue here, down in the basement."

She took Molly down the back out-of-the-way stairs to see her mother's body. She pulled the sheet back and Molly just wailed, standing there in disbelief. Slowly she got closer, wrapped her arms around her mother's shoulders, and kissed her face. Apologizing. "I knew I should've come straight here yesterday to save you. I'm so sorry I didn't get here in time."

The nurse interrupted Molly and told her, "The sheriff from Huntsville called early yesterday and had us and the local sheriff on alert, looking for you. After all, your uncle is the police chief. They've done this to your mama anyways, to teach you a lesson. You would have been caught. You need to go now, Molly. They will be back, and they will catch you. You've got to go. Go out the back door. Walk through the dark to your car and drive it back to the same door. I'm going to get a box of things that were your mother's."

Five minutes later, Molly was back at the door in the alley with the car, waiting for the nurse. She noticed a box next to the door. Molly jumped out, grabbed it, and quickly got back into the car. She was trying to see the items in the box, but it was dark, and she was crying so hard, she couldn't see. Her nose was all stopped up and she was getting little air into her lungs between her long, labored sobs and snorts. There was a note on the top from the nurse, but Molly's eyes were too out of focus to see it.

Startled, Molly looked up when someone pounded on the side of her car. "Oh no, I've been caught," she said out loud. The passenger door swung open, and Molly tried to get the car into gear to move forward. A nice-looking man in a doctor's coat poked his head in, saying, "We got a call for all doctors to go to the train crash on Black Water Road. Are you heading that way? I need a ride quickly. They say there are dozens of injured people." Before Molly could answer, he was in the front seat, telling her, "Drive! It's an emergency!" as they departed the parking area. Lights began to flash all over the buildings. The gate had closed behind them. She could hear loud sirens going off behind her as she sped away. She knew they were after her and felt glad to escape.

Back at the hospital an emergency lockdown had gone into effect at the highest level. "Red alert!" the orderlies in the hallways shouted. Everyone was scrambling, trying to calm down the crazies while they looked for Alabama's worst murderer ever: Big Jimbo Looter. His lawyer had sent him to Bryce for insanity testing, trying to get him off death row and avoid a certain hanging. "Big" had been tried and convicted for the murder of two families—altogether, seventeen people had died in a rural area. No motive had ever been given. His lawyer claimed, "He had to be crazy, since he didn't have any reason to kill anyone. He did not know anyone in either family."

Molly was so emotional about the death of her mother and being too late to save her that she wasn't thinking clearly. She was driving in a hazardous way running through intersections and weaving all over the road. Finally the doctor said, "You are in no condition to drive. Just pull over. Let me drive. Now! Now! We're in a hurry. We have lives to save."

She pulled over and let him drive. She trusted him. He was a doctor. She was absolutely exhausted and had been driving dangerously. "Where is the train wreck?" she asked.

He told her, "I'm not exactly sure. Just one county over on Black Water Road…Lots of injuries. They called all doctors in a four-county area to help. It's maybe an hour's drive." She dozed off, totally out of energy. She woke once at a filling station that didn't look open. She didn't know how he got the gasoline. Her life was spinning, and she went back out again. She woke up several more times to be told they were almost there, but this time she woke because the road they were traveling on had become very bumpy. She also noticed that it was narrow and the trees were quite close to the road. It was very dark except for the headlights.

Molly looked over to the doctor to ask where they were. She saw his eyes and knew she had made a mistake and was in big trouble. His face had changed from that of nice doctor to evil madman. He rambled, "All my medicine has worn off. I can no longer be the nice doctor." He looked like a crazy, wild dog with rabies as foam dribbled out of the corner of his mouth. The automobile came to a stop in front of an abandoned cabin. Then he slowly turned it toward a bluff and turned the headlights on high. He smirked as he said, "Over that bluff is a huge drop to the bottom. Maybe a hundred feet. I plan to kill you over here in this cabin. Then I'll put your body back in the car and push it over so I can watch the explosion when it hits."

Molly had never been so scared in her life. Why hadn't she just stayed at Uncle David's house? The madman had hold of both Molly's wrists and pulled her out through the driver's side door. Fighting as hard as her young, slender body could, she kneed him in the groin and broke away only to trip and fall to the ground. In one quick motion, he had her by the ankles. As he turned to drag her inside, a calmness that she couldn't explain came over her, and it wasn't to accept her fate. Her hand slipped up her legs. "Stop!" she shouted. "Don't you want to have sex with me before you kill me?"

This question caught him off guard for a second, and she now had her finger on the trigger of the gun she had hidden on her thigh. "Show me what you got, little lady. You might can buy yourself a little time," he said, staring at her legs as they disappeared under her dress. With her other hand she slowly started pulling her dress up, getting closer and closer, showing more bare skin. He had a sinister smile ear to ear until the four-inch barrel of the Remington revolver came into view. Molly pulled the trigger...and thought she missed him. She rolled over on the ground and kept shooting.

He was screaming while turning in circles and finally started running...toward the bluff. Madmen make odd noises when they fall that far. She heard a muffled but loud thud from below the bluff, which was supposed to be...her grave. She walked slowly toward the edge of the bluff, pushing back bushes with one hand and holding the revolver ready in the other. The car lights were not enough. It was too dark. "David Overton, this is all your fault! You pig!" she shouted. She walked back to the cabin. In the car headlights she saw blood on her arms and legs. Was it hers? Maybe she had hit him.

There was no water in the cabin. She found a bottle of moonshine and used it to clean up. Back outside, she reloaded the revolver and tied it back in the same spot on her inner thigh. That's when she noticed powder burns on her new long dress.

Back behind the wheel, she started out toward the sparkly city lights in the distance. The odd smell she remembered from her drive to Tuscaloosa told her it was probably Birmingham's steel and paper mills. A hint of daybreak indicated the sun would be rising soon in the east. She wanted to head south. Back down the bumpy dirt road, she came to the main road. She saw a small hand-painted sign that said "Heaven's Gate Hunting Club." She would always remember it as "The Devil's Hole."

She kept the sunrise on her left as she headed south. She didn't have the directions Percy had given her—must have dropped them in the cabin. Too bad, because she wasn't about to go back. Her plan was to stay south; she would come to Mobile sooner or later. Meanwhile, she munched on the doughnuts Miss Lily had given her the day before. She wondered how she had gone from having the best birthday, with the family that she wished was hers, to finding out her mother was murdered and, by the end of the night, apparently murdering some bad guy.

By midday, she was outside of Mobile. While stopping for gasoline she bought a map. It took a bit of studying and help from the filling station attendant to understand where she was and which way to go. She asked the manager if he minded if she rested in his parking lot for a few minutes before continuing her journey. She drank a Coca-Cola. This one was in a light green bottle, and it picked up her energy.

She decided to look through the box of her mother's belongings. On top was a letter from the nurse telling Molly how much her mother had loved her. Her mother was a wonderful, kind, smart person to everyone, it said. In the same envelope was a tiny brown bottle of white powder. The nurse explained that it was very safe. All you had to do was snort the stuff into your nose and it would keep you wide awake and alert for hours. The letter also said that she shouldn't stop or rest, but to just go as far away as possible to be safe. "They will keep looking until they catch you" were the nurse's final words.

Six

Gulf Shores

After many small bridges and three ferries, Molly arrived at Gulf Shores. Looking around, she said aloud, "Not one human anywhere in sight." One small dirt but sandy road headed west. Molly was still willing to push on. The ferryboat captain had said there wouldn't be another ferry until the next day. She drove for what seemed like a long time. Then she saw it: the water of the Gulf of Mexico for the very first time. She just stopped and stared. The water was emerald green, with hints of dark blue. The sand was so white, it looked like snow. Flocks of white birds circled over the water, occasionally diving down and picking up fish.

She drove just a bit farther and came upon five cabins, each a different color, just like Shasta had said: pink, yellow, blue, green, and pale orange. A big white house stood in the middle. Obviously Molly was the first to arrive. The Taylor family would have no idea that she'd been up all night and day, driving. Molly didn't know if she should go on in or sleep in her car until the group arrived the next day. She decided to walk around the house and the cabins. Off went her shoes. The sand felt like walking in a sugar bowl. Up and down the beach she went until she was sure she had all the cocaine powder out of her body. She wanted to think very clearly as she went through the box.

As she walked by the big house again, she noticed a letter on the front door with her name on it. "Miss Molly, please feel free to come into the house. The Taylor family has asked me to supply it with all necessary food and wood for the fire and stove. Sorry, no power here. They will arrive on the first ferry at noon tomorrow. The Caretaker."

She got her belongings out of the car and brought them inside. She explored the house for a bit first, noticing several pieces of incredibly beautiful framed paintings, all signed "Laura Ann Taylor."

It was time to go through the box. She found happy pictures of herself and her mother, Annie, and father, Ivan, before he died of fever. A small wedding ring. A locket with her baby hair. A picture of a beautiful woman who looked like her father...maybe a sister or aunt. Dozens of returned letters all addressed to Molly Teal Overton, Echols Hill, Huntsville, Alabama. "Return to Sender" had been handwritten on each letter. They had been opened.

In the order in which they had been written, she read them slowly, one by one. The first letters were full of hope and encouragement, saying things would be fine and that she and her mother would reunite again one day. Some of the letters were exciting, such as when her mother was waiting for Molly to turn twelve so she could decide to live with her. The hope died when she got the news that Molly had been legally adopted by her brother. The letters continued, but the tone was not as hopeful after Molly's twelfth birthday had passed. In each letter, her mother encouraged Molly to pray and keep her faith in God and said that one day soon they would see each other again.

The last letter had been written one month before her fourteenth birthday. Molly had always known that everything she was told about her mother being crazy and abandoning her was untrue, and the letters confirmed it. She hated David Overton with all her might. He was an evil pig.

She went back outside to the beach, went to the water, and walked right in, clothes and all, and kept going. The waves crashed over her head. One big wave smacked her from behind, knocking her off balance. A surge of water pushed her downward into the sand. She couldn't tell which way was up. Just as things were starting to go black, an arm reached in and pulled her out. It was Percy's. He hadn't wanted to stay in Mobile another night, so he had hired a ferryboat to make a special trip to the island.

At the family dinner that night Percy said, "Lucky for Molly we showed up when we did. She was caught in a riptide, and was fighting with all her might against it."

Grandpa Taylor took a photograph the next afternoon of Grandma Taylor, Linda Gail, Grace, Molly, and Shasta standing on the beach next to a sand dune. A few of the cottages were showing in the distant background. That night he processed the film and made two prints in his makeshift photo lab so that he could give Molly a copy before she left.

Molly never revealed that she killed a madman, but shared her experience at Bryce Hospital with everyone. She showed them pictures of her mother and father from the box, which temporarily ended Grandma's suspicions. They felt horrible for her. Had they not talked her into staying in Taylorsville, she would have seen her mother alive. She would also be in jail for stealing the car and running away from home. Who knows what would've been waiting for her at the Overton house or even in the jail? This was another day with the wonderful Taylor family. She would remember it forever. Her perfect family.

The next morning she waited for the ferry to leave the dock. Only when she was on board did she look back. She did not want to leave the safety of the Taylor complex on the beach property. But Molly knew she was bad news, and she didn't want to see any trouble coming to them because of her. Once the ferry started moving, tears flowed down again, off her face and onto her dress. She held the photo Grandpa Taylor had given her close to her heart. She sold the car for cash in Mobile to a merchant Percy had suggested.

"All aboard! This train is departing for New Orleans. Please have your ticket out for the conductor." Molly's heart was beating so loudly, she wondered if others on the train could hear it. Frightened out of her mind, she pulled out the ticket.

The Taylor family stopped at the Huntsville police department headquarters on their way back home from the family beach trip. The *Mercury* newspaper "extra" edition was printed that afternoon in July 1905 with the headline "Huntsville Police Chief Resigns Today." The article went on to say that David Overton had accepted a position as chief clerk for Circuit Judge W. T. Lawler.

That evening David Overton strongly suggested to his wife, Loretta, that it would be in her best interest to befriend Suzette, a local conniving social climber. As he chugged down his second whiskey, he went on to explain angrily, "We can use her to get revenge on the three Taylors, who just forced me to resign."

After Grandma Taylor arrived home, she summoned Percy, her eldest son, to go find Molly in New Orleans immediately. She would explain everything once he got her back safely.

Percy returned from New Orleans after only a couple days upon the news of his mother's death. It would be many years before Percy discovered the truth his mother had figured out about Molly and why it was so urgent to find her.

SEVEN

SUZETTE MILLER

S uzette was the worst kind of person you'd ever want to let into your
life. She loved to divide people, then attack. Playing games with people's minds was a favorite pastime of hers. Suzette was forever planting
seeds in weaker minds so they would carry out her devious acts. She
ingratiated herself into others' lives by trying to make herself indispens-
able…always available to help with your house, your children, your ag-
ing parents—anything to make you let your guard down. She always had
an agenda. Oftentimes, she would rather lie, even if the truth would be
more helpful to her cause.

During and after high school, she managed through her aunt and
uncle to get a job at the post office with one agenda: access to the information that came through the mail. Suzette wanted to be "in the know."
For entertainment and information about her neighbors she read letters
that she stole from her job at the post office. She had no qualms about
opening others' mail and would even carry interesting mail home to read
at night. Some of these letters were eventually delivered, some she kept,
and some she marked "Return to Sender," but most she threw away.

Suzette was the daughter of mill workers, commonly referred to as
"lint heads." She grew up in one of the homes provided by the Dallas
Mill cotton manufacturers. The houses were the same—small rooms,
small yards—and they all sat close to one another. Suzette had dreams

of living in one of the big antebellum homes in downtown Huntsville, known as the Twickenham community.

Unfortunately for the well-known, wealthy O'Kennedy family, Suzette cast her eye on the unsuspecting Michael. She followed him daily to get to know his routine, from his work schedule to his friends, and even where he went to church. She became an instant Catholic because Michael was Catholic. She knew which saloons and billiard halls he frequented and what kind of beer and food he usually ordered. Her parents were about to leave on a trip to Memphis when Suzette came down with a sudden fever and insisted she would be okay alone, that they should go on without her.

Now it was time to put all her scheming into action. Suzette went to the full bed in her parents' room and changed the sheets for her encounter later in the evening. Next she rummaged through her mother's small wardrobe and found the only pretty dress she owned. Thankfully her mother had not taken it to Memphis.

Suzette was very intelligent. In her senior year of high school she took science classes so that she could study everything from chemistry to pharmaceuticals. Not that she was interested one bit in them. She had only one thing on her mind: finding a wealthy husband to get her out of Dallas Mill village.

She had visited her old high school the previous day. The doors were always unlocked. There she found in the school library and took with her a copy of the Merck 1901 medical manual, a ready-reference pocket book for practicing physicians and surgeons. She went directly into the chemistry lab and collected all the ingredients she needed for her plan. Her parents had traveled by train, so their motorcar was available. Suzette practiced driving out toward the river. She met Percy Taylor for the first time at Ditto's Landing trading post and Whitesburg ferry. Her tire suddenly went bad, a ploy she had learned in another all-boy class. She put her best acting skills to work and acted frantic and stranded in front of handsome young Percy Taylor. He fixed her tire, as any gentleman would, and left her. She noticed when he went back to his truck that a very beautiful wife and young child were waiting for him.

Suzette took off in a real hurry. She had to get ready to bump into Michael at the exact right time. She had practiced this encounter often. Her goal was to be a part of what his family represented: community leaders and wealth. They were big-time builders and developers of Huntsville's growth in the cotton mill industry, a great family of philanthropists to the community, and supporters of the downtown Saint Mary Church of the Visitation.

Suzette parked the automobile directly in front of the Elks Theater. She waited outside her car until she saw Michael walking her way from Green Street. Suzette broke the small heel off of her shoe and stepped directly in front of Michael. He didn't see what hit him as she put a handkerchief close to his face soaked with a chemical pheromone, which her teacher believed would bring instant sexual arousal. "My foot is hurt and my shoe is broken!" she cried. Michael was not attracted to her at all. Suzette had on her mother's tight-fitting summer dress, with no corset underneath, which allowed her nipples to show. She saw that he noticed. She thought to herself, *He really likes me…Play weak and fragile.*

Michael noticed her whiny voice as she said, "I'm so afraid my parents will find out I took their Ford. How will I get it back home? I can't drive with a hurt foot."

Michael realized that Suzette was shaken and he felt sorry for her, so he did the right thing as a gentleman and offered to take the frightened girl home. "Just tell me where you live and I'll drive you home in their car." He followed her directions to her parents' home in the village.

In a pathetic little voice Suzette said, "I'll need your assistance to help me inside." Michael agreed to help her. "I'm so embarrassed to have a stranger take me home," she said. "My name is Suzette Miller." He in turn introduced himself as Michael O'Kennedy.

They pulled up to her house, where the outside light shined on Suzette. He noticed she had strange-colored orange hair and the body of a boy. "Jesus!" he accidentally said out loud. It wasn't that Suzette was ugly…She just wasn't pretty. Something from inside prevented any beauty she could have had from coming out. His plan was to get her to the door and walk back to the Elks on Eustis Avenue as quickly as possible.

Suzette played the helpless role perfectly. She had practiced many times. Michael realized he had to get her inside and near a telephone, if they had one, in case she needed to call someone later. He got her to the kitchen. In a flash, she reached into the icebox and brought out his favorite brand of beer with the glass she had cooled, just like he ordered in the saloon. Already a mixture of cerium oxalate, a sedative, nerve tonic, and Spanish fly aphrodisiac was in the bottom. She began to pour the beer and insisted that he take it. Then she poured one for herself. Before the drug mixture completely took effect, she had him walking back to the fresh linens on her parents' full bed. They almost didn't make it. His legs became rubbery underneath him a couple of times.

With some difficulty, she was able to remove his clothes. Pleased with his masculine build, she planned to give him a son. Because of the powder in his drink he was aroused. Michael was passed out, but Suzette did not care. She was willing to give herself to a corpse. They would do it not just once that night, but several times. She understood her cycle, and now was the perfect time to become pregnant. Sometime early in the morning, he started to wake up.

Michael opened his eyes to her big, wide, toothy smile. He was totally confused. He had no idea who she was or where he was, or how he had gotten there. A total blank. All he remembered was getting off work and starting out to meet some other guys for beer at the saloon. Everything was dark after that.

Suzette, on the other hand, was quite happy with herself. She tried, somewhat unsuccessfully, to avoid pushing a little too hard at first. "Where am I?" he asked.

Her version to Michael was "I was getting out of my car, and you just plowed me down on the sidewalk, and like the gentleman you are, you picked me up in your arms. We both felt intense love from that moment on. You offered to bring me home from downtown because I couldn't drive, and you spent the evening convincing me of your instant love. I gave you my virginity. After the third time, you proposed to me. The fifth time, you told me you wanted me to have many of your children. Michael, I wasn't sure at first, like you were, because I've never felt this way. Now I'm so in love too. You are such a romantic lover, so tender and attentive."

Michael put his hands on both sides of his head. It felt like it was going to explode. He was in disbelief. How could he be with her? He had no memory of their time together! His head began to hurt more, and the pounding was louder as she prattled on about their future. He got his second shoe on without a sock and fled toward the door. She screamed her name at him as if to remind him who she was. "Suzette Miller. You'll hear from me very soon, Michael O'Kennedy, my husband-to-be." Michael felt like a coward, but he couldn't remember anything. No way: she was not his type. Not a chance. *Not with her,* he thought.

Michael arrived back home. He felt dirty. He needed to get clean. He noticed his penis was red, inflamed, and sore to the touch. *What the hell happened to me?* He had no time to think. He had to get to work before he was late at the new building going up downtown.

A few days later, he saw a doctor about his inflamed, burning penis. He had a sexually transmitted disease. The doctor gave him a shot of mercury salicylate and some pills to take at home. "No sex for one month," the doctor said. "We want to make sure to get rid of this before you give it to someone else." Michael left the doctor's office confused and embarrassed.

A week later, Suzette showed up just as Michael was leaving the construction site. He was caught off guard by her presence. "How did she know where to find me? I thought I had a bad dream, but she's real," he was overheard to say. Suzette went straight up to Michael, slapped him hard on the face, and screamed, "You gave me gonorrhea, and if I weren't pregnant, I would call off our engagement."

She had staged the whole scene so that all his coworkers, family members, and others heard everything. He whispered to his cousin, "I must've poked her. Did she give it to me, or did I give it to her? I did go to a cheap whorehouse over in Decatur a couple of weeks ago."

Michael's coworkers began to laugh at him. Suzette showed up every day as he got off work. "I'm declaring my love for you, Michael," she said. "I forgive you. Our baby needs his father." The daily pressure began to work on the senior members of the O'Kennedy family, and they had "the talk" with Michael about the "right thing to do." One week later they were married. Suzette was disappointed she didn't get to have a large wedding. Both Suzette and Michael were under medical treatment and were strictly advised against any sexual activity. The treatment could cause infertility problems, but it did not occur to Michael, and apparently not their doctor, that having Suzette take such medicine while she was pregnant might be problematic for carrying a baby to full term.

Michael was totally depressed. This was not who or what he expected of his life. Suzette became very upset when she began menstruating. She had to come up with another plan after they had finished their cycles of medication. She tried having sex with him as often as she could force herself on him. He became sickened by her and would push Suzette away. She was disgusting to him. He caught her in lies and deceitfulness all the time.

Michael began to drink more heavily to dull his senses enough to allow him to go home to his wife. Suzette started to put more sexual stimulants in his food and drink. He usually just passed out, without talking. Suzette would rape him every night as he lay unconscious.

Three months passed and she still was not pregnant. She had to come up with another plan. Suzette knew of a distant relative in New Market who had fathered about a dozen redheaded children. They all looked like pretty little Michaels. The relative had had two wives who died during childbirth and was looking for wife number three to help with his children and his sexual needs.

Suzette met Red daily for sexual encounters for two weeks. He was the magic bullet. Suzette had only one problem now: how to fake being fourteen and a half weeks pregnant. She began to eat everything she could hold down and wore baggy clothing. Meanwhile, she spoke with Michael's aunt and explained that they were family now and she thought she and Michael should live in one of the family homes downtown near everyone else. Aunt Kelly Garth did not try to hide the fact that she despised Suzette. She even accused Suzette of tricking Michael into marriage. The rest of Michael's family thought the same thing. Suzette cried, wept, and boo-hooed as she walked toward the door with sunken shoulders, pretending to be a broken woman. "Arrangements have already been made for you and Michael to temporarily live in the guesthouse on Adams. My understanding was the Michael was to tell you tonight," Aunt Kelly said.

Outside, Suzette smiled as she walked across the beautifully landscaped lawn on Gates Avenue, thinking of her performance in the face of Aunt Kelly's accusations. "Time to start packing for my new home downtown," she said out loud, not caring if anyone heard. This scheme of hers was working. Now she needed a plan to explain the late delivery of her baby. Suzette rubbed her belly and said to the baby bump, "You and I are going to love living on Adams Street."

Without actually speaking to Suzette, the senior O'Kennedy family members had arranged for the newlyweds to temporarily use the Taylors' guesthouse on Adams Street until an O'Kennedy family–owned house in Five Points was available…Suzette, like a weed, planted roots immediately. The condition was that they had to move out when the new owners arrived back in town in a few months.

Percy Taylor had bought the house next door to his parents' home on Adams Street and didn't mind if the O'Kennedy newlyweds stayed in the guesthouse until they were ready to move into the main house. The house was a surprise for his wife, Linda Gail. He knew Linda Gail loved the idea of having a home downtown. Percy was having the house furnished and decorated by the absolute best decorator in the southeastern United States, Charlotte Wessberg. She loved spending other people's money on the finer things.

After moving in, Suzette began to infringe on her neighbor's, the elderly Grandma Taylor's, privacy. She had totally immersed herself in the O'Kennedys' good family name and used it to throw her weight around town at every opportunity. Laura Ann Taylor, Grandma Taylor to most, had no reason not to trust her.

Suzette was still not showing any signs of a baby, so she wore oversized dresses and rubbed her belly constantly. Suzette loved to be in the know and always wanted information about everyone around her, being a real snoop and a busybody. She showed up inconveniently every time Charlotte was at the home with new furnishings or to hang paintings. Charlotte had a professional crew unpack the wooden crates sent from

Italy. Inside the two heaviest freight boxes was marble, which was to be used in the bathrooms, fireplaces, and modern kitchen.

Suzette always interrupted the decorator. Charlotte knew of Suzette's little charm game and cut her off immediately. "Mrs. O'Kennedy told me you would be snooping around and asking questions," she said. "I was told not to inform you of anything. Which means, keep your nose out of other people's business. By the way, Suzette, when are you and your imaginary baby moving out? After I finish the main house, I need to start immediately on the guesthouse to have everything done by the time the new owners arrive."

Suzette was ahead of the game. She already knew everything, because she had befriended Mrs. Taylor next door. Charlotte knew that Suzette, as a conniving woman, was playing games. The next day, she had the men from Hayes Construction come by to build a wooden fence, closing the guesthouse off from the only access to the main house. Now the only entrance to Suzette's home was by way of the alley. Just to complete the new gift for the Taylors, Charlotte had large, fast-growing trees and shrubs planted in front of the fence. Charlotte also sensed that Suzette would use her pregnancy as a reason not to move out of the guesthouse.

Mrs. Taylor came over to chat with Charlotte and loved all the new furnishings. She knew the last box had special marble Percy had sent from his travels in Italy for the fireplace. She loved the white sanctuary marble on the outside columns that Percy's war buddy, Colonel Samuel Tate, sent from Georgia Marble in Pickens County, Georgia. Colonel Tate insisted he owed it to Percy for always having his back. "The Italian marble for the fireplace is equally divine," she said. Workmen from Sparkman Marble of Huntsville were just finishing up the installation. Percy's mother knew her son had good taste and wanted to please Linda Gail and provide a beautiful home for her and their little girl, Shasta. Grandma Taylor was excited about her granddaughter coming back from her family trip to Europe and living right next door. She had great plans to spoil her rotten.

She did mention to Charlotte that the new O'Kennedy girl was friendly and had become very helpful to her. Charlotte tried her best to warn Mrs. Taylor about the troublemaking girl, but in her grandma voice, she defended Suzette as youthful and inexperienced. "She will make a nice young lady someday," Mrs. Taylor said.

Charlotte replied, "Well, she has intruded on me one time too many, so I had a fence and shrubbery as a barrier to this house put in. I don't think Linda Gail or Percy either one will like her or her interruptions. They can tear it down once she leaves, or just put in a gate."

Grandma Taylor responded, "I know, she's already complained how she has to walk all the way down the alley and then all the way up Adams just to visit and check on me."

"Good," Charlotte said. "Maybe she'll leave you alone. She's trouble."

At five months pregnant Suzette did start to show, mostly because she exchanged her baggy clothing for some that was tighter and showed her bump more prominently, but also because she was eating like a horse.

Eight

New Taylor House, Huntsville

The Taylors arrived back in Huntsville and loved the work Charlotte had done on the new home, which was filled with the many fine pieces Percy had purchased during their time in Europe. Charlotte was correct in that the Taylors would not ask a young couple expecting a child to leave. They had only briefly met the woman. Shasta loved the new white house with its big columns right next door to Grandma and Grandpa's house, which had big white columns too. The front yard was wide and deep with a long, circular drive to the front door. Another drive to the rear of the house led to a huge greenhouse with every kind of flower in every color you could imagine. The backyard had soft green grass like a luxurious, plush rug. Big oak trees seemed to simply beg for a future swing. At the very back was a brand-new fence with bushes planted in front of it.

Charlotte had arranged an open house homecoming for the following weekend. Of course, her reputation was now solid and written in stone. Everyone loved the interior decorations of the home. At the party, Charlotte had the staff serve the absolute best beef tenderloin and roast duck from the Taylor farm. Large shrimp from the Gulf of Mexico swam in butter. For dessert, she had Linda Gail's favorite chocolate brownie pie from Miss Lily's bakery and, most important…Lily's famous doughnuts.

Charlotte was proud of her work and the beauty of the home. She was repeatedly told, "This is the best gala downtown Huntsville has seen in years." Linda Gail was pleased and surprised by all of it. Percy was also proud of himself for pulling off the surprise for his wife and daughter. He was surrounded by friends and city leaders throughout the evening.

A band from New Orleans played jazz on the front lawn. Everything was going well until Suzette and Michael O'Kennedy arrived unexpectedly. Michael looked embarrassed and had already consumed lots of alcohol. Suzette walked up, rubbing her belly, and reintroduced herself to Percy. As he was to all, Percy was cordial and did remember changing Suzette's flat tire. Percy excused himself and Suzette eventually found Linda Gail. The hair on the back of Linda Gail's neck stood up as Suzette introduced herself as her neighbor. Linda Gail was not impressed and knew Suzette was not on the invitation list that Charlotte had provided for her to review before the party. She could not get away from Suzette and was cornered. Suzette prattled, "Your rude house decorator had a fence put up between the main house and the guesthouse, and I want it torn down so I can continue using the main house driveway."

Linda Gail, surprised by Suzette's forwardness, told her, "No one is supposed to be in the guesthouse. It's due to be remodeled, but that work has been delayed for some reason."

Charlotte walked up next to Linda Gail to help her in her pickle with Suzette and said, "The new owners are home now, and you were supposed to be out weeks ago. Surely the O'Kennedy family has other residences in the Five Points area that are much larger than the guesthouse. Go leech off of them."

Suzette was furious, but she did not let it show. She was much too smart. Instead, she made the most of the moment and created a scene. She grabbed Charlotte's hand and fell backward, pulling Charlotte to the floor. Of course, she did it to give the appearance that Charlotte had pushed her. Suzette began to wail like a cow giving birth when she knew she had everyone's attention. Then came the all-out assault on Charlotte. "You pushed me! You tried to hurt my baby. You're jealous," she sobbed.

"You don't have a husband, you're jealous of me and my happiness, and you tried to hurt my baby." She lay on the floor in a fetal position.

Dr. Reynolds was in attendance, so he stepped forward to examine Suzette, who was getting all the attention she craved. Michael was onto her trick, but all he did was order another drink from the server. The doctor had Suzette moved to one of the guest rooms. The bed was outfitted with the finest of silk sheets, with custom-made bedding and pillows to match the draperies. Suzette naturally was not sick or hurt, but she used the opportunity to take in all the luxuries of the bedroom. She had hardly had a chance to appreciate the entire home's new interior before she'd created the scene with Charlotte.

Back at the party, everyone gave Charlotte the evil eye. Linda Gail had never seen such a charade and could not take it. She used a cocktail fork to tap her glass so that everyone in the room would look in her direction. "Everyone, everyone, please listen. Thank you for coming tonight and sharing with my family the best housewarming and welcome-home party. Please allow me to explain what really happened earlier. I had too much champagne and started feeling woozy, and I fell into Miss Charlotte, which pushed her into Suzette. I am so sorry. I assure you we will have the finest doctor on earth, Dr. Reynolds, take care of her. I will personally assure that Suzette makes a full recovery and delivers a healthy baby when her time comes."

Percy came over to Linda Gail and said, "You don't ever drink at parties until everyone's gone. What's this all about?"

Linda Gail winked at him. "We have a passive-aggressive scam artist on our hands, and we need to be very careful. Who knows what she's up to, but I wasn't about to let Charlotte take the fall."

Suzette played the event for all it was worth. She stayed in the main house for the next two weeks, lying in bed and being waited on. The help ratted her out to the Taylors about her behavior when the Taylors were gone. She would walk around the home, picking up every object. It appeared to them she was fantasizing about becoming Linda Gail.

Suzette's departure day came much earlier than she expected. On the final day, she begged Percy in front of everyone, "Please put a gate in the fence, so that if I need help while I'm pregnant, I'll know you're close by. Linda Gail promised in front of everyone on the night of the gala that she'd make sure my baby was delivered safely." Percy could not take her begging and pleading and caved in, agreeing to the gate. Suzette said in her sweetest voice, "I'm so happy now, Percy, knowing that our children will grow up next door to each other and can play together." But his plan was to move her out after the baby was born, because everyone became uneasy when she was around.

Percy and Linda Gail were leaving to stay at their home in Taylorsville that morning. From there they would begin another long family vacation on the shores of the Gulf of Mexico for the next several weeks. During this time Suzette's child should be born. The hunt for another home for her would have to be handled by the O'Kennedy family while the Taylors were away. Her husband, Michael, was no help. He had lost the desire to care about anyone or anything but a bottle.

The staff was told not to allow Suzette into the main house. They locked all the doors that morning before they left for Taylorsville. Suzette tried everything she could think of to get access to the main house. In her mind the main house was already her home, but no one would answer the door. Now that everyone was gone, she began parking her car in the main house driveway as though she lived there, and used it as her entrance to the guest house. In her mind, it was her house.

Michael had become a full-fledged drunk. When he could stay sober, he was actually looking forward to his baby's arrival. One week before the fake due date, Suzette hatched yet another plan. She left a note for Michael:

Dearest Michael,

I only have one week before the baby will be born. I fear for myself and the baby. No one in your family accepts me. I am going to my aunt's house in Memphis to have the baby, for safety and for her love and care. Your reluctance to protect me from the mean people in Huntsville has me wondering how important our marriage and our beautiful baby boy (I hope) really are to you. For this reason, I am leaving for the next few months. This will give me time to think about our future. My aunt's home is nice and quiet, a clean, loving environment for a new baby. I know I will appreciate her help.

Sincerely,

Your wife, Suzette

After Michael read the letter, he felt greatly relieved that she was gone. He wondered what kind of mother Suzette would be. She was so deceitful. How would that affect the child? He knew this was just another one of her strange games. After only a few days, he quit drinking alcohol. He felt much better, and everyone at work and in the O'Kennedy family noticed immediately. He was no longer sad and began to brag about what a great father he would be. Michael wished he could have the baby and Suzette would be gone, because he knew his aunts and grandma would love to pitch in to help raise his baby.

After almost three months at the home for unwed mothers in Decherd, Tennessee, Suzette gave birth to a huge, long baby boy. The baby had bright red hair like both his real daddy and his pretend but legally recognized daddy. The nuns and midwife were about to leave the delivery room with the baby when Suzette demanded, "Bring my baby to me! I've changed my mind. I don't want to give him up for adoption. He's my baby. Give him to me."

One of the nuns pleaded with her, "The new adoptive parents are outside the door, waiting for him. You promised them for months. They can hear the baby crying. They've even picked out his name. It's to be Austin."

From the moment Suzette had met the couple, she had taken emotional advantage of them. They had provided her a private doctor, special food, and lots of doting attention. Suzette had even let them hold her belly and sing to the baby.

Suzette had written Michael a letter three days before the delivery and was now ready to send an announcement of her return in three days. The baby looked like a newborn, but he was large for a newborn, and that was just going to have to be believable to Michael and his family as a three-month old baby, as her note to Michael had said. She was due to arrive in Huntsville at the train depot at eight o'clock Saturday night.

The nuns at the home were furious with her for using them and the poor adoptive family, who were devastated. Mother Elizabeth, the nun in charge of the home for unwed mothers, also tried to use shame and guilt on Suzette, but to no avail. Suzette seemed cold and indifferent to all concerned and refused to change her mind as they continued to care for her and the baby for the duration of her stay. She and the baby were taken to the train depot and caught the next train bound for Huntsville.

The whistle blew on the final bit of tracks before they arrived at the depot on Clinton Avenue. For some strange reason the train stopped before some flashing signs ahead. There was an emergency on the tracks. The train started to roll again after a very long delay. There had been an accident at the Memphis & Charleston depot. Suzette's train slowly rolled by where lots of men were gathered around a body on the adjacent tracks. Someone had tried to run across in front of a train going in the opposite direction...and hadn't made it.

It was Michael. He was dead. Suzette almost dropped the newborn baby on the hard train floor and was heard saying, "I did all of this for nothing. I had this awful baby for nothing." She then, in a slow and controlled manner, laid her infant on the floor and passed out. Passengers gathered around to care for her and the baby.

Michael's friends had come with him, running to meet the arrival of his new baby boy. They said Michael had been so excited that he was even going to try to love Suzette. His friends met her train and found out that she had just witnessed the accident and fainted. They took her back to the house. She awakened and saw the crib and the nursery Michael had made for their arrival home. She became hysterical. The screams were heard in the main house, and all the lights came on. Suzette demanded that Michael's close friends take her to the main house because the sight of the nursery reminded her too much of her husband. She just couldn't take it. They carried her and the baby up to the front door.

The Taylors were shocked and could do nothing but take her in and get her settled in the same room where she had recovered before. Why had they let Michael talk them into letting them stay a couple more months until he could renovate their new home in Five Points? Linda Gail looked at Percy and pulled him into the kitchen. "I know that baby looks big enough to be three months old, but it also looks like a new-born. What is Suzette trying to pull off now? Poor Michael. His family will be devastated."

Suzette grossly overstayed her welcome at the Taylor home again. The community came to her aid once more. They brought food, diapers, and baby toys. Some even offered to keep the baby from time to time. Suzette falsely believed that Michael's family had at last accepted her. They had not. They did, however, want to be involved in the baby's life for Michael's sake. She'd named the baby Chip.

Many times Suzette tried her manipulative charm on Percy. He regretted ever putting the gate in the fence for her and always turned down her advances. One day he got sick of her sneaking into the house just as Linda Gail left. She was always trying to interject herself in his life. He confronted her sneaking in at the back door. "Suzette, I'm laying down the law. I am happily married to a wonderful wife that I love. You are not our family, and you have taken advantage of our generosity. We are banning you from our lives and our home altogether. You are not our responsibility. You should be ashamed of your behavior. No lady I know would act this way with a married man. No more just coming into my home at any time. Don't try to pull the sad baby story on us or my parents. Stay out of my family's life forever.

"I know you won't leave Twickenham of your own free will. You can stay in the guesthouse...for now, but I want a commitment that you will seek other arrangements. If you bother us again, I'll have the sheriff evict you, and I know you don't want that embarrassment. I also know Michael's family owns several houses that they rent out in the Five Points area. You can go and stay there."

Suzette was furious. She stomped her feet and broke down, trying to use her crying trick as Percy guided her out the back door. She heard the lock click behind her. He watched as she went through the gate. He put on a tool belt and immediately headed for the fence. Percy nailed the gate closed, took out the hinges, and nailed it shut. The next day a stonemason crew with their work wagons began work on a new stone wall across the entire fence. "Done. Finished. No more Suzette!" Percy exclaimed. Suzette kept a low profile afterward, for she valued living there more than anything.

Within a couple of years Suzette had landed a new man. They had an arrangement. Suzette wanted an escort so she would not seem to others to be desperate and lonely. She grew tired of playing the part of the grieving widow. Her new man wanted a cover-up for his double life. He was homosexual but needed to play the part of a straight guy to keep his job with the Huntsville Police Department. He loved the power the badge brought to him and was willing to do whatever it took to hide his true self. He even went as far as beating up gays so that his cover-up would be convincing.

Detective Dick O'Neal agreed to marry Suzette and to be a devoted father to Chip. This became an uphill job as Chip got older. He was much taller than other children his age and used it to his advantage. He was a bully at a very young age and was especially mean to girls.

Each year Chip's behavior became weirder. Suzette's new husband frequently had to use his connections at the police department to keep Chip out of jail. He started off as a youngster going into unlocked houses…just looking around. But as he got older, he began to snoop through drawers and closets. It wasn't very long before he began to steal. More than one neighbor caught him being a Peeping Tom at their windows. He usually got away with it because Suzette would take him to the accuser's home, no matter how uncomfortable it was for the victim, and have Chip admit to his behavior and apologize to the family. No one really wanted to press charges. "He's a creepy kid…Just keep him away," they said.

NINE

BANANAS

Percy's father, C. C. Taylor, would often tell Percy Civil War stories. The story Percy could never get enough of was about the town of Americos in Brazil. When the opportunity for Percy to travel to Brazil arose, he took his family and jumped at it.

The first of the two destinations Percy had planned for his trip on the banana company's steamship, SS *Americos*, was Fort Alabama in British Honduras. Percy's research sadly confirmed the stories he had heard from his father. After the Civil War ended, many disillusioned Confederate soldiers had returned home to nothing. With farms and homes destroyed and more than half their family members killed, sadness loomed over the South. Devastated by the war, at least twenty thousand Confederate soldiers and their families packed up what little they had left and moved to Mexico and British Honduras. Even more moved to Brazil. Percy found in all locations a sad but true story. The expatriated Americans had made their new locations look very much like the prewar South they had left behind, with large antebellum homes, cotton fields, and slaves (until Brazil banned slavery).

Now, more than fifty years later, the descendants of these families were telling the stories of their parents and grandparents. Many died sad. Their belief was that the government of the United States would finally come get them and bring them all home, where they wanted to be. It never happened. The only discovery Percy found funny was that the descendants had as thick a southern accent as the people back home in Alabama. Percy met with the children, now adults, of Captain Smith, who had served with his father during the war. The family had assimilated into Brazilian culture. They did, however, enjoy American visitors.

The crop that was easiest for them to grow in this climate was bananas. Some of them had trade agreements with one of the importer/exporters at the port of Sao Paulo. Members of the young Smith family explained how bananas were easy to ship because you could pick them very green for transport with less loss of product as they ripened in shipment. Percy's new Americos friends made arrangements in Sao Paulo for him to get his exporter's license by filling out the paperwork and paying the fees.

Percy's mind was spinning with all kinds of possibilities. He went through the same type of paperwork as he made business transactions in British Honduras. The Port of Mobile would be the destination of entry to the Southeast, with Savannah and Baltimore for the East Coast ports...and maybe someday he would be transporting out of Galveston to the Southwest. From Mobile Bay the plan was to ship the product up the river system to the Coosa River and on to Gadsden. From there the bananas could be transported to the NC&STL—Nashville, Chattanooga, and St. Louis—train system to Guntersville and be loaded onto the Hobbs Island ferry to Taylorsville and then Huntsville, branching out to Memphis, Chicago, Nashville, Chattanooga, St. Louis, and beyond.

Next was to put a plan into action with Dr. Reynolds. He had shown Percy medical evidence of bananas being good for your health and had a whole list of all the benefits of eating just one banana a day. He needed Dr. Reynolds to write a letter of endorsement that would appeal to the largest number of people possible in an understandable manner. In other words, no doctor-speak, just plain English.

Next Percy took out full-page ads in the country's largest newspapers such as the *New York Times*, the *Chicago Tribune*, the *Washington Daily*, the *Commercial Appeal* in Memphis, the *St. Louis Gazette*, and more, spelling out a list of the health benefits of bananas, backed up by the research of Dr. Reynolds of the outstanding Vanderbilt University. The ads would run for four Sundays in a row and then one Sunday a month for a year. This cost Percy a small fortune. As it turned out, the money was well spent. He was now into a very profitable shipping and importing business. He and Doc Reynolds celebrated over the future good health of the country…thanks to bananas!

After the banana boats, trains, and shipping took off, Percy began to take a closer look at importing rum and other libations from outside the country. His connections told him the Prohibitionists were becoming more influential and powerful in Washington, DC, every day. They told him, "Don't be surprised if Prohibition gets passed through both houses and the president signs the amendment." Percy was preparing for the worst: Prohibition in America.

TEN

NEW ORLEANS

Once Molly's train departed Mobile, a family of con artists from Chicago tried latching on to her. She did everything she could to shake them, including having the conductor move her to another car, to no avail. They followed her. Sensing their dishonesty, Molly wore an apron with large pockets underneath her long skirt, which is where she hid all of her valuables. As expected, Molly's small bag disappeared about the same time the Chicago family disappeared. Fortunately, Molly had placed books from the train's library in her smaller-size luggage and that's all the thieves got that day.

Molly realized that day she did not have a lot of street experience and would have to be more on guard around strangers. She needed to find a safe place to live and get a job immediately. The train's arrival into New Orleans was especially slow, which gave Molly a chance to look around. On one side of Canal Street sat the French Quarter, and out the other window was Basin Street, with the most beautiful four-story mansions she had ever seen. Before the train rolled into the depot, Molly noticed the Metairie horse-racing course. They all looked like great places for Molly to live and work.

Because it was still early in the day, Molly decided to stop at the racetrack to see if she could get a job before looking for a place to stay.

The first gentleman she spoke to asked her if she knew anything about horses. Molly replied, "No, I don't, but I'm a fast learner."

He dismissed her with a wave of his hand, saying, "I'm not here to be a teacher, honey."

Refusing to let her first encounter discourage her, she saw two very well-dressed women without a male escort and decided to approach them. She waited for them to conclude their betting business at the window. "Hello, ladies, my name is Molly Teal. I'm new to town and looking for work. Do you think you could help me?"

"Our names are Lulu and Minnie White," one of them said. "Turn around and let us get a good look at you. How old are you? Where are you from? Are you a runaway in trouble with the law? Who have you worked for before? Look at her, Minnie. You know how men like those child-looking girls. They pay extra."

Molly's face turned from innocence to confusion, and then reality set in. "I don't want a job like that," she said. "That's why I ran away. I want a job where I can work hard and pay for a place to live and buy my own food."

"Oh, that's all you want," the one named Minnie said. "So you won't do kinky sex tricks with men or animals or with other people watching? Well, good for you, Miss Young Little Girl. Why don't you go down there on Basin Street and see if you can buy yourself one of those big mansions, or maybe one of those nice people will give you a job." The two women snickered and laughed as they went on about their way to watch the race.

Molly thought to herself, *What a good idea!* She had noticed one of the homes with lots of bay windows and a tulip-domed cupola. She would try there next...the Arlington house. Molly went straight to the front door and knocked, intending to ask the first person she met for a job. The butler opened the door, but unbeknownst to Molly, he hadn't opened it for her but for the homeowner, Josie Arlington, who was walking up the sidewalk right behind her. "Hi, my name is Molly Teal," she said to the butler. "I'm new to the city. I picked your house because it's the most beautiful on the block and I thought you might employ me."

From behind her she heard, "Where did you come from? I just get home from the coast, and I have strangers knocking at my door. What do you want, young lady?" Josie laughed, knowing she had scared the young woman. Molly turned quickly and stood there frozen, not knowing what to say. "Come in and tell me your story," Josie said. "I'm going to tell you I'm not hiring anybody as young as you." She extended her arm for Molly to come into the lavish front parlor.

Molly realized she had a very limited time for an interview, and the words came pouring out of her mouth. "My mama and I were living in Nashville when my daddy died. My horrible uncle kidnapped me, put my mother in a crazy hospital, and took me to his house. He raped me, night after night. So did his stinky friends, Judge Lawler, the sheriff, the district attorney, and two others. I couldn't take it anymore. Went to find my mama. They had killed her. I'm just a kid, and I want my life to start over. That's why I'm here."

Josie, remembering she had been only ten when she was forced into prostitution, had a soft spot in her heart for Molly and appreciated her directness. "Molly, dear, this is a sporting house, a bordello, a brothel, a whorehouse—all the same. Do you know what that is? Of course you don't. This house is exactly why you ran away!" Josie continued, "I've always said, the life of a madam chose me, I didn't choose it. I knew the only way I could survive being taken advantage of by men was to learn their weaknesses and get to them first. Life as a prostitute kills most young women."

"Ma'am, please," Molly replied. "I just want to work and have a safe place to live. I don't want to do 'sporting' with anyone. I will work real hard and do whatever needs to be done around here for you."

"My very first employee that doesn't want to screw anyone. That's unheard of in this business. Okay, Miss Molly Teal, you can be my niece and be my eyes and ears around this sixteen-bedroom house and on the streets of Storyville. You're hired!"

Molly and Josie got to know each other better that afternoon at another house that they would call home. Over the next few weeks Josie did as she said and treated Molly as her very own special niece and taught her everything about the business. Almost everyone was surprised at Josie's soft side. She was usually no nonsense and strictly business.

Within just a few weeks, Molly was Josie's closest friend, other than her lover, Tom Anderson. Mr. Anderson was a businessman, state legislator, and the unofficial mayor of Storyville, the world-famous red light district of New Orleans.

To Josie's surprise, Molly was extremely helpful in the bookkeeping department, pointing out areas where she was losing money and offering other ideas on how to increase profits. Now she had Josie's attention. Anytime the bordello was open, Molly was at the madam's side like a student, taking in all the information and learning from it.

It didn't take long for Molly to realize how bitter Josie was toward the men who made her rich. Josie was respected and sought after inside the walls of the sin city, but these same men shunned her on the streets of New Orleans. Molly noticed that very powerful men, such as mayors, senators, governors, lawyers, surgeons, and riverboat owners, would pay any amount of money to get inside the walls of Arlington. It had become a status symbol of the ultra wealthy to be seen coming or going through Josie's doors. Her house was well known all over the United States. Her reputation was to have the finest of everything, from the interior of her parlors and elaborate bedrooms, to the most expensive liquors, wines, and exotic drugs, to a very sophisticated and cultured staff of ladies from every nation, ready to satisfy any sexual desire of the patrons.

ELEVEN

CAPTAIN PALMER

Early one evening before things got too busy, riverboat captain Palmer Graham came boisterously through the front parlor. His loud voice carried through the halls. Josie was curious about all the excitement when she heard him, and came running out of her office. He was one of Josie's first customers and always treated her like royalty openly on the streets. Her arms went flying around his neck and his around her waist. They had remained very good friends over the years. It was the captain's investment money that had helped Josie in the beginning. After their initial greeting, Josie noticed his face change. His body language became more reserved and gentlemanly. "What just happened in the last five seconds? You look like you've just seen a ghost," she said.

He pointed down the hall at the girl who stood out the most because, unlike most of the prostitutes, she wore a dress covering her legs rather than being draped in French lingerie. She wore sleeves over her arms, and her collar covered up her neck and was buttoned. Her beautiful dark hair was pulled back tight, unlike the loose hair of the working girls. "Who is that girl? Is this some kind of sad joke, Josie?" he asked.

"No, Palmer, she's my niece and does my book work for me. I know she doesn't exactly fit in, does she? But no, she's not available. Says she not going to do the sporting stuff with *nobody*!"

"Good," Palmer said. "Now go get her and your evening jackets. I'm taking you two ladies to the Commander's Palace for the finest dinner in all of New Orleans." He left twenty dollars on the table as a house tip for his usual girls and walked outside, lighting a fine cigar as he waited for his dinner companions to join him.

At the restaurant Palmer arranged to have a private room so as not to be interrupted. The two adults ordered the house special trout amandine, but they started off with fresh fried oysters. Molly confessed, "I've eaten dinner already, but I still have room for dessert."

Palmer's face became soft, although he had a huge lump in his throat at the same time. "Please let me order that for you—Molly, is it?"

"Yes, sir," Molly replied.

He turned to the waiter. "She'll have the bread pudding soufflé with whiskey sauce." The waiter thanked him for ordering early, because soufflé takes a long time to bake.

Finally the conversation began with Palmer. "Josie, Molly, I have a confession. I got off the ship with only women on my mind. Now all I can do is think of the past. When I was a young man, I took a wife. I was gone a good bit of the time, but we had a real nice marriage. We had a child. My wife died when I was out to sea. I took it upon myself to be a good father and brought my daughter with me everywhere I went... including this restaurant. It was her favorite. She often claimed she had had dinner already but always had room for the bread pudding. She was about your age—fifteen or so—and we were on our way to Panama when we hit a bad storm and she went overboard. We searched for her all during the storm...even lost a couple of deckhands looking. Stayed in the area for weeks. We had help from other ships. I lost both of my ladies to the sea," he said in a fading voice.

"They say everyone has a twin in the world somewhere," he continued. "You, Molly, are my daughter's twin. That was more than twenty years ago...before I met Josie. I haven't thought of them in a good while, until tonight."

Molly looked at him and said, "Captain Palmer, I'll be glad to come with you anytime to this fabulous restaurant and remember your daughter while we enjoy dessert. I'm just relieved you aren't one of those dirty old men who want to have sex with me. Yummy—here comes our food now."

Once every six weeks or so afterward, a package would arrive for Molly. It was usually an exquisite, age-appropriate dress from a far-away place. Captain Palmer usually arrived in town within a week of the delivery, and they would enjoy a father-daughter date, always at the Commander's Palace. One night he took her to the ballet. He introduced her to the star of the performance, Della Downes. Della was Palmer's wife's sister. She was shocked at Molly's resemblance to her niece. The two hit it off and became good friends.

TWELVE

SAN FRANCISCO VIA DENVER

Molly stayed at Josie's for a couple of years before she decided to move out west to Denver. She had heard Denver was a boom-town. She wasn't sure what she would do once she arrived, but she had enough savings to last for a while. Anything would be better than the freakish people who visited New Orleans's Storyville. Josie had become difficult to deal with because of her age, paranoia, lifestyle, and declining health. Molly knew it was time, so she took all that she had learned and said a few good-byes.

On the train to Denver she noticed at one of the stops that someone had followed her. It was Bruce, the feminine-acting boy from the kitchen at Josie's. He confessed to Molly, "Yes, I'm following you. I had to get out of there before I was killed. Those people are crazy. You were the only one with any sense. I figured you had a plan in Denver and I could tag along...maybe help you out. Actually, I saw two of the working girls on the next car up. I think they're following you too! So what did you have in mind once we get there? Thinking of opening your own house?"

Molly was in disbelief. She'd thought she had left all that behind her. "I don't have a plan. I just had to leave," she snapped.

Deciding she would be safer in a group, Molly was able to find rooms at the luxurious Brown Palace Hotel. While enjoying high tea Bruce becomes chatty with the bartender Roseanne and they discussed locations for Molly to set up her business. Roseanne introduced them to her uncle, who was a law professor and owned a building on the 2000 Block of Market Street. A simple barter arrangement was made for renovation and rent…a written contract was not necessary or desired according to the professor. Altogether fourteen of them had left New Orleans that day. It wasn't what she had originally had in mind, but soon Molly was operating a bordello in Denver. She and Bruce formed a friendship that would last a lifetime.

Being from the Deep South, Molly never could adjust to the brutally cold winters in the Rockies. Captain Palmer Graham always stayed in touch by letter. He suggested Molly take the small fortune she made in Denver and move her business to San Francisco. He had a brother of great wealth living in the Bay Area who owned several large vacant houses that had been rebuilt after the disastrous earthquake and fires in 1906. Palmer and his brother had expanded into the international shipping business in anticipation of the Panama Canal opening in a few years.

In January 1910, after five years in the "sporting" business, Molly, Bruce, Roseanne, now bordello manager, and every single one of her working girls left for the coast, never to be cold again, to the city with the nickname Paris of the West.

Upon her arrival Molly was met by her good friend Palmer and his brother Pete. Bruce was instantly attracted to Pete. The feeling was mutual. Pete was surprised at Molly's young age. He had heard many stories from his brother and had expected her to be much older than her years. Pete was delighted to help his new adopted niece set up shop in a Nob Hill home near the Flood Mansion on California Street. He chose this house mainly to irritate the snobs in the neighborhood, people Pete despised. The location was excellent, for it held the city's richest clientele to help build Molly's business. Pete introduced Molly to Pierre, his personal decorator, and they became immediate friends. Molly now had in place the support to run one of the best brothels in San Francisco for the next ten years.

SECTION II

1910–1920

After World War I, the United States of America was for the first time considered a world leader. Child labor problems were shameful. Sports and music dramatically drove the direction of American culture during the prewar and war years. Fans cheered as the famous Wrigley Field was built in Chicago. The National Hockey and National Football leagues were formed. There was a wave of college stadium building for Saturday events. Blacks popularized ragtime, jazz, and blues music. President Woodrow Wilson served two terms as a progressive, during which time the federal income tax was enacted and the doors of the IRS were opened. Ford employees celebrated as they produced each Model T on the assembly line in only ninety-three minutes. Across the Atlantic Ocean times were hard in much of Europe because of political instability, restrictive religious laws, and deteriorating economic conditions. Many people were immigrating to America. In Belfast, Northern Ireland, the shipbuilders Harland and Wolff were constructing an 883-foot-long, 25-story-high, 46,000-ton passenger steamship, the largest ever built at that time, the unsinkable *Titanic*.

THIRTEEN

LETTER IN A BOTTLE, 1910

Shasta was ten years old. A storybook she loved spoke of a bottle with a letter in it. Shasta's mission of the day: to write a letter, put it in a bottle, seal it, put it in the river, and hope someone from a faraway land would find and read it.

After a few false starts Shasta had a better idea. Railroad Bob, a family friend, was an engineer for the Nashville, Chattanooga, and St. Louis Railroad into Taylorsville. Bob had written and published an article for the National Railroad newsletter that described Taylorsville, including the history of the land and its founder, C. C. Taylor. He described the beauty of the expansive river and the mountains that surrounded the small, quaint community. "The love the citizens had for the Taylors was remarkable," he said in his article. Bob also mentioned the important function that Taylorsville played in transporting freight and passengers upstream. There was actually an incline used to roll the train cars onto a barge while the passengers boarded a steamship for a twenty-one-mile journey upriver to Gunter's Landing. This trip may have been the only time the railroad had a "navy." She rolled up the paper, pushed it into a bottle, and sealed it with a cork. Then she went looking for her grandpa. He would know what to do next.

Grandpa was packing for a trip to see his sister in Tennessee, and he was glad to take a break. Anything for Shasta. He dearly loved his granddaughter. Grandpa was often sad since his wife had died suddenly five years earlier. Her death had been unexpected. Shasta had a way of distracting Grandpa for hours at a time. He loved it when she snuggled up next to him on the couch and fell asleep with her little arms wrapped around his waist so he couldn't go anywhere.

"Okay, Grandpa, let's go down to the river and throw it in the water," she said.

"We need to seal the cork with wax first, but before we do that, you need to write a special note on the newsletter, welcome the recipient, and then sign it," Grandpa told his little Shasta. Shasta signed her name at the bottom of Bob's article and wrote in big bold letters "COME SEE US." Afterward, Grandpa helped his granddaughter drip wax from a candle, sealing the cork.

Grandpa knows everything, Shasta thought.

"Shasta, let's say a little prayer for whoever finds the bottle...May they always be welcome in Taylorsville," he told her. Shasta held the bottle close to her heart and closed her eyes. "Dear God...please bless and keep safe anyone who finds my bottle...and tell them to come see me and Grandpa in Taylorsville...amen...is that okay Grandpa," she asked, looking up with her big green eyes. "I think that will be fine," Grandpa replied.

That day was Shasta's last memory of Grandpa Taylor. He went to see his sister, passed away a few days later, and was buried by his wife's side at the Hobbs family cemetery in Green's Cove, between Taylorsville and Huntsville.

FOURTEEN

BOTTLE FOUND

The bottle meandered down the Tennessee, Ohio, and Mississippi Rivers and eventually into the Gulf of Mexico. The Gulf storms took the bottle around the tip of Florida. Atlantic currents pulled it northeast to Europe. The bottle's journey took more than a year. Some say such a trip is impossible or at least improbable. However it got there, it eventually washed ashore in a small town in Poland off the Baltic Sea.

After another fourteen-hour day at the shipyard, Stanley "Jagi" Czachowski walked home along the shoreline. He was not looking forward to getting home, because he was hungry. At home there would be very little or nothing to eat. Every bit of his pay went to his parents. His father farmed. His stepmother raised chickens and sold the eggs. She kept only a few for her family. Jagi knew he had no future. With three older stepbrothers he would never own land. He had heard great stories of America. Jagi daydreamed about going to the United States to be able to work, buy food with his money, and eat all he wanted.

He looked up ahead in the rocks and saw a bottle flash in the setting sunlight. Out of idle curiosity he decided to pick it up for a closer look. Red wax had been melted and dripped down the sides. The top had the letter *T* stamped in it. He wanted to know what was inside but didn't want to damage the wax stamp. A small knife was all he had to pull out the cork. He was surprised to find that after loosening the wax with the knife around the edges, he was able to lift it off in one piece. The cork came out easily. Carefully he pulled out rolled-up pieces of paper.

Jagi had been forced to quit school at age twelve so he could start to work. His choices were a coal mine or a shipyard. He had chosen the shipyard, thinking he might live longer. While he was in school, all of Jagi's teachers had considered him a wonderful student. He was advanced for his age in German, Russian, and English, along with his homeland Polish. Reading different languages was more difficult than speaking for him, and he scanned down the papers, able to interpret only certain words. The best he could understand from the contents was that this place called Taylorsville was a beautiful place with nice people. The note was signed "Shasta." He wondered to himself if this name belonged to a boy or a girl, a man or a woman. He could visualize in his mind steamboats, trains, and forest-covered mountaintops, and the beautiful farms with orchards, vegetable gardens, strawberries, blueberries, grapevines, chickens, goats, pigs, cows, lambs, and horses...all in one place! Enough food for everybody. *All you can eat,* he thought. His mouth began to water.

Jagi arrived home to potato broth and a small slice of bread. He closed his eyes while he ate and just imagined being full on something called fried catfish and corn-bread hush puppies. This was the most satisfying meal he had eaten in a long time. That night Jagi went to bed full...in his mind. While trying to fall asleep, he kept thinking about the letter. He planned to take it with him to work the next day for his cousin Alfred to reread for him. After all, Alfred had stayed in school until he was thirteen, so he was book smarter.

The next morning Jagi got up earlier than usual. His stepmother had made porridge, which wasn't enough to fill him, so he pretended he was eating a southern peach. He was out the door in a hurry so he could go by Alfred's house in time for him to read the letter and explain it better to him. The more Alfred read, the more excited they both became. Together they walked to the shipyard. Their shift was from 4:00 a.m. to 6:00 p.m. with one thirty-minute break for lunch. The two cousins worked separately but always had breaks together. Sometimes one of the older workers brought extra bread and cheese for them. Some days they ate nothing at all. Today it didn't matter. The two boys chatted their entire break about how to get to America. How could they save extra money for the ship ticket costs to Ellis Island, New York City, United States of America?

After their work shift ended, the boys went to talk to their supervisor, Kimal. "I really like you two, because you work hard, you don't complain, and you always show up on time," Kimal said. He listened carefully as they told of their plan to find Taylorsville.

Kimal knew the boys were doing the right thing, because they would never get to keep their own money—they would always have to give it to their parents—and they couldn't afford to do anything else. Leaving was their only chance to find a brighter future. "Sir, what we'd like to do is work two extra hours a day and work Sunday for an extra twelve hours," Jagi said. "That would be twenty-four additional hours a week. Would you put that extra money aside and give the regular paycheck to our families?"

Kimal agreed. "All your hard work will pay off. When do you plan to leave?"

Alfred spoke up. "By the end of the summer, sir. We want to make the journey across the ocean before it gets too cold, and if we don't have enough money saved by then…maybe next March."

"Do you have any idea how long the journey will take?" Kimal asked. "I believe it could be up to thirty days. You could have stops in Sweden, Belgium, Great Britain, Ireland, Greenland, Iceland, and Canada before you get to America."

Jagi said, "I hope we can be gone by winter. Food is even scarcer, and the possibility of starving is on everyone's mind at my house."

"My house too!" Alfred acknowledged.

Kimal went on, "We all know Poland is the fighting ground between Russia and Germany. Our economy has been unstable because of this continued fighting. Regular work is hard to come by, which is why I think you will have a better chance if you leave. Hell, if I wasn't married with children, I'd go with you!" Everyone started laughing as Kimal finished talking.

"You can have that old wife of mine; I'll go with the boys," said a man listening in.

"I hope, when the shipyard hires more children, they work as hard as Alfred and Jagi," another man said. "Usually the coal mines get the children first."

The two cousins worked sixteen hours a day, seven days a week for eight months before they had enough money saved. They survived another winter in Poland. During that time, they learned more English and the steamship system. Alfred was able to contact an uncle in Newark, New Jersey. "We can stay with my uncle until we find work or are able to move south to Taylorsville," Alfred told Jagi excitedly.

FIFTEEN

THE JOURNEY TO AMERICA BEGINS

It was a cold, windy day in March when the boys were finally ready to depart. There was no fanfare or great emotion at Jagi's home. He simply told his parents and siblings good-bye and walked out the door, ready to begin his new, better life. He had no regrets, because he was really not leaving anything behind.

At the shipyard, some of their fellow workers threw a bon voyage party of sorts. Some pitched in and packed supplies for the boys' long voyage, including beef jerky, smoked fish, dried fruit, boiled eggs, and loaves of bread. "This is more food than we've ever seen in one place in our entire lives," Alfred said proudly.

Kimal had the best surprise of all. "I've had a talk with the head boss of the shipping line, and they have agreed to upgrade your tickets from storage and freight to the regular passenger compartments." Everyone cheered. Some were even envious.

"Thank you each and every one so much. We feel like Christopher Columbus going to discover America!" Jagi said.

Kimal explained, "With these new tickets you will be provided some meals, blankets, and cots. I have one more surprise for you: all the money, for the extra hours you have worked for eight months, I am matching. Good luck!" Kimal walked away. He was sad and would miss them.

As they picked their things up, Jagi said loudly, "I will never forget the kindness I learned today."

On board their ship they met people from all parts of the world. The ones who would listen heard all about their journey to find Taylorsville. Those who could read English took a look at the article about Taylorsville. Most were excited for the two.

The women worried that they were too young to be out in the world all alone. Jagi was only thirteen when they departed. He had a young man's body...underweight but strong and muscular. His face was that of a young boy, heart shaped and cute, and he wore a cotton top and always a big, friendly smile.

They encountered some off-duty clowns on the ship who were from the world's most famous circus. They had been to Taylorsville and confirmed that it was real and very beautiful, and that the people were especially nice. The founder, C. C. Taylor, had died two years earlier. Jagi was happy and sad to hear this news. He had really wanted to meet Mr. Taylor to ask him about the Civil War and how he had become an injured POW and then been taken to a hospital in Illinois. The clowns told Jagi that the surviving sons ran Taylorsville and that one had a daughter. He knew it before they said her name. "Shasta," they said in unison. One of the clowns said, "The daughter often travels with her father around the world. She is very nice...All of them are. They call it southern hospitality."

The infirmary was the place on the ship Jagi found the most interesting. The ship's surgeon took a liking to the young boy and allowed him to stick around and ask a lot of questions. Later, the quote he remembered best from the doctor was *"Wash your hands often, and you will never get sick."* That saying stuck in Jagi's mind. He learned how to clean wounds and how to apply bandages and splint broken bones. Jagi visited the patients in the infirmary every day. His smile and the twinkle in his eyes worked a special magic on them.

Late in the evenings Alfred and Jagi would meet with a storyteller named Story. Story was a watchmaker; he smoked big cigars and told them he was from a state called Pennsylvania. Since they had so much time on board the ship, Story taught the boys how watches were made and how to repair them. The boys loved to listen to Story telling tall tales in his American accent. He enjoyed talking while he observed them taking apart tiny watch pieces that his old hands could no longer handle well.

By the time the ship arrived in New York, the two had quite a list of names of people they had met on board, along with where they lived. By now, of course, everyone on board knew about the southern river and train town of Taylorsville.

The most memorable passenger Jagi met on the voyage was a woman named Madam C. J. Walker. She was a first-class passenger who boarded in London for New York City. He thought she was the most beautiful woman he had ever laid eyes on. She told him she was forty-six years young. He didn't know exactly what she was called in America. Would it be black, colored, Negro, African? He didn't know. Her skin was soft and silky. Her features were fuller than dark-skinned women he had seen before. Her cheeks were round like small apples and her lips were big; he almost wanted to touch them when she spoke. She had a large chest and wide hips. Jagi was from a country that was so poor, he had never seen a full-figured woman before. This was his first hard crush on a woman.

Madame Walker was very flattered by her young suitor. Sometimes he would just show up at her cabin and offer to help move her shoes or her luggage around the room. She thought it was a cute boy crush. Her cinnamon smell reminded him of a bakery. Madam Walker was a very generous person and tried to give him a gratuity. Jagi would bow, wave his hand back and forth, and refuse, saying, "No, thank you" or "My pleasure." His English was improving every day.

One day he noticed that Madam Walker's feet would swell when she wore a certain type of shoe. He tried his best in broken English to tell her he would fix her shoes. She didn't understand much of what Jagi said, and he didn't understand her either. What she did understand from their conversations was that he was poor, from Poland, thirteen years old, and going to America to find Taylorsville. "You are such a brave boy, Jagi. I would like to help you," she said.

She admired his will and determination. Madam Walker had been very poor when she was a child. Married off at fourteen years old, she had immediately started having children. She knew Jagi had what she had…a drive to have a better life. At the moment she was glad she had not been able to get a first-class passage ticket on the new ship everyone was talking about, the *Titanic*. She was happy to have met Jagi, and she gave him her address in New York.

In a bold move, Jagi took her shoes to the ship's maintenance room. He had an old leather belt in his knapsack. He used the ship's tools to split the belt right down the middle, took the extra leather, measured the old strap, and made new straps that were much longer. He then went to the ship's surgeon for some large needles and strong surgeon's string. He sewed the new straps onto the shoes. When he was finished, he used a cloth to buff the shoes until they and the new straps were polished and shining.

Back in Poland, when Jagi was younger, he had helped his uncle at an upholstery shop by sweeping the floors and helping with simple repairs. Jagi took the shoes to Madam Walker. He handed them to her and motioned for her to try them on.

She kissed him right on his forehead. This brought him great pleasure. He knew she was happy, although he never understood much of what she said. Jagi eventually learned that she made chemicals to straighten Negro women's hair. She told him this made her lots and lots of money. *Why would women want to put this chemical in their hair? I don't understand,* he thought.

SIXTEEN

NEW BEGINNINGS

It was a beautiful spring day and there was standing room only on the deck as the SS *Canada* approached the Statue of Liberty. She was as big, beautiful, and welcoming as they had all heard. Tears streamed down all the new immigrants' faces. The two cousins' plans were to arrive at Ellis Island and fill out papers, take the ferry to Staten Island, take a train into New Jersey from New York, cross a large bridge, and walk twenty-two and a half blocks to Alfred's uncle Joseph's house.

Things didn't go smoothly on the first stop. The cousins said their final good-byes to all their new friends. New immigrants went in one direction, and US citizens made their way in the other. First, all immigrants' health was checked. The more suspicious it was, the more closely the medical staff examined them. The boys passed through this area quickly.

At the next stop there were papers to fill out: twenty-nine questions to answer. Alfred was so nervous during this interview that he forgot his English altogether. Jagi stood silently. Alfred noticed his palms were wet, and that sweat rolled from his head and neck, down his chest and back. He wasn't sure why he felt this way—nervous, excited, and scared all at the same time. Now it was Jagi's turn for the interview with the immigration agent. To speed things up he told two small lies. In his very best English he said, "Alfred is my brother. I am fifteen. All information is the same." This went well, except now he had a new identity, Jagi Czachowski Butler. *I'll fix this later,* he thought to himself. When the interview was over and Jagi stood up, he was so wet with sweat that his clothing stuck to him. Jagi confessed to Alfred, "I overheard another agent tell a young boy you had to be at least fourteen if you were traveling without an adult. If you and I were brothers, we couldn't both be fourteen."

Jagi and his new "brother" Alfred had all their necessary papers. The whole process took almost six hours. The ferry departed in fifteen minutes. Next stop…New York City, New York, United States of America! The two boys held their hands up in triumph. They vowed to learn better English immediately. "We are Americans!" the two shouted.

They arrived at New York's Pier 54 at 9:00 p.m. to a crowd of forty thousand people. Scheduled to arrive at 9:30 was the *Carpathia,* the ship that held the survivors of the sunken *Titanic.* On board the *Titanic* had been more than 2,200 passengers and crew. Of those privileged, yet unlucky, few to make the maiden voyage of the *Titanic,* 1,502 hadn't survived. Immediate relief in the form of clothing and transportation to shelters was provided by the Women's Relief Committee, the Travelers Aid Society of New York, and the Council of Jewish Women, among other organizations.

The noise of the crowd was deafening. It seemed as though everyone's lips were moving, but all you could hear was a loud roar. Jagi was so overwhelmed, he could hardly remember to breathe. Neither he nor Alfred had ever seen such a large crowd of people in one place. As far as they could see in any direction, there were people. On one street alone you could see heads for hundreds of blocks…maybe farther.

Real panic set in once Jagi realized he'd lost Alfred. "I can't show up at Alfred's uncle Joseph's house without Alfred," he said, unable to hear his own voice. His head was light, and his knees didn't want to keep his legs straight. The crowd kept moving him in different directions. He had never felt this way before. Nearby were a man and his daughter, who looked about Jagi's size and age. No other young people seemed to be in the crowd.

Someone touched his arm. He turned around quickly. It was his cousin. Alfred noticed the pale white face, and just as quickly Jagi's legs folded and he went straight to the ground. The crowd seemed to swallow them. Jagi's head landed next to Percy Taylor and his daughter, Shasta. He came to after a man had given him smelling salts. Jagi woke to see big green eyes inches from his, staring. Shasta spoke to him in English, French, Italian, and Spanish. His tongue was so thick, he couldn't answer her. For some reason Alfred couldn't speak either.

The boys noticed that although the man and daughter were very nice, they had very worried looks on their faces. Percy told Alfred to get Jagi out of the crowd and into some fresh air. He told them to go down the street five blocks to a man who sold cooked sausages and bread with mustard. Percy knew the German he was sending them to understood many European languages. He gave the boys some money and pointed them in the direction of food.

It was very difficult for the two boys to travel against the crowd, as more and more people kept arriving to meet the ship. Finally they found the sausage man Percy had told them about. His name was Deter, and he did speak some Polish. The two cousins understood his German very well also. They ate slowly to savor each bite of their first meal in America. It was wonderful!

Deter explained the reason for such a large crowd. He told them of the great unsinkable ship, named the *Titanic*, on its maiden voyage across the Atlantic. The *Titanic* had hit an iceberg and sunk. A passing ship, the *Carpathia*, had picked up only 700 survivors of the 2,200 or more people on board. Everyone else had died at sea. Jagi had heard Madam C. J. Walker speak of the ship *Titanic* and that she had not been able to purchase first-class passage. That was why she was on the ship with Jagi.

Deter asked the two boys to stay the night. "I can put a pallet on the floor in my upstairs apartment. Besides, my family would enjoy meeting you two," he said. Deter, like Percy, couldn't believe how young these two boys were to have traveled alone from halfway around the other side of the world. Jagi had a young-looking, innocent, and sweet face that caught everyone's eye. People just wanted to help him. The cousins took

Deter up on his offer and would be on their way early the next morning to Uncle Joseph's home.

They lay quietly on the floor that night, but neither could sleep because of the loud noises of the city. Jagi was totally exhausted and wide awake at the same time. He thought of the girl with the green eyes who had been wearing a green dress. He closed his eyes the first night as an American, in America.

SEVENTEEN

UNCLE JOSEPH

The next morning the crowd was not as large as the night before, but the noise was still loud. Once they arrived at Uncle Joseph's in Newark, he had them put away their knapsacks and other belongings in a small room. Uncle Joseph was the maintenance manager of an apartment building. He explained to the two that he was happy to provide a roof over their heads and all the food they could possibly eat. In return they would work for him in the building, each of them doing a twelve-hour shift alone. Their job was to supply the furnace in the basement with coal twenty-four hours a day. They would keep busy by carrying coal from outside in a wheelbarrow. Their job: Keep the fire burning. One load after another after another.

The cousins didn't see each other except at shift change time. One would usually show up early or stay past shift change to catch up with the other. It was a very isolating job. No one ever came to check on them or even visit. After only a few weeks, Jagi began to miss the shipyard back in Poland. At least there he had other human beings to talk to. Jagi hated being alone.

During his time off he wrote a letter, as best he could, to the watchmaker, Story, in Pennsylvania. He asked for employment as they journeyed south to Taylorsville. Meanwhile, he wanted to see Madam Walker. She had a home on the Hudson River in Irvington, New York. While walking the streets during his off time, Jagi met people in the neighborhood, most of whom were from Poland. They filled his head with all the great things they had discovered in America.

Wanting to practice more English, Jagi ventured into other neighborhoods. He noticed that people in other neighborhoods stayed to themselves. The Germans stayed with the Germans, the Italians with the Italians, the Irish with the Irish, and so on. He wanted to find the English-speaking neighborhoods. Everything in this place, America, was so loud. So many people everywhere. He made friends easily because of his cherubic face.

At a newspaper stand he became friends with an Irish boy who sold daily extras. "Buy bananas for longevity, good health, and taste! Extra! Extra! Read all about it!" he shouted to the fast-moving sidewalk crowd. His name was Toby. He showed Jagi maps of New York and how to read them. Toby received most of his education by reading the newspapers he sold. He tried to explain to Jagi how the national debate was about assimilation versus multiculturalism. Jagi understood assimilation to mean that he would be an American from Poland...not Polish in America. *Is this all I am asked to do to stay here? It seems reasonable and not too much to ask*, he thought to himself. "I will be an American from Poland," he said out loud.

Next to Toby's newspaper stand was a bakery called Maltoid. Toby explained to Jagi that they made Milk-Bone dog biscuits, the only business of its kind on New York's Lower East Side. *Only in America*, Jagi thought. *Dogs getting their own bakery.* In Poland, most dogs died of starvation. Jagi wanted to have a dog of his own one day. He couldn't wait to share this with Alfred. He continued studying the maps of New York until he could determine where Madam Walker lived. Her house seemed too far for him to walk there and back in his twelve hours off. Maybe he could work something out with Alfred.

Jagi had an idea that if he worked extra hours for Alfred, then Alfred would return the favor. They shared their idea with Uncle Joseph. He was furious with them and responded by open-palm slapping both of them in the face, and across the room they went. He ranted, "How ungrateful you two are for everything I've done for you." Jagi had been pushed around and had sometimes wrestled with his older stepbrothers, but never before had he been hit in the face by an elder.

The cousins saw fury in Uncle Joseph's eyes. They were afraid of him. The next week, Uncle Joseph punched Jagi in the stomach so hard, it caused him to double over and cry in pain. On Jagi's fourteenth birthday, he decided it was time to leave. Alfred shunned Jagi for some reason Jagi didn't know about. So he wrote Alfred a letter. The letter said he was going to try to find Madam Walker and see if she could help them find work that didn't require them to live in a black hole all day with no one to talk to. He asked Alfred to forward any mail he might get from Story the watchmaker.

He was tired, and his stomach hurt like everything, but he decided to stop by and see Toby at the newspaper stand to look at the map one more time. "Jagi, you can't leave yet," Toby said. "The grocer over in Hoboken is friends with my pa. He wants us to give out samples of new cookies from the National Biscuit Company today. We can eat all of them we want. Are you coming with me?"

Jagi wished Alfred was with him. "Okay, I'm ready," he replied.

At the grocery store, a table was set up near the front door with a big sign that read "Oreos." The two made sure everyone tried each of the two flavors, lemon meringue, and chocolate with a crème middle. The grocer was kind enough to leave a jug of milk for the boys, which they shared with the others. Some people just drank the milk, but one little girl with no front teeth dipped her cookie into the cold milk to get it soft first. Others pulled the two cookies apart and licked the crème out first, then ate the cookies. Only the adults liked the lemon cookies.

Toby and Jagi did such a convincing job that the store sold out before noon. A delivery truck was sent to refill the shelves. Word spread around the neighborhood, and a third truck of cookies had to be sent within the hour. The grocer had record sales of milk that day. He thanked the boys by giving them each a bag of cookies. Toby gave his to Jagi, because he didn't feel too good. They went back to the newsstand.

Toby's mom came out to the street to get him for dinner and insisted Jagi join them. He accepted and enjoyed a delicious beef stew with the family. Toby was still too full to eat dinner, but not Jagi. He was also invited to spend the night. It was the first time Jagi had slept in a bed with a mattress, and the mattress had feathers in it. There were also pillows. He had never used one of those before either. He went to sleep thinking, *What a great birthday!* He slept like a rock that night.

Toby joked with him in the morning about snoring so loudly that it drowned out the city noise. They laughed and laughed. Toby's mom made hotcakes with maple syrup and sweet blueberries on top. Jagi had never had those before either. Everything in America was new to him. He couldn't help but smile.

Once they were outside, Toby's dad gave Jagi trolley tokens he had bought for him. He also wrote directions step by step all the way to Irvington. Jagi's mouth stayed open in awe all day as he rode the electrically powered trolleys through New York over bridges and into tunnels. His neck hurt from looking up and out the window at the big, tall buildings. People were everywhere. Each block smelled like a different kind of food. The trolleys took him through Harlem. He had never seen a place where all the people were of color. The ride through Chinatown smelled the best. He decided that he would have to revisit one day.

Toby's dad's last direction read, "Get off trolley at Irvington Station." Time to get off and walk. Jagi noticed that all the homes were large… almost like office buildings or shops. The front lawns were perfect. The city noise seemed far away, thankfully. It was hard for him to think with those loud sounds in his ears. After asking directions several times, he found the right street. Never had he seen such beauty all in one town.

The sign in the front yard read "Walker Mansion." "I found it," he exclaimed as he jumped in the air with delight. Through the gate, across the very green lawn, and up to the enormous front door he went. It was painted bright red. A woman in a uniform and hat opened the door. He had noticed that all the women in America wore hats. So did the men, now that he thought of it.

He told the uniformed lady in his well-rehearsed English, "I'm here to see Madam Walker." The lady gave him a look-over and raised her eyebrows. She took a feather duster to his clothes and shoes, and then she brushed his hair back off his face and out of his eyes. She took a cloth out of her apron and began to wipe his face. *This is so nice of her,* Jagi thought. She placed him on a bench and told him to wait. She came back with a fresh white shirt for him to change into, so he did.

About the time the uniformed lady was pushing his hair back again, she looked into his eyes and said, "You must be Jagi." He smiled. "You made a big impression on Madam Walker," she continued. "She spoke of you when she returned home from Europe. You look exactly as she described: a blond angel boy." His grin grew even bigger and stretched from one ear to the other. She remembered him. This validated Jagi. No one had done that before. Another new thing in America.

EIGHTEEN

MADAM WALKER

"There you are, you sweet little angel. Come give Madam C. J. a big hug." Jagi felt safe. He felt her love. He had not known these feelings until now. His mother had died when Jagi was very young. His father had married her sister, who had many children already, and that's when the home had become a very crowded house. There was no love. Just existence.

Jagi never wanted to let these new feelings go. Madam Walker squeezed him tighter and rubbed his hair and head. Jagi thought, *Please don't stop*. He was filling up his soul with the love she was showering over him.

Over the next few hours she took him on a tour around her very regal showplace. Meanwhile the uniformed lady had another uniformed lady do some cooking per Madam Walker's requests. Chicken was made from her childhood Louisiana-style recipe...fried with crispy crust and spices, along with red beans and rice and butter-soaked biscuits with honey. The wonderful food was like a tranquilizer to Jagi.

Madam Walker had a room prepared and a warm bath drawn for her young guest. Jagi noticed the bed was big enough for six people. After his bath, he jumped into the bed. The mattress was so soft, he sank into it. The sheets smelled good, and so did Jagi.

The next thing he knew, Madam Walker came to his room with a book. He opened his bag of Oreo cookies and gave her one. She had the uniformed lady bring them milk, and he showed her how to dunk them first. She read to him until he nodded off. She felt that fate wanted her to know Jagi better, rather than letting her get on a sinking ship.

The next morning, their conversation was about Jagi's dismal circumstances at Uncle Joseph's. Jagi felt awful about leaving Alfred. He hoped to hear from the watchmaker he had met on board the SS *Canada*.

The next few weeks were like a whirlwind for Jagi. He was taken around in chauffeur-driven luxury cars and went everywhere with Madam Walker. Every single black beauty shop within a hundred miles of her home got a personal visit. Jagi participated in classes and saw demonstrations on the hair products Madam Walker had invented. He learned to wash hair and give scalp massages. "Wash your hair often," she told the women.

Unless the women spoke slowly, he didn't understand much of what they said. Jagi told Madam Walker, "These women speak so fast. They all talk at the same time and, the most curious, they seem to understand one another in different conversations going on across the room."

"I agree, Jagi. It seems that only women use this special power," she said as she chuckled.

Madam Walker worried about Alfred. The next day she had the chauffeur take them to Newark, stopping in Chinatown on the way for the great food Jagi had smelled when he had come through on the trolley. Madam Walker ordered sweet-and-sour pork and spicy Mongolian beef for him. Jagi loved them both. She instructed the driver to tour through Central Park. After the park, Jagi wanted to show Madam Walker the dog bakery before heading over to New Jersey. The driver went inside and bought dog biscuits to satisfy Jagi's curiosity. Then they stopped at the Hoboken grocery for cookies.

The driver parked right out in front of the apartment building where Jagi had recently lived. Together he and Madam Walker walked in and went down to the furnace room in search of Alfred. Alfred's back was to them as he shoveled coal into the flames. Madam Walker saw his beaten face first and gasped. She reached out to him, but he rejected her comfort.

Alfred explained that he couldn't go with them because this was his dad's brother. He could not disown his family. "Blood," he said, as though this had been beaten into his head.

Jagi shouted, "I am your family. I am your brother. Remember? We are family. My dad is your mother's brother. We are family too. I went and got us help from Madam Walker. She will help us. We must leave. We are a team. We got this far together. Please come with me, Alfred. We will get other jobs and make our way to Taylorsville."

"You have to go!" Alfred told them. "I need to get to work. You're a fool, Jagi. There's no such place as Taylorsville. It's made up; this is real life, here."

"It is real, Alfred. I saw it on a map at the Irish newsstand on the corner. I was in the post office the other day and saw Taylorsville on a large poster on the wall. Taylorsville is on Hobbs Island Road on the Tennessee River in Alabama. Look at this. It's in a timetable of the railroad, right here." Jagi pointed down at the train schedule pamphlet that included Taylorsville.

Madam Walker said, "Baby, God did not put your sweet self here on this Earth to be someone's punching bag. He has bigger plans for you. I can help."

Alfred turned his back and continued to work as his eyes began to swell with tears. He knew she was right. "Leave," he shouted. They didn't know his uncle was sick and about to die. He was sworn to secrecy about it.

Before they left, Alfred pulled a letter out of his back pocket from the watchmaker and gave it to Jagi. "Will you go to Pennsylvania with me?" Jagi asked.

"No," yelled Alfred. "Please leave."

After they were gone, Alfred fell to the floor, curled up like a baby, and cried until his ill but still cruel uncle came in and kicked him so hard, it caused his teeth to hit the floor and crack. Taylorsville was his dream too! He had to stay and take care of his dying uncle Joseph's family.

A few miles passed without a word from either Jagi or Madam Walker. Then Madam Walker asked, "Jagi, would you like for me to read the letter to you?"

He nodded. "I forgot to give Alfred his cookies," he said sadly. The letter was very positive. Story, the watchmaker, wanted both boys to be his apprentices. He looked forward to their arrival and was ready for them whenever they could get to Philadelphia.

Jagi stayed another week with Madam Walker. She enjoyed spoiling him with every luxury. During her busy days she always made time to be a generous contributor to good causes. She gave generously to the needy and indigent. She also had a scholarship fund. Jagi had never seen someone with so much, who worked so hard and gave so much away.

Before Jagi departed for Philadelphia, Madam Walker helped him write and send two letters. The first letter was to Story, the watchmaker, accepting his offer of apprenticeship and to thank him for the opportunity. Sadly, Alfred would not be joining him. Included was the time and date of his arrival.

The second letter was to an unknown Mr. Taylor of Taylorsville, Alabama. "My name is Jagi Czachowski Butler from a small town in Poland off the Baltic Sea," he began. He told the story of how he had found a bottle with a letter in it about Taylorsville. Included was an invitation signed by Shasta. He mentioned events of his traveling journey so far, where he was going, and that eventually he wanted Taylorsville to be his final destination. He never mentioned his age. Mostly he wanted them to know he already loved their town and was enjoying being an American now. He was working his way toward them.

Madam Walker took Jagi to Penn Station. She paid for a train ticket and put some money in his hand, then wrapped her hands around his. They spoke of Jagi starting his new life. She mentioned that she traveled the country often, sometimes as far south as Atlanta, and that she might come to Taylorsville one day. The good-byes were sad, yet the two were joyful about having met each other. Jagi promised to write her letters during his journey. As the train pulled away from the station, Madam Walker realized that she thought of Jagi as one of her own children, going off on his own in the world.

Nineteen

Next Stop: Philadelphia, 1912

The *Broadway Limited* was Pennsylvania Railroad's premium passenger train departing from New York's Penn Station for Newark Station and then going to Philadelphia North. It was inauguration day for the new train, and of course Madam Walker had purchased a sleeper car at an extra fare. The train had an open platform observation car named Continental Hall. The inside of the observation car reminded Jagi of Madam Walker's home. Luxurious things such as panels made of fine walnut, large upholstered chairs, and bouquets of flowers were everywhere. There was even a writing desk with engraved stationery and a secretary to take dictation. Jagi had the secretary first write a letter to Madam Walker. It was a very heartfelt thank-you letter. The second letter was another to Taylorsville to tell them his journey south had begun.

Story picked Jagi up at the train station. He noticed right away that Jagi's appearance had brightened up quite a bit. Story could not believe how much Jagi's English had improved in such a short time. However, the most noticeable change in Jagi was his self-confidence. Story realized Jagi's previous host had had a very positive influence on him. Jagi explained Alfred's situation with great detail and sadness. The watchmaker's shop was at the corner of North Broad and Berk streets behind the Baptist Temple. An apartment was directly above the shop. The temple was the largest Protestant church in the United States and the dream of Temple University founder Russell Conwell.

They entered the shop, which was very neat and organized except for a few boxes in the corner. Story said, "Oh, before I forget, let's go over here to the desk. I had a key made for you to the front door of the shop, Jagi."

"Gosh" was all Jagi could think to say. "What trust you have in me! I could be a thief."

"I don't think so," Story said.

Upstairs was the apartment, and it was definitely that of a widowed man. After being at Madam Walker's feminine home, Jagi could see that this place could use her decorating touch. Story told Jagi that his wife had been pretty and very bright. Story believed she had been given a sedative or poison by an envious man next door when she rejected his advances. He could not prove this, but then again, he said, "That neighbor disappeared one day." He told Jagi they had never had children, and he had never remarried. He mentioned that he'd had occasional girlfriends, but not the kind you take to church. Story showed Jagi a room with two small beds. The other was intended for Alfred. The beds looked new. There was a washroom, Story's bedroom, a small living area, and an unbelievably large kitchen, which seemed out of place.

Story's late wife's dream had been to have a restaurant downstairs. She had planned to do the cooking upstairs in her beautiful, modern kitchen. Story had made a pot of potato soup with pieces of sausage and stale bread. The soup was filling but very bland. Jagi said, with no ill intentions, "So your wife, she didn't teach you to cook?" They laughed out loud together. Story knew the meal was tasteless. With great eagerness on his face Jagi said to Story, "The cook at the house in New York taught me a few things. How would it be if I tried to make them for you? It couldn't get any worse."

Story laughed and said, "Down the street is a butcher and a grocer. I have an account, and I'll put you on it. Then get all the supplies you need. Things are already looking up." Story smiled.

"In the next week I'll have an employee working in the shop," he said. "So for the first time in twenty years I'm going to take time off. I want to show you everything Philadelphia has to offer."

Jagi asked, with a slight grin, "Philly baseball?"

"Yes," Story replied, "and the Liberty Bell and the Declaration of Independence and dozens of other places that I want to show you about America's first big city and all her history."

Story was elated. He had just been given a second chance at having the wonderful son or grandson he had never had. He was going to make the most of it while Jagi stayed with him. After the first week of sightseeing and eating various foods in different parts of town, it was as though the two had known each other their whole lives. Jagi mattered to Story. Story mattered to Jagi. Throughout their activities Story told stories, some of them real...some of them made up. The stories sounded like music to Jagi's ears.

After a few failed attempts at cooking, Jagi finally got it right: Louisiana-style Cajun fried chicken. Jagi made enough for eight people, so they had chicken for a few days. Jagi would have to remember not to cook so much the next time. His best dish happened to be sautéed shad caught in the nearby river. He had learned how to cook it from the nice men at the fish market. Everywhere the sweet-faced boy went, he made friends. He liked Philadelphia better than New York. New York had many more immigrants and not as many real Americans as Philly. His English became better with time. In the evenings Story began teaching Jagi the art of being a watchmaker and a watch repairman. Story was pleased with how quickly Jagi learned the trade.

Meanwhile, Story wanted to continue to explore and show Jagi all the city had to offer. They both agreed Philadelphia baseball was the best and most fun thing they did. Story bought two gloves and a ball. The two of them threw daily while Story told tall tales of all the baseball greats.

Although it had been just a few weeks, Story was quite proud of how well his apprentice was coming along. Together through their sightseeing and museum visits they learned a lot about American history. Jagi explained that back in Poland, they had never gotten over the effects of the wars that had been fought back and forth across their land. Here everyone seemed to be better off after a hard-fought war.

"Tomorrow I'm taking you to the best birthday party you'll ever go to in your whole life. It's the Fourth of July, America's birthday! We have parades during the day and fireworks at night," Story explained. Jagi's face lit up. Then he described that back home there were no happy fireworks; there was only the constant firepower of the war between Germany and Russia with Poland in the middle.

Jagi had a good night's sleep and woke up early on the Fourth of July. That morning they watched the parade from the corner in front of the church. Parade participants wore patriotic colors, and flags and banners decorated the streets. More than once Story looked at Jagi, whose face glowed with joy. "I am so happy to be an American!" shouted Jagi over the noise of the crowd.

That night, after a neighborhood feast, they all walked down to the Schuylkill River for the spectacular fireworks show over the water. Story spent most of the time watching Jagi's reaction to the fireworks lighting up in the sky as the band played "The Star-Spangled Banner," "America the Beautiful," and many more American patriotic songs. Jagi felt like he loved this country so much, he would die for her freedom—something he could never say of Poland. He knew he was in the right place for the moment. He also knew he had made the right decisions so far to leave Poland and to leave Uncle Joseph's and Alfred behind. Leaving Madam Walker was the hardest to move past. He also knew there would come a time when he would leave Story, but not yet. He had too much to learn.

"Story, when we get home, will you teach me the Pledge of Allegiance to my flag, and can I add *of the United States of America*?" Jagi asked.

"Of course I will, and I think adding *the United States of America* would be appropriate," Story said with great pride.

TWENTY

BACK IN TAYLORSVILLE

Percy had received two letters from a man named Jagi from Poland. He decided not to tell Shasta just yet. Maybe the next letter would have more information. He was intrigued that this man had come so far to America to see Taylorsville because of Shasta's notes in a bottle.

He and Shasta had made it home from New York with Olivia and her twins, Oliver and Opal. The entire world was devastated by the sinking of the supposedly unsinkable *Titanic*. "How could this have happened?" was the question on everyone's mind.

Percy's biggest problem now was how to best help Olivia. She had witnessed her husband and father perishing in the sinking of the *Titanic*. They had refused to get into the lifeboats until all the women and children were taken care of. Olivia would love to have gone down with them rather than live without them. If it hadn't been for her children, she would have stayed with her husband. Her father, Linal, was one of Percy's most trusted friends in the world. They had served together during the Spanish-American War. He and Percy had vowed a long time ago, before Linal's wife went crazy and Percy's wife, Linda Gail, died, that they would take care of each other's family if something were ever to happen.

Percy and Shasta were in New York on rum and banana business. He was trying specifically to acquire a building for his friend Emilio to expand his rum distillery business to New York. By coincidence, he was there to greet the Howard family on their move to America from France when the tragedy occurred. He promised Olivia he was making all the arrangements for her and her twins. She didn't care what happened; she only wanted her husband, Deval, to be alive. Olivia was in shock and a deep depression.

Her family had previously visited Percy and his family in Taylorsville. Because of those visits, Taylorsville or nearby Huntsville was one of the primary areas they were considering for permanent residence. The Howards were a black family of means and education, but even Percy had concerns about whether they would be accepted in Alabama. Percy and Shasta had always stayed with the Howard family when they were in France. Shasta and Opal, Olivia's daughter, attended the same women's schools in Paris and New Orleans. Shasta thought of Olivia as a beautiful royal princess. She loved having the Howard family around and thought of them as her royal family.

The twins were a bonus and were very bright. Their French education was more liberal than that of American schoolchildren of their age. Deval and their grandfather Linal had had a hand in teaching them reading, math, and science. Olivia and the children took turns reading to one another daily. While in Europe, the children had great opportunities to learn several languages.

Percy by now owned several homes in downtown Huntsville. They would live there as well as in Taylorsville until Olivia could decide her future. Percy thought living in town would give Olivia a sense of being with more people and provide conveniences and variety in shopping, entertainment, and churches. The two white-columned houses on Adams Street were chosen. Shasta knew of Olivia's nightmares and, since the twins wanted their own rooms, asked if it would be all right if she and Olivia shared the bed in the large master bedroom downstairs. Under Shasta's pretense that her daddy had agreed to help her redecorate her room and it would not be ready for a few months, Olivia readily agreed. Percy was happy with this decision because it was the room where his wife, Linda Gail, had died. Percy, Shasta, and their newly extended family would bring life and happiness again to the vacated house.

Olivia was numb and didn't care what happened, but she did sleep better with Shasta in the bed. She lay wide awake and remembered the first time the two had met in New Orleans after Shasta's mother had died unexpectedly. The little girl's life was shattered without her mother. Olivia was older, but completely understood, since her own mother had been sent away to a crazy house for putting an island voodoo spell on the mayor and refusing to take it off. Olivia was raised by her father only. She understood and tried to comfort Shasta. Now this little girl was a few years older and trying to take care of her.

Slowly, everyone began to adjust to this new way of life. Percy felt like he had four children now. He loved family life. Chase, Percy's brother, noticed a huge difference in him. After Linda Gail died, Percy had seemed to drift and wander the earth, all with the intent of showing Shasta everything the world had to offer, like he had wanted to do with her mother. Now Percy had a reason to focus more. He was proud of his enlarged family. They went everywhere together as a group.

Olivia and the twins were mulattos. Because of this, Percy knew it was possible that some misguided racist local might want to do them harm. He hired extra staff to keep an eye on them. Percy just dared someone to deny his family any service or courtesy. He would put them out of business, and the town folks knew it. He could and would destroy. This did not change the fact that some people would up and leave a restaurant, department store, or even the Big Spring Park when they came around. Percy knew some people were strongly prejudiced, and he felt that he could change it in some and not in others. His family meant everything to him, and he would do anything to protect them.

A racist from Scottsboro once spit on the ground in front of all of them. Percy took his hand as though he were greeting him with a shake. The man howled in pain as the bones in his hands were being crushed. Shasta asked, "Daddy, why do you do that to the men you don't like… break their fingers?"

"Oh, honey, some people like to poke you in the eye and need to have their poker broken…that's all." The man came up missing one day soon afterward, and someone was heard saying that he had moved out to Dallas, Texas.

Slowly the negative behavior began to stop. Only a fool wanted to be on Percy's bad side. He was very powerful and rich and, most important, knew all the boys from Cloud's Cove. The folks who came up missing in Cloud's Cove were often thought to have moved to Texas. The police chose to never go into Cloud's Cove unless there were two patrol cars with two officers in each one. This seldom happened. One of their own decided to join law enforcement. On his first official police visit he made to his own people, he went missing.

Four other officers went to investigate the disappearance. They stopped the postman to ask him if he knew anything about the missing officer. He told them, "I've been told Joe was moving to Texas. Haven't seen him around lately. You officers need to be careful. I just saw one of the boys from around here jump out of his truck and stomp a rattlesnake to death. He had a gun on the rack in his truck, and I asked him why he didn't just shoot it. Do you know what he told me? 'Postman Parsons, you know this is more fun!'" Most of the Cloud's Cove folks were good people just trying to make a living, but some were crazy dangerous. The patrol cars turned around and sped away. Postman Parsons just laughed. He loved telling the rattlesnake story. It was true!

After just a few weeks, the townspeople accepted Percy's new family additions. After all, he often had visitors from all over the world come see him anyway. This was really nothing new to his friends. He liked to see the good in all people, no matter what foreign land they came from. He thought Huntsville should accept all people, locals as well as those from any nation. At present he also had a guest from China, Mr. Yong, staying with his family until Percy could set him up in business downtown with a living area above. Mr. Yong was an acupuncturist who helped Percy greatly with his injured back. More important, Mr. Yong taught Shasta self-defense, strengthening, and meditation exercises. He said they were "good for balance."

Another of Percy's frequent visitors came from the Middle East. Everyone called him the sheik. Shasta loved the sheik's wardrobe, starting with the turban on his head. Because she was a little girl, she got away with pestering the sheik until he taught her how to tie a turban. She loved to feel the cloth from which his clothing was made. The cotton was so soft, you could snuggle in it. His silk robe was from a faraway land called Hong Kong. He wore sandals, so his toes showed all the time. Shasta thought this was silly. The sheik loved Huntsville's hospitality. He also invested in businesses and land in the county, often on the advice he received from Percy.

Percy's Italian friends came to visit and never left. Their family kept expanding as more came to stay and start businesses. Constantine, Alberto, and Gino were opening an Italian restaurant. Percy thought they made the best meatballs on earth, and for this reason he wanted to make sure they stayed and were successful. He had met them on a visit to Sicily. The three brothers laughed at Percy for gaining so much weight while in Italy. He loved the food and was delighted when the brothers decided to stay in America. Percy learned the hard way to stay out of their way while they worked in the kitchen. He interpreted loud voices, screaming, and yelling as a fight brewing. Alberto corrected him: this was "Italian love." The Italians used his house next door in Huntsville while they built a house in Taylorsville near the farm.

Another of Percy's friends from afar was Carlos, who was from Brazil. He was very helpful when Percy visited the Brazilian town of Americos, translating Portuguese during meetings with businessmen. His passion and craft was that of a master stonemason. When he arrived on the farm, he helped build a bunkhouse and finished out the front entrance with a beautiful stacked stone design. Percy told him the bunkhouse was his advertisement, because everyone who saw it wanted to hire him for buildings all over town.

Olivia, Shasta, and the children took it upon themselves to help all new arrivals learn English. Sometimes, during slow periods at the Taylorsville depot, they taught English in the waiting room, where there was plenty of seating. Shasta loved to take the women dress shopping on English-speaking-only outings. They loved it. The twins played with and taught the other children. The international children, of course, learned English faster than the adults.

TWENTY ONE

WASHINGTON, DC

A third and final letter was sent to Taylorsville by Jagi, who continued to fill them in on his journey and the details of his upcoming arrival.

Story decided Jagi should see Washington, DC, before he journeyed southward. They arrived at Union Station, which was the jewel of railroad stations. Having opened only six years earlier, the terminal was celebrated because it connected the Pennsylvania Railroad with the Baltimore and Ohio Railroad under one roof. Washington finally had a station large enough to handle crowds and beautiful enough to serve the capital of the United States of America. The second reason the city benefited was that both railroads removed their tracks from the National Mall, site of the Washington Monument. Also, only a few months earlier, the construction of the Lincoln Memorial had started near the Reflecting Pool.

That afternoon, Story waited at the bottom of the Washington Monument while Jagi climbed the 897 steps and fifty landings to the top. That night they stayed at the Hotel Harrington, which was the capital's newest and most modern hotel, at Eleventh and E streets N.W. Rooms with running water and bath cost two dollars per day. The hotel had six floors with an elevator and a negative draft system using fans on the roof to draw air from the hallways. Each guest could open the room window and use an adjustment lever to open a panel over the door so that outside air could circulate through the room during the hot summers. The architectural firm of Rich and Fitzsimmons had designed the building to last a hundred years. While enjoying dinner at the full-service fine dining room, Story and Jagi met Augustus Gumbert. Mr. Gumbert was a hotel regular and hoped to be the general manager someday. He was a veteran of the Spanish-American War and had a peg leg from a war injury. During the course of the dinner, they discovered Augustus had shared a hospital stay with Percy Taylor while under the command of the famous admiral George Dewey. Jagi soaked in all the new information he could.

The next morning sightseeing continued to the Capitol and then on to the White House, home to the president of the United States. Jagi took it all in, photographing everything with his eyes and preserving the images in his mind.

Finally Jagi's departure day arrived, a sad day for Story. They reminisced how just a few short months earlier they had met on a ship crossing the Atlantic Ocean and had grown close since then. "Jagi, you never knew why I was in England when we met on the ship. I had gone to London to buy the world's best watch: a Rolex. I want you to have it. Give it to your grandchild when you are old."

Jagi gratefully accepted the gold watch, not completely understanding the magnitude of the gesture. He did know it was really nice and that it was Story's personally prized possession. Jagi promised to keep in touch and write letters to Story often. Story confessed how much he would miss Jagi and wanted to visit him in Taylorsville. He felt like he was losing a newfound son. "If I don't like it there, Story, I will come back and live with you in Philadelphia, if that would be okay," Jagi said.

"Of course, my dear boy, of course" was all Story could say.

The two sat silently at Union Station, waiting for Jagi's train to arrive and head south.

TWENTY TWO

JAGI ARRIVES IN TAYLORSVILLE

After nearly seven hundred miles and three days on a train with many stops in between, Jagi completed the land portion of his trip in Guntersville. The last leg of his journey involved a steamship for the train passengers while the emptied train passenger cars were pushed onto a barge and then pushed by the steamship for twenty-one miles to the final destination. Jagi was nervous and hoped his letters had arrived. He thought he might nap on this final part of his trip, but there was just too much to see that he didn't want to miss.

Traveling on the Tennessee River, Jagi felt like the first American explorer going through wilderness. There was more wildlife than he had expected. As they passed a cave at the water's edge on the right, a passenger told him that every night at dusk thousands and thousands—maybe millions—of bats flew out. A few more miles down the river, he witnessed a show of two American bald eagles teaching their young to fly for the first time. Walking on the sandy mud beach was a seventy-pound dirty white bobcat strutting his stuff. Off in the distance, he could hear howling. The captain of the steamship told him the sound was from coyotes. The biggest surprise was through a narrow stretch of the river where an eight-point deer swam to the other side. He didn't know what it was until the deer reached the shore. *Wow! Deer can swim*, he thought.

Jagi's heart sank as he remembered that Alfred was supposed to be here witnessing all of this with him. They came around a bend in the river, and much to Jagi's surprise, huge cliffs jutted hundreds of feet straight up out of the water. The captain told him the locals knew them as Painted Rock, named by the Indians. Then they passed by Paint Rock River and a smaller river known as the Flint. Many small boats were in this area, all loaded down with produce mixed with moonshine from Gurley and Cloud's Cove. The people in the boats all seemed to know Captain Lindstrom and waved or came to the side of the barge and hitched a ride. The captain didn't seem to mind. He pointed ahead to Jagi and said, "At the foot of that mountain straight ahead is Taylorsville." To Jagi's surprise along the east side of the riverbank a well-dressed Negro entertainer played back and forth between a harmonica and a saxophone as background music. *Wow, this must be America's South,* he thought.

It seemed to take forever to travel those last few miles. Once they arrived, his patience was pushed to the limit for it seemed to take another forever for all ten train cars to be pulled up the incline one at a time by the train's engine. To his amazement, the deckhands used a boatswain whistle like they did at the shipyard back in Poland. He was on the top deck looking out at the beautiful farm that awaited him. All the passengers were then taken off the ship and boarded back on the train for the short ride to the depot. He seemed to have gotten a second wind by the time they pulled up and stopped.

Jagi was first in line to get off. Unknown to him, one of the locals had accompanied him down the river and walked through the fields to the Taylorsville Depot, giving the town an hour's "heads up" that their guest was aboard and what he looked like. As the doors slowly opened, he was met by a crowd. The warm air rushed over him, and it smelled very sweet. Several men were holding a huge board painted white, and in bold black letters it read "Welcome to Taylorsville, Jagi." He looked behind him to see if someone else had the same name. Percy had arranged for the town folks to meet the man from so far away who had found Shasta's note in the bottle. Sometimes, when it is least expected, fate has a way of rewarding.

Before he could take one step off the train, two large men hoisted Jagi onto their shoulders. Another picked up his trunk. They carried him over, in a parade-like fashion, to meet his host. He didn't want to cry, but he couldn't help it. He had never before felt so special. They didn't even know him.

There in the center of the crowd stood the girl and the man from Pier 54 in New York City. Jagi was surprised and thought it strange that he should see them again. He wanted to thank them again for the help they had given him and Alfred in New York City. Jagi couldn't help but notice that he was being carried directly toward them. To his surprise, the men set him down in front of them saying, "Mr. Butler, this is your host, Mr. Taylor, and this is his daughter, Shasta."

Before Percy had a chance to say a word, Jagi looked directly at Shasta. "You sent the bottle?"

Her beautiful green eyes opened wide. "You're Jagi? The boy I met at the pier in New York?"

"Yes, yes it was me," Jagi replied. "I woke up. You were trying to talk to me. Yes, it was me..." Jagi was so excited, but caught himself as he started rambling in Polish. He turned to Percy and began speaking in the best English he had, saying. "Mr. Taylor, I am Jagi Czachowski... Butler. Thank you for helping Alfred and me when we arrived."

"Son...son, no need to thank me. Like Shasta's bottle, fate just brought us together that day. Welcome to Taylorsville. Is the other boy with you?"

Before Jagi could answer, Big Mama took him in her arms and smothered him into her chest, a giant breast covering each ear. Her appearance reminded him of Madame Walker. She finally let go and whispered in his ear, "I'm going to make it my job to put some meat on your bones."

That night there was a unique Taylorsville party. Everyone, including Percy, had been expecting a man, not a boy. The men had whole pigs with apples stuffed in their mouths turning over open wood pits. The smell was incredible to Jagi. The ladies busied themselves carrying food and drinks back and forth between the homes, and a huge tent with tables was set up. The Taylors took Jagi into the house to let him put away his things and freshen up. Inside the house, he met Olivia and her two children. That night Jagi went to bed feeling so full and happy, he didn't care if he never woke up. His last thoughts before he fell asleep were of Alfred.

The next few days were a whirlwind. Shasta and her father took him by horseback on a tour through every inch of the farm and up and down the river and over the mountaintops. Percy looked at Jagi as though the world wasn't so cruel after all. He had been given a son. Jagi's big smile and the twinkle in his eyes intrigued everyone.

While they were high on top of a mountain, looking out as far as they could see, Jagi asked Percy, "Where did all the open fields come from? Did someone clear all the trees?"

Percy told him, "Local legend has it that before the white man came with their guns, this area was the Indians' greatest hunting ground. They gathered at one end of the forest, set the other end of the woods on fire, and then waited for the animals to run out where they would club them or shoot them with arrows. The burned forest became fertile ground for the newly arriving white settlers and farmers, who didn't have to do all the work required to clear the fields. That's how Alabama got its name: *Alabama* is the Indian word for 'Thicket Clearers.'"

Jagi seemed to understand English better than he spoke it. "Why do it look so green here as to other parts of the country?" he asked.

"Jagi, I guess the Indians wanted to leave some of the trees for us to enjoy. That or the white men drove them out before they finished burning all the trees down," Percy said, chuckling.

Jagi said, "Mr. Taylor, I want to have job and pull my own pounds around here."

"Weight. You meant to say *weight* instead of *pounds*. I understand you have been working for the past few years to help feed yourself and your family. As you can see, we have plenty of food around here. I'd rather you catch up on your schooling. That is why we will spend the school year downtown. Shasta, Olivia, and the twins will reside in the white house on Adams Street. Chase lives in my parents' house next door. I could not stay in the house where Shasta's mother died. I recently purchased a house right around the corner at Franklin Street and Williams

Avenue. It's a great big house with a secret cave under the basement. It will be you, me, and sometimes Doc Reynolds. Doc usually stays when he visits. Of course Big Mama will be with us too! All three houses have plenty of help.

"Dinner's at six o'clock every night at my house. We go over the events of the day for every person and discuss current local and national news. We will spend the weekends at the farm. Shasta is going to help tutor you. Olivia and the twins will help teach you, too. You can start your career over the summers or on the weekends. What kind of job would you want?"

"Story, the watchmaker I met on ship coming over to America, taught me his trade and gave me the tools for repair shop here if I can. He gave me his personal watch...See," Jagi said, showing Percy the beautifully crafted watch. "Also, I noticed the Negro women's hair around here could use my help. Madame Walker, another friend I met on ship, lives in New York. She is a Negro woman and taught me how to work in a booty shop to relax hair. Why they do it, I am not really sure, but they willing to pay good money. Do you think Miss Lily would let me do her hair?" Jagi asked. He continued, "I brought plenty of the product Madam Walker gave to me. She will send me more if I need it."

"Jagi, I am glad that you want to work. Sounds to me like you have good ideas. How about we get you caught up on your book learning for your age first? Now, about Lily's hair: you do that at your own risk. I'm not so sure she will go along." Percy again chuckled softly.

The next Saturday afternoon Jagi ran into Lily as she was leaving the general store. She could hardly understand anything he said to her. He had a good soul...she just knew it. "Miss Lily," he said, "see how my hair is limp, soft, and straight?" He looked at her, waiting for an answer. Lily looked at him, wondering what would make him think she would understand being burdened with straight hair. He smiled real big, touched his hair, and then touched hers. He continued, "I do for you. Straight hair. You like?" He pulled combs and brushes and a bottle of Madam Walker's product out of his bag. He then read off the bottle, "'Negro hair relaxer. Professional use only.'"

Lily caught on and said, "I only wear a scarf on my head. There is nothing I can do with this hair." As she showed him her hair twisted up against her scalp, he smiled and took her by the arm. "Let's me and you do booty shop."

Lily looked a little reluctant, but for some reason she trusted this young boy with her hair. "It can't be any worse. Okay, Jagi, let's do beauty shop!" she said.

By the time Lily went to singing that night, Jagi had transformed her life. Her hair was long, straight, shiny, and soft. She couldn't keep her hands out of it. She wore a special dress to church to go with how she felt about herself that night. "How much do I owe you?" Lily asked.

"Would one dollar be asking too much?" Jagi replied, unsure if he was offending her.

"No, honey, I'd gladly work the rest of my life to look this good. I bet all the ladies tonight will make a big fuss," Lily said, beaming.

Early the next morning, before the sun had had a chance to come up properly, Jagi heard a tapping at the back door. He jumped up, eager to see who might be visiting at this hour on a Sunday morning. He looked out through the stained-glass window to discover four Negro women in the yard. When he opened the door, the tallest one stepped up and said, "Are you Jagi? I have my one dollar and fifty cents. Will you do my hair to look like Miss Lily's? Before I go to church?"

"Mine too?" asked the second lady.

"Us too," said the others.

Jagi pushed the screen door open and held his arm out to welcome them into the kitchen. "Did Lily tell you one dollar and fifty cents?" he asked.

"Yes," they all said together.

"Is that enough?" one asked. "I have more. It is my extra money. I made it ironing. No children of mine will be doing without."

"That is a good amount," Jagi said, smiling. "It's what they pay in New York City." He wondered why Lily hadn't told them he charged one dollar.

Before he knew it, one of the ladies had started coffee to boil and the others were rolling out biscuit dough. He looked up from the sink, and out in the yard were more women. Standing in the doorway was Percy... smiling. "I knew when I saw Lily last night that you were starting something," he said. "Good morning, ladies. Step right up. In no time at all Jagi will have your hair looking beautiful too!"

Jagi had to turn them away after the last bottle was empty. He had made twenty-five dollars, he hadn't even dressed for the day, and it was nearly lunchtime. "Mr. Taylor," Jagi said as he handed him all the cash, "will you help me write a letter to Madame Walker? I want to ask her to please send more bottles."

"I'll do you better than that: let's call her on the telephone, long distance," Percy said.

"Long distance?" Jagi inquired. He couldn't quite comprehend how he could talk to her if she was so far away. It took some time, but the operator came through. Madame Walker was on the other end of the line. Jagi couldn't speak. Percy took the phone and explained who he was and why they were calling.

"How's my baby, Jagi?" Madame Walker asked. "Are you taking good care of him? He is very special. You know that, right? Very special. I hated to see him go."

"He's fine and has started quite a business today," Percy replied as he looked down at the pile of cash Jagi had made in a few hours. She assured Percy she would send a package the next day. He put Jagi on the phone. It was sweet how Jagi kept touching the box on the wall like he was touching her face while she spoke. He mostly just smiled, grinned, and nodded his head up and down while listening.

After the phone call was finished, Percy said, "Do you want to see a very special pocket watch? It was my daddy's. He was the one, with Shasta, who sent you the letter in the bottle." Percy opened a desk drawer and pulled out the pocket watch and an old billfold. The old leather billfold was still in very good shape, so Percy opened it up and put the twenty-five dollars in it. "Jagi, this was my daddy's billfold and now it is yours." Jagi could not speak, but Percy understood. His daddy would have approved.

Jagi carefully pulled a handkerchief out of his pocket that revealed a red piece of wax with the letter *T* stamped on it. "This was on top of the bottle I found that Grandpa C. C. and Shasta sent." After he showed it to Percy, he placed it in his new billfold.

Jagi preferred time at the farm in Taylorsville to downtown Huntsville. He understood why Percy and Shasta insisted he stay in school. Shasta worked with Jagi every day on his studies, especially his English.

At the farm, Jagi focused on his social skills, mainly at the depot or one of the general stores where the locals would sit around and swap stories while they whittled wood with their pocketknives. The old-timers always made Jagi feel welcome and tried to include him in their conversations.

Two men Jagi liked the most happened to be Negroes. Mr. Herman Deeley was a traveling music man. He had a sign painted on the back of his truck that was decorated with musical notes and read, "Music Man: Tell Me a Song and I'll Play You a Tune."

Most of Mr. Deeley's instruments were homemade, such as the drum. It looked to be a bottomless pot with cured deerskin stretched across the top and the bottom. The sticks were crudely made. The guitar was fantastic, Jagi thought. It consisted of a small wooden crate with river cane stalks added to the side and tight strings of some sort tied to both ends. Although it was sometimes out of tune, Jagi danced around in circles singing in half English and half Polish. The only store-bought instruments Herman owned were harmonicas. He gave one to Jagi for Hanukkah one year, because for some reason he thought Polish and Jewish were the same. Jagi carried the treasured gift in his pocket always. Mr. Deeley's most prized possession was a brass saxophone he had inherited many years earlier from a previous employer.

Mr. Love was the other fellow Jagi took a liking to. "I'm a moonshiner…That's my business," Mr. Love said. He drew in the smooth, dry red dirt a diagram from the top and side view of his operation. The dirt picture showed the oak barrel, the thump keg, and the condenser. There was a copper boiler buried underground, sheet metal, iron pipes, and firewood. One day he showed Herman and Jagi his stills and went into great detail about how moonshine was made. Mr. Love said, "Moonshining is an art and takes a real craftsman to make. It is an unlawful, clear liquor made from corn, sugar, and water that has to ferment. The fermented mixture is run through a still. Sixty gallons of water, fifty pounds of sugar, and a half bushel of cornmeal makes four or five gallons of 'shine. I make it right—that's why my business is good. People come to me because I make whiskey that's fit to drink."

Mr. Love gave Jagi a small mason jar filled with his "white lightning" liquid as a gift. Jagi tasted it, immediately spit it into the air, shouted something in Polish, and pointed to his mouth.

The other two men laughed and took a swig, swished it around their mouths, and then swallowed with big grins on their faces. "Try this, Jagi," Mr. Love said. "It's 'shine I make for the women. It's called apple pie."

Jagi tasted it and licked his lips. "That tastes just like pie...No alcohol taste. I like that," he said.

"Be careful, that's a hundred and eighty proof," Mr. Love said.

"Fine 'shine! White lightning," sang the music man, and Jagi finally caught on and began to play the harmonica.

It became a weekly ritual for the three to meet at the depot. Moonshine Man, Music Man, and Polish Boy were a bit of an oddity in the small town but completely harmless to all—except one local, R. H. Craft. He would often try to bully the three. It really bothered him that Percy allowed Jagi to befriend the Negroes. Percy had to finally deck him in the jaw one day to get him to leave the three alone. This made for bad blood between the Taylor and the Craft families. Percy regretted the day his daddy had ever sold land to the racist bully and his family.

The nightmare began for Jagi in Taylorsville on the cold afternoon of Monday, January 18, 1915, when he was sixteen. He went out earlier than usual to bring in firewood because it got dark so early that time of year. He had gone back outside for a second load when he heard loud voices from around the corner of the depot. His gut told him something was wrong, so he yelled into the house for Percy and took off running toward the screaming. He recognized the voice; it was that of his dear friend Herman Deeley. Jagi approached the crowd of men and could not believe his own eyes. There was Herman, scared and begging for his life as R. H. Craft tightened a noose around his neck from atop his horse. He had Herman standing in the back of the wagon.

Herman's last words were "If I am to die here today, I put a curse on this land and the Crafts for one hundred years!" Bass Cobb and Will Craft held him in place. In a flash the two men let go of Herman, jumped out of the wagon, and slapped the horse hard on its rear. Jagi screamed, "*NO!*" as he pushed his way toward the oak tree from which Herman dangled.

Immediately, Jagi started to climb the tree to cut the rope and save Herman. R. H. Craft swiftly turned his horse around and almost pulled Jagi off the tree, delaying his cutting of the rope. Jagi would not give up. One more hack at the rope, and Herman dropped to the ground as Jagi jumped from high up in the tree, landing next to Herman's body. Percy arrived about that time and fired a gun into the air to break up the frenzy of the Crafts trying to stop Jagi from coming to Herman's aid. Percy then placed the gun next to Craft's ear and said, "The next bullet goes into your brainless head!" as all three men raised their hands in the air.

"Someone call the sheriff!" Shoving the three men to the ground, Percy shouted to the bystanders, "We have murderers in our custody."

Jagi desperately tried to cut the rope off the lifeless Herman, who had suffered a broken neck, but it was too late. Jagi looked up at Percy and asked, "Why...why?" Percy couldn't explain it. He himself didn't know why. Although caught red-handed, Craft was able to get off when tried for the crime. It appeared someone in high places needed him to owe them one.

TWENTY THREE

SUGAR

Percy's seizures became a real nuisance. He never knew when or where a seizure would happen. Most of the time they happened with little notice for him to sit or lie down. The military doctors, and now his good friend Dr. Reynolds, explained to him that the bullet left near his tailbone was leaking lead poison into his bloodstream and that it would someday kill him. The apothecary prescribed cocaine. Cocaine was widely available and used, along with moonshine, for many ailments. It seemed to keep Percy more alert, and the seizures seemed to be less frequent. However, it made him lose too much weight. Everyone would take notice and fuss at him about it, but when he stopped the cocaine, the seizures returned.

It was another splendid day along the Tennessee River at Taylorsville. Percy was traveling from the orchards to the cattle in another pasture, farther away from where all the food was being grown. These were the livestock areas…turkeys in one field…goats in another. Farthest away, because of the smell, were the chickens, pigs, and cattle. The more Percy made in the banana business, the more he invested in expanding his farm. He and his brother had a dream. This was just the beginning of what Taylorsville could be. He stopped by the cornfield to investigate a unique irrigation system his brother, Chase, had set up after returning from Auburn. He had great respect for his brother and really leaned on him after the death of their mother, which was soon followed by the passing of his wife, Linda Gail. Chase helped Percy hang on and focus on being a great father.

Suddenly, Percy felt himself falling backward and his chest felt tight. He blacked out. Not knowing how long he'd been lying out there in the field, he was beginning to come to. His brain was foggy and slow. His eyes would not open. *This time did I wake up in heaven, or do I have another day on this earth?* he thought. He felt thumping on his chest. He couldn't shake this one off. More pounding was followed by a wet tongue licking his mouth and more thumping. The licking, wet tongue was all over his face now. He thought maybe some kind of wet instrument entered his ear. More pouncing. Now he was starting to breathe. He could feel his chest expanding with deeper breaths. Out of focus, his eyes gradually began to open. *Is a pretty blond woman looking into my eyes?* he thought, still fuzzy in the head. Something was licking his face and walking on his chest.

Finally, able to breathe and think better, he could see more clearly. It was a golden yellow puppy. Since she was so sweet and determined to lick him, he called her Sugar. They would never part for the rest of their lives. She slept in his bed and rode in his car or buggy. Sugar went everywhere with Percy. She was about seven weeks old and weighed about eight pounds. Sugar had golden eyes and blond fur, and her back haunches and tail were covered in long white hair. Her belly was so soft to rub, it felt like putting your hand in a bowl full of flour. Percy thought it was funny that a puppy had come from nowhere and jumped on his chest until he came back to consciousness…At least he liked to tell that story. It probably just hadn't been his time.

Sugar spoke to Percy by using long, exaggerated yawns, with highs, lows, and several different kinds of yelps. She never used a full-fledged bark for communication. Barking was used for danger, fear, excitement, and notification. The most important sound Sugar made was a whiny sound with pulses. During these sounds, she would also use her nose and paws. That was the only time he ever noticed her being forceful with him.

One morning Percy put it together. She acted this persistent only before he had one of his many seizures. He once thought she was causing them. He decided to take notice and document the occurrences with her behavior. It became very obvious what was happening. Somehow she knew when Percy was about to have a seizure and would begin whining. He began taking his cocaine medicine the moment Sugar nudged and whined. He was convinced that she was a gift from the heavens, sent just for him in his time of need.

Percy had to share this discovery with Doc Reynolds. To his surprise, the doctor was not surprised. Doc had read of something like this occurring in Scotland. Scientists there had documented numerous cases as they were training German shepherds for combat in the European conflict that soon would become the First World War. Unusual canine abilities that were noted showed that some of the dogs with the keenest sense of smell could be used to detect land mines and other explosives. Several of the adult handlers had different ailments, and their dog partners in training could apparently smell chemical changes in their human partners. No follow-up information was available.

Dr. Reynolds wrote the author of the article to share Percy's observations with Sugar. After corresponding for months, Hudson Limbaugh, professor of veterinary medicine at the University of Glasgow, arrived in Huntsville on the NC&STL train. He was on his way to Mudville, Missouri, where he had family, but he wanted to stop in Taylorsville to observe Sugar's behavior for his research. Doc was surprised that the professor was of German descent, because he had thought Limbaugh was Scottish or Irish. They had coffee and doughnuts from Miss Lily's downtown bakery while they waited for the train to Taylorsville.

Sugar enthusiastically greeted the professor. Truth be told, Sugar was excited to meet anyone, and she covered his face in dog kisses. She was not usually allowed this sort of behavior, but the professor insisted it was okay with him. Percy had planned the professor's visit, so he did not take his regular dose of maintenance medicine that day, thinking he would be more likely to have a seizure and the professor could witness Sugar in action and perhaps run a few smell tests with her.

The professor actually stayed several days in Taylorsville, hunting and fishing with Percy and Dr. Reynolds. He spent hours speaking in German with Jagi, catching him up on things in Europe. Before continuing his trip to the Midwest, the professor wanted to closely observe the relationship between Percy and Sugar. He noticed there were a few words and sounds that only they seemed to understand. For example, Sugar made a certain sound when she wanted ice to crunch. Percy would chip a piece off a large block and then offer her a stick, a small piece of bread, or the ice. She would pick the ice. When she sounded (spoke) her word for fetch, he would give her a choice of three objects: a cloth, a stick, or a ball. She would pick the ball and run to the door, tail wagging. Percy just knew that Sugar was thinking, *Let's go outside and fetch.*

As they continued to talk, the professor noted how agitated Sugar became when Percy ignored her. Was she pawing and trying to tell him he was close to an attack? Percy hated to ignore Sugar. He knew an attack was likely to occur soon, although he felt great at the moment. He told Doc and the professor to catch him if he slumped out of his chair. It happened. They let Percy's now-limp body down to the floor gently. Doc questioned if having a seizure on purpose was advisable, but the professor also saw and documented how Sugar reacted when Percy was unconscious. Sugar, now at eighty pounds, climbed with all four paws on top of his body. Then she began to pounce on his chest forcefully with her front paws. No one knew exactly what she intended to be doing, but it seemed the dog thought her actions would cause Percy to regain consciousness. The performance completely amazed the professor.

Departure day gave one more example of Sugar's unique gift. The three men, plus other guests, were having lunch at the Russell Erskine Hotel in the main lobby restaurant near the Memphis & Charleston train depot. The restaurant's manager would absolutely not let Sugar sit quietly under the table. He said the city health department would not allow it.

They were all enjoying their lunches while Sugar was stationed outside the front entrance of the hotel. Hotel construction workers and other witnesses said the dog suddenly and desperately tried to scratch her way through the door. Without Percy's knowledge, she was going crazy outside the hotel. The front doorman was under strict orders to leave her outside, no matter what. Sugar refused to stop. She ran down to the corner, circled around the building and into the car garage, and ran up through the receiving door to the kitchen, which was open. She tore through, not knowing where she was going. She was looking for Percy. The chef and the kitchen staff started chasing her. She found the swinging door into the dining area with the kitchen crew in close pursuit. Through human legs and under tables, she ran across the room to a place near the window where Percy was lying on the floor next to a table. He was surrounded by Doc Reynolds, the professor, and others. Sugar burst into the crowd, jumped on Percy's chest with great force, and began her dog resuscitation.

Percy awoke to Sugar's beautiful golden eyes and her long, wet tongue cleaning his face. The commotion drew a crowd of about twenty or thirty witnesses, including the restaurant manager, the kitchen chef, the hotel manager, and two of the hotel's financial investors. Most important, Mr. Russell Erskine himself, president of Studebaker, was there.

Mr. Erskine had driven up to the front entrance in his brand-new black Studebaker about the time Sugar was trying to gain her way into the front door, but he had not paid her any attention. After Mr. Erskine arrived at his table, in the Heritage Room restaurant, he noticed the dog being chased by the kitchen staff to the group of people gathered around a man on the floor. He saw it all firsthand. It appeared to him she saved the man's life and would not take no for an answer until she got to him. Impressed by this rescue by a dog, Mr. Erskine declared Sugar the hotel mascot, welcome inside at any time. The crowd applauded.

The stories of Sugar spread all over town. Of course, the truth got stretched each time they were told. The professor left for Mudville, Missouri, satisfied with his stop at Taylorsville. His research on animal services to humans had another chapter added.

Sugar had a few bad habits also. She thought she had to be with her master even in the bathroom…Men just do not want a girl present at times. Sometimes, in the middle of the night, she would give the alert bark, meaning there was a deer outside. More often than not, Sugar would eat snacks of rotting fish parts off the riverbanks. This would require getting up in the middle of the night to take her out and watch her get sick, eat grass, get sick again, then come inside, drink lots of water, and finally go back to bed.

Once the story of the Sugar rescue got around town, she was allowed everywhere…any restaurant, grocery store, or hardware store and even at Percy's men's meetings, where she was accepted as the only female creature allowed. Sugar became the town's celebrity dog. Percy would go to Mr. Yong's for acupuncture treatments for his back pain, and Sugar would snore loudly while she waited. Mr. Yong explained to Percy, "It her only time off duty, so she sleeps soundly on floor and snores."

When Percy received fancy invitations to the town's big society balls, theaters, and concerts, or even to a casual dinner at a friend's house, the invitation was always extended to Sugar too. As a joke once, a party committee sent a formal invitation to Sugar and had a handwritten note inside saying she could include Percy. Everyone in town had put a bid into Percy if she ever had pups. A good friend, George, put folding money into Percy's hand and said, "I'd give anything to have a female in my house who would listen to me."

His wife, Lynn, just laughed. "I listen to you, George!"

TWENTY FOUR

MISS GUNTERSVILLE VS. TAXIS

It was no secret to many that Judge W. T. Lawler, Police Chief Kirby, former police chief David Overton, Sheriff Philipps, assistant district attorney Sheldon Pleasants, and a couple others used the front of a taxi service owned by Chief Kirby to run liquor out of Ditto's Landing into Huntsville. They knew their biggest competitors were Hobbs Island Road moonshiners and especially Taylorsville importers. One steamship like *Miss Guntersville* could bring in a lot of rum. Fortunately for them they knew most of the rum from Cuba was going to other states, but between the rum and moonshine, their business was affected.

The downtown crowd knew only one way into Taylorsville from Huntsville. They had to go through Whitesburg and Ditto's Landing… the front line of defense. Taylorsville always knew when the law was coming. Percy made sure the port at Ditto's Landing was connected to the Huntsville Telephone Exchange twelve miles away, and he used his own money to get the lines extended to Taylorsville about two miles away.

One evening at the crowded Taylorsville Depot, a gathering spot for locals, Chief Kirby entered with Judge Lawler and announced, "The Honorable Judge W. T. Lawler."

Percy stood up in front of the desk and held out his hand to Lawler and said, "Honorable Judge Lawler?"

This irritated Kirby. Percy looked at the judge now before him and said, "I'm the honorable judge to you, Lawler. I may have retired, but I earned the title Honorable Judge."

Lawler squawked back, "You're a farmer and a bootlegger."

"How are things at Ditto's Landing, Judge?" Percy asked, referring to the judge's involvement in the alcohol taxied service out of Ditto's Landing. Lawler's face got all red, as Percy had called him out in front of everyone. Percy waited for the train to stop and the crowd to quiet, and then he said, "I chose not to be a judge of dishonor, which happens to be what Huntsville and the Madison County Courthouse is full of these days. Dishonesty runs amok."

Lawler tried to get the last word in and almost shouted, "I am a Prohibitionist! There are many sins of alcohol. In this great state of Alabama, it is *illegal*! Alabama is bone dry."

"Forever campaigning, aren't you, Judge?" someone from the crowd shouted.

"I will jail any of you who get in my way!" Lawler screamed with no one listening.

They would attempt to turn the town upside down looking for anything illegal. Percy knew that without a search warrant, or probable cause, they could not search. Occasionally he would let them peek, but not touch anything, inside the warehouse or barn. He knew nothing would be found anywhere. The sheriff would try twice sometimes in one night to surprise Taylorsville's residents. "Our informants can't be this wrong," said the police chief.

"R. H. Craft is on our payroll, living here among them, and he owes us for saving his butt after he lynched Herman Deeley," complained wimpy Officer O'Neal.

Captain Tom Lindstrom of the steamship *Miss Guntersville* was always pleased to arrive at what he liked to call the Port of Taylorsville. Percy Taylor was his friend and on many occasions Percy would instruct the dock hands, while unloading, to leave a case of cargo on board.

He would go past the landing to spin the barge downriver to gain a better angle when going back upriver to snuggle the barge up against the left bank. Another reason for the maneuver was a young Indian woman named Kimtumpka, which meant "soft smoke" in her native language. She lived on the south end of Hobbs Island with two elderly Indians, Standing Bear and his wife, White Dove. Everyone assumed she was somehow related to the couple, but no one knew for sure.

Kim was said to be the great-granddaughter of William Simpson, the owner of the island in the early 1800s. The Indians considered him a giant at nearly seven feet tall. She took after him in her height and in her brown hair with its golden streaks. Her skin color was lighter than most Indians'. She would stand tall at the downriver point of the island to watch the dockings. Captain Lindstrom pulled closer and closer to the island each time to get a better look at her.

The captain got too close once and hit a sandbar that trailed from the island. It took some skillful operations, with the full weight of all the train cars, to fight against the current and pull the barge back off the sand. He looked back at the Indian woman, and she clapped her hands. He bowed and waved back. The captain pulled ahead with a big, embarrassed smile on his face. Percy was at the dock laughing. He saw the whole thing. "I swear Percy. I have not had a drink in two days," Captain Lindstrom said. Percy still with a shit-eating grin replied, "Tom there are some things even stronger than alcohol and she may be over there on that island."

The Captain was always good at lining up the barge against the railroad incline and giving one loud honk to let the dock hands know to tie down. The engines never turned off in case of an accident because of the strong current. Now they could let the ramps down on the barge and attach and lock several sets of brakes. Two whistle blows from the train and she was ready to disembark. One car at a time, the train's engine pulled them up the incline. There were only seven cars to unload, and then another train stood by with ten cars to take up the river to Guntersville Landing...about a four-hour trip.

Captain Lindstrom took this train-switching downtime to leave his boat, walk over to the depot, and find out what he could about the island woman. He had never gotten that close to her. He was not sure why, but he felt his heart beating faster. He talked to a few of the town's people on the street. They all referred him to Shasta. One woman said, "Shasta will know everything." Shasta was known to swim, or at times wade, across and stay on the island all day. In the afternoon the Indian girl would bring Shasta back across the channel in a small canoe. Captain Lindstrom was told Shasta wasn't in town at the moment. "She's gone trail riding up on Wallace Mountain with her favorite stallion, Duke."

The captain had to wait, but long before the sun got too high that summer day, Captain Lindstrom, who for some reason had never learned to swim, waded across at the shallows to meet Kimtumpka, with Shasta as his escort. He swam back across with his new Indian bride. The elderly couple had given their consent and, in a ceremony, married them that day with Shasta as a witness. The town folks could not figure out which was the strangest...the captain getting married that day or the fact that he swam back across the river. Captain Lindstrom and his new bride lived aboard the *Miss Guntersville* and traveled up and down the Tennessee River for many years. He liked to call her Kim. Kim and the captain brought the old Indian couple supplies until one day the old couple just disappeared.

Twenty Five

The Bad Seed

Chip learned from a professional liar, his mother, how to look some-one in the eye with apparent innocence and lie his way through anything. His mother was a true master of the devious and deceitful arts. It was no secret where he learned his corrupt behavior, and she never called him out on anything except perhaps his Peeping Tom fetish, and even then, only when he got caught too close to home. Chip often went with his stepfather on sneaky stakeouts where he learned techniques of hiding in the shadows and watching everything without being seen. Most of his life, his mother, Suzette, was very detached and couldn't have cared less where he was at any given hour. During the school year she really did not keep track of his whereabouts. His stepfather usually stayed gone a lot, somewhere in the Lacey's Spring area. He found there the kind of company he liked to keep, without everyone knowing his business.

Without parental restrictions, Chip ran the streets and jumped the trains from one part of town to the other. His Peeping Tom activi-ties continued all over town except close to home…He didn't want his mother, under the pretense of being a concerned mother and neighbor, to drag him to a neighbor's home to apologize when he knew she didn't really care. He often tried to get into a brothel, and they turned him away for being too young. One summer he took a job for pennies a day at a local house of prostitutes, so that his Peeping Tom needs were met. He was a very strange boy.

One night, all of the girls got together to have the madam fire him. He was gross, and often spit on unsuspecting girls as they came near him. More times than they could count, he would be nearby, watching the prostitutes earning their pay. They felt he was dangerous. Two weeks later, after the brothel had closed for the night, everyone was sound asleep as the house burned to the ground. The madam and five other women burned to death that night. The firemen never really knew what started the fire. Bad electrical wiring was often to blame, but the scene still smelled of gasoline the next morning. It was concluded that a local Christian group must've thought they were doing the neighborhood a favor. Case closed.

One of Chip's favorite pastimes was to hop the train in Huntsville and go down fourteen miles of track to the town of Taylorsville. Everyone was happy there and very friendly, even to Chip. His reputation was not known there yet. He would disappear into the woods near the incline ramp for the Hobbs Island ferry train to Guntersville. Chip had overheard that his stepdad and other officers were trying to clamp down on any bootlegging in Taylorsville. Not only was it illegal in Alabama, but it was cutting into the profits of the police chief as he ran a taxicab bootlegging service from Ditto's Landing to downtown Huntsville. Chip became their scout, coming across as a lonesome boy. He would often hide in the background of scenes and report back what he saw.

This day he watched the paddle steamer line up with the land anchors and slowly bring the barge up to the track. A tailgate let down, chain was attached to the barge, and, as it had done many times, the engine pulled one car at a time up the incline track. If the barge was loaded down with ten cars, this could take up to an hour. Chip watched each car carefully to see if anything fishy was happening. Next, the passengers were taken off the steamboat and reboarded onto the relinked cars of the train.

Something different was happening this day. On the far side of the barge with the last row of train cars still waiting to be offloaded, there seemed to be some movement. Chip quickly came down the tree where he'd been watching, getting bark burns on his chest. He sneaked behind the last cars and then climbed across the barge as the crew was eyeballing the pretty young ladies getting off the steamer. As he climbed through the cars, he saw the last of four flat-bottom boats with small, quiet engines moving away upstream, toward the Flint River. Usually this kind of transfer occurred while under way at the mouth of the Flint River opening. Today, thunderstorms had interfered with the small boat operations, so they were much later than normal. Such missed connections rarely happened.

The next day, Percy was interrupted by Police Chief Kirby with a search warrant for the inbound Hobbs Island ferry train. Percy already knew there were no scheduled special arrivals that day. "Go right ahead and look in the cars," he said. "Now, gentlemen, this search warrant applies only to this train at this station. I am more than happy to comply. However, this warrant does not permit you to walk down that train track, and even if you had a warrant down the train track to the river, you could not board the vessel. To board a vessel is against maritime law without the permission of the captain. I can guarantee that when Captain Lindstrom arrives, he will not permit you aboard. Go ahead. Try it. Just to see what happens." Percy had been expecting this little trip out of their jurisdiction from the Huntsville Police Department after he'd seen that good-for-nothing Chip climbing up a tree Monday as the ferry train arrived. Captain Lindstrom was also given a heads-up, as were the counterparts of his team upriver.

Police Officer Dick O'Neal stepped up and gave his word: "The informant is reliable." He was the stepfather to the little weasel Chip O'Kennedy. Detective O'Neal was never even bothered by his wife's decision to keep her late husband's name instead of his. She thought the name O'Kennedy was more prestigious. That family despised her and thought Chip didn't look anything like his father, Michael. Chip was standing in the back of the crowd, acting his usual weaselly way. People were beginning to gather at the depot to meet the train's passengers or inbound freight. Others were already starting to arrive for the departure for downtown Huntsville in one hour.

The police chief illegally ordered the officers down the track, where they waited at the incline for the *Miss Guntersville* steamship to arrive.

The *Miss Guntersville* was busy lining up the barge with one long boatswain's whistle for the onboard crew and a loud docking horn for the onshore crew. Captain Reb Beck pulled up in another ship and tied off along his starboard side. Captain Beck was in on this standoff for the team...not Percy Taylor. They didn't particularly like each other...over a woman. Captain Beck had won the woman, Diane, a long time ago.

Altogether there were twenty-five men between the two vessels. One beautiful Indian woman sat near the ship's wheel, sharpening a large blade across a stone. Other ships idled nearby, waiting for activity, ready to jump in and assist. They all bore their weapons, daring the rogue members of the Huntsville police to try to board the *Miss Guntersville* with only five officers and the police chief. The boats' crews knew the law of the water; defending it was their honor. Ship captains on the rivers always stood together when local police tried to throw their weight around. The waterways were the bootleggers' open highways to distribution, and most local police knew they had no jurisdiction.

Percy arrived as the situation was getting tense. "Captain Lindstrom," Percy hailed. "Would you consider making an exception this one time and allowing the police chief to board?"

"Mr. Taylor, that would be highly unusual, but I will make an exception...this time," Captain Lindstrom replied.

While the police, boats' crews, and train's employees were all gathered at the river's edge, eighteen fully loaded automobiles drove straight through Taylorsville from the Flint River to the Lily Flagg depot, the distribution center of sorts for the south end of town.

Percy's day was made when Police Chief Kirby had to leave empty-handed. Dick O'Neal was about to get an earful on the way back to the police station. Chip's and his stepdaddy's credibility were shot. The depot broke out with laughter as the squad cars pulled away.

Chip wanted to get even. His mother had hated the Taylors for a long time. She told Chip they had often mistreated her when he was a baby. He also wanted to hurt Shasta for personal reasons. She had really embarrassed Chip in public at the Big Spring one afternoon. He had tried to push his way into a circle of Shasta's friends to bully her and Jagi. One quick, swift action of Shasta's right hand and Chippy was flat on his back on the ground. No one saw what she did. They were just laughing at him lying there. She spoke to him in French. "Little wussy boy, you touch me again and I will have to kill you." Olivia and her children spoke French and laughed hysterically.

Percy had first hired Mr. Yong in Paris. Because Mr. Yong's ancient acupuncture always seemed to bring great relief to Percy's back pain, he on many occasions became part of the family, traveling with Percy. It was Mr. Yong who believed it necessary to teach Shasta nonaggressive self-defense. She had an athletic build and, with her dad's permission, had learned Mr. Yong's techniques quickly. Chip was heard saying under his breath, "I will beat you, Shasta, and set you on fire one day." With Shasta's encouragement, Jagi started daily self-defense lessons from Mr. Yong that very afternoon.

Officer Dick O'Neal dropped by Taylorsville, often alone on his way to Lacey's Spring, sometimes with other officers. Mainly he just wanted Percy to know he had the power and authority to do whatever he wanted, or so he thought. On one of his many harassing visits, Percy had a crowd around and couldn't help but tell the story of going up San Juan Hill in Cuba during the Spanish-American War. He was busy firing with the rest of the Americans when he took a bullet in his lower spine. As he lay there bleeding, waiting for a medic, he saw Dick O'Neal, who had also been in the battle. Percy pointed to the officer. "Dick here was running away and hid in a grove of trees until the firing stopped and the battle was over. Only then did he come out. Little Dickie over here was a coward that day when other good men risked their lives. He should've been court-martialed for going AWOL during the battle...after he shot me in the back."

"It was an accident," O'Neal said.

"Perhaps, but you did say you would do anything to protect your 'little secret,'" Percy replied. Percy then spoke in Spanish to Dick. "You pig-sucking coward wussy, I will kill you one day for shooting me in the back." No charges had been pursued against Dick during the war. Mainly, Percy had just wanted to get out of the hospital and back home to his beautiful young bride-to-be. Percy continued, "Dick is one of those loose ends in life that always comes back to bite you in the ass." The crowd broke into hysterical laughter.

Most people knew Percy suffered seizures because of the lead leaking from the bullet. The doctors didn't want to remove it, for fear it would cause permanent paralysis. Now they knew how he had gotten the lead.

Twenty Six

Murder at the Steel Bridge

Grace Ann Taylor Thomas, sister of Percy Taylor and wife of a preacher, loved everything to do with her Methodist church. She helped the needy, volunteered at all fund-raisers, taught Sunday school, held Bible study classes, and, most important to her, helped her husband practice for sermons before Sunday services.

Very much like her mother, Grace was loved by all. She missed her mother, who had died only a few months after the last big family beach trip when Grace wasn't even fifteen. Shortly after her mother's unexpected death, Linda Gail, Percy's wife, died. No one knew what had happened. Of course, it had devastated the entire family: two great women from one family lost within such a short time. C. C. had gone into shock, and Percy had shut down for a while. Chase had had to care for Shasta. After Linda Gail's death, Percy took the life of traveling the world with Shasta in tow. He had a private teacher for Shasta, Big Mama, and other staff to assist him. Grace prayed for them every single night of her life. She did a lot of praying. Grace had a difficult time sleeping, often waking up with terrible nightmares. She prayed a lot…It was about all she could do sometimes.

On Wednesday, June 14, 1916, Grace and her husband, Pastor Travis Thomas, had a wonderful evening. Church services, revival preaching, and singing were followed by a potluck dinner for a huge crowd even though there was also a Chautauqua meeting downtown. They enjoyed their lives together and their church. Grace and Travis picked up two different families for church services as their usual practice. Because of this they had two automobiles. After the services that evening, Grace took the family riding with her to their home at Whitesburg, near Taylorsville. She hated to drive alone at night, but there was no better reason to do so than the Lord's calling.

Just before she got back to the bridge at Whitesburg, her car began to shake, and then she heard *clop, clop, clop. Oh no, another flat tire,* she thought when she got out and looked. She knew she was in a fix. Being a good pastor's wife was her calling...not changing bad tires. It was not safe out here in the middle of nowhere at night.

Grace always wore a revolver under her skirt. A good friend had taught her to do so years earlier. She decided to wait until a car came along and flag it down to assist her. Two taxicabs raced by in the direction of Huntsville. She knew she saw uniformed police officers driving both taxis and thought she recognized one as Dick O'Neal. Grace was fuming that neither stopped to help a woman in distress on a dark, lonely road. She would give Police Chief Kirby an earful the next day.

Grace just stared at the tire. She was truly clueless about what she should do. "Yeah!" Grace shouted as headlights approached. She stood in the middle of the road to make sure this car didn't miss her, waving for help. The car slowed, but continued on past. She thought the driver was Sheldon Pleasants, but there was no doubt she saw David Overton in the backseat with Judge Lawler beside him. *How odd. All you see in the papers is how these two men hate each other and called each other "bootlegging crooks" during the recent election,* Grace thought. She was fit to be tied. *How dare they pass by a preacher's wife in need.*

She had no choice. She would walk farther down the road across the steel bridge and maybe have one of the men at Ditto's Landing help her with the tire. She reached down, felt the gun on her thigh, and began walking. The car that had passed with Overton and Lawler had turned around. It came back across the bridge, pulled forward a hundred feet, and cut the headlights. The two men got out while the driver stayed in the car with the motor running.

Grace for some reason felt the need to be sneaky out of curiosity and crept up on them by staying off the road and hidden in the woods. Her approach certainly showed that she lacked stalking skills. If their car's motor had not been running, they surely would have heard her. She got close enough to hear the voices clearly. At first, the conversation pertained to covering up anything the grand jury had on both of them. They started accusing each other of stealing from the operation. Lawler seemed to stumble over his own feet as they walked toward the bridge. "What did you put in my coffee in the thermos?" he asked.

"I don't know what's in the coffee. I don't drink it. Loretta made it for you. It was a nice gesture," Overton said.

"Tastes like crap. My stomach is starting to hurt," Lawler said as he poured the rest of the coffee over the bridge into the water below.

This was when Grace's ears really perked up. "Molly? What does that little slut niece of yours have to do with our operation here and getting the grand jury off our backs?" Lawler asked.

"You're the one who set up the deeds, the land trust, and the bank accounts all in her name," Overton said. "It's been eight years since those letters came and twelve years since she ran off. The other guys and I are tired of putting our part of the cut into the blackmail account. She's not coming after it. We can divide it up six ways. There's got to be a hundred thousand dollars in cash by now. That bitch wife of mine found out that the deed to our house is in Molly's name and she wants it back. Now! Next week you need to fill out some papers so we can have her sent to Cedar Craft Sanatorium like we did to my sister and your first wife. Maybe that'll straighten Loretta out."

Lawler wanted none of this and shouted, "I love my wife, and I don't want anything about Molly to come out. I wasn't even married when all this happened years ago. No, this cannot come out. It would ruin me, my career, and my marriage!"

"Hell, Judge, your career is already ruined. You've been indicted for election fraud, and you're going to be impeached. We're all a little concerned you're going to blab your mouth," Overton said. A cocky

Overton got right in Lawler's face. "You see, *Judge*, you're the one who had to make this election all nasty. We agreed, way back in the beginning, that this would be my turn to be circuit court judge, but you just couldn't let go of all the power. Now, you see, you're outnumbered here. We don't want to pay any more, and we want all the money in that account of M. Teal in our hands."

Lawler, feeling a little woozy from the coffee, said, "What a rookie mistake...to drink from the cup of your enemy. You're the one who set me up with a wholesale-size amount of liquor in my barn."

"You set me up first, Judge!" Overton shouted.

"Well, David, you've already been prosecuted once for buying votes and bribery."

"Yeah, Judge, you're one to talk," Overton snapped back. "Money has come up missing ever since you've been in office. You're as crooked as they come."

They continued arguing back and forth about how a stupid tramp girl had gotten the better of them. "I don't know what her problem was. She always liked it when I did her," Lawler said.

"Bull crap, Judge," Overton said. "I saw her face after you were through with her."

Lawler, even woozier and not thinking straight, was feeling pushed into a corner. He pulled out a large knife, took a swing at Overton, and hit him in the neck. Overton swiftly responded, pulling his pistol and putting a bullet straight into Lawler's chest. Lawler crumpled to the ground. Panicked, Overton dragged the body into the woods and dropped it within ten feet of Grace. He returned to the car with the driver. "I thought you were going to wait until the drugs got him, then flip him over the bridge," the driver said.

"Well, Sheldon, plans changed. The son of a bitch stabbed me. I had to shoot him instead. Let's hurry and get back to Sheriff Phillips' office and have him cover this up."

Grace had kept her hand over her mouth the entire time, fearful she might inadvertently make a noise. She watched the car speed away and went back to the body. She had to know for sure if this servant to the Devil was dead. It was dark, and she stepped on Lawler before she knew it. His body was all twisted up between a huge boulder and a big piece of steel left over from the bridge, or was it a railroad rail? She tried to pull him out by the feet, and he moaned. He was "the Devil," as Molly had put it, but she was a good Christian and just had to help. It was what the Lord wanted and the right thing to do. He was stuck. She tried from the other end. No luck there either. "*Shit!*" she said, and then immediately followed with, "Forgive me, Jesus...Bless my heart."

The boulder was too large for her to move it aside. She tried to get the steel off of him. Without thinking, Grace began to speak to the unconscious Lawler. "I heard everything you and David Overton said tonight. You both are nothing but the Devil. I have the Lord Jesus Christ in my life, and only because of him am I trying to help you. I think you should be ashamed of yourself. You are supposed to be a community leader, and really, you're nothing more than a common crook. You claim to be a Christian Prohibitionist. You lie! You sell alcohol for money. The worst sin of all is what you and the other five men have done to Molly Teal. I'll tell Police Chief Kirby everything tomorrow. Overton is now a nobody with the police department, so he will not get away with it."

Meanwhile she had gotten the steel moved about five inches off of Lawler. He surprised Grace by saying, "You stupid, easy piece of tail, friend of Molly Teal's. She liked it. So would you."

Grace wasn't really sure she had heard him correctly, but she knew that whatever he had just said to her, it was not nice. "Whoops," she exclaimed as the steel rail slipped out of her hands because of its incredible weight. It landed on top of his skull, crushing it.

Grace wiped her hands clean on her skirt, took a deep breath, and began walking in the direction of Ditto's Landing for help. She looked down and saw a large amount of blood on the bottom of her skirt. She took the wet spot over to the rail on the steel bridge and wrote "Devil" in blood. She continued to walk. Then she ran back and smeared the word *Devil* off because it felt sinful.

She looked up and saw headlights approaching, pointed directly at her. It was Travis. He pulled up and said, "I began to worry and came to look for you. Good thing I did—saw your broken-down automobile back there." He noticed the blood on her skirt. "Grace, are you okay?"

"I'm fine," she said as she motioned toward the body, "but Judge Lawler was murdered." Before she could get out, "And I saw the whole thing," she burst into tears.

Travis wrapped his big ol' arms around her. "You didn't see anything," he said. "We need to stay out of this. It's dangerous out here. Let's get you home and come back for the car in the morning." Travis was her hero.

After Grace went home, there was a third encounter with Judge Lawler. It was Asa, from Gurley, who now worked at Ditto's Landing. He had been seeing headlights go off and on at the bridge and thought he would investigate.

Asa hated Circuit Court Judge Lawler. Lawler had gone out of his way to help convict Asa of a petty crime. Then Lawler had sentenced Asa severely for unknowingly being in a car carrying moonshine. Lawler liked to show his strength to his competitors by making examples even of people convicted of misdemeanors. Asa had served hard time. His wife was at home during his imprisonment, dying of tuberculosis, unable to care for herself or for their small child, Harmony. After Asa's wife died, Judge Lawler had arranged for Harmony to be adopted by one of his wealthy family friends who wanted a child.

Asa didn't live in Cloud's Cove like most of his kin. He had had a disagreement with the family and moved to Gurley. It didn't matter that he did not then live in Cloud's Cove. His family there was furious to know that one of their kin had been adopted out to some rich strangers. While Asa was in prison, and without his knowledge, they kidnapped Harmony and brought her back to Cloud's Cove. No one needed to know the details. No one talked, and strangers were at risk of not leaving if they entered Cloud's Cove to snoop around. The whole clan protected this child because she was "special." She didn't speak with humans...only to animals.

When Asa got out of prison, he went back to Gurley. He started on a violent rampage all over that end of the county, looking for his daughter. There was still some bad blood between him and his family, and no one broke ranks to tell Asa they had Harmony. He spent every night after his release from work prison looking for her. He worked in a coal mine near Gurley as the front man in the line with the pick and ax. Because he was really large, Asa could do the work of two men. He spent so much time in the mines never taking a bath that he looked like a Negro.

Asa looked at Lawler's head crushed in and the wound from the gunshot to the chest and was sorry he had not gotten to him first. He would've demanded to know Harmony's whereabouts. Lawler's hand moved, and it scared Asa. He got down close to Lawler's face and asked real nicely, "Judge Lawler, sir, my name is Asa, and you put me in prison three years ago. When my wife, Julie, died, you gave away my daughter, Harmony. Where is my daughter? Please. Mister Judge. Sir. I beg you... She is all I have. Do you remember my wife, Julie? She has a trouble-maker cousin, Tullie. Julie's kinfolks were all politicians who lived up in Washington, DC. They didn't think I was good enough for Julie. Which one of those rich bastards did you give my Harmony to?"

The judge, barely alive, half his skull and eye socket crushed in, whispered, "You monster" as he tried to spit in Asa's face.

Asa pulled Lawler's limp body out from under the steel with one jerk. He had Lawler's shoulders, screaming at him, "Harmony! Harmony! Where is she?" He jerked Lawler's body so hard that Lawler's neck broke, which caused his head to dangle. Asa had seen this as his last chance, and now it was gone. He took Lawler's body and treated it like a rag doll, grabbing it by the ankles. He began to beat it into the ground, over and over. He spun around a few times and let it go back into the woods where he had found it. He walked away, weak, into the darkness. He gave up on his last hope and decided to go home to his long-forgotten kinfolk in Cloud's Cove. He was a broken giant, in for a surprise.

Headlights came alive on a car in the lot at Ditto's Landing. It was Candice Pleasants, wife of the assistant district attorney. She had followed Overton, Lawler and her husband, Sheldon and was impatient with all the activity around Lawler's body. He had too much on her husband. Candice pulled her car right up to the body's location. She went straight into the woods, put another shot into Lawler's chest, got back into the car, cool as a cucumber, and drove away.

What killed Lawler? Poison from Loretta? The gunshot from Overton? Having his head crushed by Grace? Having his neck broken and his body abused, courtesy of Asa? The final bullet from Candice?

Overton, bleeding heavily from his neck wound, went straight to his good ol' buddy and best friend, Sheriff Phillips. The sheriff temporarily bandaged the knife wound while Overton told him, "I shot Lawler, but the judge attacked me with his knife first. He just wouldn't budge on the Molly Teal account and had to be dealt with immediately." The sheriff sent Overton to a surgeon in Chattanooga and then sent Silas Niles, Overton's replacement as circuit court clerk, to pick up Perry Brooks at the Whitesburg ferry. Together, they were to get rid of the body. After all, they were all in this together.

Niles and Brooks arrived at the bloodbath near the bridge. Niles took one look at Lawler's body and said, "Oh, hell! Overton said he shot Lawler one time…my ass." They both looked at the corpse. There were two large gunshot wounds in the chest, half of the head was crushed in, and the rest of the body looked like it had been run over with a truck. They used the steel beam next to the body that looked like part of a railroad rail. Brooks had a spool of wire in his truck, so they used it to attach Lawler's body to the steel. It took both of them to drag his body out of the woods and to the bridge since the beam was so heavy. They angled it so that the beam would flip off the bridge and into the creek below. Brooks said he was certain the water was at least fifteen feet deep. They reported back to Sheriff Phillips and told him the gruesome details. Phillips realized he had a big problem with David Overton. His trigger-happy friend may have just exposed them all.

After years of searching for his baby girl, Asa was a broken man when he went back to his roots in Cloud's Cove, only to discover that his family had rescued his daughter Harmony three years earlier. Asa and Harmony, now much older, went to church to pray for forgiveness of his horrible sin, but mostly to thank the good Lord for returning her to him.

The *Huntsville Daily Times* reported on the following Sunday that Judge Lawler's body was pulled out of the muddy creek attached with wire to a railroad beam, with gunshot wounds in the chest. The death certificate written by the coroner had the rest of the story: "Two gun-shots to the chest, broken neck, crushed skull, abused body, and thrown into the deep creek."

TWENTY SEVEN

JUSTICE FOR FIVE AND ONE TO GO

Candice, wife of a prominent lawyer, the assistant district attorney, often used the God-given ample blessings of her body to gain things otherwise out of her reach. Her husband, Sheldon Pleasants, had a very smart brother. Howie Pleasants was a druggist and operated his own apothecary. However, he was also socially inept. He could only speak to women professionally about pharmaceuticals. Other than that, he stuttered, mumbled, and grunted to women.

Candice knew Howie's weakness: her very large, round breasts. He could not keep his eyes off of them. She would often walk into the drugstore, lock the door, flip the welcome sign to closed, draw the blinds, and walk right over to Howie, slowly unbuttoning her blouse. One shoulder at a time, she would pull her arm free of the sleeve and the undergarment at the same time. Howie just stood there with his mouth half open and his tongue partially out as she bared her chest. Howie's eyes would always pop at the sight. As usual, Candice had to take the initiative and pull his hands into hers. She rotated her body so that she was standing directly in front of him with her back to his chest. She then placed each of his hands on her nipples. He was able to take over from there.

At this point she would lead him, with her breasts in his hands, toward the different drugs on her list this week. She would ask each time, "Now, what does this do to the body? For how long? How much do I use?" She needed different things for different reasons…none of which mattered to Howie. Candice would complete her shopping list, remove his hands from her breasts, replace her undergarments, button her blouse, straighten her hat, and leave. Howie would lock the door behind her to relieve himself. This was a win-win process for everyone, Candice thought…Howie, on the other hand, thought he and Candice might have a future and that, with some encouragement from others, he would eventually make his move.

Candice was wicked. Possibly incapable of feelings for others. She gave Loretta powder to put in the coffee for Judge Lawler to make him dopey. It was pure poison. Intended to kill. Candice had an agenda.

Early on Monday, June 19, 1916, the papers were flooded with information about the murder of the missing Judge Lawler. His body had been found Saturday in fifteen feet of muddy water under the steel bridge over Aldridge Creek at Ditto's Landing and Whitesburg.

On Wednesday, June 21, Grace decided to visit Sheldon Pleasants, a church member friend and the assistant district attorney, at his office on the North Side Square. The office staff had no appointment for Grace, but they assumed the visit was about a church fund-raiser. She was chairwoman again this year.

Later, shortly after Grace's midmorning visit, Candice visited her husband at his office. Loud voices were overheard. Candice brought Sheldon some cool water to calm his ever-unsteady nerves, and then she left. This was not an unusual visit between the couple. In her pleasant, calm voice, as if nothing was wrong, she spoke to several of the employees as she made her way out the door. Candice was down the steps and almost to the corner when she heard the gunshot coming from the direction of Sheldon's office. She continued walking. *Rats,* she thought. *Now there will be a big mess. He should have just waited until his medicine took effect. Then there wouldn't have been any bloody mess. What did he and Grace talk about?*

Early Friday morning, June 23, Grace visited with Sheriff Robert Phillips. Only a few minutes after she left, Loretta Overton arrived to see him. They were overheard arguing. Then Loretta stormed out of the sheriff's office. Deputy Ward went in and had a short conversation with the sheriff. Ward noticed that the sheriff looked weak and sick. When

Ward started to leave for lunch, he overheard others whispering, "The sheriff has taken his life, and Ward was the last to see him alive."

When Loretta heard the news, she was disappointed that her method hadn't had a chance to work first. She was also a little bit angry. She had had to throw a fit at the sheriff's office just to get him to drink a Coca-Cola...all for nothing. *Wonder why he shot himself,* she thought. *What did the preacher's wife have to say to him?* Now she just had to hope someone would shoot her husband, David Overton, for the reward money; all her human obstacles would then be eliminated. Niles and Brooks were weak players in the situation, but she could deal with them later.

Loretta was the only person, other than the six involved men, who knew about the secret Molly Teal money account and the other assets. She had plans to get it all. Candice might know something by now, but Loretta would take care of her when the right time came. She would use and set up that conniving worm Suzette to do the dirty deed.

On Wednesday, June 28, Grace was on the downtown square early, delivering papers for her brothers to the Cotton Row merchants, when she decided to make a visit to Police Chief Kirby. One stop at Harrison Brothers Hardware store to pick up cigars for the elderly, homebound Mr. Weeden and new locks for the church, and then she would be on her way across the street to the police station.

Grace stood there in the police department headquarters wearing her religious righteousness and giving Chief Kirby the third degree. "On the night of the murder, your men saw me standing there in the dark on the side of the road, alone, with a broken-down car. Their heavy-ended taxis just sped past me. I saw the officers' faces. One was Dick O'Neal. He just stared straight ahead instead of looking at me and stopping to help.

"This was around the time that the Lawler murder was happening near the bridge, close to the same spot where I was broken down. Thank the good Lord Jesus my husband backtracked after me when I didn't come home right after him, so I wasn't there very long. I was scared, and your taxicab drove right past me. I'm a Christian woman in need of help, and they just sped right by me. What were your men doing down there anyway? Do y'all know already who killed Judge Lawler?" The police chief stopped her and then escorted her toward the door. He had had all he could take of her ranting. He also knew that she knew more than she was saying.

An officer came through the door with such urgency that he practically knocked Grace over. He hurriedly apologized to her. The officer announced to the chief that the Lawler grand jury had just censured him on the accusations just implied by Mrs. Thomas, who was conveniently out in the hall but close enough to hear. "I'll resign today...right now!" the chief said, knowing all the money he had been raking in would now be going into someone else's dirty hands.

Grace had done this one for her brother Percy. *To even the playing field*, she thought. She was thinking of the many times Police Chief Kirby and Sheriff Phillips had shown up with their entire force for a raid on Taylorsville. Everyone in Taylorsville would be expecting them, and the scene would be as clean as a whistle. No rum from the islands, no vodka from the Shoals, and no moonshine from Cloud's Cove. No stills burning on the mountains, and traffic was normal. Just a quiet and peaceful country town.

Grace felt good about her accomplishments lately. She began to sleep through the night. No more nightmares. After a couple of weeks of sleeping through the night, Grace was finally able to give her virginity to her husband of two years. They eventually had many children together.

Widow Candice Pleasants made several visits to a young twenty-seven-year-old Niles. Her plan worked well. She counted on him through her time of grief. He succumbed to her sexual experience. Eventually, he was unexpectedly paralyzed. He could not speak. Later that year, Niles was the first in Huntsville to die of the Spanish flu. The Spanish flu killed four hundred people in Huntsville within a year. Only four of the town's doctors survived the deadly virus.

Candice moved on in her put-on grief cycle to entertain men of influence from all over the state. Loretta and cohort Suzette used the power of suggestion to plant evil seeds. Loretta's plan was to rid herself of one more person getting a cut of the secret bootlegging business and the M. Teal account. They knew a very smart pharmacist who needed to use his knowledge of drugs as a way to marital bliss. The social circles of Huntsville were surprised when Candice settled down with her socially inept former brother-in-law, Howie. Candice thought she was the only one to manipulate outcomes with pharmaceuticals, only to become a slave to the sexually deviant druggist for decades.

Brooks was a real piece of cow manure. He was one of those men that even the good old boys weren't too happy to be seen with...especially around women. He embarrassed all the other men. It was hard for them to get around the truth. Brooks had been convicted of the attempted rape of a young lady schoolteacher from a prominent family. He was currently on a suspended sentence while his attorney appealed the case. Brooks was a known creep. Most of his victims were ashamed of what happened and didn't pursue criminal charges because this brought a label of shame to them and to their families. Usually, nothing was ever done about rape cases.

After the Lawler murder trial, Brooks got off the hook. He received a mysterious envelope that had a strange odor and was full of white powder. Suzette had delivered the letter as part of a plot Loretta had set in motion in reference to the money in the secret Molly Teal account. The money was the bait to get Brooks where Loretta wanted him to be at a particular time. Greedy to get his hands on this huge amount of money, he eagerly jumped on a train to Muscle Shoals, according to stipulations in the letter. Brooks' instructions were to cross the tracks at precisely four o'clock and meet someone at the Depot Café in Muscle Shoals. Brooks arrived at the Shoals Depot lightheaded and forgetful. He looked down at his watch and had just enough time to meet a stranger at four o'clock. Without looking, he walked straight in front of the train bound for Iuka, Mississippi. Instantly the world was better off.

No one in his family knew why he was in the Muscle Shoals area or anything about his finances. By the time his estate was settled, every member of his family except one had died of the Spanish flu. The niece who lived with the Brooks family, whom he often raped, found herself with a large amount of bootlegging money in the bank.

Of the six men involved in the Lawler murder, five were now dead and Overton was convicted of murder, awaiting execution in Birmingham. Many thought that with the money he had accumulated in his illegal alcohol business, he would hire a good lawyer and appeal the sentence. No one could have predicted what fate was to bring David Overton.

Twenty Eight

The Circus Comes to Town

Meanwhile, at the Taylorsville depot, Percy was planning for the three-day visit of the circus. Every year when the circus came, Percy invited the ringmaster to come and relax at the farm for a few days before getting back to the never-ending, tiring daily train travel and the hard life of the circus. Everyone in Taylorsville looked forward to circus weekend. The merchants and salesmen made out well financially. Mostly everyone enjoyed all the animals. The circus crew enjoyed fishing and hunting as well. Percy had it set up so that the animals had a little more freedom to play. Elephants went to the ponds, and the giraffes just relaxed, eating tree leaves, while zebras were allowed to freely graze with the farm's horses, and lions enjoyed the sunshine and fresh air coming through their cages. Most spectacular were the beautiful show horses.

Percy and the ringmaster had an argument. The conflict was not normal. It was about whether or not to shoot a newborn baby elephant with a clubfoot. One of the fortune-tellers told the ringmaster it must be killed or it would bring bad luck...in the way of fire. To save the infant elephant, Percy had to bribe the ringmaster, Agee, by promising him a trip to town for a high-stakes poker game.

Agee agreed, and Percy sent someone to Cloud's Cove to get Harmony. No one had ever heard her speak, although she did hear quite well. Harmony's special connection with animals enabled her to communicate with them without talking. The ringmaster agreed to let Harmony take the clubfooted baby elephant to raise back in Cloud's Cove. In the past the ringmaster had given her a very old zebra, a toothless lion, and some mean birds called emus that everyone in the circus hated.

Chase and Jagi had been planning for the event for three days, preparing barbecue with time for fishing, swimming, and partying for the circus staff. They were ready to relax. Olivia and the twins had been down at the arena enjoying the breeze off the water and looking for four-leaf clovers. They found several, but apparently not enough.

Among the circus activities was the scheduled train from Gunter's Landing on the barge, now docking. The *Miss Guntersville* steamship had a very structured timing of events while loading and unloading. Two whistle blows indicated that the train was to move forward to load. One loud blow meant the train was to stop. Three whistle blows signaled that the train was to start offloading the barge. This process of bells, honks, and boatswain whistles was the only communication between the boat captain and the train engineer. For safety reasons, passengers had to remain on board the steamship until the entire process was completed. After the train cars had been successfully transferred to the land, the passengers were allowed off the boat and were then immediately directed back onto the train. Although the depot was only eight hundred yards away as the crow flies, no walking was normally allowed, because of safety concerns on the direct path through the fields and pasture lands and because part of the distance to the depot by way of the train tracks was on a high timber trestle. For the safety of everyone, this part of the track could certainly not be walked across.

Chip O'Kennedy took after his biological father in size. Although a teenager, he was now the size of an adult, at six feet tall. He continued his Peeping Tom habits all across town. It was his form of releasing pent-up anger. He would be outside a woman's window and masturbate while watching her undress. Then he moved on to watching couples have sex in their bedrooms.

The weekend the circus was in Taylorsville, Chip O'Kennedy sneaked around on the outskirts of the busy events. He wanted to be a part of this traditional party in his own way. Toward evening, when the last train of the day came down the river, he watched the cars being unloaded as he had done many times before. Chip had heard a rumor going around, alleging that a large black man had gone on a violent spree from Gurley to Cloud's Cove. He noticed one of the doors was open on a train car, and that a woman was climbing inside. He figured she was probably a hobo, jumping trains. The train's whistles and horns were going off. Two loud whistles and one long horn blast as a response signaled that it was time to unload the cars and move them up the track. It would take at least another hour.

For fun and entertainment he decided to harass the female hobo. She was already passed out from too much liquor, which he could smell the moment he climbed into the car. This was a dream come true for Chip. The loud sounds of the ship and train's horns and whistles provided a great cover. He pulled his pants down and tried pushing her dress up. Eventually he just ripped the dress completely off of her. As he was raping her, he fantasized that she was Shasta and became more aroused by hitting her hard in the face and chest. He kept up this brutal rape until he finally climaxed in her during the beating. Chip left her there in a pool of blood but still alive. In the future, he would recall this night many times, and it always brought him great pleasure.

He walked back to the depot area and saw Olivia with her twin children. Olivia's son, Oliver, had gotten quite tall since the last time Chip had seen him. Chip decided this would be the perfect time to put the uppity Negro in his place once and for all, with the added benefit of upsetting the protective Taylor family.

The reconnected train cars departed from the riverbank and were pulling into the depot. Passengers were getting off while others were waiting to board for the trip to Huntsville and beyond. Chip went around to the empty car with the woman inside. To his surprise, she was sitting up, sort of on her side, looking at him desperately. "Help me! Help me!" she moaned. Her teeth were broken, her mouth was swollen, and it appeared her blackened eyes could barely open. Her breathing was ragged, as though she was in intense pain with every breath or movement she made.

Chip put his plan into action. "Oh my, what happened to you, woman? I'll get you some help!" he said as he leaned in and pretended attempts to comfort her. "I saw a large Negro man getting out of the car... He did this to you? Now say it with me," he commanded. "Large Negro man. Now, you have to say it before I will get help. I heard your screaming, and I came to help you."

The woman mumbled something, but Chip could not understand her. "Listen, lady, the police don't like me. I will get you help, but I can't be involved. Do you understand?" She nodded, still unable to speak. He tried to help her sit up, and she screamed in pain. With one swoop, he picked her up, climbed out of the train car, and laid her on the ground near a fence post where she could be seen. The woman screamed and moaned loudly. Chip put his hand over her mouth, but she moaned even more. "Listen here, lady, I'll go get you help, but you better tell them what I said about a big black Negro. The cops won't believe me. They're trying to nail me for bootlegging. You mention anything about me and they won't believe you. Do you understand that? They won't believe you if you mention you saw me," he said.

She put her hand to her broken mouth and uttered, "Big black...," and as her voice trailed off, she fell onto her side.

Chip quickly scurried away before he was seen by anyone. "Large Negro man," he shouted over his shoulder as he disappeared into the darkness.

Twenty Nine

King Earl

Earl was very abusive to his wife, Lily. He was real nice when he wasn't on the moonshine, but that was not very often. Lily was missing several teeth on her left side because of his right hook. Although both were black, Earl became mean when he drank and demanded that she serve him as if she were a slave. He demanded that she refer to him as King Earl. Lily would usually cave in just until he passed out, and then she would continue making her special doughnut batter for the next day.

She dreaded the nights when he came home after being out drinking. The next day she would always make excuses for her bruises, but everyone knew her situation. One night Lily decided she wouldn't take it anymore. She was going to get beat up anyway, so tonight she would show him she could hit him back. She put a rolling pin and a small iron skillet on the kitchen table within easy reaching distance. Lily also got out a kitchen knife. She hoped she would not have to use it, but if things got out of hand, she was not going to let him kill her.

Lily never knew what time Earl would come home or what kind of mood he'd be in. The longer she waited, the more she started thinking this was a bad idea. Her back was turned, so she was startled when Earl finally flung open the screen door. He was confrontational and mumbling worse than usual. "You come any closer, Earl King, and I'll hit you with this skillet," she said.

"Woman…ye ah youuu jus tryy…," he mumbled as he tried to raise his fist. Lily was about to give Earl a frying pan between the eyes when he stopped midword and fell straight back onto the stone floor. Earl didn't move. He wasn't breathing. This was not moonshine. He had been drinking methyl alcohol, which was poisonous.

Lily, always levelheaded, was now in a complete panic. Knowing that she had planned to fight back, she felt guilty, because she always wished him dead when he was drunk. First, she went to find Percy and was told that he and his longtime buddy, the ringmaster of the world-famous Barnum & Bailey Circus, had gone to town for a poker game at the Huntsville Hotel. Lily knew Percy would see her if she asked, but should she drive to Huntsville? Confused about what she should do, she went back to the house. Earl still lay there on the floor. *Dead as a doornail,* she thought.

Lily came up with a plan to get him into the trunk of her car, which was parked close to the front door anyway. Being so busy with Earl, she forgot to turn off the fire under the hot frying oil, and it was beginning to smoke. She stepped over Earl's body to turn off the heat. Suddenly, he grabbed her ankle on one leg and the calf of the other leg, causing her to stumble. She fell against the large handle of the frying oil pot, and down it went onto Earl's entire upper body and face. She kept tumbling until she came to the closed door to the cellar. Although lightheaded from the collision with the door, she immediately knew what she was smelling. Crispy King Earl! Unable to control herself, she ran out the front door to throw up. King Earl was now King Crispy. Lily made several attempts to go back inside, but each time, she returned to the grass on her knees at the point of dry heaving.

THIRTY

THE HANGING

A couple from the traveling circus was sneaking off into the woods for some private time when they stumbled across the half-naked, beaten woman. They began hollering as loud as they could for someone to come and help. A circus medic showed up and immediately gave her smelling salts. The blood-soaked woman spoke clearly: "A large black man did this to me." She fell over and passed out again. A crowd gathered around, and quickly there was an uproar for justice.

Chip was so proud of himself for getting away with this heinous act, but he wasn't finished yet. He pointed out to some strangers from the circus staff, "This must have been done by Oliver Howard Taylor. He's the only large Negro around. He's missing now...He must be the one."

A well-known racist in Taylorsville, R. H. Craft, and his emotionally beaten-down son, Will Craft, stepped up. Like a mouthpiece for his dad, Will proclaimed, "This is how Negroes behave—like savages to our white women."

"Time for lynching," the father shouted.

Almost everyone in Taylorsville knew Oliver was not capable of such a horrible crime. Even some of the old-timers from the circus refuted the accusation, for they had been stopping in Taylorsville for three days each fall for many years and knew him well. "Shut up, Craft," Lim Hobbs said. "Everyone around here knows you're the one who's been trying to get the Ku Klux Klan to come to town to get Percy Taylor because he befriended Olivia's family. Even heard your name is already in their sacred book of brothers. You seem to have forgotten how you dragged us all into court when you lynched Herman Deeley. We all liked Herman. Black or not, he was one of us. Remember that, Craft? Remember what you and that son of yours that you bully around did? You also seem to have forgotten the ass whipping Percy Taylor gave you. Hell, you still can't walk up straight. That black boy is his adopted son. I bet you won't live to talk about it this time."

Yes, Hobbs was a good friend of Percy's, and he would not let up. He continued, "Somebody needs to go find Percy Taylor. Go away, Mr. Craft. You are nothing but a religious hypocrite and have embarrassed all of us at the Whitesburg Pike Church for the last time. You claim to be a Christian, and yet every chance you get, you bully someone less fortunate, down on their luck, or a different color. We all remember how you tried to run over that Chinese family for cutting through your field. According to the *Huntsville Daily Times* you were as guilty as sin of murdering Herman Deeley. Your wife, bless her heart, got up there and lied, pleading your case for you. She got you off."

"The judge too!" someone yelled.

At the trial Craft's wife had moaned and wailed to the jurors in her fake squeaky voice. The all-male jury couldn't take it, and it appeared Judge Lawler's position over the trial had been compromised. After all, he was known to be a womanizer, and it wouldn't be the first time a little hanky-panky back in his private chambers had gotten someone off, so to speak.

The same Bass Cobb who stood trial for murder with the two Crafts stood up and said, "Ladies and gentlemen, Craft is not on trial here today. We have a dangerous Negro boy running around raping our white women. We need justice, which means there's gonna be a lynchin', and I'm going to go find that boy now. Who's with me?"

Chip just sat back and beamed with pride as the events unfolded. The wheels were in motion; not even Percy Taylor could stop this hysterical crowd. Chip couldn't wait to share this with his mother.

Jagi joined the crowd late, but it didn't take him long to figure out what was going on. He had to warn Olivia and her children, Oliver and

Opal, as quickly as possible. He had talked with them earlier, and they had been heading to the arena to do a little night fishing for catfish. He jumped into the Taylor company truck and took off as fast as he could without raising suspicion. But Olivia and her family were not at the arena. He had forgotten they were also going downstream a little farther to look for Indian arrowheads on the riverbank until it got too dark. There were some good fishing holes down that way also.

He had heard more disturbing rumors about the KKK trying to become relevant in the region again. Jagi found an oil-soaked, big white cross a couple hundred feet away from the arena, the Taylor family picnic area by the big oak tree. Jagi was sure it was intended for an upcoming membership rally.

Suddenly, in the middle of the field, Miss Lily drove up. He was not sure if she saw the cross, but her face was almost white. Lily got close to Jagi, and he could smell throw-up and burned grease. Before he could tell her about Oliver, she started rambling on and on to Jagi about how she thought that although Earl should have died for being so mean when he was drunk, she hadn't meant for him to die. She told him that earlier, after she was able to pull herself together, she had wrapped Earl in a sheet and dragged him into her automobile trunk, and about how she had gone to find Percy, but he was away in town at a poker game. "I really thought he was dead, lying there on the floor. I didn't mean to spill the hot doughnut oil on him." She rambled on about the accident with the doughnut oil until finally, almost exhausted, she concluded, "Earl is still wrapped in a white sheet in the trunk of my car." She pointed to her car.

"He's in the car? Dead?" Jagi asked.

"Yes," she said, "and I'm not sure what to do. Do I throw his body into the river or take it down to the police and confess to everything?"

Lily and Jagi agreed they needed to search for Percy, but judging by the noise of the crowd at the depot, Jagi knew they might not have time. Yes, they needed Percy's help with the white cross Jagi had found and what to do with Earl—or "King Crispy," as Lily called him—but more important right then was the lynching party forming for Oliver.

Jagi told Lily about the woman being raped and Craft and Cobb working the crowd up to lynch Oliver. "Jagi, Oliver would not do that,"

Lily said. For a moment she forgot about Earl, and her thoughts went to how she could help save Oliver. Craft had hanged Herman Deeley, and they knew he wouldn't hesitate to hang Oliver. Jagi told Lily to go down the river to find Olivia and the kids. He would go to the depot to find Shasta or Doc Reynolds, who he heard was in town for the circus. Everyone would meet at the oak tree.

Jagi started running for the depot only to remember halfway there that he had left the company truck back at the arena. *Never mind*, he thought. He could probably run the distance faster than the time it would take to go back and get the truck. Near the depot in the darkening gloom of the evening, Jagi walked smack into the worst piece of horse dung of a person he had ever known: Chip O'Kennedy. Jagi knew that Chip was nothing but a troublemaker who sniffed around Taylorsville for information he could take back to his stepdaddy, the crooked homosexual detective on Huntsville's police force. The detective wanted to put moonshiners and bootleggers out of business so that he and his bosses could control the entire county's liquor business and make all the profit. Chip was claiming, "There's a woman who's been raped. She can identify the Negro as the guilty party." Chip was just like his mother, using the power of suggestion to point a guilty finger toward Oliver. He repeated to Jagi, "Bass Cobb told everyone we need to have a lynching."

Jagi tried to look calm as he scanned the crowd. He felt a hand on his shoulder. It was Doc Reynolds. "Jagi," he said, "you look worried."

"I am," Jagi mumbled softly. "Let's step back from the crowd so we can talk." Jagi knew that Doc Reynolds would help in any way possible, so he blurted out the whole story. Doc knew of Chip's wrongdoing in the past and told Jagi he suspected that Oliver was being framed to divert attention from the real guilty party. Jagi asked him to ride over to the arena, where Miss Lily was waiting. As Jagi and Doc left to find Doc's car, they ran into Shasta. She saw the look on their faces and demanded to go along. Whatever was going on, she wanted to help.

As they were riding over to the arena, Jagi gave Shasta the short version of what was happening. Shasta was horrified but determined to stop a lynching. Jagi said, "Why Herman or Oliver? If anybody deserves to be hanged, it's Earl."

Doc said, "Jagi, you may have something there. Let me think." They reached the old oak tree at the arena where Lily was standing by her car. Olivia and her family were hiding in the bushes until they knew who was in the car. When they saw Doc, Shasta, and Jagi, they came out.

Doc called everyone together. He had a plan. "First," he said, "Miss Lily, can we talk privately behind the oak tree?" Minutes later, the two returned, having apparently reached an understanding. Doc then talked with Olivia. He came back and addressed Oliver. "Son, your mother and I have talked, and we need you to come home with me to Huntsville tonight. Jagi, you and Lily are going to hang Earl in place of Oliver, and when the crowd shows up, Opal, you and your mom are going to cry your eyes out, saying the body is Oliver's. You need to be convincing. Oliver's life depends on it."

Doc then turned to Shasta. "Shasta, while the crowd is focusing on the hanging, you must pretend to console Olivia and Opal. At first chance, Lily will offer to carry you and them home with Oliver...I mean for Earl's body to have a proper funeral in Huntsville. Don't go home. Lily will drive you to the Memphis and Charleston depot downtown. Walk out the back door and go over to the Nashville, Chattanooga, and St. Louis depot. Take the train to Chattanooga and go to the Chattanooga Hotel next to the train station and check in. Shasta, if anyone has a problem with accommodations for colored people, tell them your help is traveling with you. I don't think there will be a problem, but as a last resort, don't hesitate to throw around your daddy's name. I will meet you there with Oliver." Shasta had long ago planned a quick getaway for Olivia and her family for whatever reason. She had a trunk ready and waiting in the storage locker at the depot. In it were clothes, lots of cash, gold, and a contact list.

Doc continued, "Jagi will hide the company truck and slip away during the commotion to track down Percy and the ringmaster at the Huntsville Hotel and bust in on their poker game. Percy has to know what is happening. Jagi, does the company work truck have any rope in it?"

"Yes," replied Jagi. He had just gotten some rope at the seed store for the company.

Jagi returned with the rope, and with Doc's direction everyone worked feverishly to prepare the scene. Jagi tied the rope around Earl's neck just like the one he had tried to cut off Herman nearly three years earlier. He looped the other end over the lowest limb of the big oak tree. While the others were going to get the cross, Jagi took a moment, got down on his knees beside the oak tree, and prayed. He wondered if Earl would understand. He was doing this to save another young man's life. "Oh God, please have mercy on Earl's soul, and God...please help Earl forgive me," he pleaded.

It took everyone to get the huge oil-soaked white cross upright. They were able to stabilize it with stakes hammered into the ground and some fence wire that was also in the work truck. Jagi took the truck and hid it out of sight in the woods nearby.

After a few more adjustments to the rope, they carefully and slowly pulled Earl into the air so that his feet were about three feet off the grass. The rope was tied in several knots on the backside of the tree. Jagi looked at the beautiful stars above, and for the second time he asked God's forgiveness for what they were doing.

The scene was set. Off in the distance they heard the crowd by the train depot becoming louder. Jagi looked at Doc and said, "It is time, isn't it?"

"Yes," Doc confirmed and added, "Jagi, I'm counting on you." Tearful good-byes were said, and Oliver got in the trunk of Lily's car, where Earl had been. Doc got into the driver's seat, and they left, headed for Huntsville. Jagi pulled a box of matches out of his pocket and looked at Lily and Olivia. "God willing, this will work."

He struck a match, and in an instant the entire cross was ablaze. Jagi began to think of Earl as a hero. The fire on the cross drew the crowd's attention. Jagi realized they were heading in the direction of the arena. Right on cue, Olivia and her daughter began the performance of their lives, with Shasta and Lily pitching in. Truth be known, they were not acting. Many hours of pent-up emotions came flowing out. Mother and daughter began crying, chanting in French, and howling in Cajun, with Lily in the middle. Jagi was crying also. His emotions finally got to him. Shasta did as her father would have and tried to comfort them all.

Lily looked traumatized as she looked at Earl's body hanging from the rope. Finally she couldn't cry anymore. The crowd drew closer. Lily had a bag of doughnuts in her hand. She looked at Jagi. "King Crispy dough-nut?" she asked. Jagi stared at the emptiness in her eyes and realized that Lily used doughnuts as comfort and therapy for herself. She had escaped Earl's abuse by making doughnuts. She gained acceptance and pleasure by selling and giving them away. Doughnuts were her prop and crutch in life. Doughnuts defined Miss Lily. He reached out and took one. Jagi wasn't sure, but he thought he saw a slight calm now in Lily's face.

The crowd gathered around the hanging man. Before anyone got close enough to verify that it was Oliver under the white sheet, the wind shifted direction, as though it were planned. A spark landed on Earl's oil-soaked sheet. The blaze quickly took over his body. The rope caught fire, and Earl's burning body fell to the ground. Olivia ran up to the flames and cried for her son, "Oliver!" Screams and crying came from the crowd. *This wasn't supposed to happen*, many of them thought. How had it gotten this far out of hand? Everyone just knew that the KKK had to have been behind the supposed lynching. Fear spread through the community.

Jagi went to get the truck he'd stashed in the woods earlier, but it was gone. He came back and whispered to Shasta that the company truck he had hidden in the woods had been stolen. "Here are the keys to my car. Go get Daddy!" she exclaimed.

Jagi ran quickly to the Taylor house to get Shasta's car. He heard his heartbeat inside his ears so loudly that it drowned out all other sounds. His feet were numb as they thumped down on the hard ground. With surging adrenaline, Jagi finally reached the house, completely soaked with sweat. He looked back in the direction of the burning cross as the crowd managed to knock it into the river. Jagi wondered to himself if this deed was his one-way ticket to hell. He could almost hear the priest at his own funeral mass.

Driving as fast as the Model T would go, he almost bounced out of his seat several times as he hit every pothole on Hobbs Island Road and on the Whitesburg Pike into Huntsville. He thought about tying a rope across his lap so his head wouldn't hit the roof as he sped over the bumps, but there was no time to stop. His mouth was dry, and he was still breathing heavily. Jagi desperately needed water. His mouth and tongue felt like a dried leather belt. He thought this must be how it feels when going to hell. He felt that he would be punished.

Finding Percy was his first priority. Then they would pick up Oliver later. He knew Oliver was safe with Doc Reynolds. Jagi was a smelly, sweaty mess by the time he parked the car at the hotel. He knew that in this condition he should not use the front door, but to his surprise the doorman let him in without objection. He went directly to the elevator and asked the elevator operator to take him to the poker room. At first the young operator was reluctant to help because of Jagi's appearance. He even denied knowing anything about a poker room. "I need to see Percy Taylor now! It's a matter of life and death," Jagi told him.

"They made me swear not to let them be interrupted," said the elevator operator.

Jagi reached into his pocket and pulled out a smelly, sweat-soaked dollar bill and put it into the operator's hand.

"You say it is a life-or-death situation for Mr. Taylor?" the operator asked.

"Yes," shouted Jagi.

"Yes, sir…Top floor," the operator replied.

Not one of the card players noticed when Jagi came in. The cash pile on the table was tall, and they all had serious looks on their faces. Percy had just peeked at his last hole card. Two women, sparsely clothed, were bringing them drinks. Jagi walked over to Percy, quietly tapped him on the shoulder, and whispered, "I hate to intrude, Mr. Taylor, but it's Oliver. They are trying to lynch him."

Percy's face dropped as he stood up and said, "Gentlemen, something extremely important and urgent has come up, and I must leave immediately. Please continue your game. I'm going to let Miss Dawn here play out my hand." He motioned for her to take his seat. "Darling, if you win, it's all yours to split with your friend," he said as he and Jagi turned to leave the room.

Jagi turned to John Agee, the ringmaster of the Ringling Brothers circus, and said, "Mr. Agee, you may need to head back to Taylorsville. There was a fire and your people are spooked."

"Damn it, the fortune-teller was right. She predicted fire if we didn't put down the infant elephant. 'Bad luck,' she said."

The ringmaster took Shasta's car back to Taylorsville. Much to his surprise, he found that most of the equipment, tents, animals, and crew were loaded into the train cars and ready for departure. Just a few were still sweeping the animal poop into large holes and covering it with sawdust. The ringmaster said his farewells at the depot. He also said, "I will never come to Taylorsville again!" He was off to the Huntsville fairgrounds downtown. The traveling circus train left within the hour.

Jagi was telling Percy the whole story as they drove to the beautiful Taylor home at the corner of Williams and Franklin. Percy was totally silent as Jagi told every detail, without taking a breath, from Lily's "King Crispy" Earl accident, to the smell that came along with it, to setting the cross on fire and hanging Earl. Also, he said, the work truck was missing.

Percy found the time to tell Jagi how proud he was of him. "Jagi, you've done a really good job taking care of our family. I'm proud that you were able to think on your feet and act so quickly. I'm not sure I could've done as well."

"I never want Madam Walker to visit me here, Mr. Taylor. She would only be put in danger. I do not understand this issue some people have for colorful people. In the hot summers here my skin is much darker than Oliver's or Madam Walker's."

Percy had no answers for Jagi as he loaded up four suitcases from the other house into the brand-new Studebaker. As at the Chattanooga train depot, two always-ready, packed suitcases were taken to the Studebaker from Shasta and Olivia's room and two more from Oliver and Opal's rooms. Percy even put a couple of cases of wine Shasta was starting to like in the car. "My good friend Emilio from Cuba sort of shorted me of some of my island rum," he said. "He sent me this twenty-something-year-old Rothschild wine instead...said he thought I might enjoy it. He meant well, but I would just as soon have had the rum. But since Shasta is starting to drink it, maybe where she is about to go they will like this kind of stuff," he mused.

Percy was in control now. With the information he had from Jagi, he quickly developed additional plans and filled Jagi in on all the necessary next steps. Oliver was still hiding at Doc Reynolds's house. Percy arranged with Doc to come by to get Jagi, switch automobiles, and drive with Oliver to Chattanooga. "Y'all need to take only back roads to Chattanooga, and then go and meet up with Shasta, Olivia, and Opal at the Chattanooga Hotel next to the train station. Come back home a different way."

When Doc arrived to pick up Jagi, Percy thanked him for all his efforts and praised the plan Doc had initiated. "Hurry along now, Jagi, and get poor Oliver out of town. You and Doc try to explain everything to him. I hope he understands," Percy said. Then he left in Lily's car for Taylorsville and began putting his plans into action, making several middle-of-the-night stops to see acquaintances and allies on his way back to the river.

To keep awake, Jagi, Doc, and Oliver talked all the way to Chattanooga. Between taking some back roads and a flat tire, the sun was rising by the time they reached Chattanooga. Oliver did ask, "Why did the trunk of Lily's car smell like burned fried pork rinds?"

"Oliver, you really don't want to know," Jagi said.

Oliver had come closer than he knew to being framed and lynched. The hobo woman eventually recovered. She stayed in town, and some of the kind locals took care of her. Nine months later the woman was seen carrying a redheaded baby...not a colored baby. She was often seen with another hobo woman. They both stuck to the story of her being raped and beaten by a large black man.

And Earl? Rumor was that Earl had left his wife and run off to Texas or somewhere. Oh, and by the way, it appeared Miss Dawn didn't have the poker face that Percy and the other high-stakes gamblers had, or thought they had. Percy had a pair of sevens and an ace showing. Looking nervous, Miss Dawn sat down and slowly looked at Percy's hole cards, and started smiling. She reached down into her corset, pulled out all the money she had, and put it on the table...No one would call her. She still got a large pot without showing her cards. Every man around the table eventually asked Percy what had been in the hole. "She made the decision not to show her cards. Ask her," he would say with a smirky smile.

THIRTY ONE

THE BAD SEED AT IT AGAIN

Percy shared his cocaine with Jagi. "Just put a little bit in your nose, and it will keep you alert and on your toes," he said. The white powder made him sneeze, so he dumped it into a bottle of Coca-Cola and chugged it down all at one time.

Doc, Jagi, and Oliver met the group at the hotel as planned. Wide awake and sticky, Jagi was pushed into the bathtub to get immediate improvements. Shasta did take a peek, and talked to him all the while he bathed. "The arrangements have been made for the New Orleans train at ten. We have two hours." After Jagi got dressed, she privately took him aside and said, "I have plans to meet with Olivia's mother in New Orleans. Duval, her husband, and her father, Linal, were on the *Titanic*, and they went down with the ship. Olivia and the twins had to spend the cold night in a lifeboat until they were rescued. Daddy and I were already in New York City on rum and banana business. We were there to meet them after the tragedy happened. We brought them back to Taylorsville, where Daddy adopted all three, and they became Taylors and a part of our family. That was the first time I laid eyes on you."

"Yes, I know the story," Jagi said.

"Yes, I suppose you do," she said without slowing down. "Anyway, I never completely trusted that strangers would not do something to them because of their color. So I devised this escape plan. I met with

Mark and Faye Howard, Olivia's aunt and uncle, on one of Daddy's business trips to New Orleans. They wanted to meet Olivia and the twins in Taylorsville way back then. That day is here, but it will be in New Orleans. Only a few months ago, Mark was able to get Olivia's mother out of the crazy house. Now her mother, Sylvia, is a practicing and successful psychic in New Orleans."

Jagi unloaded the luggage from the car, including the two cases of wine. "Percy packed this wine for you, thinking maybe you would enjoy it wherever you were going." Jagi tried to hide his tears, wiping them onto his sleeve as the train with Shasta, Olivia, and the kids left the station in Chattanooga. He would miss them terribly. They were his new family, and he loved them each and every one.

Saddened, but happy with their successfully accomplished mission, he and Doc were soon back in the car and headed to Huntsville. The journey took a few hours longer than he expected. Doc had to drive completely around through Winchester, Tennessee, because the ferry that crossed the Paint Rock River there was out of service. It was late by the time they came into Huntsville on Meridian Pike. Then they ran into the traffic of the circus. All the animals were being walked back to the tents from the fairgrounds at the corner of Church and Wheeler. The holding tents were over across West Clinton. Doc and Jagi watched the animals parade past as they sat on the hood of the car, parked at the Armor meatpacking plant, across the street from the NC&STL train depot.

Suddenly, a great commotion broke out. A cigarette smoker with red hair was seen at the back of the horse tent. The beautiful white horses with all their fancy decorations and outfittings were stampeding chaotically, and some were coming straight toward them. The horses and their outfits were on fire! The horse trainer was able to mount one of them and blow into a bugle, the command to line up. Twelve of them lined up, and he shot them each in the head as they stood there blazing. The tent burned to the ground as bystanders stood by, watching helplessly.

Jagi saw John, the ringmaster, who was screaming, "Don't panic! Everyone calm down!" No one listened. Jagi overheard the ringmaster say, "The mystic fortune-teller was right! I should've listened. She said there would be fire. Now it's my fault for not listening. I'll never bring the circus back to Huntsville again. EVER! The wooden portion of the Huntsville Hotel is on fire too! That's where we stayed last night and were going to stay tonight. Not now. I want to get on the train and get the hell out of this town."

One hundred and thirty horses died or were humanely put down that day, after running on fire in every direction. Only one elephant was lost. They found him the next morning and buried him near the road, on the side of Clinton Avenue.

As the sun set on this second consecutive day of fire with the stench of burned flesh, Doc dropped Jagi off at the Taylor home on Williams Avenue. Jagi was exhausted, but he still couldn't sleep for reliving all the horrors of the past two days. The poor woman who had been beaten, raped, brought to the depot, and dropped off out back by the fence. The redheaded freak Chip snooping around, stirring up the stupid and racist elements. The odd baby elephant. Earl King drinking himself to death. His wife, Lily, frying him. The hanging, the cross, and the fire. The truck was gone. Driving Oliver to Chattanooga and having to let go. The horses and the hotel on fire. All were burned into his memory for life.

Again Jagi cried. He hated fires. Fire had destroyed his family when he was a child. Jagi was the only survivor from a farmhouse fire. Five sisters, his mom—all gone. The fire was suspicious. His father had been with Jagi's soon-to-be stepmother at the time the blaze was set.

Jagi realized that there was no use trying to sleep. Where was Percy, Sugar, or Big Mama? He headed to the kitchen to get something to eat. Luck was on his side. A huge pot of chili was still warm on the woodstove and so spicy that it burned his mouth. Shasta and her spicy cooking, no doubt. She had made the chili the morning before, when everyone was supposed to get back from Taylorsville that night. She must've used some of those little orange habanero peppers that Carlos's family sent from Brazil. Jagi's eyes began to water from the hot pepper on his tongue, half on fire, half numb. His ears were starting to itch, and his nose would not stop running.

Jagi opened one of the remaining bottles of Rothschild wine that Percy was trying to get rid of and drank it straight out of the bottle. The wine reminded him of Shasta. It did nothing for the burn in his mouth, but he finished the chili anyway as he guzzled the wine. Jagi brought the last of the bottle of wine with him to bed in case he got dry mouth during the night. Finally, the cocaine wore off and the effects of the wine kicked in, and he was able to sleep.

A few hours later, Jagi was awakened by two sheriff's deputies standing over him. One of them shouted, "We've been knocking and banging at your door for a half hour. We finally climbed on top of the cruiser and jumped to the balcony. Get up! We're taking you someplace." Jagi slowly got dressed. He just knew they were on to him about Earl.

The two deputies had no idea what was about to happen. They had just been told to pick him up and bring him to the Kildare Mansion on Oakwood Avenue. On the short ride over they passed the smoldering remains of the Huntsville Hotel, and one of the deputies asked, "Did you or Percy give Chip O'Kennedy permission to drive the Taylorsville company truck? The fire department reported Chip was driving away from the burning hotel when they arrived to put out the fire."

Jagi didn't know how to answer, so he remained silent. The three drove up to the sprawling estate in the patrol car. "Jagi, we've done our job and got you here," one of the deputies said. "The meeting is downstairs in the basement. The house is seventeen thousand square feet and has forty rooms, so don't get lost, because I heard this place is haunted." Jagi reluctantly opened the car door and figured the end was near for him. While he stood on the porch, he doubled over as stomach pains kicked in. He just knew by now it was the Klan and they were here to lynch him. Even worse, he thought they might have brought him here to persuade him to join their cause.

The burning hole in his stomach turned to cramps. The heartburn was so bad, it felt like fire in the back of his throat. Fear took over. Bullets of sweat began to pop up on his forehead. He wished he had kissed Shasta in Chattanooga earlier in the day. He loved her. He understood the expression *deathbed confessions* now. He took a deep breath and entered through the front door. He saw nobody as he walked by a grand piano and looked into the dark dining room with a table big enough for twelve people.

Each room was fancier than the one before, with fireplaces everywhere. Some were angled into the corners. Finally he saw the staircase down to the basement, but not before he heard footsteps behind him. There was no one there. He flew down the steps, afraid that he might hear a second noise. All the lights were on, but still no people were in sight as he walked through a third kitchen and past a double-sized cast-iron stove. Around the corner appeared to be a wine cellar filled with wooden wine racks that stretched from floor to ceiling and the entire length of the wall.

He opened the only door he could find and walked through. "Holy crap!" Jagi said under his breath. Everybody who was anybody in Huntsville and the surrounding area was in the basement. This was an enclave of Huntsville's important people: the bank presidents, the Chamber of Commerce president, a couple of Catholic priests, the O'Shaughnessy brothers, old Mr. Pratt, the Weatherly elders, the Walkers, and even Dr. William Hooper Councill, the black college president and Methodist minister. "What!" Jagi looked around, puzzled. The new sheriff, the mayor, the worshipful master of the Masonic Lodge, the Elks president, several prominent black businessmen, Baptist preachers, a Jewish rabbi, and other important leaders of Huntsville all turned to look at him.

At first, Jagi could hear noises and people speaking. Then the sound became only a hum. His stomach continued to rumble. He thought he was having bad gas when he realized it was the hot habanero chili. He had to go to the toilet...now! Pushing people aside, he ran to get back outside. Seeing no outhouse, he headed for the woods and barely made it. Hanging on to a tree trunk with a sick, nauseated feeling, he promised God he would never eat a habanero chili again. Or was it really the KKK trying to poison him? He had no idea what was going on at this gathering. His mind tried to focus on the faces back in the basement. *A Jewish rabbi? What in the world is going on?* he thought.

After a lengthy delay, during which he made even more promises to God, he was able to pull up his pants. After three tries, he was able to make it back inside and to the basement with the town leaders. Someone began to speak about the cross from the night before. Earlier in the meeting all had agreed that together they would fight the Klan as it tried to organize in Huntsville. It was especially important to keep politics clean. The city had been through enough with the Lawler murderers. United, they would stand against the KKK to prevent it from taking a foothold in Huntsville. Percy was the person who had put this whole meeting together. However, he was not in attendance.

Then it hit Jagi again…the chili. Poison? The room started to spin, and all the faces became a blur. Jagi passed out and fell straight to the floor. Several people rushed to his aid. Huntsville's most prominent surgeon, Dr. Reynolds, came to assist and had everyone back away to give him air. Some feared it was the deadly flu spreading across the country. The largest of the men picked up Jagi, got him into Doc's car, and carried him to the house on Williams Avenue. Dr. Reynolds gave him a couple of different shots and other medicines to keep him asleep while his body fought off the fever.

Down in Taylorsville, Percy was in the panic of his life over Sugar. He was missing the enclave meeting. He could not find his dog. He had let her out after she had begun her alarm bark. Her fur was standing from the top of her head all the way down her back to the tail as she tore out the door. Percy had thought nothing of it at the time. It was her usual behavior in response to a visiting pair of coyotes. Now she'd been gone far too long, and he needed to get to the meeting at Kildare Mansion.

As Percy came around the side yard, he saw Harmony trying to get something out of Sugar's mouth. Harmony looked up, terrified, and pointed to Chip, who was hiding behind a row of scrubs. Percy took off and tackled him from behind with a full body blow. He dragged Chip's limp, lanky body over to Harmony and Sugar's apparently lifeless body. Harmony had wrapped herself completely around Sugar. She was taking long, deliberate breaths, then exhaling loudly and with great effort. Percy sat beside her with his hands all over his beloved Sugar. She had saved his life so many times, he had lost count. "I can't lose her, Harmony," he said, his voice cracking. She took his hands and put them over Sugar's heart and had him make small circles. Her deep breathing continued for a few more minutes. Then all of a sudden their bodies began to convulse in a rhythm as Sugar started to throw up the contaminated meat. After what seemed like hours to Percy, Sugar started breathing on her own, her legs began to move, and she tried to lift her weak head.

Harmony pointed to the nearby well, and Percy jumped up to get some water. Out of the corner of his eye he saw Chip try to sit up. Without blinking, he said, "This one is for Sugar," and he stomped his boot across Chip's kneecap to keep him stationary. Then he turned to get the pail of water. Next to the well, a roofer had left half a bucket of fresh tar. He picked that up also.

Sugar was unable to hold her head up to drink. Percy brought the pail up to his own mouth, took in as much water as he could hold, cupped his hands around Sugar's lips, and transferred the water into her mouth. He stopped when she tried to give him her tongue and her tail began swishing on the grass. Then the three heard for the first time Chip wailing behind them about his broken knee. Sugar jumped to her feet. She almost fell, but that didn't stop her from growling at him, showing him every one of her big teeth. Percy stood over Chip, waiting for the coward to quiet down, and then slammed his foot over the other knee, saying, "This one is for Oliver." That started the wailing again. "You and your disgusting mother and that pathetic excuse of a human being that you call your father have done it this time," Percy said as he began pouring the tar from the bucket all over Chip's body. "I am not going to kill you now, because I don't want killing a child on my conscience, but where I am sending you, you'll wish I had."

Percy dragged Chip over to the train depot and dropped him within inches of the track. Percy, Harmony, and Sugar stood guard all night, waiting for the early morning train heading north to Toronto. Chip cried himself to sleep. Percy couldn't take his eyes or hands off of Sugar. He did notice the company truck parked at the side of the depot. Jagi may have been mistaken about where he had left it parked, but he assumed Chip had been involved in its disappearance.

Percy waved down the early morning train as it rolled inches from Chip's head. When the train stopped, Percy picked Chip up by the collar and dragged him down to a train car full of bananas. Chip's screaming became so loud that it began wearing on Percy's nerves. He reached down to the ground, scooped up gravel, forced it into Chip's mouth, and then picked up a short piece of rope from the ground to tie tightly around the loud mouth. Harmony helped lift Chip into the banana car. Percy pulled off Chip's suspenders and used them to tie him and his hands to a wooden crate. He took a pen out of his jacket, unfolded a piece of paper, wrote a note, and put it above Chip's head. As he closed the railcar door, he looked back at the tar-covered lump and said, "If the deadly Brazilian spiders don't get you, maybe the elements and the frozen landscapes of Canada will."

After the train departed, Percy turned to thank Harmony. "I am forever very grateful to you, Harmony. How did you know Sugar needed you?" She wore a big smile, held her hand up to her ear, and pointed at Sugar. "Let me take you back home. The truck is over here," Percy said. He noticed a gasoline container lying empty in the truck bed. He started looking around and noticed that gasoline had been poured all around the outside of the depot building. He searched further, only to find the same at his home. Sugar had saved his life again. Before he took Harmony home, he stopped by the volunteer firehouse and arranged for the depot and house to be hosed down.

Four days later, Jagi awakened to find Heather, Dr. Reynolds's assistant, tending to him. "Am I dead?" he asked.

"No, but your house has been quarantined off in case your fever is infectious or contagious."

"Then why are you here?"

Heather began to speak slowly so that Jagi could understand. "Percy told me he gave you cocaine, and then you drank old wine, which probably had sulfites in it. You ate Shasta's special chili with habanero peppers. You then went to the secret meeting that everyone in town is talking about. I think you had an allergic reaction to the world's hottest pepper or maybe the old wine. You were probably paranoid at the meeting because of the unknown, and Doc thinks you may have had a panic attack."

"Panic attack?" Jagi asked, looking confused. "The kind that old ladies have when they're going through the change of life?"

"No, I mean you were overwhelmed by everyone at the meeting," she said. "Some of the men said you looked like you'd seen a ghost when you came through the door."

"So there's nothing wrong with me?"

"Oh, there is something wrong with you. Your bottom has the worst case of poison oak I've ever seen. Wiped your tail with some leaves, I reckon," Heather said, almost laughing. "If you're going to live in the South, you'd better learn what it looks like." She grinned. At that moment his rear felt the fire. Heather gave him another shot to put him out of his misery. Then she rolled him over and put more calamine lotion on the necessary areas.

THIRTY TWO

THE SPEECH

With no sleep, Percy had been in nonstop mode since Jagi interrupted his poker game four nights earlier. That afternoon he had attended the ground breaking for the new Masonic Lodge. He was honored to help lay the cornerstone for the fifteen-thousand-square-foot building.

"Meeting at Dark," the recently printed fliers read. "Poplar Grove Mansion, 403 Echols Hill. All city and county officials, business leaders, civic leaders, social leaders, and religious leaders should attend."

The Spragins family was kind enough to host a meeting in their spacious backyard, with its perfect view of Huntsville's beloved Monte Sano Mountain. With the mountain to the speaker's back, a podium and loudspeaker were set on a small stage. Two hundred chairs were brought from the nearby First Presbyterian Church and set in front of the stage for the elderly and the women.

To almost everyone's surprise, more than a thousand people showed up to hear Percy Taylor speak. The town was desperate for a strong leader. The Lawler trial had everyone mistrusting and suspicious of the law and the court system. The rape and the subsequent hanging, thirteen miles away in Taylorsville, along with indications that the KKK was trying to move back in, the tent fire at the circus that had killed all the horses, and a mysterious fire at the hotel had not been solved. People needed hope. Former judge Percy Taylor was here to deliver.

Everyone respected the Taylor family. Yes, they were rich and ran a business that wasn't completely on the up-and-up, but they always acted like everyday, normal folks. They were kind and extremely generous farmers. Every Saturday morning they set up a stall at Cotton Row on the downtown square just to give away bananas for free to everyone, not just the needy. All thought Percy, while in office, had been the best, most honest judge Huntsville had ever known. The city had been shocked, not about the political corruption, but about the walk-out of the only honest man remaining…He had up and quit.

During the trial of David Overton for murdering Judge Lawler, the honest people in town kept bringing up Percy's name. He finally went to the *Daily Times* again and confirmed, "I am not interested in replacing Lawler."

Now he stood at the podium looking out over the crowd and began, "Tonight I would like to thank the good Lord above for such a pleasant temperature on this twentieth day of October. Thank you all for coming. Thank you to the Spragins family for hosting this event. My aim this evening is for us to pull together as a community, all of us together, to drive out graft, corruption, and, yes, I might add, evil from Huntsville." The crowd was silent. They wanted and needed to hear more.

"We have been invaded by evildoers. The KKK has come to my town!" The crowd gasped. Percy continued, "To *your* town!" He walked across the stage with his head down in contemplative thought and back to the podium again. "They are here to divide us. They don't like anybody different or anyone they think is not one of them. You may think that because you are white, Protestant-born, and raised in north Alabama, you have no reason to fear the Klan. Think again. The Klan is controlled by a few, with the rest being misguided followers. If the few have misguided agendas, they will use their control of the many to put you in line for their own self-interest…even if you are a white Protestant.

"This great county of ours, Madison County, was named after a great president, James Madison, the fourth president of the United States. He is hailed as the father of the Constitution and author of the Bill of Rights. We have quite a reputation to uphold. We don't need to let out-of-towners tell us what to do and how to think, do we?"

"No!" the crowd shouted back.

"A walking cane like mine here"—he held the beautiful cane with its removable brass horse-head handle in the air—"made of shittim wood from Taylorsville, was given by my daddy, C. C. Taylor, to President McKinley four months before he died. My great-great-grandfather George Taylor, who lived in Pennsylvania, was an immigrant from Ireland. A 'nobody,' he signed the Declaration of Independence. Hell, folks, half the streets in Huntsville are named after presidents and our Founding Fathers, who were immigrants or descendants of them. Let's see, we have Washington Street, Andrew Jackson Avenue, Madison, Adams, Jefferson, Lincoln, Franklin, and Monroe streets. Betcha the Klan wouldn't welcome any of them either. No streets here are named Klux or Klan." The crowd laughed.

Percy turned and looked at Dr. Reynolds. "Where was your great-great-grandfather from, Doc?"

"He was Turkish," Doc answered.

Percy had the crowd going. "So you're a turkey?" The crowd laughed. All the townspeople loved Dr. Reynolds and appreciated someone of his great talent being in Huntsville from Vanderbilt University Hospital. The laughter continued on for a few more moments, and Percy followed up with, "Anybody want to run our Dr. Turkey out of town?"

"No," the crowd shouted.

"How about Jagi? This poor boy came halfway around the world alone to become part of our community. Everybody in town loves him. Name me somebody who doesn't like him. Who would fix those fancy watches? Heaven knows, all of our Negro women's hair would never be soft and beautiful again. My own daughter would disown me if I allowed harm to come to him. Do we want to send this young man all the way back to Poland?"

"No," the crowd roared.

"I didn't think so. The Klan doesn't like Catholics either. If we don't have priests and nuns, who's gonna take care of all those unwanted babies that keep showing up on the doorsteps of the Catholic church? Mr. Yong, sitting over there, came all the way from the faraway land of China. He helps me with my back pain. Anybody here need help sometimes for back pain? The KKK would send Mr. Yong away."

"Keep Mr. Yong!" they shouted.

"All you ladies out there who like that fabric, the cloth, and the rugs that Sahara the sheik brings from Persia—should we send him away, never to come back?"

"NO!" the women replied.

"The one group nobody wants to talk about is the Negroes. For crying out loud, we already had a war involving slavery and lost half the great young men in this country. Huntsville initially opposed secession from the Union, and about half our population had family members that served in the Union Army. Eight generals were from here...four on each side. Are we going to let the Klan tell us all that was for *nothing*? I don't think so.

"Look at Big Mama. She's got more hugs and love than anybody else on this planet. She fed me and kept me alive when her own baby had died just a few hours before, all while my mama was too sick to feed me. Everybody in town knows I'll stand in front of a bullet for Big Mama." Percy stood with his hands on his heart as he looked directly at her. Her eyes were big and wide as she looked at him with swelling pride. "Last question. Who here tonight wants Huntsville to be a town without Miss Lily's doughnuts?" There was a long pause. "As I thought, not a one of you! We are all different, and together we help improve the lives of those around us. Can we celebrate the diversity in that?"

As Percy finished speaking, behind him the sixty-three-foot white cross on Monte Sano was lighted for the first time with a gigantic American flag waving in the wind on a pole to the right for all of Huntsville to see. It didn't matter which direction you approached Huntsville from—east, west, south, or north—you would see the white cross night or day from miles away. Percy looked over his shoulder at the unveiling and said, "This is Huntsville's message to the KKK: STAY OUT! We will fight back." He finished with, "God bless America."

Everyone in the crowd stood together and began singing, "*O beautiful for spacious skies, for amber waves of grain, for purple mountain majesties, above the fruited plain! America! America!*" It seemed to work. There hasn't been another lynching in Madison County since.

THIRTY THREE

NOT A JUDGE, 1917

I n late March, David Overton, in his escape from the Birmingham jail,
was killed in a shootout just outside the city in a place called Heaven's
Gate Hunting Club. Rumors consisted of two different theories, with
both alleging he had had help or was set up. There was never any proof,
but it was Suzette's so-called stolen car that was used in the escape. He
told some other fellows who broke out of jail with him, "I need to sneak
back into Huntsville to pick up a large amount of money and take care of
some unfinished business named Grace." Overton believed Grace had
ratted him out to the grand jury as a witness. Either way, fresh out of
jail, he had an automobile, guns, money, and steamship tickets to South
America on him when he was shot to death. Everyone in the justice system and law enforcement was under suspicion. They concluded it must
have been a sharpshooter from a long distance who had gotten him first.

The replacements for the six Huntsville dead men's public positions
of circuit court judge, police chief, sheriff, circuit court clerk, a deputy,
and assistant district attorney took office with scrutiny from all sides.
With its politically liberal-leaning slant, the *Huntsville Daily Times* newspaper could not accept that their former publicly-endorsed Lawler had
been a crook. Every article the *Times* ran about the crooked judge came
with such praise and admiration that their readership fell sharply. They

felt that if they kept repeating good things about Lawler, the gullible public would finally believe it.

On the other hand, the *Huntsville Mercury* newspaper couldn't print enough copies to keep up with demand. During the height of the murders and suicides and the associated trial, they often had daily extras printed that sold out immediately. The *Mercury* printed it all…the truth, rumors, and the gruesome details. With each printing, they would go all the way back to the election fraud and finish with the blow-by-blow final details of the shootout. Although the *Mercury* had endorsed Overton during the election, they held back nothing on him or Lawler. The more smut, the better the sales. Advertising had never been more lucrative for the *Mercury*.

Judge Jones, Lawler's replacement and a once-honored citizen, was now in the spotlight of an investigation. He resigned. The other offices saw face changes as well during this crooked time in Huntsville that garnered so much national news coverage.

The few honest leaders who remained in power, along with many prominent citizens, tried to persuade Percy Taylor to fill the circuit court judge position. Percy was not interested in the least. He refused to be a hypocrite like so many others holding public office at the time. Percy understood that one of his most profitable businesses clearly broke the Prohibition laws of the state of Alabama. The writing was on the wall that within a few years, Prohibition would be US federal law.

"I'm honored you would consider me, but pick someone else," he would say. The pleading never stopped. Olivia and the children had left for their safety, and the KKK had been at least temporarily run out. Percy never thought of himself like the others—a crook—but he knew he did not want to be a "crooked" politician. If he were judge again, that might restrict his rum business. He had retired many years earlier after meeting with Mr. Pierce of the *Huntsville Daily Times*. He had announced to the editor, "I will be leaving the position of judge because the court-house is full of crooks and religious hypocrites. I want no part of the corruption going on downtown. "I never want to step into the crooked Madison County Courthouse again," he told the editor. "You can quote me on that, Mr. Pierce! Put that in your paper."

Thirty Four

Court Business

After the murders, the world war continued, the Spanish flu also took many lives, and the Madison County court system was in shambles, considered nonfunctional by the public. The citizens had no confidence in the local legal system at all. The position of the circuit judge had been filled and vacated several times. No one wanted the job. Those who took the position regretted it a short time later. The caseloads of the judges were an all-time high of 870 cases as attorneys delayed and stalled proceedings to await improvements in the court system.

Percy had been in negotiations with the local power company for some time. The power company wanted to strip-cut across the top of Wallace Mountain into the Green's Cove area. Percy wanted a road over the mountain, and he had a plan for the timber on it. He knew his ability to negotiate was limited. After all, the power company did have the right to use eminent domain and take the right-of-way for fair market value. He also knew that they knew he could tie it up in court for a long time. However, he understood they would prevail in the end. Percy had suggested up front to the company that he was thinking about building a hotel in that area, like the one on Monte Sano Mountain. He would use this point later.

As he stood at the door to the conference room before their next meeting, he decided to take a lesson from Miss Dawn. Three power company executives were in the room. They wasted no time getting to the bottom line. "Mr. Taylor, if we could come to a deal today, what would you need for a hundred-foot right-of-way across your land?"

Percy looked up at the ceiling as if thinking hard. Then he said, "First, as in all business matters with me, I want to be paid in gold coins."

One of the executives started to say, "Out of the question," but Percy stopped him and said, "Please let me finish. Second, I want the timber you will have to cut for the power-line path and for you to store it dry until I need it." Percy quickly looked around for a reaction, and as one of the men started to say something, he continued, "Next I will need you to make the logging trail and your future maintenance path for the big trucks to be graded at a full sixteen feet wide. The crossings over streams and ditches and wet weather springs have to be permanently stabilized with concrete bridges and pipes…and gravel needs to be put down on the roadbed surface." Percy knew the logging road followed the already-existing horse-riding trail and would not be that hard to up-grade. Before one of the men could say how unreasonable he was, Percy added, "The final and most important condition…"

"There's more?" one of the men said.

"Yes," Percy said. "I want the power company to use local labor."

The executives looked annoyed, and one said, "Mr. Taylor, we can't do that. First, we don't pay in gold. We don't even have a system in place to pay in gold."

"I'm only asking for twenty gold eagles. Surely a company as big as you are can come up with that," Percy said.

The executive computed twenty gold eagles in his head and realized the total was actually less than they had planned to offer. "Well, perhaps we could come up with a way to pay in gold, but Mr. Taylor, we don't grade and gravel most of our maintenance roads or put in concrete pipe or bridges."

"I thought you did," Percy said. "Perhaps I was mistaken, but since you already have the equipment and labor on-site, what if I supply the pipe and you supply the equipment and labor?"

"Are you supplying the gravel also?" one asked.

Percy knew sand and gravel was right there at the bottom of the mountain with barges full of cheap gravel. "I'll pay for half of it," he said.

The executives knew they could use local labor, and they didn't want the timber, but they had no facilities for dry storage of timber. One spoke up. "Mr. Taylor, even if we agreed to all that, we're a power company. We don't have a building to store timber."

Percy pretended to be thinking and said, "I have a big building down on the farm. You could put it there."

The executives looked at one another, and one said, "You have a deal, Mr. Taylor. We'll draw up a lease contract, and you can get your gold in a couple of days. It will be a few years before we put in the road, but you will have the timber."

"A few years?" Percy said. "That is unacceptable." He knew they had only so much in their budget. He also knew they hadn't planned to put any of the power poles in the ground until perhaps as late as 1927. Percy had an agenda. He wanted to speed up the process and use the improved logging road as soon as he possibly could.

"Mr. Taylor, surely you don't expect us to build a road now, one that we don't need for a few years," one said, knowing he did not want to divulge that it could be seven or eight years. They knew he had the money to build a hotel. They had to get the right-of-way, now.

Percy pretended to be thinking again and said somberly, "Gentlemen, I guess we are at an impasse. I kind of wanted to do the hotel anyway."

One of the executives started to explain eminent domain to Percy, but he was also starting to realize that this man was playing them. Taylor would get an architect to design a hotel, he would work out some unrealistic cash flow values, and they would have to abandon this route or pay a hundred times what it would cost now. "Mr. Taylor, if we put in the road now, would you maintain it until we need it?" the executive asked.

Percy pretended to fight with the decision. "I suppose I could," he said finally.

"Unless you're going to hit us with something else, Mr. Taylor, we have a deal. Our attorneys will draw it up."

"Thank you, gentlemen," Percy said as he shook hands. "I wouldn't want to impose on your attorneys; my attorney will draw it up."

The right-of-way was granted to the power company for a hundred-year lease beginning in 1926. The details had finally been ironed out to everyone's satisfaction.

Before Percy signed, he wondered to himself what the world would be like in a hundred years—in 2026. He loved and fought hard for his country. He hoped it would only get better. With the human frailties he knew to exist, his biggest fear was that government would get too big and bossy. He hated the Sixteenth Amendment making citizens pay an income tax to the government from their hard-earned wages. During the world war Percy had given an enormous amount of money to the war fund. It was his duty as a wealthy man and his honor as an American citizen.

Percy never trusted a politician. He knew they were power hungry and would come back for more and more money to buy support from their constituents by providing government funds for people and favored projects. They could always come up with a reason for a tax and would try to make anyone who didn't support it seem un-American. Even though American citizens already had tariff taxes, sales taxes, property taxes, privilege taxes, business taxes, use and toll taxes, license fees, and more, the politicians had added an income tax. "Hell, I wouldn't be surprised if the income tax rate didn't reach 15 percent one day," Percy would say.

Percy was often heard spouting off about how much he disliked President Woodrow Wilson because he was a racist who had showed a KKK film at the White House on the same day he removed all Negroes from the White House staff. President Wilson had even segregated the military between black and white. Percy thought this was nonsense. It had been his privilege to fight side by side with a Negro, and he had already done so with Hugh Freeman in the Spanish-American War.

Later in the afternoon, after Percy's meeting with the power company executives, the new mayor of Huntsville, the new police chief, and the new sheriff met with him at the Taylorsville depot. Once again, they pleaded with Percy to help bridge the distrust between the citizens and the law and the court systems. All citizens knew and trusted Percy Taylor...colored or white. Percy had prepared well for this meeting too.

"Gentlemen, I don't believe it was much of a secret that I distributed rum through Taylorsville for many years...It was legal when I began it. Then the entire state of Alabama went bone dry. I had to resign as a judge. I didn't want to be a hypocrite like Lawler. I finally was able to move the distribution to New Orleans, where for now, it is still legal. With the movement toward national Prohibition, who knows how long selling alcohol will be legal even there." He looked the men straight in the eye. "Do any of you have a problem with that?"

"No," they all said.

"Appears it's legal where you operate," one said.

Percy stood up and walked to the window, where he said while look-ing out, "I don't see anything wrong with having a drink. A few in this nation are trying to make laws that, as a judge, I would have to enforce. They want to impose their morality on everyone. Hell, the way things are going, they will one day make the cocaine I use for my back pain illegal." He again looked them straight in the eye. "Legal or not, I still have a problem judging some of those young kids you've got in that jail up there for the same things that I do. I would have to take each case on its own merits and consider all extenuating circumstances. But, where I thought it justified and legal, I would just slap some of them on the wrist, especially the first-time offenders, and get them back to their families, giving them another chance to lead a productive life. Do any of you have a problem with that?" Each sincerely told him they did not and that they found his position refreshing, considering what had occurred in the past.

The three men were then pleasantly surprised. Percy told them he had reconsidered their offer and would once again become a judge, tem-porarily, in Madison County under certain conditions. He would be con-sidered a "visiting" judge in the inferior Huntsville City Court, which would give him more flexibility than the current judges holding office. Percy knew the three men were so desperate that they were willing to agree to almost anything. The state was also eager for Madison County to reduce its caseload by referring cases to the inferior court. They had failed in the past when using outside judges to do this work.

Percy told the men about his idea: "Let me pick and choose over the cases on the docket that I know I can settle immediately. That way I can reduce the overall caseload on the county. I believe that in six months, I can significantly reduce the backlog. If so, I will retire again and return to my family and business. Under no circumstances will I work more than a year. I want discretion on punishment, fines, and sentencing. Also, as a visiting judge, I want your word that I have absolute immunity from anyone in the city, county, or state, even if you have to get approval from the governor. I want to be held harmless as a volunteer who would receive no pay."

"We will be glad to pay you, Percy," the mayor said.

"No thank you, gentlemen," Percy said. "I do not want to be financially indebted to this county or city in any way. I am strictly volunteering my services back to my great state in a free and wonderful country." He did want a staff to be paid by the county, so that everything could be recorded properly and legally. He shook hands with the three men and told them he would begin work immediately.

As promised, he started for work the next day at 5:00 a.m. By the time Percy entered the courthouse, the word was already out. The people came to him with praise and appreciation for coming back to help right all the wrongs that had happened over the many years of crooks destroying the place. Mr. James, the longtime courthouse custodian, came to greet Percy with great emotion and became all choked up. "These are tears of joy," he said. Percy had gotten Mr. James hired when he was still a judge many years earlier. Judge Percy Taylor was welcomed by everyone in the courthouse.

Word spread quickly: "Judge Taylor is back." The mood among all the courthouse employees and staff became much lighter. Even the other judges welcomed the change. Brighter days were to come. Judge Taylor was trusted—which was exactly what the town needed.

Percy asked Mr. Green, the oldest postal worker in town, why some of the letters to his office seemed to have been opened and resealed. "Mr. Taylor, I've been noticing that happens whenever Suzette O'Kennedy works in the post office. I said something once to her aunt, and nothing ever was done. So I don't say anything."

"Tampering with the mail is a federal offense. That is going to stop today!" Percy told Mr. Green.

Other than reinstilling trust, Percy got absolutely nothing accomplished that first day. He left for home on nearby Williams Avenue after a long twelve hours. All his family and close friends were there when he arrived. "Time for a Bacardi rum and Coca-Cola. Alcohol is legal to own. You just can't buy or sell it in bone-dry Alabama," he said in a toast to everyone.

After his dinner guests had left and the family was making their way to bed, he sent a wire to Molly Teal in San Francisco. Percy got Jagi, who had recovered well, and back to Judge Lawler's office they went. It was late. There were few people to disturb them at this hour. He and Jagi went straight to work on the case files. They went through the stacks, putting defendants' files in several different categories. Many were bootleggers, moonshine still operators, bar owners, and bar employees. Many of the younger men were drivers of the moonshine delivery vehicles. They always tried to outrun the law. It was a quick way for them to make easy cash. Otherwise, they couldn't find a job.

Percy knew he couldn't just dismiss the cases because he thought they were without merit or based on laws he did not agree with. That was where his long-term plan kicked in. The offenders in the past were usually met with a six-month to one-year jail term, along with fines of fifty to two hundred dollars plus court costs. The city could not afford to house and feed that many inmates for such long periods. These young men needed paying jobs to help themselves, their families, and the community.

Percy had devised his plan well. The men with good strong backs would be offered a chance to complete their jail time in a work-release program, doing public works or charitable work throughout the county. They could help build bunkhouses at his farm for the work-release volunteers. After that they would work on the power-line roads or the logging roads, clearing timber and building new roads and bridges. With good behavior they would stay in the bunkhouse for six months instead of jail.

The best part of the offer was that they would be paid ten dollars a week and eat better than regular jail inmates. The money for this would come from public and private sources when available. He thought he could convince many people that this was a good idea and in the public interest. If he couldn't secure pay for them, he would pay them out of his own resources. The more trustworthy and affluent offenders could stay at home with their families, with an honor system for house detention, but their fines would be higher, to pay for the salaries for others.

Percy's first court date was set for three weeks later. Three different times during the day for court hearings were set. No jury was required. Nearly 300 of the 870 people on the case docket were to appear that first day. Percy preferred to handle group court sessions, with each one an hour long and a thirty-minute break for the paperwork in between. He gave each group a short speech on the options. If they were to choose Percy's plan and follow it through to completion, their records would be wiped clean. If not, they would go to jail, pay court costs and fines, and have criminal records. Percy made it very clear that they had a choice. "This is not a Louisiana-style chain gang. You will be paid. You will have a job and may learn new skills. You can quit the work-release program at any time and return to jail to serve out whatever remains of your sentence," he would say when his court was held.

Before that first day of the inferior court session was over, all 287 defendants had signed up with Percy's plan. They would be sent court papers telling them when and where to sign up for duty. In one day he had unloaded a third of the backlog of old court cases, helped employ nearly three hundred men for the benefit of the county, and given the area something positive to look forward to.

Percy outlined again his grand plan to those selected to work in Taylorsville on the day they showed up at the depot. He would pay them ten dollars a week. He wanted the bunkhouse completed as quickly as possible. Chase had already designed the project and had volunteered to be general contractor when a local contractor volunteered to do it for free. Percy supplied the materials that were not donated.

The contractor's son had been injured in the European war, and he liked Percy's plan to build some bunks for the soldiers who were hurt overseas and had no one to come home to. Many had lost arms and legs and were never going to work again. Percy had a list from

Washington, and he read out loud to the prisoners the names of the hurt soldiers who would be coming to Taylorsville to live. It was very important to Percy to take care of these men who had volunteered to fight for this great country. He didn't expect the government would take care of the injured war veterans. Percy took this task upon himself. He was overheard saying, "It is my honor to help these men in any way I can. After all, I've made a lot of money and expanded this farm to support all its inhabitants with fruit, fresh vegetables, cows, hogs, chickens, goats, fish, and freshwater springs. Why bother to have all this if I can't share with those men I honor the most—the men who defended my freedom?"

In less than a week Percy called another meeting at the depot and invited the press to disclose another of his plans. He had built it up to be the biggest thing south Huntsville and Taylorsville had ever seen. The crowd could not wait to hear what he had to say. "I want to make the roads over some of my private property a training ground for bootlegging drivers," he started off.

The crowd went crazy laughing. They loved the idea, but one man said, "Judge, you serious? You know the press is here."

The judge acted surprised and finally said, "Yes, I know. I invited them. We won't be training future alcohol runners. Automobile racing is becoming popular around the country. We're going to give some of our boys something to do that is legal instead of running 'shine."

He continued to give them the details. "We'll call it the Bootlegger Race. Annually. Invitations will be sent out around the region and fliers placed at all the train depots. The flier information will include directions and details. Twenty-five miles over the top of Wallace Mountain, through the boroughs, smaller mountaintops, over through Philips Pass around to New Hope, and back to Wallace Mountain in Taylorsville. Fifty dollars to register, and a five-thousand-dollar grand prize." He had hopes of getting fifty contestants. "Different vendors will come to sell their goods. The vendors will be charged to participate. This will cover the grand prize money. Having a large crowd will be good for the merchants in both Taylorsville and Huntsville. This project will take some time to complete." The Huntsville city leaders were in support of everything Percy had in mind. He didn't mention that he would have tents set up for gamblers betting on the races.

In just a couple of years the Eighteenth Amendment would take effect, and alcohol would be illegal in the nation. Prohibition would set in. Percy hated the idea of religious zealots running a social experiment on the nation. He hated the fact that they were getting away with pushing their ideas down everyone else's throat. The politicians who voted on the amendment made lots of money in the states that had already enacted Prohibition by participating in bootlegging or being paid off to turn their heads the other way. They just stood to make more money.

As Percy planned ahead, assuming that Prohibition would happen, his good intentions of promoting the sport of automobile racing in his proposed Bootlegger Race would be training drivers to become part of the enormous illegal business of transporting 'shine and importing alcoholic beverages across the country.

THIRTY FIVE

TELEGRAM FROM HUNTSVILLE, 1917

Molly eventually found herself in San Francisco running a very profitable brothel, one of the town's largest. Most of her clients were from the rebuilt Nob Hill and Pacific Heights area. Sex was only for business, as Molly took no pleasure in it herself, perhaps because of the scars from her past. Many of the brothel's better clients had offered her exorbitant amounts of money for one night with her. Although flattered by their offers, she wasn't emotionally ready to participate, and she certainly didn't need the money. Molly herself mainly focused on the business aspects of the house and her staff of girls.

She was looking forward to the ballet tonight. Her friend Della Downes would be performing for a sell-out crowd at the San Francisco Opera House.

Earlier that day, Molly, working in her office, had received a knock at the door from a Western Union agent, who delivered a telegram. It read, "Beautiful Molly. The yellow-bellied coward you hate so much is dead, as are most of the scoundrels with whom he associated. They left you something, Molly. Time to come home. Time for you to come back to Alabama." It was from Judge Percy Taylor.

She began to think back to 1905, the year she had left Huntsville, and all the horrible men who had stolen her childhood. Uncle David had kidnapped her and had her mother locked away in a hospital for the insane. She had gone to Judge Lawler for help, only to have him become one of the regular rapists. Next, she had reached out to Sheriff Phillips. Big mistake. He and two of his followers, Perry Brooks and Silas Niles, became regulars at the Overton house. The sixth visitor was Sheldon Pleasants, the assistant district attorney. Molly wasn't sure all six men had actually climbed into her bed. Many times the room was dark or she kept her eyes closed, but she hated them all. She had wished them all dead, along with Aunt Loretta, who had gotten away with murder. It was no wonder sex had never been a pleasure to Molly. It could only be a business that might have provided a way to get back at men for what she had suffered.

She laughingly remembered that while she was at her own first brothel, in Colorado, friends had encouraged her to continue her book education because they all thought she was the smartest woman they had ever known. One of Molly's dearest friends was a professor at the old law library. One of his favorite thrills was to have sex with one of the women from the brothel, standing up against shelves of law books in the last row of the east wing, while other people were only a few feet away. He also liked to use the top of his desk for that purpose, as well as doing it at night in the dark auditorium in front of the podium from which he would lecture only a few hours later. Molly accused him of wanting to get caught. She began to study parts of law and economics, often sitting in on his classes and lessons. This, too, turned him on, knowing her occupation.

As a joke one night, the professor helped Molly compose six blackmail letters to her Huntsville rapists. Little did Molly know how seriously the recipients took the letters. They all reacted by doing exactly as she demanded. One started a bank account for her at First National on the square in downtown Huntsville. Some of them put Huntsville property in her name. Others had gold coins put in a safe deposit box at the same bank and included deeds to several properties. She wasn't even eighteen years old when the letters were sent. She had done it completely as a laugh, to scare them.

Almost ten years had passed since the letters had been sent. She had lived in three cities after leaving Huntsville. Only Percy Taylor of Taylorsville knew of her whereabouts now. The six men had all but forgotten about her until the day they received the blackmail letters. But she had never forgotten about them. They were all repetitive rapists who had probably victimized other girls as well. The wives of these men were either in on the cover-up or had chosen to look the other way. Not one of the six men had ever tried to make contact with her over the years. Probably they were hoping to never hear from her again, at least not in person on their home turf, where their reputations could be destroyed if she told anyone of their past activity with her. They wanted her to stay away, hoping that she was dead.

Molly Teal called Judge Percy Taylor the morning after she received the telegram. She held in her hand a picture from long ago of five women on a beach.

Percy filled her in on Huntsville's politics that had led to so many murders and related suicides. He told her he was temporarily helping out the city by cleaning up the courthouse and the backlog of cases. He further explained that he had been using Judge Lawler's old office when he found the key to a safe deposit box taped under the desk. This was after the police department had scoured his office for information about Lawler's murder. "I took the key to all the different banks. It was from First National, and I opened the safe deposit box. It contained all these different property deeds in the name of M. Teal and had account numbers to different banks. So I went to my friend and confidant Victor Webster, the bank president. He looked up the different accounts for me. We were both shocked to see that there was more than a hundred thousand dollars in the combined accounts. Molly, apparently there have been monthly deposits for years, and a lot of cash and gold is in the deposit box."

Molly didn't say a word. He finished, "You also own a partially burned Huntsville Hotel, thanks to your uncle David Overton. You are entitled to the insurance money from the fire. Also in your name, Molly, are two homes, one on Echols Hill and the other in New Market with more than two hundred acres and a paying tenant. The hotel is on Walker Street. You're rich, Molly."

"Percy, I am already filthy rich. I sort of know what this is about. I promise to fill you in one day. Now, this partially burned hotel: how bad is it?"

Percy said, "Remember my younger brother, Chase? He is a talented architect in town now. I'll have him go over and look at it, and we'll get back with you."

"Percy, I guess I'm going to need legal representation," Molly said. "Would you be able to do that for me, and would Chase be able to assist in the reconstruction of the hotel?"

"Sure, Molly," Percy replied. "That is why I sent you the telegram. I want to help you and would like to see you come back home. We'll take a look at everything and get back with you in a few days."

Molly hung up the phone and had the best laugh of her lifetime. She laughed so hard, tears were coming over her lower eyelids like waterfalls. She would almost catch her breath, and then she'd start laughing again. The sides of her face actually hurt, and the muscles around her ribs began to tighten. She laughed and cried for almost an hour. Those pig men were actually threatened. Who knew the power of a seventeen-year-old with a pen?

It had been a few years, but she had always kept perfect, secret records of all her clients. Molly couldn't resist and picked up the phone to call her former professor and client in Denver. He laughed with her and remembered that he had used the letterhead from when he was an attorney general of Colorado. It had obviously been effective. "Molly," the professor said, "those letters must have scared the hell out of those men. Actually I forgot all about it. I heard of the case in Huntsville about the political murders. It made all the national newspapers for months. I just never connected them with those letters."

"There's an old burned hotel there," Molly said. "I am thinking about fixing it up and relocating my business after it's finished. What are your thoughts, Professor?"

He replied, "I've always wanted to see the South. Book me a room when the hotel has been completed. I have retired from teaching, and the winters here in the Rocky Mountains are really getting to my old bones. Promise to keep me filled in, okay, Molly?"

"I will. You're the only person on the planet who knows my story, and I just had to share it with you. Thank you for being my friend."

Molly talked to Chase about the hotel. He told her, "Only the top three floors were damaged by the fire and needed to be gutted. Most of the exterior was brick and stone."

"Great," replied Molly. "Since the top three floors need to be torn out any way, I want to have the top two levels renovated into a secure penthouse and office for me and a special area with a private ballroom, billiards, bar, lounge, and card room for select clients. The fifth and sixth floor I want renovated into nice apartments for some of my girls."

"I know exactly how to do it," Chase said enthusiastically.

Molly laughed. "You architects are all alike, aren't you. Percy said you were good, but we'll see if you're reading my mind."

Over the next few days they spent hours on the telephone by long distance. They pored over every detail. The hotel would be the first in Huntsville to be fully air conditioned. She wanted the top floors with her penthouse, office, and special clients' area to have lots of windows. The first floor would have a first-class bar and billiards. She wanted the fancy pool tables with red felt and fringe hanging from the pockets. Also on the first floor would be a barbershop, a shoeshine stand, a men's magazine stand, a cigar stand, and a full bath service. A cashier would be posted at the rear of the bar near the elevator and grand staircase.

The next three floors would consist of working rooms. The rooms would be semiprivate, meaning that it would be mandatory for the door to the room to always stay a quarter of the way open for the women's protection.

Existing rooms would be remodeled and the walls covered in smooth leather. Some rooms would have two beds per room to accommodate those customers who would pay to watch. Small lamps would be placed near the headboard, and dark draperies hung at the foot of each bed. Community baths and washrooms would be down the hall.

Some of the rooms were especially luxurious with large beds, mirrors on the walls and ceilings, and chandeliers above the masterfully carved headboards and tables. The finest of fabrics were to be used for the sofas and draperies. Gas fireplaces would all have marble mantels.

A washroom with a claw-foot bathtub was to be an amenity in these rooms.

Most transactions took place in and around the grand lobby on the first floor. The girls mingled with the clients for drinks, dinner, or just talk, and if there was interest, they would escort them to the working rooms above via the grand staircase or the elevator.

There was also an exclusive level on the seventh and eighth floors. It was not cheap, but there were a lot of clients ready to pay the cost. After clients had paid a private access fee, the elevator operator would carry them to the seventh floor, where the elevator would open up to a two-story grand ballroom with mirrors from floor to ceiling, huge crystal chandeliers, rare oil paintings, fine china and crystal, expensive wines and liquors, a cigar girl, and six poker tables, with two private poker rooms in the rear. A gentleman would be playing a grand piano.

On a schedule, beautiful women would line the grand staircase all the way to the floor above. The working women would always be dressed in elegant long evening gowns, with their hair professionally styled, their nails polished, and their makeup flawless. They would all wear high-heeled shoes. It would be mandatory. The women would not mingle with a client until he chose one. Or, the gentleman could go to the bar and have a drink first. The sign behind the bartender would read, "Manhattan Club: Entertaining and Agreeably Serving Visitors."

As on the first-floor lobby level, once the woman was selected, the john could choose to have a drink with her at the bar or by the fire, or have a chef prepare dinner. Of course, many clients chose to go directly to the room. The client could pay by the hour...publicly or privately. Some customers would eat and drink after their transaction time was up. Molly knew she made as much money in this part of the business as she did in the working rooms. Once the lady was chosen, she would take the client on the elevator up or down, as the case may be, to one of the working floors and direct him to an available room.

Wood flooring throughout most of the floors was to be made of mahogany. Arrangements were made to obtain the wood once used in a manufacturing building in Seattle before it closed. The same wood was planned for the seventh-floor ballroom. The thirty-to-forty-foot beams were imported and stored at the south end of the Dallas Mill weighing station.

The Hayes Construction Company was doing the renovations. Most of the workers couldn't wait for this place to be open and to see all the fancy women coming all the way from California. They were ready-made, built-in customers, along with many of the local cotton mill workers who observed the renovation activities and furnishings as they were delivered.

Molly thoroughly enjoyed shopping around San Francisco and the Bay Area for interior furnishings for her new special-purpose hotel. Most of her shopping adventures included Bruce and Pierre, Bruce's boyfriend. Pierre had connections with every estate auction house within a hundred miles. Decorating was his passion. Pierre had a huge clientele on the West Coast. Although he was a homosexual, he absolutely loved Molly. His spiritualist told him they had been lovers in a previous life. He just knew it was true. He would have followed Molly anywhere.

Bruce, on the other hand, was a different story. Bruce enjoyed the living arrangements they shared in the bordello with Molly. It was very luxurious. Bruce's niche in life had to do with women also. Lots of them. All day. He loved to play dress-up with the working girls. Before anyone went on duty, they had to pass Bruce's inspection. His need for control of everything sometimes drove the women nuts. "Perfection!" he used to say. "That is all I want from anyone! Perfection!"

Molly knew that Bruce's personality was demanding, but it was his handiwork on the women that gained Miss Molly Teal's Lady Luck Inn the reputation for having the most beautiful women in America. Bruce let nothing slip past him. He believed that the hair should be meticulous, makeup flawless, fingernails and toenails always a perfect match with the dress that he chose. He taught the girls personal grooming too. Bruce would sometimes hold refresher classes on how to properly shave legs and underarms. No stubble was allowed. Moisturizing lotion had to be applied daily to the entire body, especially to the darker-skinned women. He thought this made them glow. He loved soft, glowing skin.

Once a month he had "bush" control. He thought the idea of having pubic hair grow down one's inner legs was unacceptable. Bruce invented a procedure of spreading melted wax over the unwanted hairy areas, then placing a dry cloth over the wax, letting it dry into the towel, and in one smooth move, ripping it off. More than one mutiny was resolved after he demonstrated the procedure on his own chest. He would say, "This is how Pierre likes it—smooth" as he ripped the hair off his chest. He loved to put moisturizing lotion on himself and walk around shirt-less. He also used his hot wax method on Pierre's hairy back. "Yucky!" he told the girls.

Everyone complained, but they still loved Bruce—even though he carried tweezers in his pocket, ready to pluck out someone's unruly eye-brow hair. "Girls, I love perfume. Only jasmine for my ladies. Gardenia smells and reminds me of virgins and grandmothers. Do we have any of those here?" he would say in his giggling and laughing way. Sometimes he would allow the girls from the Orient to wear a cinnamon scent. Bruce laughed at the thought of Molly moving to Huntsville and said, "She would never do that to me. We left the South once already to-gether, when she branched out on her own after leaving New Orleans for Denver."

In spite of Bruce's reservations, Pierre told Molly that, if she really wanted to return to Huntsville, Alabama, they were both on board for the move. Thirty-five of Molly's best girls trusted her and decided to make the move with her. The other seventy or so stayed in place with Roseanne, Molly's current and highly trusted manager, running the operation.

Many of the girls would travel back and forth between the two cit-ies after the positive feedback from the first group. This pleased Molly, because she had already trained all the girls under her rules, and yes, they were in fact the most beautiful women in America.

Molly flashed back to a conversation she had had with the dearly departed Judge Lawler. *Bless his heart*, she thought as she laughed with an evil grin. Lawler had explained it to Molly. Her beauty was a burden she would just have to live with. He told her it was not a man's fault if, after he saw her, he wanted to behave badly. He even went further, explain-ing to the twelve-year-old that she should not complain, for there were many ugly women who would be grateful to have Molly's beauty. He had raped her for the first time that night, after Uncle David had unlocked the door to her room for him.

Molly shook it off and looked around at the girls busy getting prettied up by Bruce for the rush crowd. They were all-American beauties; many of them had had this same "burden" as they grew up. Maybe, just maybe, the old dead judge was right.

Molly found herself looking forward to the long-distance calls she shared with Percy on the telephone every day. After one particular phone call, she explained to him her concerns about letting anyone in Huntsville in on the new business coming to town. Molly didn't want any roadblocks once she arrived and had the business up and running.

Thirty Six

Sugar Land Properties

"Good morning, Molly. I have been putting together a business plan that I thought you might like," Percy said with a little excitement in his voice as they spoke on the phone. "I want to be your partner. I know you've got great business skills and a lot of experience on top in your profession," he said. "Wait," he stuttered, "I didn't mean it that way." They both started laughing. She took it as a compliment. He remembered Molly was a child prodigy in mathematics.

"Here's my idea, Molly. I want to open a business as equal partners. Fifty-fifty. I would like to name it Sugar Land Properties. We would start with the company owning the hotel. Not the business—that would be yours. It would protect your assets and limit your liabilities. I will reimburse you for half what you have in it or the appraised value we agree on. With you investing that money in Sugar Land, and with me matching it, we should have enough start-up capital to invest in companies all over town that need capital to grow and expand. The company ownership would show on records as P. Taylor and M. Teal, just like your other properties and bank accounts that were set up for you. You've been gone so long that no one in town knows who you are anyway, and no one would ever suspect there being a woman owner. This arrangement will work out wonderfully for the both of us. We can keep our finger on the pulse of everything going on in the city—privately and publicly. 'Knowledge' is priceless."

They both agreed. The first investment by Sugar Land Properties would be the hotel, to be called Hotel Alabama on the northeast corner of Walker Avenue and Meridian Pike, which was conveniently outside the city limits by one block. "Percy, besides the hotel, let's also invest in an automobile dealership," Molly said. "Here the girls don't really need private cars, but they are all looking forward to driving and owning cars in Alabama. I'll bring the built-in customers…maybe open a real-estate office too. The women who have children will want to buy their own homes. After all, they can afford it."

"I like the way you think, Molly. I will get to working on that before your group arrives. Hugh will be trustworthy partner for a profitable automobile dealership." Percy's anticipation was growing.

Molly was laughing at Percy and said, "Horse or dog?" He was noticeably silent. "Percy, tell me about the name of the company. Is it named after a horse or a dog?"

He smiled and said, "Oh…dog."

Molly responded by saying, "Let's make her president of our new company. President Sugar Taylor or 'Pres. S. Taylor' on her new desktop nameplate."

Percy laughed back with Molly. "I'll draw up the papers. I'm not aware of any absolute reason a dog can't be president, but we may be challenged on that if discovered. We won't give her any stock. She will be powerless if she attempts a corporate takeover." They were both laughing and then Percy said, "She is beautiful, Molly, and she saved my life. I can't wait for you to meet her. Let's talk again tomorrow." She agreed and was smiling again when she hung up. So was he.

Percy was quite enthusiastic about his new business partner and their many plans. Most of his money had been made in investments that were not in Huntsville, such as rum, bananas, oil, steel, Ford Motor Co., and his favorite, gold. His daddy had told him after the Civil War that they had only worthless paper money. "Always buy gold if you can, son, and more important, get paid in gold," he said. Percy knew to diversify, but often he would ask to be paid in gold or would buy it. He kept some of it in safe deposit boxes in several banks, but he also stashed a lot of it in the secret cave below the basement in his house on Williams Avenue.

His other favorite hiding spot for gold was behind a spring in a cave at the farm. Bananas were the best gold crop.

After the hotel remodeling was completed, the next call to Huntsville had to do with the house on Echols Hill. Molly had Chase send a landscaper to remove all the shrubs against the house, add new planting beds, place fruit trees throughout, and cut down the overgrown old trees to add sunlight for grass. Next she wanted the old gravel drive removed, replacing it with a circular paved driveway leading up to the front door. She also wanted the front door replaced and the entire house painted a lighter color of green that Pierre had picked. Her goal was to change the exterior for a completely new look. There was nothing she could do about the large windows that looked like they belonged in a church.

On July 10, Molly's birthday, Loretta Overton came out to her front lawn to pick up the morning paper and was met by several different work crews starting their day. "Who are you? What is going on here? Why are you in my yard digging up my flowers and bushes? I demand to know who is in charge!"

Right on schedule, a deliveryman got out of his car, gave the woman a package, and had her sign for it. "What the hell is going on?" she screamed at the painters placing ladders against the side of her house while she opened the envelope. A sickening feeling came over her as she locked her eyes on the red ruby ring from a time long since forgotten.

The letter informed her that the illegal adoption of Molly Teal had been nullified. The residence in which Loretta lived was not in her name, and she had twenty-four hours to vacate the premises. An added handwritten note said that the ruby ring was being returned, and that she might need to sell it someday to make ends meet. There was also a veiled threat to initiate a murder investigation into the death of Molly's mother.

Just as Loretta was shoving the letter back into the envelope, a sheriff's deputy drove up and served her the official eviction notice.

An unknown car slowly drove past the house on Echols Hill with a very satisfied passenger sitting in the backseat who quietly said to herself, "Happy birthday to me!"

Molly never set foot in the house of horrors again. After the renovations were completed and the occupant had moved out, a Taylorsville real estate agent hammered a "For Sale" sign into the yard.

Shortly after Molly returned to Huntsville, the Hotel Alabama held a grand opening. The hotel stayed full every night of the week, rightly earning a reputation for world-class women with southern hospitality. Percy again resigned his position as judge.

The Colorado professor kept his word; he moved to Huntsville and was one of the hotel's first and most frequent visitors.

THIRTY SEVEN

JAGI COMES HOME FROM WAR

President Woodrow Wilson committed the United States to war in 1917. Every able-bodied man in the county went to the war registration office to show their patriotism, with four hundred men in Madison County signing up. Percy thought his services and his time in the army during the Spanish-American War could be helpful at headquarters in Washington, DC. He knew he could be of great help behind the scenes.

Germany blew up one of our ships, and the captain was someone Percy knew. No wonder the professor who did the study with Sugar wanted to relocate to the United States and away from Europe.

Percy knew a pirate, in his banana navy in the Caribbean, who could facilitate things in the war effort that the United States Navy could not. His banana boats and friends were available at a moment's notice. Jagi was in Europe and acted as an interpreter in missions behind the enemy lines. He kept Percy informed about the war effort from his perspective. Washington finally said, "What the hell could it hurt to provide this southern gentleman enemy ship movement information?" Percy did forward this information to the right hands in the banana navy. German records would eventually disclose that two German U-boats and several surface craft were unaccounted for in the Caribbean. Percy's books also showed some banana shipments that didn't arrive.

Percy usually had lunch with Dr. Reynolds at the Twickenham Hotel. He liked to arrive early so he could poke fun with Henry, the head cook. Without going all the way into the kitchen, Percy would say, "Excuse me, gentlemen in the kitchen, do you have green beans today?"

"Yes, sir, we have the best green beans in town" was a typical reply.

"Where do they come from?" Percy would ask.

The kitchen staff would reply something like, "Our vegetables all come from Taylorsville Farms. The best-tasting green beans around these parts, sir." Percy would always smile and give Sugar the okay to go into the kitchen to get bone scraps from Henry, her other best friend.

Percy generally walked through the restaurant to meet everyone. He always said hello to Tracy Pratt, who was considered by many to be Huntsville's "first citizen." Pratt, along with Wells, Wellman, and Ward, had transplanted himself from South Dakota. They brought much-needed money and ideas that changed Huntsville for the next fifty years. In addition to their own money the four partners often accepted more investment capital from the Mayo brothers and T. Coleman Du Pont of the Du Pont dynasty in Delaware.

As the war came to an end, nobody had heard anything from Jagi. He was supposed to be coming home. Percy sat quietly reminiscing about the day Jagi left for the war. Jagi had given Percy the Rolex watch that he cherished from Story. He also made sure Percy had the only other things of value to him: the cheap harmonica that had been a gift from Herman Deeley and a bag of Milk-Bone dog biscuits sent from New York City by Madame Walker. Jagi daily practiced the Pledge of Allegiance to the flag, and he sang "The Star Spangled Banner" and "The Battle Hymn of the Republic." His last words to Percy as he boarded a train heading off to war were "I am an American. I know all these words, but I feel all of them more!"

I wish I could've stopped him from enlisting, but all he could tell me was that he was proud to be an American. It was his honor to serve this great country, Percy thought as he opened the Western Union envelope. The telegram was from Jagi's commanding officer and said Jagi would arrive in Taylorsville on Wednesday, escorted by another soldier. The letter asked that someone meet the soldier at the train depot in Taylorsville for his release, because of medical conditions.

"What the hell does this mean?" Percy asked, handing it to Doc Reynolds for an opinion.

"Forty-seven maple trees were planted today in downtown Huntsville on the south end of Madison Street in memory of the men we've already lost from Huntsville," Doc said. "At least our Jagi is still alive. In what condition, we don't know. I've read a lot of medical reports of soldiers coming back from the war. We won't know until he gets here if he has any legs or arms. Maybe head injuries." This was the most brutal war of all time—the war to end all wars. More than eleven million soldiers had died worldwide...116,000 from the United States. It was the ones they were shipping back alive and hurt that the country needed to worry about now. Many believed President Woodrow Wilson's exit strategy was dangerous. "Get out while the getting is good" left the world open for future conflict. Percy was going to do whatever he could for Jagi. "I know you feel like he's your responsibility," Doc said.

"No, Doc, he is like my son. He's not a burden. I'll do whatever it takes for him," Percy said.

When Jagi's train arrived on Wednesday, Percy, Shasta, and Doc Reynolds were there to meet him. Jagi looked skinny and frail, but most obvious was the look of shell shock. Fear, fright, and terror best described his face. Doc Reynolds had done a good bit of research on Pentothal, a truth serum, and its uses for soldiers coming home from the war who were traumatized. Jagi showed no excitement about arriving in Taylorsville or seeing Shasta, Percy, Sugar, Big Mama, or anything.

Later that morning Doc explained to an anxious Percy and Shasta that he had done a basic psychiatric evaluation of Jagi. Doc concluded that Jagi had witnessed or participated in something horrific that had caused him to shut down emotionally. "Damn! Doc, we can't leave him like this. What can we do for him?" Percy asked.

"Well, what I'd like to do, Percy, is use truth serum. It may help him remember things his conscious mind doesn't want to remember. If we can determine what caused the trauma, possibly, after the drug is out of his system, we can help him deal with it emotionally."

Later that day Doc treated Jagi with Pentothal. Percy and Shasta stayed with them for the treatment. Jagi revealed that he had been taught to use dynamite to blow up bridges in front of the advancing enemy troops. One day a bridge in the French countryside didn't blow up as planned. Jagi ran back to the bridge within rifle range of the German soldiers. He desperately tried to repair the fuse and thought he had no choice but to light the short fuse and run for it. He described how the bullets were hitting the ground all around him. He knew it was his time to die when, at that exact moment, the bridge blew. The dozens of soldiers on the bridge were blown to bits. He was buried alive and assumed to be dead by his own men. When things were quiet, he started to dig his way out. Finally reaching the top of the debris, he saw blue sky out of the darkness. At the same time he saw a blue-eyed head with no body attached. That was when his brain had flipped the "off" switch. The blue-eyed head with a helmet belonged to a child soldier, maybe twelve years old.

That night, for the first time ever, Sugar left Percy and went into the bedroom next door. She snuggled into bed with Jagi and stayed all night.

It took almost a year before Jagi got back to normal, with Shasta's help. She was always by his side. A family friend, Molly, had moved back to Huntsville during the war. She and her beautiful employees were a great distraction to Jagi. He once said to Shasta, "You seem to be so indifferent to how all these women work and live. Why is that? Does it bother you?"

"Oh, Jagi, I have known Molly my entire life. She knew my mother. We saw her in business all the way back, from New Orleans and Denver to San Francisco. I have no judgments, because I never had to live through what these women did, which may have led them to this lifestyle. Growing up in great privilege as I did doesn't entitle me to look down upon women who did not."

Jagi and Shasta grew closer. Jagi confessed to Sugar that he was in love. He knew she would not tell his secret. Shasta confided in Percy that she secretly wanted to marry Jagi. Percy told her, "Honey, I already figured that much out."

Thirty Eight

The Wedding Dance

Shasta's version of her wedding dance, which she told a few close friends about, was short and to the point: "My mother wrote to me not to give away the cookies until you know you have the right person." So, she and Jagi had a naked, "*look, but don't touch*" dance under the old oak tree. It soon afterward led to Jagi asking Shasta's father, Percy, for her hand in marriage. The next weekend, after Jagi purchased a ring from her uncle at Hobbs Jewelry store, they were back under the big magical old oak, and Jagi went down on one knee and asked her to be his wife. She accepted.

Jagi's version was a little more detailed. Shasta had danced very erotically for Jagi, and he was sure she was waiting for the proposal. First, he needed to ask her daddy, the imposing Percy Taylor, for her hand in marriage.

At first chance he asked Percy if he could talk privately with him. "Mr. Taylor," Jagi said, holding his head high. "Because of recent developments, I would like to ask for your daughter, Shasta's, hand in marriage."

Percy, not being the least bit shy, asked Jagi, "Is it a mandatory wedding?"

"No, no, sir, not at all," Jagi stammered. "I have always been fascinated with Shasta, and it's true, I've been attracted to her for a long time now. I love her...have loved her ever since the first second our eyes met at Pier 54 in New York."

"So," Percy persisted, "how did you come to wanting a wedding because of...what did you say...recent developments?"

Jagi confessed, "Mr. Taylor, I might be under some magical spell. No, I'm not kiddin' around. Last night Shasta and I had an outing down at the arena by the big oak tree, and we discussed the likelihood of our relationship moving forward. She told me she had concerns about our body types not matching."

Percy interrupted, "Body types not matching? Magical spells? Son, you need to tell me what happened and why you think you're under a spell before I can consider the question."

This isn't going so well, Jagi thought. "Well, Mr. Taylor, I swear nothing happened...nothing happened much...Well, something happened, but it's not what you're thinking."

"Son, perhaps you should tell me what happened so I won't be thinking what you think I'm thinking." Jagi thought he was in a pickle. He had not intended to tell her daddy about the dance, but now, that appeared better than him thinking they had done something.

Jagi started slowly, "Mr. Taylor, I'll tell you what happened and let you be the judge, but in my eyes, it was the most beautiful evening of my life. Shasta and I discussed a 'no-touch' peep show of our nude bodies. No hanky-panky, sir, I swear. We were parked at the arena, close to the old oak tree down on the riverbank. There were millions of stars in the sky last night, and we decided I would go first. She just sat there on the hood of the motorcar and watched me undress.

"First I took off my shirt. I know this sort of pleased her. She had kind of a grin on her face. After all, I'm quite a pleasing man to look at, with a big chest and shoulders and tight stomach here." Jagi held his arms out to show his strength and thumped on his hard belly. Then he continued, "I think I had her attention at this point, but I continued on, showing her my strong back...Now, mind you I've never undressed with someone watching me before. I took off my shoes and socks pretty quickly, and as I was turning around, I thought, *Oh, what the heck,* and down came my trousers too!

"You know, sir, I'm a bank walker, so I was feeling good about myself...you know, down 'ere. I walked back and forth in front of the fire a couple of times. She smiled at me in approval with a slightly downward smile. So, I pulled my clothes back on slowly, as I knew she was enjoying watching every move I made. If this was a test, sir, I wanted to do my best to pass."

Percy looked at him and said, "Well, I guess that was not so bad. So y'all came home then?"

"Not exactly," Jagi replied. "I walked right over to that automobile, looked her right in those beautiful green eyes, and said, 'Your turn,' and we held the look for quite some time. She stood up and walked around to the back door and reached in and pulled out a crank Victor Victrola. She turned on the music...loud New Orleans jazz. Then she walked back by, between me and the fire, gently swaying from side to side.

"Mr. Taylor, I know this is a bit much, but I've just got to tell you the truth. She turned her back to me and reached around to unbutton her dress, and before I knew it, it had fallen onto the ground. Then her slip seemed to be pushed off one shoulder and then the other. She wiggled out of her corset and bloomers to the rhythm of the music. Mr. Taylor, I know she's your daughter, and there's no doubt in my mind that I love Shasta, but when that slip hit the ground, she had me. A train could have run me right over, and I would not have noticed."

Jagi had perfected the English language, but he was talking really fast now and was anxious enough that his Polish accent emerged. Percy was finding it hard to contain himself and chuckled under his breath. "Please continue, Mr. Czachowski, if I may use your real name?"

"After her clothes were all off, she began to sway this way and that way. I never noticed before now, but she has this real long back and the most beautiful round bottom. I wasn't even sure if I'd thought to take some air into my lungs. At this point she moved her hands along her sides and her hips, and then all that long, golden hair was untied and flowing down her back. All the while, her hands were moving to the silhouette of her body.

"As the music changed, she began to turn her front side to me. Thank God I had my pants back on at this point, sir, or she would've noticed my excitement for her. Then her hips started moving forward and at the same time from side to side. Her hands were moving as if showing me where to look. So, I looked!

"Then she used her hands again, and they were circling around both breasts without touching them. One hand went straight up into her hair, pulling it up high, and then it fell right over her nipples. Her hips never stopped moving in the shape of two circles…maybe more like the shape of the number eight.

"And then all of a sudden, she turned her bottom back at me and stood on her tiptoes and began shifting her weight, back and forth, faster and faster. Her entire body began to shake and shimmy. I was afraid to blink. Afraid I might miss something. The music got faster and so did she. I wanted to reach over and touch…no, grab, handfuls of her bubble-shaped butt. Back around she turned her bare chest to me. Then she got closer, and I wanted two handfuls of those too. She began to spin in a circle, her hair chasing behind her. This was too much for a man, Mr. Taylor. Her body. The fire. Her dancing this way and that way…in the moonlight.

"The song ended. She stepped into her undergarments and dress all at once. It was over. I think she put me under a spell, Mr. Taylor! I've never wanted anything so much in my life. I can't think straight. I cannot eat. I cannot sleep. I go to closing my eyes at night and I see her dancing in the moonlight…a beautiful sight. If I died right here and now, I would die a happy man." Jagi looked out into the air with a huge smile on his face.

Percy, unable to control himself any longer, burst out laughing. "No, you're not under a spell. She did the wedding dance on you, Jagi. My answer is yes, marry my beautiful Shasta."

"What dance?" Jagi asked, looking confused.

"Her mother did the same thing to me," Percy said, laughing. "I'm trying to figure out how she knew to do that. She was so young when her mother died. Maybe it's something she inherited in her blood. Good luck, Jagi. I know you'll be a fine son-in-law and will be very happy, as her mother and I were." Percy thought to himself that Linda Gail's sister, Shasta's aunt Kelly Garth, had some letters that were written when

Shasta was just a baby. In all probability her aunt Kelly had given them to her.

"Just a warning to you, Jagi. Between my side of the family—the Hobbs and Taylors—and Linda Gail's side of the family—the Weatherly, Lanier, Hayes, Strong, and Garth connections—you won't have a chance to have any input into the wedding. Those women have been planning Shasta's wedding at the Monte Sano Hotel since the day she was born. For family unity, just let them do whatever it is they want for a real big shindig, and your marriage will be smooth sailing. That was the advice my mama gave me...Let the women do all the work and fuss, stand back, don't interfere, and tell them how pretty everything looks. Best advice she ever gave me. 'Men just need to show up looking real nice, clean and shaven,' Mama said.

"Now, you do need to go see my family over in Athens, John and Judy Hobbs. They own a jewelry store. If Judy hasn't designed a ring yet, she'll get it done real quick-like, and John will make it in no time flat. They are also her godparents. Knowing those two, a ring has been sitting in the window with Shasta's name on it since the day they opened the jewelry store."

The wedding was just as Percy predicted: designed by a bunch of women who had been looking for a reason to have a large family event at the old Monte Sano Hotel. Shasta went along with it all, mainly to hurry up and get it over with; she had been in love with Jagi since sparks flew when their eyes met at the pier in New York.

Story had already relocated from Philadelphia to Huntsville and would be Jagi's best man. Madam Walker would of course be in attendance, although Jagi worried for her safety.

Jagi was especially thankful that his cousin Alfred was coming to be a groomsman. Although they had written many letters, they had not seen each other since Jagi had left New York six years earlier. Alfred stayed working for a few years at the apartment building after Uncle Joseph died until he landed a better-paying, more exciting job at the Harvard Bar in the Coney Island section of Brooklyn.

Jagi stayed busier than he intended with the wedding arrangements. Alfred got a chance to get to know Percy. "Mr. Taylor," Alfred said, "I know the people I work with are dangerous, but I'm a straight-up guy. My boss, Yale, is in the mob. His partner, Torrio, a guy from Italy, moved to Chicago to run the crime business for his uncle Colosimo. The last time he was in, he told us he was looking for an unknown, reliable bootlegger from the South before Prohibition starts in 1920. Jagi told me what you did with the banana import business and a rum distribution company in Louisiana. I told someone at the bar, and they asked me to deliver this to you…said they thought you might be interested. That is all I know. Here, I have all the information for you." He handed Percy an envelope.

Percy was very interested but also cautious and wary. He read the contents of the letter and thought about it for a couple of days. Yes, Prohibition was almost certainly coming, and Percy knew it would be impossible to ban something that was a norm for most people. Someone was going to supply this nation. He had already resigned as judge after he and Molly went into business together, and someone was going to step up and do it…He could do it cleaner and more safely than the crowd likely to step forward if he didn't do it.

He met again with Alfred and told him to be alert and attentive. He handed him an envelope to deliver and said, "These are my prices. Give this to him. And one other thing: I only accept gold. Here are the schedules I'm currently running to Chicago by train and water. We may have to do some adjusting as time goes by, but only through you, Alfred. Is that understood? Otherwise, no deal. You keep your hands clean and make a nice profit." He discussed code words with Alfred. "I'll be known only as 'the Ron.' It means 'rum' in Spanish. Your guy will be known to me only as 'the Fox.' If there is a problem, everything stops immediately. The code for that is 'high cotton.'"

"Mr. Taylor, call me 'the Cousin,'" Alfred said. "Ron, Cousin needs to warn you of something. The Fox has some real bad people who work for him in Chicago. I know them too well. They used to work at the Harvard Bar. Names are DeStefano and Capone. They are wanted for murder in Brooklyn." Percy understood Alfred all too well. It was the nature of this business.

"Now let's get going," Percy said. "I was supposed to have you fitted for a tuxedo this morning. Alfred, it goes without saying, this goes no further than you and me. Not even Jagi needs to know too many details."

Percy escorted Molly and Big Mama to the wedding. People talked. He couldn't have cared less about the gossiping. Jagi made only one toast at the wedding reception, and it was to Percy with great gratitude: "Thank you, Mr. Taylor, for allowing me to come to your town, Taylorsville, in America. Thank you for trusting me with your only daughter to be my wife. She is the only woman I know you taught how to think, not what to think, which to me shows what wonderful, loving parents you and her mother have always been to the beautiful Shasta. *Salute!*" He raised his glass.

The wedding guests responded, "*Salute!*"

As Jagi and Shasta left the reception, Shasta pulled the wedding bouquet out of the bottle that had brought them together. Throwing the bouquet she laughed, "You can't have my bottle."

SECTION III

1920–1926

The year 1920 was the beginning of a lawless decade permeating all of society, including baseball and sports. The Nineteenth Amendment was ratified, women were allowed to vote, and the prohibition of alcohol led to speakeasies and the era of flapper girls. Ordinary working-class people had more money in general, giving rise to a more prosperous population as occupations shifted more into mechanization and industrialization and away from agriculture. President Warren G. Harding was victorious by the largest vote percentage in a hundred years, and his win was the first in history to receive more than ten million popular votes. He won by running against outgoing President Woodrow Wilson's failed progressive policies.

Thirty Nine

Beach Trip, 1920

A teacher from the men's University of Huntsville stored a rowing boat called a scull behind the train depot at Taylorsville. The teacher and a friend had won the 1904 Olympic gold medal in St. Louis in the men's double scull race. "To whom do I report a crime?" he asked Percy.

Percy had just finished a month's worth of paperwork, a job he hated. "Not me," he joked. "What happened, Frank?"

"The dock we built to launch our boat is missing again," Frank replied.

"Yes, the dock," Percy said. "I saw it yesterday down around Ditto's Landing. It was loaded down with seven teenage kids floating down the Tennessee River, Tom Sawyer–style. Lots of whiskey and big imaginations."

"Do you know where they took it?" Frank asked. "We worked hard on building that dock, and this makes the third time someone has sawed through the chain."

Percy couldn't help but laugh. "They said they were going to the beach! Who knows," he said, "they might pull right up to that shrimp shack on the Florida-Alabama state line. I can just see them, peeling royal red shrimp, shucking oysters, and chugging cold beer while listening to some local music. State Line Bar is the name of the joint."

Percy stared off in the distance and said, "Frank, why didn't I think of that? Just the thought of some fresh shucked oysters on the half shell with some horseradish on top, and Frank, my stomach is talking to me!" As he walked away rubbing his stomach, he looked back and said, "Good luck with your dock, Frank. Time for me to plan a family trip to the beach. I'll let you know if I run into the dock joy riders." Percy shut the door behind him and looked down at Sugar. "Sweetie, you're going to love red snapper, and if we do this right, so will Molly."

Percy left the train depot with Hugh driving and Sugar sitting up-right in the middle. Typical for Percy, he confided his plans to Hugh, talking out loud to himself, going over details and strategy for his plan for the beach trip. "Hugh, don't forget what we read in the paper."

"Which article?" Hugh replied. "The new Piggly Wiggly supermar-ket on the east side square? Did you know J.S. 'Bubba' Connors is the new manager?"

"No, Hugh," Percy replied. "I was talking about the new speed limit. They are writing tickets for anyone going over twelve miles per hour." Hugh pulled the big Studebaker up through the gates into the porte co-chere at the front door of the Hotel Alabama. "Pull into a parking space, Hugh. I want you to walk in with me. I'm half owner with Molly. We want you to feel okay about walking in through the front door."

"I am not sure this black ass should be seen walking through the front door of Miss Molly's place," Hugh said.

Percy looked right at Hugh and said, "Now Hugh, that is silly. I'm sittin' right here in the car until you get out and come in with me." Sugar was hot and panting, letting dog drool stream off her lower lip onto Percy's shirtsleeve. "Come on, Hugh, it's worth it just for the air-conditioning."

"You've always been such a hard head, Mr. Taylor," Hugh said.

"Percy is my name, Hugh...Percy. Please stop that 'Mr. Taylor' busi-ness. That was my daddy."

"You know the rules in public," Hugh replied. "Percy, you've always been the one to stir the puddin' to get people all crazy. Who knows, the KKK could be back in town, and I don't want them to think that I'm acting all uppity."

After a silent standoff they got out. Right away they noticed Fat Dan, hog-tied with a long rope and hanging by both his feet out a third-floor window. He was buck naked, his backside facing the traffic on Meridian Pike and "PIG" written in black ink across his ass. Cars slowed as they went by, the occupants honking and yelling things out their windows. A small crowd gathered below him laughing, and one shouted, "That's what happens when you hurt one of Molly's girls, Fat Dan!" Another man shielded his eyes from the disgusting sight.

Percy and Hugh walked into the elaborate lobby together. In the center of the lobby, Victoria, the seductive songbird with long, flowing auburn hair, charmed the men as her fingers danced across the keyboard of the grand piano. Each time Percy entered the Hotel Alabama, he was amazed at the success Molly had brought to the hotel. The hotel manager came over to greet them and shook hands with both men. Sugar held out her paw. The manager bent over and shook it as Percy asked, "What's with Fat Dan hanging outside?"

"You need to ask Miss Molly," the manager said. "She is expecting you and has asked that you meet her in her office." He extended his hands toward the elevator. Of course, Percy knew the way. The elevator operator carried them up to the eighth floor where the door opened to a small but well-decorated foyer. One door led into Molly's office and the other into her penthouse. A third door opened up to a grand balcony and staircase that led down to a private floor for special customers only. The door to Molly's office was not locked since the door to the balcony was always locked; the only other way in was the elevator, and the elevator operator was well aware that not just anyone was allowed on this level. Few knew, but he carried a pistol and was sworn to not allow unauthorized access to the eighth floor. Percy opened the door to her grand office to find Molly working hard on a stack of papers next to piles of money.

"You making us lots of money, honey?" Percy said with a huge grin as his eyes locked with hers. They both acted starstruck whenever they saw each other, but neither had done anything about it yet.

She smiled over at the men. "We've been making a lot more since you've gotten the Huntsville police off our backs and on our payroll. Hello, Hugh. Please come in and have a seat."

"Hiring off-duty police as hotel security is a good business practice. What about the chief?" Percy asked. "We did have to cough up a membership for the chief, didn't we?"

Molly smiled. Percy sauntered on over to Molly's side of the desk and said, "I hear all the girls really like him a lot."

"Word is, Percy, he's…Shut my lips. I'm not going to talk about clientele even to you, Percy Taylor. So, yes, you're right, he gets along real well."

"Well, we will just have to keep him in office," Percy said as he looked out the window at the traffic below. "Noticed Fat Dan hanging outside," he said inquiringly.

"Percy, you know how I feel about someone who mistreats my girls, especially pretty Dana," Molly said. "He treats all women with disrespect, even his own wife. He trash-talks his best friends' wives. He is permanently banned. It's common practice in this business to hang scoundrels out to dry. He is a no-good backstabber and runs his mouth about us both anyway. Fat Dan was never your friend."

"You know," Percy replied, "someone smart once said, 'Stupid people talk about people. Brilliant people talk about ideas.'"

"Okay, Percy, then stupid Fat Dan is permanently banned," Molly replied.

"He may end up floating down by the Whitesburg ferry when all the regulars hear about their favorite girl. So how is Dana?" Percy asked with much concern.

"Heather is with her now. She is still unconscious. He hit her across the head and face—looks like her nose and jaw are broken. Her arm hit something when she fell. They set it, and it's wrapped in plaster. She may have some scars for the rest of her life. I don't care if he does come up floating in the river," Molly said with tremendous disdain.

Changing the subject as he walked across the room, Percy asked, "Where did this safe over here come from?" He looked at the enormous doors.

"Taylorsville. You remember—thieves broke into the general merchandise store there. They took supplies and vandalized the glass cases. Only thing that was left behind was this large safe. It weighs two tons. I told Mrs.

Parsons I'd keep it for 'safekeeping' until they return from their travels in Egypt. They're going to the ancient pyramids so they can see King Tut's tomb. She said when they returned, the store would be renovated and I could either return the safe or buy it if I wanted to keep it. Hayes Construction had to reinforce the floor and take the window out over here to get it into the room by using a big crane." Molly pointed to her left toward the window.

"I bet you put more money in that safe than they ever did at the store," Percy said, laughing.

"In one day, I bet. Maybe we should open another hotel in Taylorsville," Molly said as she continued with the papers on her desk.

"No, that's why Hugh and I are here," Percy said. "I have a brilliant idea! Everyone needs a break, Molly, especially you. You work all the time, and so do I. Let's take some time off and go to Gulf Shores. We can rest, relax, eat lots of seafood, play on the beach, swim, take boat rides...You remember when we went there a long time ago, don't you?" Percy stopped talking.

She opened the drawer, pulled out the old picture she had treasured for all those years, and handed it to him. "Yes, I remember," she said.

Percy stared at the old tattered photo, which showed, from left to right, Molly; Linda Gail; Shasta; Laura Ann, his mother; and Grace. "Daddy took the photograph with a gigantic camera he just had to bring along on the trip. He must have developed one for you that night. I had no idea you had this photo, Molly. I have a duplicate from the same negative, and it is what I used to look for you in New Orleans."

"Percy, I'd love to go. I just have too much...," Molly said.

Percy put his index finger over his lips to shush her and said, "We'll close the hotel so everyone can have a paid vacation. My treat!"

"I suppose you've already put the wheels in motion," she said, suspecting he was not going to accept no for an answer.

"Some," Percy admitted.

"What exactly?" she pushed on. He took a deep breath, and at the same time, Sugar and Hugh did as well. Sugar circled three times and then plopped down on a new spot on the Oriental rug.

"The train will leave two weeks from Saturday from downtown Huntsville at seven o'clock to Taylorsville. Departing Taylorsville at nine o'clock, we will go up the river to Guntersville. From there, we take the train to Gadsden, traveling by steamship down the Coosa River, connecting to the Tallapoosa River to the Alabama River to the Mobile River and finally into Mobile Bay. We'll purchase our supplies in Mobile and stay there for a couple of days at the Battle House Hotel, which is very luxurious and right on the riverfront downtown on Royal Street. You'll love it, Molly, and I'd like to learn more about the city on the water. It may help us plan for a harbor down at Taylorsville.

"After a couple of days we'll board the ship and head to the Shores, unpack, and stay forever. Here's a list of folks I'd feel privileged to have join us. Please feel free to invite any and all of your girls plus the two girly boys and all your other friends and staff."

"How big is the ship?" Molly asked.

"It's big enough. It's the USS *Americos*, now in the banana navy. It's the rainy season in Brazil, and the ship will be in Mobile for maintenance anyway. Start telling the staff that they'll be off for a while. If you like, I'll have a meeting with everyone after lunch in the dining hall," Percy concluded.

Molly looked at Percy in disbelief and said, "Glad you were waiting on my answer before planning anything." She started smiling and said, "Percy, thanks. This trip is like a gift from heaven for me right now. Since we opened the doors twenty-three months ago, I have not stopped. I could really use a break. I might even stay a few extra days and let the staff take care of everything here. Heather runs the place like clockwork, and the boys will not let anything slip by them. I'm so ready for some relaxation and sightseeing vacation time." Percy hadn't seen her with a grin on her face like that in a long time, if ever. He left the Hotel Alabama on a cloud, thinking, *If only she will say yes later!*

FORTY

IF SHE SAYS YES

Percy met with Shasta and learned she had already been to Monroe
Printers. Wedding invitations were being prepared for delivery the
next morning. Of course, she also had the staff at both houses preparing
for the trip. They would travel to the Gulf a few days ahead of all the
guests—everyone except Big Mama. She had traveled with Percy since
he was a baby. Big Mama was getting up in years. She didn't do as much
as she would have liked to, but she stayed on top of the help at both
houses.

Hugh told Percy that he wanted to bring his oldest son but they
would travel only as far as Mobile. "Are you sure they will have the USS
Alabama battleship docked?" Hugh asked.

"Sure," Percy said. "During June and July. She's been doing recruit-
ing and training missions up in Chesapeake Bay and along the Atlantic
seaboard. She is making this one trip along the Gulf of Mexico. But
are you sure that your son is ready for the military? You and I were two
crazy kids when we went into the army for the Spanish-American War.
I still can't believe you joined with me and have been by my side every
day since then. Hugh, you are aware that there has been no change in
President Wilson's segregation policies?"

Hugh did know that the military was still segregated. "President
Wilson, a so-called progressive, did this and ran all the Negro staff out

of the White House too!" Percy said. "He made Washington into a 'sundown town,' where blacks are officially, and unofficially, not allowed after sundown. Wilson and his supporters advocate controlled purity of the white race and help segregation flourish," Percy continued, fussing. Neither Hugh nor Percy could understand why people had kept such a racist in office for so long. Percy complained, "What kind of country are we becoming when we let a known racist become our president? No wonder the KKK felt so entitled to walk into every town and set up shop."

Hugh answered, "I know, Percy. It's not just the segregation issue. I think the president wants the government to control everybody's life because they think we're too stupid to make decisions for ourselves. They think they know what's best for us since they went to elite schools up in the Northeast."

Percy added, "Yes, Hugh. They think we don't have higher education in the South. I'm sick of politicians thinking the geography of their birthplace somehow makes them superior. Those folks up in Washington somehow forget what the rest of America sent them up there to do. I feel like one day we, the citizens, will have to go and clean house in our nation's capital and get rid of all of them and start over. Then, just maybe, the next group will have learned the lesson of needing to listen to the people and implement the will of the people, not the will of the politicians."

"Let's change the subject from the depressing stuff," Hugh said.

"Yes," Percy agreed. "I don't mean to get all choked up, Hugh, but I have something real special to ask you."

"You know I'm not that way, Percy. Don't go gettin' on one knee and embarrassing yourself. I've already got a wife—kids too!" Hugh chuckled as he held out his left hand, his ring finger extended.

"I think the sun must be getting to your head, Hugh. Put your hat back on," Percy said as he reached into his pocket and pulled out a wedding ring box from Hobbs Jewelry. "It's for Molly; I'm going to ask her at the beach. If she says yes, I'll ask the girly boys to set up the perfect Cinderella wedding at the Grand Hotel in Point Clear. That's why I have something to ask you. Will you be my best man at the wedding?"

"What do you mean *if* she says yes? You know she will. You two are always starry eyed with each other. You haven't been fooling anyone with that 'she's my business partner' routine. She will say yes. I'm going to pack my tux. Percy, I would be honored to be your best man. Maybe my color won't be a big issue in Mobile."

"Hugh, your black ass has saved my white ass more times than I can remember. Anyone who does have a problem doesn't need to be at my wedding anyway," Percy declared. "So, now you need to modify your plans. Have your wife and other kids meet you and your son in Mobile. Shasta will talk to her. She wants your daughters as the flower girls. I'm sure glad your brother-in-law owns a suit store. Shasta says we all have to wear tuxedos and that this is going to be a real fancy, elegant Southern wedding. She can't wait to see Bruce and Pierre's flowers, the cake, and who knows what kind of other decorations. Shasta knows the designer dressmaker Silas of New York City. She's planning to have the girls from the hotel wear flapper-style dresses made of beaded silk and chiffon. They'll wear flapper-style rhinestone evening caps too.

"This dress stuff is likewise right up Shasta's alley. It's her dream to design clothes. That's why she can't wait for each issue of *Vanity Fair* magazine. Who knew clothes could make someone so happy? You should have seen her going on and on about the bridesmaids. They'll be wearing cotton with tulle and gold metallic lace evening dresses with fishtail trains and silver beading. They'll also be wearing rhinestone evening caps. Oh, and the shoes, Hugh, are Perugia velvet with metallic gold trim. The shoes are already on their way from Paris."

Percy walked on his toes and swung his hips like a woman as he demonstrated for Hugh. They were both laughing out loud when Percy continued on. "Everything is being shipped to the Grand Hotel. I'll admit I did have a diamond tiara made for Molly from Tiffany's. I hope she doesn't think we have gotten too carried away with everything. Shasta and the boys are going to a wedding seamstress in Nashville tomorrow. I think they'll buy the store out, just to make sure they have enough choices for Molly. The Garth family is shipping down the family china from the Monte Sano Hotel. We've reserved the entire Grand Hotel for this event."

Hugh had to interrupt. "You're acting like an excited teenage school-girl, Percy, or you've taken too much of your pain medicine. Calm down. But I am glad to see you happy. It's been a real long time."

The Huntsville area was abuzz with the secret. Percy was about to bust with anticipation. His friends all over town were happy for him. Percy had felt empty inside since Linda Gail died. No one dared mention what Molly did for a living, and only a few even knew Percy was in on her business, a half owner of the hotel and a silent partner in many other area businesses.

FORTY ONE

THE BEACH

The final leg of the trip from the battleship in Mobile to the Shores was uneventful. It was a beautiful day. The water was flat and emerald green. A cool front had arrived, and the humidity was unusually low for the beach. Percy announced, "The farmer's almanac predicted lower than normal temperatures for June and July and sweltering heat for August."

As the family cottages came in sight on the horizon, Percy gave Molly a telescope for her to see the place more clearly in the distance. He was wondering how well she remembered the place. After all, it had been fifteen years. He told her, "Everything had to be rebuilt after two hurricanes in 1916. They hit Mobile Bay real hard too. The rule usually is to stay away from the coast in September. The first one hit that year in early July, and the second one hit in late October."

"Percy, it all looks different from how I remember it," Molly said. "Of course, the pastel colors all look the same. I bet that was your mother's touch, when they first built the cottages." He was smiling as he remembered it, and nodded. The boat dropped off everyone at the first brand-new pier near the cottages.

Percy had Molly stay on board. She was more than ready to get unpacked and swim on the beach. Just a short way up the beach was a lagoon, which is where the second pier was. As they approached, Percy heard Molly saying, "Oh no, someone else has built a house, and so close by. Why did they have to make it so big? Show-offs! Did you know about this? Why didn't you stop them, Percy?" The main house, in the middle, was the largest. As Molly looked more closely, she noticed the house was up in the air. So were the two smaller houses on each side. They were connected by bridges. "Tree houses?" Molly asked with a puzzled look on her face.

"Pier houses," Percy told her. "It just looks like they are tree houses. They're built that way with the hope that the next hurricane surge will just roll right underneath the house without all the damage. The new cottages are built on stilts too; they just look like two-story houses. This is my dear brother, the architect's, idea—something they were working on at Auburn University. Chase should be here already."

As they were walking down the pier, Percy put a nervous hand on Molly's shoulder, and they stopped. "Before we go on, Molly," he said, "I do have a question for you."

"Anything," she shot back.

"Good. I don't know if you know this, Molly, but I'm in love with you." She stopped, took a deep breath, and stared at him, surprised. Percy continued, "It took me a while to realize what all these feelings I had for you meant to me. I'd wake up thinking...*I wonder if Molly is awake.* I would think all morning long about seeing you for lunch. The more lunches we had together, the more intoxicated I became with you. All afternoon, I think about how beautiful you were at lunch. Then comes dinner. Wow.

"Anyone with any sense could catch me staring at you all the time. You glow and sparkle from the inside. At bedtime, I think of your face and lie there awake, repeating in my mind every word you said and every scene we shared together that day. I know your life, your past and present, and I want to be part of your future. I want us to be a family. This is why I had this built for you...for us." Percy knelt down on one knee with a small box. "Molly Teal, would you do me the honor of being my wife? Will you marry me, Molly?"

The sun was right in Percy's eyes, which made them look ocean blue. "Percy, I had no idea you felt this way," Molly said. "Since I've been back in Huntsville, I guess I did notice something, but I was afraid of being hurt again. I've done everything I can think of to cover my feelings for you. I've been crazy in love with you ever since my fourteenth birthday. You were my hero. I did think you were too old to love me, though."

"Molly, I'm only a few years older than you are," Percy said.

"I know that now, Percy," Molly replied, "but back then, a few years seemed different from how it does now. You were my hero. Somehow you seemed to find me in New Orleans, Denver, and then San Francisco… always there, trying to rescue me. I felt like I'd been bad luck for you. So I never took you up on getting me out of all that mess. Looking back, I wish I had left with you the first time you found me in New Orleans. I was so embarrassed when you found me living in Storyville. It wasn't what it looked like. I just took off out west. You were all mixed up anyway, having just lost both Linda Gail and your mother unexpectedly.

"Yes, I was far too young to be in the prostitution business, which is crazy, because that was why I thought I couldn't leave with you…I thought I was too young for you to ever want me. I didn't want to love any other man, and I never did. All I wanted was to save myself for you. On many long, lonely nights I dreamed and fantasized about you."

Percy was still on one knee. He looked up at her, opened the box, and asked, "Molly?"

"Yes!" she squealed.

He stood, and she almost knocked him into the water as she threw her arms around his neck. They had never touched that way before today, and now they held the overdue embrace for a very long time. Neither of them wanted to let go of this long-awaited touch. At the same time they each felt an undeniable sexual need for the other and pulled back before it got out of control.

Applause erupted from the trees, the beach, all the decks around the big house, and the bridges. All were covered with happy people clapping and cheering for them. Big Mama Ruth had always thought of Percy as one of her own children, "no matter how white he is," she used to say. Shasta and Jagi were the first to arrive, with Shasta immediately throwing her arms around both of them. "I love you, Daddy," she gushed. Then she kissed him and turned to Molly. "I love you too, Molly. You've given me my daddy back since you've been in town. I know you will be good together, and you will make each other very happy."

Molly finally had a chance to stop and look at her ring. "Percy, could you not have gotten the ring a little bigger?" she joked. "I don't know if I have the arm strength to hold up these heavy stones."

Percy took Molly's hands in his and looked into her eyes. "This ring was made to represent the intertwining of life and family. It has four large diamonds to represent the phases of our lives. The first diamond acknowledges our past. The second one represents our today, and the third diamond looks to our future. The last one, the largest, means everything to me. Molly, it represents our family. My family and your family will be one. I love you totally. My life would be nothing without you, and you are now part of my family and I yours. Molly, you will keep us all on your finger, forever being a part of our joined lives." He looked down toward Sugar and said, "You too, darling!" The crowd closed in with joyous backslaps and congratulations for Percy and with crying and hugging for Molly.

Eventually the crowd started to thin out and go to their cottages. At the front door of the tree-house-looking pier home, Percy stopped and reached inside his pocket. He picked up Molly's hands. "I forgot, this is *your* house," he said as he put the key in her hand. The key chain held a big letter *M* made of gold.

"What if I had said no to you, Percy?" Molly asked.

"It would still be your house, sweetheart. Chase designed it with concrete to withstand a hurricane. The Hayes brothers had a great time at the beach while they built it. I remembered when we left San Francisco. You told me how much you would miss the ocean. This isn't the Pacific Ocean, Molly, but it is the Gulf of Mexico. Beautiful water, white sand that looks like sugar, and great deep-sea fishing, which means great food. I love everything covered in butter—shrimp, crab, grouper, flounder, scamp, yellowfin tuna, and red snapper."

He looked over to Molly. "Let me show you around the house." After he realized he had been babbling on about food, he leaned over and pressed his lips against hers just as she was about to speak. She followed his lead and kissed him back. They both felt a sizzle in this simple touch and tingles in other parts of their bodies. "I want you, Molly Teal, but I'm going to be a southern gentleman and make you my wife first. What about June twentieth?"

"June twentieth is five days away. Can you wait that long?" Molly asked, smiling. Then she added, "I plan on driving you wild until then."

"You're wicked," Percy said.

Molly continued, "I've been celibate for many, many years. I can wait a few days longer. In a different way, you will be with a virgin. This will be my very first time to make love to a man. Yes, I know I've been around sex all my life. I became a madam first, but I have never been a prostitute. I didn't have to. I was busy running the business, and I didn't want to die young of a venereal disease, either. A while back, I met a man...thought he was the one. I would've thrown away the business for him until I found out he was married. I was just a challenge to him. He just wanted what he couldn't have. Now that I'm with you, Percy, I am so glad I waited."

Percy was a little shocked to hear this information. What if it had worked out with Molly and that man? He stared deeply into her eyes and said, "I know you, Molly, and you know me. We both have a past. I want you, no matter where we have been before. Our lives begin together, from this day forward. I don't want you to change anything. I want us to keep the hotel open and running as it is...Heck, running a brothel is quite profitable for us.

"Speaking of money, the day we get back to Taylorsville, I need to take you and Shasta to a cave. I'm not sure anyone could find it by the map I left with my will...probably need Chase to draw up a better map. Anyway, the cave is where I have many years' worth of gold hidden. Oh, and under the basement on Williams, there is another stash of gold. If something ever happens to me, you get half and Shasta gets the other half. I've already made arrangements for my extended family. Every time I envisioned my future, Molly, you were in it. Now, let me show you the bride's room."

This house was new to both of them, so together they looked around at the finishing and the contemporary furniture that Pierre and Charlotte had picked out.

The view of the Gulf was breathtaking upon entrance into the master bedroom. Percy put Molly's trunk and other luggage out of the way in the corner. He blew her a kiss and closed the door behind him as he said, "See you in an hour at the beach. Come on, Sugar. Let's find our room."

Molly unpacked quickly. Shasta had picked out a European swimsuit for her. It was not yet well known in America, being a two-piece suit, but its origins were linked to before 1400 BC by archaeologists who found artifacts depicting such a garment on Greco-Roman female athletes. It was much smaller and covered a lot less skin than Molly expected, but she was not shy about her body, which seemed to be quite pleasing to men. Besides, this suit did come with a matching hat. She took a large scarf, wrapped it around her back, twisted it at her chest, and tied it around the back of her neck to make a dress cover-up. As Molly walked back through the main room, she had to take a moment to let it all sink in.

Sure, she'd had nice things before, but this house was a gift…a gift given out of love. These kinds of feelings were all new to her. Outside the large floor-to-ceiling windows were trees to provide shade for the inside of the house while allowing breezes to enter. The breeze off the water kept everything pleasantly cool.

At the beach, under a sideways-growing palm tree, Percy set out a large blanket. He had a basket with Molly's favorite goat cheese from the farm, a chilled bottle of Chardonnay, and a loaf of French bread that he had picked up on the River Walk earlier in Mobile. He remembered Molly telling him she could eat a loaf of this bread every day. Also in the basket were frozen bunches of grapes and some bananas. Lying against the side of the basket was a handmade guitar. It was made of shittim wood, from the trees found all over the farm. It was believed to be the same kind of wood that was used to make the Ark of the Covenant and Noah's ark. Some said that the cross on which Jesus was crucified was also made of it. The only other known location of this tree was in the Middle East, where its popular use in shipbuilding finally drove it to extinction there. Who would have thought it also grew in north Alabama?

Percy looked at the guitar, which made him think of his father's handmade canes. As a soldier, Percy had watched his father when he gave a cane to President William McKinley at the Memphis & Charleston Railroad depot in downtown Huntsville a few months before McKinley was assassinated.

Percy looked up to see Molly standing there looking absolutely radiant. She noticed the spread of goodies he had prepared for her on a blanket. "Let's drink wine and walk in the surf," she said to him. Molly turned her back to him, lifted her long, dark hair, and asked him to untie the scarf around her neck. He eagerly jumped up to assist her. As he helped with the scarf, she let it fall off her body and onto the sand. He leaned over and kissed her bare neck very softly. Chills of thrill ran down her shoulder and chest. He noticed the scent of Molly's lotion. It smelled like coconut. He would remember this smell forever. He really wanted just to lick her but restrained himself.

He took her hand in his and said, "A beach walk for my lovely Molly." He handed her a large glass of wine, poured one for himself, and said, "That swimsuit is very pretty on you!"

"Thanks," she responded. "Shasta gave it to me. Glad you like it so much."

"I love the way you fit into it," he replied.

"Why are you so surprised?" she asked.

"Well," Percy said, "you don't dress provocatively like the women at the hotel. You don't have to. I am convinced that if we held a beauty contest of all the women we know, you would easily win first place. Molly, you're a real beauty queen. Ask Pierre or Bruce; they won't lie to you." She laughed at Percy. They enjoyed their walk, and they talked of the future together.

"Oh, Molly, I need to tell you: Shasta, the boys, and many others have arranged our entire wedding at the Grand Hotel in Point Clear," Percy said.

"Mr. Taylor, when were you going to tell me this? Seems like everyone was in on it," Molly said, laughing.

Percy put his hand on his side and said, "Yes, we did keep the secret well, if I do say so myself. Anyway, it will be a fancy, elegant southern wedding. The San Francisco boys are decorating, preparing the flowers and a special cake. I can't wait to see what they come up with. You just know it will be wonderful. I hope you don't mind that I gave the three of them total control of it all. They think that they know you well, and none of us wanted you to stress over the decision making. I just want you to relax and let them tend to all the details. Shasta has brought a couple dozen dresses for you to choose from. All of us menfolk are wearing white tuxedos with tails. Is this all okay with you, Molly? We can stop now, scrap everything, and start over with a clean slate if that's what you want to do."

"Percy, wow! This is a wonderful surprise, and I know it comes from the heart. I would not want it any other way. Now I won't have any of the headaches that most brides have in planning their wedding," Molly said.

"I know! This will be great," said Percy. "Shasta and Charlotte love doing this kind of thing. I think it's like a real-life dress-up tea party on a real big scale. This means the world to Shasta, since she didn't get much of what she wanted at her own wedding. She has been shopping in New York and Nashville. I know she has some things coming in from Miami and Paris. This will be her debut into the designing world on a big scale. Thank you, Molly, for letting her roll with this. I'm sure it will be any socialite's dream wedding to attend. I couldn't be any happier. You're finally going to be my wife!

"I can't seem to get this smile off my face, according to Big Mama," Percy continued as he turned directly in front of Molly with a big cheesy grin. "I'm having Hugh stand up for me as my best man. I sent word to Captain Palmer Graham. Thought he would be your first choice to fill in for your daddy and walk you down the aisle. He was in the middle of the Pacific Ocean, already heading toward the Panama Canal. Palmer has sent word that he would move heaven and earth to be here for his Miss Molly. Doc loves you like a daughter too, and he would be honored if he needs to stand in at the last minute."

"Percy, you are so sweet. You've thought of everything," Molly said.

Molly and Percy held hands and continued to talk as they walked into the surf holding their wineglasses up as the waves rolled in chest high. They scampered like little kids running back to the beach when a big wave crashed over them. He looked down on her wet skin as she came out of the water. Her top was off and in her hand. She looked at him and said, "What? I don't want to have any suntan stripes."

Percy acted like a teenage boy. He stared for a moment, and then looked away.

"I don't mind if you look at me," she teased.

"I want to be a bad boy…not just look at you," he said in a serious voice, "but I am a gentleman, and I will honor my word to you." He winked. "Until we get married."

They walked back to the blanket and poured more wine. They sat close as they fed each other bread and cheese. Molly lay back on the blanket while Percy fed her ice-cold grapes out of his lips and into hers. They kissed passionately until he pulled back, reached for the basket, and poured more wine just for something to keep his hands properly occupied.

Molly pulled a banana out of the basket and peeled it. She pushed part of it into her mouth and slowly pushed it back out, then back in for a second time. Her lips were pressed hard on the banana as she sucked it in, and she began to gently nibble on the tip with small sexy bites. His face was so close to hers that she put the fruit to his lips, saying, "Do you want some? Banana?" Her teeth seemed especially white when she smiled, because she was already turning brown from the sun. "You're not the only one who knows fruit tricks," she said.

He caught his breath. "You are wickedly good and have forever affirmed my commitment to be a distributor. However, I don't think I can ever look at a banana the same way again. I've always said it's my best cash crop. Looks like gold to me now! We may start a whole new approach to advertising the benefits of bananas."

Percy was very aroused. He reached over to pick up the guitar and held it across his waist as he began to strum the strings and hum a song. He finished humming and sat down close to Molly again. He whispered, "Do you want to play another fruit game?" He gently pushed her shoulders back on the blanket so that she was lying down. Then he began placing cold grapes on her flat, brown stomach and lined some up between her breasts. He used his tongue to lick up the grapes one at a time and eat them off her body. He circled his tongue around her ribs. Then he moved up higher with several grapes in his mouth, kissing around her breasts as he cupped them together with his hands. She inhaled deeply, as though taking in her very first breath. With a mouth full of cold grapes that were quickly warming from his own rapidly rising body heat, he moved back and forth and from side to side.

Molly was able to take in another breath and say, "I thought you wanted to wait," wishing that he didn't.

He replied, "I'm going to wait to have coitus with you, but right now I'm going to play and please you in every way I can think of. By Saturday you'll be screaming for me to jump your bones."

"*Coitus* is about the most sterile word for sex that I've ever heard, and that's saying a lot, considering my business. Have it your way then!" Molly answered. She laid her head down in surrender. He got back to kissing his way down her taut belly. As he moved even farther downward, he tucked some grapes into her swimsuit bottom by pulling the cloth down with his teeth, and rolling the grapes out of his mouth with his tongue. Molly continued her irregular breathing, interspersed with a few *ahs* and *ohs* as the grapes rolled around, pushed by his tongue. His hands were all over her.

Exploring every inch, Percy slid his fingers into the suit bottom across her waistline. With fingers on both sides, he slid the bottom down over her hips and thighs and pulled her feet through. He again teased his way down from Molly's belly button with more grapes. In a few more minutes he was able to drive Molly wild as she thrashed about and went over the edge in short, quick jerks that made her toes curl up. She caught her breath, looked at Percy, and said, "I'm really going to like being married to you!" Then she stretched back out over the blanket, having just enjoyed a sexual act focused upon her own pleasure for the first time in her life.

For dinner that night they enjoyed Percy's perfect food, royal red shrimp. Percy wasn't a man to miss explaining something. "Molly," he started, "the shrimp boats have to go out about fifty miles from shore to find them, where the sea shelf drops and the deep blue water begins. These shrimp are better than lobsters from New England. The trick, Molly, is to cook them with their heads on, until they turn bright red. Peel them while they're hot and dip them in lots of melted butter with a touch of lemon juice and some spice."

Percy took the hot shrimp to an outside table, put down old newspapers, and dumped the shrimp out next to a huge bowl of warm spiced butter for dipping. Molly brought out a bowl of red new potatoes and boiled corn that Big Mama had prepared for them earlier.

Just as they finished eating, Shasta and Jagi came out as Percy and Molly began to clean up. Sugar was on the bridge of the deck nearby, licking the last taste of butter off her paws. Molly looked at Shasta and said, "Yes, Percy peeled an extra pound for his other girl, with some extra butter for a shiny coat!"

The next morning Jagi had plans for the other men to take Percy deep-sea fishing. "I wish we could instead go fishing for oysters on the half shell. You know what they say they do for your sex life," Percy said.

Shasta interrupted, "Daddy, we know."

Percy responded with, "I'm getting married to a woman a few years younger than I am. I need to be ready!" They all laughed together.

Shasta told them, "We've prepared the wood for a bonfire on the beach. At sunset we should go down and light it, sing songs, and play guitars. Doc has some sort of steel drums that were on the banana boat. Jagi has his harmonica, of course. I'm not sure he'll ever leave, being so at home here on the beach."

The later it got, with more rum and fruit drinks, the better they all sounded. That night Molly went to Percy's room with butter. She rubbed him down with it and said, "You said everything's better with butter. Honestly, I think you're right."

The next morning the guys went fishing as planned. Shasta kept Molly occupied for most of the morning by reviewing her numerous dress choices. Molly was delighted Shasta was taking on so much, relieving her of the stress, but most important, Molly was thankful that Shasta was so supportive of her dad's desire to remarry. All the women went to the beach and wore the revealing two-piece European swimsuits that Shasta had picked up in Miami for them…the latest risqué new fad. Shasta convinced everyone that it was 1920 and a pale complexion was out…They needed a healthy tan look for the wedding. They all wanted to get a nice brown suntan before Saturday.

The wedding dress was a Shasta original. "Molly, I've taken parts of fourteen dresses that look the best on you and made one fabulous dress," Shasta said as she looked away…"I think." Yes, it looked as great as Shasta predicted. The top was strapless. It had sleeves that transitioned to sheer at the same level as the dress bust and ended up with finger loops on the hands. The waist and hips were very snug, which showed off Molly's fit body. Unheard of in the wedding dress industry, the hemline stopped well above the knees. The veil was attached to the back of her long dark hair only, and there was a detachable train from the waist to the floor. Shasta had sewn pearls around the trim just above the bust. She also had tiny sparkly beads sewn in accent points of the dress body and in the trim of the veil and the train. The short dress really emphasized Molly's long, lean, brown legs.

The men had great success fishing, catching mostly grouper and yellowfin tuna, with some red snapper as well. Molly and Percy took an outdoor shower together. The fresh water was warm from the tank sitting out in the sunshine. At first they were just rinsing off the salt water, but it turned into a sudsy splash fest, thanks to Percy getting carried away with the hair detergent.

At first he wanted to wash her long hair. He began by massaging her head, and then he went to her neck and shoulders. He just kept going right down to the small of her back and stopped at her soft bottom. Percy was really enjoying this body part, and slowly turned her around and began on her front side. Starting at the neck while adding more soap, he gently rubbed her shoulders and moved to her chest, spending a generous amount of time cleaning those obviously dirty breasts. He worked his way around her waist and to the sides of her hips.

By this time Percy was also covered in suds. With both of his hands he rubbed her thighs—one at a time, moving down to her knees and calves. Displaying a devilish grin, Percy proclaimed, "Just getting started with you, my beautiful Molly." His soapy hands pulled her backside up against his chest and waist. Hip to hip, his arms wrapped around to her front as his hands kept moving down past her navel until he heard her sigh out loud. He began nibbling her ear from behind and kissing her neck and shoulder. Her back tightened and straightened up and slowly relaxed. His fingers were busy pleasing Molly and didn't stop until she exhaled with sounds of pleasure. Her knees really did give way, and her soft rear pressed hard into him. It was all he could do to keep from losing it. He held her up in his arms as the water rinsed away all the suds. Afterward he put crème rinse in her hair and very slowly combed away the tangles. Then they napped in a nearby hammock until her hair dried.

Forty Two

The Wedding

The weather could not have been more perfect on the wedding day: puffy white clouds, with a bit of sunshine; a gentle breeze, with low humidity. The Grand Hotel at Point Clear southeast of Mobile on Mobile Bay was absolutely the best choice in the South for a big wedding. Chase, Jagi, and Hugh had brought Percy the thirty miles from Gulf Shores early in the day. Bruce already had the staff jumping at dawn. Pierre had extra servers brought in from Mobile. Shasta asked Pierre to make bouquet balls of white flowers with long ribbons. Two hundred and fifty flower balls were tied upside down to the low-lying limbs of the huge live oak trees with Spanish moss draping everywhere. There was one bouquet for each guest. It gave the effect of a low ceiling.

Hundreds of white chairs were lined up in the shade under the ancient trees. The gentle breeze rustled through the flower balls and stirred the Spanish moss, which together gave off a mild, pleasing fragrance. Surprisingly, the old trees had taken and survived a direct hit by two different hurricanes in 1916. The hotel had suffered great damage, but it had been rebuilt to be better than ever. The old oaks were just fine, as live oaks typically thrive for hundreds of years along the Gulf coast.

Guests who didn't have a room at the Grand Hotel began arriving in boats from Mobile by mid-afternoon. The five bars were open, with four bartenders each.

At twenty minutes before six o'clock, someone shouted, "Banana navy ship in sight!" The ushers finished seating the late arrivals and those who were enjoying cocktails at the bar. The wedding party came in as the ship drew closer. Molly could be seen at the bow. As the captain docked at the pier, a crew attached a ramp for Molly to walk ashore. Captain Palmer Graham had arrived and was waiting to escort Molly from the ship to the ceremony. He made a striking figure on the dock with a head of thick dark hair and the same big sky-blue eyes as Molly. They walked across the beach together, with Sugar leading, as the orchestra played "The Wedding March." They met Percy at the altar with the ship's captain, Randy Keefer, who was officiating.

The wedding party stood up with them. Grace, the matron of honor; Shasta; Della Downes, the dancer; Heather; Lily; and Bruce completed the bridal party. Hugh was standing as the best man, and the groomsmen were Chase; Jagi; Victor, the bank president; Oliver; and Doc Reynolds. Oliver caught stares from everyone. Most folks thought he had been hanged four years earlier.

Captain Palmer kissed Molly on the forehead and turned to Percy. "I've had you checked out, Taylor, and I understand that you're a decent fellow. Otherwise, I would not be here today giving you my precious Molly. She tells me she loves you like no other, and your job is to make sure she always feels that way." He kissed Molly's hand and placed it in Percy's.

It was hard for anyone to take their eyes off Molly. She was brown from the sun, her teeth seemed white as snow, and her long, dark, flowing hair was pulled around to one side, falling off her shoulder in the front. The dress fit just right everywhere. Shasta had worried it would be too loose. Percy just stood and stared at the beautiful sight. His bride-to-be was just gorgeous, and he looked up to the sky and said, "Thank you, God."

The menfolk looked mighty fancy, thanks to Jumbo, the tailor, outfitting them in white tuxes with tails and fashionable telescoping crown Panama hats. Hugh's and Grace's daughters were the flower girls in all-white dresses, with their hair in pigtails and spiral white ribbons. The girls carried baskets of white flower petals, which they held above their heads so that the breeze picked up the petals and blew them around like magical summertime snow.

Big Mama was seated in the honorary front seat, crying and grinning simultaneously. She remembered nursing Percy as a newborn only hours after her own baby had passed away in her arms. Laura Ann had nearly died during childbirth and hadn't been able to care for Percy. He loved Big Mama like his own mother and Hugh, her son, like a brother. Lily, Big Mama's baby sister, was Percy's best female friend, next to Molly.

The vows were finished. They kissed. Captain Keefer announced, "Ladies and gentlemen, may I present to you Mr. and Mrs. Percy Taylor!"

At the same time up walked Jude, Emilio Bacardi's six-year-old nephew, who gave his uncle a pretty blue pillow from Tiffany's of New York City. On the pillow was a tiara made of diamonds...their specialty. Percy winked at Jude and whispered, "Good job." Molly was stunned. She knew quality. Percy placed the tiara on Molly's head. He picked up her hand in his and looked at the guests. "I introduce to you, my queen!" As if right on cue, Sugar threw her head back, neck straightened, and howled as flashbulbs went off and the music began. Together they walked down the aisle, followed by Hugh and Grace and the rest of the wedding party.

The reception began with a champagne toast. A new champagne was on trial from Moët et Chandon, named after Dom Perignon, a monk. The champagne was a crowd pleaser. Fletcher Henderson of New York City's Cotton Club played big-band jazz and swing...more of a dance band than jazz.

The food was abundant. Servers walked around with trays of shrimp cocktails. One whole area was set up just for oysters, on the half shell, fried, steamed, or baked, some with cheese, bacon, and bread crumbs. There were huge rounds of roast beef, with an attendant slicing for the guests. More tables had fry stations serving scamp, shrimp, snapper, and chicken. A whole roasted pig, surrounded by all the fixings, adorned another large table. Several tables had imported fruits, cheeses, and sweets, offering world-famous delicacies rarely seen in the area.

The bride's cake looked like a princess's castle with a miniature bride and groom on the top. A smaller chocolate groom's cake looked as if it had been hand-painted with little brushes. The cakes and desserts were all from the Commander's Palace of New Orleans, famous for its exotic imports and creations. From his knowledge of Molly's favorite New Orleans dish that Palmer Graham had gotten for her, Percy had had them make their signature dessert of bread pudding soufflé with whiskey sauce, enough for Molly and all of the guests.

The attendees who were not from the South were surprised that there wasn't a formal sit-down dinner, but they were pleased with the variety of self-serve, buffet-style tables and the party atmosphere in the garden setting.

The first dance of the newlyweds was remarkable, like that in a fairy-tale book. If anyone had grown to be coldhearted, looking at these two made them believe in true love again. Jagi came to Percy and said, "I've never seen so many beautiful people in the same place at the same time." He had his innocent smile back again after Doc Reynolds had helped him with the truth serum and because of Shasta becoming his own bride.

Emilio Bacardi had been able to bring his entire family from Cuba, including aunts, uncles, grandparents, children, and grandchildren. They had loved Percy and his entire family for many years, and both men cherished their business partnership.

Molly was radiant all evening. Her tiara seemed to catch any lights and make her sparkle. The bride and groom held hands all night. They held a reception line to meet and greet all the guests and well-wishers. Neither had a chance to eat or drink until late. Shasta had arranged for a dance company to teach the latest dance crazes, the Charleston and the tango. Everyone seemed to be having the time of their lives. All of the working girls were off duty but having a great time dancing and keeping the party lively. They especially liked the new short flapper dresses that Shasta had brought from New York City.

The service at the Grand was excellent. It was a well-known, posh place for members of the southern elite along with movie stars, wealthy entrepreneurs, politicians, and socialites. The Grand was also known as the Queen of Southern Resorts. The crowd in attendance at the wedding was probably the most diverse group ever to grace its doors.

In walked Tullie with her father and grandfather, Congressman Bankhead and Senator Bankhead. She made her usual grand entrance, although she was not trying to steal the spotlight from the newlyweds. It was just the way things were for Tullie. She came straight to the front of the reception line to hug and congratulate the two happy love-birds. "Darling, you are just beautiful," she kept repeating in her new Hollywood actress voice.

Molly had to ask, "What have you done with your hair, Tullie? It used to be so long and blond."

"I cut it all off short and dyed it black. It shows up better on the screen than blond. I go by my given name Tallulah now, not Tullie," she replied.

Percy lovingly smacked her on her backside. "I remember not too awfully long ago when we couldn't keep you out of the hotel. You said you were dressing up and practicing your actress skills. Who knew it would actually help."

He reached over to shake the hands of the two political dignitar-ies who had just joined them. "Congressman, Senator, thank you both for coming." Turning back to Tullie, he said, "How many times do you think I had to toss you out?"

"Darling, you just touched my derriere. I could take that as an invita-tion to join you two in your bedroom tonight," she shot back at Percy with a seductive look.

Embarrassed by her forward behavior, along with her wearing her strong sexual appetite on her sleeve, Grandpa Bankhead stepped in and said, "See, this is what happens when a girl doesn't have a mother around to teach her right from wrong."

Of course, this did not faze Tullie. Nobody was ever sure if she was in character or just being herself. She continued, "By the way, did I tell you I flew on an airplane all the way from California to Mobile? It scared the beeswax out of me, but it sure beats sitting around on a boring train for days. Now, Father, be a dear and fetch me a bourbon straight up," and Tullie gently pushed him in the direction of the nearest bar.

"Tullie, I'm truly afraid that all the made-up characters and lifestyles that you and your fellow actors shovel out of Hollywood will someday be considered normal by everyday folks in America," Percy said with sincere concern.

There were other politicians at the wedding, including the governor. "Governor Kilby," Percy said, "so glad you could make it. Please meet my queen, Molly."

The governor felt caught off guard since, taken by her beauty, he had been staring at Molly. He turned and said, "Percy, did you have to have booze everywhere? It is illegal nationwide now, in case you forgot!"

Looking around and enjoying himself and almost shouting over the loud music, Percy replied with an "I dare you to say no" smile on his face. "We are not manufacturing or selling it, just giving it away. Drinking is not prohibited. States are at liberty to enforce the law. Most like you do not. The bar is up high enough to keep children from seeing anything. Now, Governor, let's me, you, and my lovely bride go and have ourselves a libation." Percy put his hand on the governor's back as he escorted him along with Molly over to the bar.

Shasta came to Molly's rescue. "Hello, Governor. May I steal the bride and groom so that we can all have some wedding cake? The photographer is waiting on us." Shasta knew the governor, like all politicians, did not have boundaries. He would be in campaign mode, hustling her dad for donations even at his wedding.

After the pictures and the cake cutting, the children did a maypole dance in the bride and groom's honor. After applauding the children, Percy asked for a fresh rum and Coke and decided to take a walk on the beach before anyone else engaged him in conversation.

Shasta pulled Molly away from the celebration and up to a suite. She had handmade a special departing dress in royal blue. Linda Gail had mentioned in her journal that she had given the same color dress to Molly on her fourteenth birthday in Taylorsville. She had noted how beautiful Molly looked in it that day. Shasta's dress fit Molly perfectly and matched her sky-blue eyes…just as her mother said the gift dress had years earlier. The front fit Molly's body closely. The back was bare all the way down to her waist. She kept the tiara on.

Molly thought of Linda Gail and wondered if she would approve of Percy remarrying.

Shasta gave Molly a gift, saying, "Here, Molly, open this before you go back out to the reception. It's a bottle of perfume from Gabrielle 'Coco' Chanel. She sent this to you from Paris. She said to tell you it hasn't even hit the store shelves yet."

"When did a famous Paris fashion house start to create fragrance?" Molly asked.

Shasta said, "It's for clients only. You're one of her favorite people."

Molly laughed and thought of all the dresses she had purchased for her brothel in San Francisco as she stuck her nose to the bottle with delight. "Chanel Number Five. It smells great! I'll wear some tonight. I bet Percy will love it!" She dabbed small amounts on her wrist, then her neck and shoulders.

Grace arrived as Molly was about to return to the reception. "Molly, I've finally gotten all the children into bed. They were so excited to participate in your wedding. Before you go back downstairs to the reception I have a gift for you." She presented Molly a beautifully framed painting. It was a scene of a woman on a beach, rubbing the feet of two little girls with sand. "I found this in my mother's attic and had it framed. Look at the writing on the back!" Grace squealed.

Molly flipped the painting around and read it out loud: "'Grace and Molly, three years old.'" Puzzled, she asked, "How can this be? We didn't meet until I moved to Huntsville years later."

"I don't know, but it doesn't matter—we've always felt like sisters. It goes back even further than we thought. Now you're married to my brother, and we are finally family." Although she and Molly had very different lifestyles, Grace held her arms out, and the two had a heartfelt embrace.

Smoke filled the reception ballroom. It was Tullie, burning a marijuana cigarette. She passed it around to all the girls. Tullie observed boundaries about as well as politicians. The band continued playing while the food kept coming, and the bars kept flowing until the wee hours of the next morning.

Before the newlyweds departed, Percy found the headwaiter and bartending captain and gave them a most generous tip. He was not aware of it at the time, but this big event at the Grand would be the talk of the town for years. To some it seemed out of place and time, but to Percy Taylor, everything seemed in place and normal. History would show he was a man ahead of his time.

FORTY THREE

HONEYMOON

The banana boat departed from Point Clear back toward the Taylor compound at Gulf Shores around midnight. Captain Keefer and his wife, Carolyn, had only two passengers and one dog. Sugar stayed on deck with the captain. The hotel staff had prepared the master stateroom with lit candles, fresh flowers, champagne, strawberries, and chocolate.

Molly wanted to wait until they got back to the tree house to consummate the honeymoon. Percy didn't. Percy won. In the short time it took for Molly to use the head, Percy had all the amenities off the bed, the covers pulled back, his shirt off, and his birthday suit on. Two filled glasses were in his hand. He gave her a glass, and they toasted. She took a drink, looked around the room and said, "You're quick!"

"No, no, I'm not, and I want to prove it to you," he said as he unhooked her dress at the back of the neck and let go. It fell to the floor. Much to his surprise and pleasure, Molly was totally naked, except for the tiara. He had two thoughts: go slow or gobble her up. At last the bodies of these two starved souls connected for the first time.

The next morning, they awoke to the sounds of the waves splashing the side of the ship. Everything was perfect. Percy was amazed at how happy he was around Molly. He loved being in love again. Molly, for the first time in her life, let her guard down. She loved Percy with everything she had. Being so passionately in love was something new for both of them.

"Let's go for a swim, and then we can head to the house for something to eat for breakfast. I'm really hungry," Percy said. When he heard Sugar whine from outside the stateroom, he opened the door and said to his other girl, "Good morning, Sugar Baby, are you ready to get up and swim?"

"Arf, arf" was the reply as she bounced off her front paws and onto her hind legs.

"Come on, Molly," Percy said as he smiled at his sleepy, beautiful bride.

"I don't have anything to put on to swim in," Molly replied.

"You don't need anything to put on. We're on our honeymoon, honey. The only thing I want to see on you is me." His smile stretched across his suntanned face. All three dove into the cool morning water for a refreshing swim.

While they were still in the water, Big Mama walked up with towels and robes. "Percy, even whens you was a baby, yous take all your clothes off to swim. I just 'spected things haven't changed one bit. I was right. I see your bare bottom sticking out, even from over heres. I'ves got bacon, eggs, and grits likes at home. Biscuits are on too. Y'all dry off and come ons this way."

Molly went back to the dock and put her tiara back on. "I'm going to wear this until we go back home," she said, laughing.

Big Mama giggled as she walked back up the dock with Sugar, who was sniffing her bacon-smelling apron. She leaned over and pulled a piece of bacon out of the pocket. "I made extra for you, baby." Big Mama turned back around and said, "Ya know, Molly, you gunsta have a problem with him keepings his clothes on."

"You're supposed to be on vacation. What are you up cooking for?" Percy asked Big Mama as he dried off Molly's back.

"That's all I knows, Percy, takin' care of people," she said.

"Then you're fired," he shouted, "until we get back home. Let the younger ones do the work, and you relax."

Big Mama didn't pay Percy much attention. She went on as if to ignore him. "Can't. I'ves had corn soaking in lye all night long for hominy. Gotsta clean it and hasta cook a coupla hours before dinner."

"With corn bread?" he called.

"Yes," she said, giggling.

"Pole beans too?" he asked. Big Mama nodded. "Banana pudding?" he added.

Still walking and treating Sugar, she said, "'Nana puddin', and 'nana bread…maybe some 'nana ice cream too, if I can get someone to turn the crank."

He shouted back to her, "Then you're fired after dinner!"

Each day became better than the day before for the newlyweds. All the family and other guests had gone back home. Percy sent the crew of the banana ship to Mobile. They were scheduled to come and pick them up in two weeks. A ferry dropped off supplies every other day. They took long walks on the beach every day, with Sugar leading the way. That dog was usually in the surf or digging for the ever-elusive crabs. "Sugar, you're going to catch one of those, and it will bite your nose," Percy would say, and laugh. She would stop digging and turn around and look at them, her nostrils packed with sand, only to become distracted by the flock of seagulls circling close above and diving in and out of the water with small fish in their beaks trying to wiggle out.

On a long walk one afternoon Molly hollered above the squawking white birds, "Let's just stay forever…just the three of us."

"I think there are more than three of us," Percy replied. "When I went into the woods yesterday looking for wood for the bonfire, I had a feeling something was watching me. Maybe it was nothing…it being so quiet with everyone gone. Sugar ran after something for a good long while. When she came back, she had this guilty look on her face. Anyway, I loaded the Remington Rolling Block rifle above the fireplace just in case. I left more ammunition right there on the mantel. Let's do some practice shooting when we get back."

"I love that big smile you always have on your face these days," Molly said with just as much of a grin on her face. "Okay, we can practice with the Remington in the morning, but I'm not that concerned about some poor wild animal Sugar chases. I don't want to miss the beautiful sunset. Besides, I'm pretty good with a gun. That's one thing a southern girl never forgets. My daddy would take my mother and me target shooting. He made sure we could handle a revolver pretty well, too, before he died. Too bad I didn't know to use it on my aunt and uncle so long ago, but you know what? All the terrible things that happened brought us to this point in our lives. I guess I'm trying to say that as bad as it all was back then, I wouldn't change anything. I have you in my life. That's all that matters now. You too, Sugar!" she added as she reached over to rub Sugar's belly. "Look, Percy, at all the colors in the clouds above the horizon. They look like a basket just waiting to catch the sun before it falls into the water."

They stayed watching until the very last bit of sun disappeared. "Percy, I remember the words you said when you found me in New Orleans. Do you remember?" Molly asked.

He turned toward Molly. "You remember what I said in 1905?" he replied.

"Yes, I do. You said, *'Molly, I don't know who said this, but it applies to you today. The time will pass anyway. You can either spend it creating the life you want or spend it living the life you don't want. The choice is yours.'*" Her face was close to his as she finished. "Finally, I am creating the life I want, with you, the sunset, the beach, Sugar, and all of it. This is the life I choose." The hatred Molly had carried with her all her life for the six men who had stolen her childhood was replaced by her love for this man from Taylorsville, Alabama...Percy Taylor.

The smell of gumbo simmering as they walked through the front door was terrific. "I'm so hungry," Percy said, rubbing his stomach. Molly got the bowls as he tore off large pieces of the French bread that she liked so well.

Molly woke to an empty bed the next morning. There was a misty rain outside. The smell of New Orleans coffee and chicory filled the air. She looked out the front windows and didn't see Percy at the beach or the lagoon. She settled on the covered back deck to enjoy her brew and listen to the small birds chirp and whistle under the canopy of trees. Suddenly far off in the distance she heard Percy screaming at the top of his lungs for Sugar. Then she heard her name. *"Molly!"* She heard panic in his voice this time.

Without thinking, she reacted by jumping up and going inside to grab the Remington from over the fireplace. She picked up the extra ammo while she was at it. Running back outside, she yelled, "Percy!" And then "Sugar!" In a clearing a couple of hundred yards away she thought she saw a flash of Percy's white shirt and a few seconds later a big black blur. She saw Sugar running full speed in the direction of where she thought she had seen Percy's white shirt. Molly didn't know what to do next, so she watched and waited with the rifle to her shoulder, braced on the upper deck rail, and her eye looking down the sight. For what she was waiting, she didn't know.

She saw Sugar tear into the woods, barking and growling. From out of the woods, into the open area, came Percy, running for his life with what looked like a three-hundred-pound black bear following in close pursuit. About the time she thought she might have a clear shot, Sugar had caught up with and attacked the bear. Percy turned around and saw the dog on the bear's back. Sugar had latched her teeth into the bear's neck. The bear was swatting in the air, trying to knock Sugar off. Percy knew the bear would kill Sugar. He managed to forget that the bear could kill him also and ran back to help Sugar. The bear was going around and around, trying to shake Sugar off. Percy was circling the bear with a rock in his hands. Molly was still up on the deck. All she could see was black and white and blond turning in a circle.

Finally, Percy grabbed Sugar by her back legs. Her body was stretched straight out. Percy was desperately trying to shake her loose from the bear's reach. As he pulled back, Sugar let go, and both went flying backward, landing on the ground. The bear quickly turned and rose upright on its hind legs with teeth bared. Percy heard a swish...a thump, and then the report of the Remington across the field. He sat up, still holding Sugar, while staring in disbelief at the lifeless bear. He knew the sound a bullet made traveling through the air and the report of his Remington, but only one person could have squeezed that trigger.

It seemed like an eternity to Molly as she ran, adrenaline surging through her veins. She reached Percy, and with one hand pulled him up.

With her other hand she pointed the rifle at the motionless bear. Her heart was pounding so hard, she could almost hear it. Percy let Sugar go, and she began her low growl. However, she didn't go in for another attack. "Good girl," Percy said.

"You *are* a good girl, Sugar," Molly repeated as she pulled Sugar closer.

"I meant you, Molly," Percy exclaimed. "Hell, to think I wanted to give you shooting lessons. I think it needs to be the other way around. You need to teach me. That has to be a two- to three-hundred-yard shot you made."

"It was easy because I was up high on the deck. When you pulled Sugar off and went backward, it was safe for me to shoot without hitting her or you. I admit, I did pray to God not to hit the white shirt. I just became your wife and her mother only a week ago. I wasn't about to let some stupid bear take all that away from me."

Panting and still out of breath Percy stared in disbelief across the field at the deck. "Dadgum, Molly," he said, "that deck is at least two hundred and fifty yards away! Where in the heck did you learn to shoot like that?"

"Believe it or not, Bruce and I used to climb the bluffs in Colorado and shoot the wild pigs. They were destroying his flower gardens. He would get so fussy about it. I had to show him how to shoot. Every day at dusk they would come out by the dozens, and we would pick them off from up high. The local miners loved it. They would take the pigs to their smokehouses and then have plenty to eat during the long winter months. The trappers loved them, too. Not me. I thought they tasted awful, gameylike and tough to chew. I like the hogs at Taylorsville just fine." Her heart rate was finally slowing down.

Percy stood there staring at his beautiful wife in disbelief. She had just saved his life. Sugar's life too. Close by, from under some of the low-lying scrub, came a whimper, then a whine. "Sugar, no!" Percy yelled. "You've done enough for one day." She ignored him and went to check out the sound anyway. "What has gotten into you today? You never ignore me," he said. Sugar came back to his feet, put her paw on his leg, and looked back toward the sound.

"She wants you to go see what it is over there, Percy. I'm making sure this bear doesn't move." Molly poked at it with a long branch. "I've got you covered in case it's the bear's angry husband." As she held up the rifle, she added, "It is loaded, I promise."

Percy was a little leery, but he went over and lifted the dense foliage with a stick. "You're right about it being a husband, Molly," he said as he went down on his knees into the brush with Sugar leading. Molly heard him say, "It's okay, boy. I'm going to help" in a soft voice, as though speaking to a frightened child.

Out from under the bushes came Percy, Sugar, and a large dog. It looked just like Sugar, only black. He was hurt, with a bleeding wound across his shoulder. Percy told Molly, "Let's see if we can get him to the house and get his shoulder fixed up. I saw Jagi sew up the leg of one of our farmhands once. All he had was some fishing line and a big sewing needle from the leather shop. We have plenty of fishing line, I know." The rain finally started to lighten up. The four of them slowly headed back to the house.

Doc had left them an emergency medical kit. They gave the big dog something labeled "Knock Out" and hoped it wouldn't kill him. There was a needle in the kit, and Percy did the best he could with the gash across the dog's shoulder. He finished by pouring rum across it several times. The dog slept for the rest of the day. Sugar stayed close by. Actually, they all did.

After all the commotion settled down, Percy recalled running into the bear and two cubs, but black bears don't usually attack humans. Had the black dog or Sugar already spooked her when he was slowly trying to walk away from her and her cubs? He speculated that after he foolishly began to run, when he thought the bear was about to attack, that the black dog showed up for some reason to protect him and the bear got a hard swipe at the dog while barely slowing down her charge...until Sugar attacked from nowhere.

Now that he thought about it a little more, Sugar had been disappearing into the woods for long periods of time, then slinking back home in time to eat. Percy started talking to both dogs. "You looked guilty of something, Sugar, when you came back yesterday. Is this a boyfriend that you've been going to see? Where did he come from? You can only get here by boat. It's too far for him to swim here. Did you fall off someone's boat, boy?"

As she looked at the snoozing dog, Molly said, "I know one thing for sure, Percy. We're keeping him. He saved your life. What do you think of the name Bear?"

He looked up at Molly, grinning like a child on Christmas morning, and replied, "That's a really good name...Bear. Now let's hope he makes it. I hope I didn't give him too much of that knock-out medicine."

The look on Molly's face became sad. "What is it?" he said with concern.

"What about the babies? You said there were two cubs. How will they survive without their mother?" Molly pleaded.

"Better question than that, Molly. Where is the papa bear? She probably could swim here from the mainland. Bears can swim long distances like that. You want me to go out there in this pouring rain to look for two baby bears, don't you?"

She nodded. "We can all go. It will be safer. He looks like he'll be sleeping for a while. If we find them, we can take the baby bears back home. Harmony will know what to do with them. Until the ship comes back for us, we can fence them into an area on the bridges between the houses so that some bigger animal won't get to them. Big Mama made sure she left enough cows' milk for a month. They will probably drink it. At the farm I saw Grace feeding a calf by soaking a cloth in milk and letting it suckle it. We also have bananas, or maybe they'll eat fish."

"Okay, okay, Molly. How could I ever say no to such a pretty face? Where is your tiara, queen of the animals, tame and wild?"

She thought for a second. "It must have fallen off out in the woods by the bear. We have to go find it; I don't care if it's raining. The cubs are scared and hungry. We need to find them quickly anyway."

It didn't take much to find the cubs or the tiara. The tiara had fallen off on the stairs where Molly had nearly fallen down running to Percy. The cubs were playing next to their dead mother, as if all was well. Percy wanted to have the mama bear stuffed and brought to Huntsville. He brought a blanket with a rope block and tackle to hoist the bear high into a tree to prevent damage.

After lunch, Percy spotted a familiar ship in the telescope that he had brought outside to the front deck. He had a white flare in the air a few moments later. The ship changed course to the direction of the dock in the lagoon. After the usual nautical chatter, Percy explained his position with the bear. He went further to explain that he was on his honeymoon. The cooperative captain and crew took the bear's body to Mobile that afternoon. Percy made sure the ship was well stocked with rum and champagne left over from the reception.

FORTY FOUR

MOBILE, ALABAMA

The new family of two humans and their two dogs arrived at the waterfront in Mobile at the end of the two-week honeymoon. They could already see that Waterfront Street was filled with tourists, shop-keepers, fishermen, and others, all busily moving about in their different ways in life. Sugar and Bear were at the bow with their noses twitching at all the different and new smells. One of the deckhands had made leashes for the bear cubs and walked them down the gangplank onto the wooden dock. They seemed to mind him. The two dogs followed behind the newlyweds. "One big happy family," Percy said as he helped Molly down the last step off the boat. He took one cub leash and handed Molly the other.

"The crew will be busy stocking the boat for a bit, so let's walk down Royal Street and eat at one of the outdoor cafés," Percy said.

Before going too far, they found themselves surrounded by the curi-ous. The cubs loved all the attention. A woman in the crowd yelled out, "Look! It's them!" She held up a magazine from the nearby stand as the crowd turned toward her. It was the first edition of *High Cotton*, a lifestyle magazine of Alabama. On the cover were Percy, Molly, and Sugar. The headline read, "Mob, Madam, and Mutt," and in smaller print, "Grand Wedding at the Grand Hotel."

Percy and Molly looked at each other and said simultaneously, "She's not a mutt," and busted out laughing. Their laughter became contagious. Some people just liked the way they felt when they laughed, so they joined in the fun.

The next move was to get to the bottom of the cover story. Both Molly and Percy deeply valued their privacy. Their businesses demanded discretion, and this kind of exposure could be very costly to their operations. Percy bought every copy at the little stand. He found out from the owner where the magazines were printed. The owner also told Percy that he was usually the first on the delivery route and had had them only a few minutes. He was even kind enough to write down the contact information on a piece of old newspaper. Within a few hours, Percy had bought up all the copies scheduled to go to Montgomery, Birmingham, and Huntsville. He realized that all this bought him was time. The remaining copies had already been distributed throughout Mobile.

Clearly the cover story was an all-out attack by one of his competitors. Now he was going to be under the watchful eye of the revenue man. "Molly, I still haven't been able to get a long-distance telephone line to Huntsville. I've sent a Western Union to Chase just in case I don't get through. Our code word for 'Red alert! Shut down all operations' is *high cotton*. Coincidence or an inside job? Which distributor do I know who's willing to stab me like this? We've got to get word to the hotel, too. This was aimed at you as much as it was at me."

"Percy, I'm already on it. While you were at the printer's, I got through to Heather at the hotel. She had the police chief in her office while we were talking. He was there to arrest Fat Dan's sons, Ronny and Rickey. They had planned to hurt the girls and tear the place up in retaliation for what happened to their daddy. The off-duty Huntsville police officers took care of the situation before any real damage was done.

"After this magazine article, we'll have to live straight for a while. The hotel will still make money as a legitimate hotel. It's all my girls that I'm worried about. Some can relocate to San Francisco, at least temporarily. The others still want to work. They need the money. This will drive them to the streets or to work from their homes. That would be dangerous for them without our protection. Percy, let's get back home as quick as we can, before anyone gets hurt."

Percy agreed as Molly continued, "I read the article. It was actually very flattering about all of us, especially you, and Shasta's debut into the clothes-designing world got rave reviews. It said I was 'an overpriced, overrated, West Coast socialite madam.'" She added with a wink, "Oh, Percy, never in all my days have I had something so…I don't know…so nice written about me."

They loaded up all the critters on the boat and headed home. At each stop along the way they picked up local newspapers. Each one's headline over their story was as corny as the first: "Bootlegger, Bordello, and Bitch" said one, and "Hustler, Whore, Hound!" was another. They all had the same photo from the wedding: Percy introducing his queen, who was wearing a diamond tiara, his arm holding hers up high and Sugar by his side.

"We're going to be as busy as bees when we get home," Percy said. "I'd really like to get the motorcar racetrack finished ahead of schedule. The weekend of the bootlegger race alone the girls should make a month's worth of money. I know we will with the vendors, gambling tents, and ladies."

Harmony met them at the Taylorsville depot with her father, Asa. Asa had been scrubbed, his face and hands were white, and he was clean shaven, with a new haircut, presentable clothes, a hat, and shoes. Asa now lived and worked at the barracks for wounded soldiers. He was so strong that he could easily pick up the helpless heroes with little effort. Harmony loved him very much. She was delighted with the cubs. It was hard for Molly and Percy to let them go. They didn't realize how attached they had become and had even given them names, Teddy and Molly.

Without even looking at Sugar, Harmony announced, "Sugar's due date is August fifteenth, and she'll have eleven puppies. That's fifty days from now. Make sure she eats a lot of meat." Harmony couldn't help but notice the puzzled looks on their faces and continued, "I just know. Don't ask me how. The new black dog, Bear, he's healthy."

As if she wanted to catch up on years of not speaking, Harmony continued, "My grandma told me to never open the door to a stranger wearing shiny shoes…that a hardworking man's shoes will always have a little dirt on them, except at church. Grandma was right. The federal revenue men have been snooping around here and asking a lot of questions about you two. They busted Mr. Love for moonshine and fined him two hundred dollars. Mr. Love only had two gallons."

Percy was stunned. "Harmony, I've never heard you speak!"

"I know…Guess I didn't have much to say before. Daddy thinks it was the traveling preacher man laying hands on me," she replied as she rubbed her cheek against Molly bear's fuzzy chest.

Jagi walked up, and Bear, the dog, jumped up on his hind legs, chest bumped him, and licked his face. That's all it took. Jagi was in love. The dog he had always wanted had just arrived. Percy and Molly went back to having only one animal. Jagi told the dog, "Bear, I'll have my cousin in New York City send us some dog biscuits from a dog bakery up there."

FORTY FIVE

BANANA BUSINESS

Doc Reynolds and Percy were at the private bar in the Elks Theater. Percy was in a happy mood and made a toast. "Doc, this past year has been absolutely wonderful. I married the most beautiful woman in Alabama...hell, in the country. She and Shasta got to vote for the first time a few months ago. Sugar had eleven beautiful puppies and is as happy as she can be. They all have new homes. And the racetrack for motorcars is just about finished." Percy was looking forward to the race-track. He was consumed with its progress.

He continued with his toast, "At first, when our identity became public last year, I feared the worst. It has all turned out better than we could have imagined. Thanks to Molly's great idea, we now have our MMM logo, and our famous picture has been added to the label on all the rum bottles. Sales have tripled. People buy the bottle as a novelty item more than they buy it for the booze.

"Molly also came up with the idea of putting a flask inside teddy bears with the letters *T* for 'Teddy' and *M* for 'Molly.' With each bear comes the story of their lives and how they came to live in Cloud's Cove with Harmony and the other orphaned animals. All the profits go to feed the animals. People have more spending money now than ever before in this nation. Did you know that, Doc?"

Before Doc could answer, Percy said, "But the main thing I want to toast with you tonight is…bananas. My favorite song is playing on radio stations in all the big cities: 'Yes! We Have No Bananas.' We couldn't have gotten better free advertising. I bet it will become the best song on the charts. Yes, there's a blight on all our farms in Brazil. But thankfully we bought property in British Honduras and shipping rights out of Orchid Bay. The land is actually better in many ways. It was all old forestland that had been cut for the mahogany wood over the years.

"I'm proud to tell you, Doc, that we are now the world's largest importer and exporter of bananas. Congratulations to us both!" Their glasses clinked in the air in celebration of their good fortune. Sugar woke up at the sound and poked her head out from under the table. "And while we're celebrating…Here's to the new home for abandoned children in Taylorsville we funded." The members of the Saint Mary Catholic Church were so grateful, they had committed to praying for the two men's souls for all of eternity. Doc and Percy figured they might need the prayers, so they had accepted them gracefully.

They were at the theater early to meet two women: Molly and her ballerina girlfriend Della, the star of that night's sold-out show at the Elks Opera House and Theater, which could seat a thousand people. Molly joined the two men first. She was thankful and very excited that Della was stopping in the South after her just-completed world tour. From her stops in Madrid, Baghdad, Hong Kong, Sidney, San Francisco, Denver, and New York City, she was in great demand. Neither she nor Doc Reynolds remembered meeting at the wedding at the Grand Hotel. When Della walked into the room, she and Molly embraced. Doc's mouth dropped open in absolute delight. "There's my soul mate!" he leaned over and told Percy.

The two women walked over to the gentlemen, and Della looked at Doc. She told him, "I remember you now. I noticed you at the wedding, but we never talked. Molly, why didn't you introduce me then?" She then leaned over to Molly and said, "He is kind of sexy. Is he married?" Both Molly and Percy sensed the instant attraction and the tense arousal between the two. Electricity was definitely in the air as the sparks flew between Della and Doc.

The show was the absolute best, and the last, of Della's career. When the curtain came back up for her to take a bow, Doc Reynolds looked over at Percy and said, "Old friend, I may need your support if I totally embarrass myself, but I'm going to ask that woman to marry me." Before Percy could say, "Doc, you've had too much to drink…Let's go out to dinner" or something else first, Doc was up on the stage down on one knee and before the entire audience, asking her to marry him. To his and everyone's surprise…she said yes. They had known each other for three hours and fifty-eight minutes.

FORTY SIX

THE SÉANCE

S hasta and Jagi lived in one of the big white houses on Adams Street, and her uncle Chase lived next door in her grandparents' house. Percy, although married to Molly now, did not care too much for this house because it was where his first wife, Linda Gail, had suddenly died. Shasta loved the house because it was filled with memories, photos, and things her mother loved. But now, night after night, she awoke with nightmares of her mother screaming.

Shasta didn't have any strong memories of her mother because she was only five years old when Linda Gail died. Molly contacted Sylvia, a widely known and respected psychic in New Orleans. She was also Olivia's mother. Josie Arlington, Molly's first employer in New Orleans, had often used her to see her future. Percy would do anything to help his daughter and agreed, along with Molly, Doc Reynolds, and Jagi, to participate in a séance at the home where his wife and his mother had died. Della declined the invitation.

Sylvia had already caused quite a stir since her arrival in Huntsville. She had seen two ghosts of black men in Taylorsville. One, she said, was a music man, and the other a king. She also saw what she believed to be the son of the Devil floating above the water at Ditto's Landing. While traveling up Whitesburg Pike to Huntsville from Taylorsville, Sylvia had one of her most memorable local psychic sightings. It was that of a young girl named Sally Carter, age fifteen or so, playing in the yard of Cedarhurst, a mansion near Drake Mountain. The girl never wanted to leave the beautiful estate and loved playing pranks on unsuspecting visitors. No one paid much attention to these revelations. After all, they had been written about or were known local legends and lore already. It was also possible that whoever had hosted a séance with Sylvia had unintentionally given her the information.

The stage was set for calling upon the dead at Shasta's house. The house was dark except for candles on the buffet and the dining room table. Percy let it be known to everyone that he was going along with this nonsense only to give his daughter some peace of mind. All of them were seated around the dining room table when Sylvia first spoke in her Caribbean accent. "I would like to ask now that everyone hold hands and clear their minds of any thoughts or activities." After a long period of silence, she continued, "My name is Sylvia. I am a spiritualist here today to contact those who have not traveled to the other side. If there is someone here from the spirit world, please contact us now by knocking on the wood table." After another long period of silence, Sylvia stood up from the table and declared, "This house has been cleansed by a priest. It will be hard for any of them to make contact. Have any of you here this evening ever used or heard of the Ouija board?"

Percy opened his eyes and stared at Sylvia. She had his attention now. "My wife and my mother had a Ouija board and used it for entertainment. If no one has moved it, it is upstairs in the attic of this house."

Jagi considered himself a rather intelligent young man and looked around, puzzled. "What exactly is a Ouija board? What does it do?" Jagi was wide eyed and did not realize there were mystics in America. He knew his stepmother and some of the old ladies in Poland would get together when the men were at work and speak to the dead. As a small child, he had been caught listening to a séance and was made to swear to never mention it again. He thought it was the Devil's work.

The spiritualist spoke. "It is a flat board marked with letters of the alphabet, the numbers zero to nine, and the words *yes* and *no* and *hello* and *good-bye*. It uses a small heart-shaped piece of wood—a planchette—which is a movable indicator that, with our help, spells out the spirits' message in automatic writing. Some Christians consider it to be demonic, but it is just the natural order of things. Many have used it since the war to contact their loved ones."

Shasta returned from the attic with the Ouija board. Everyone kept their seats, mainly out of curiosity. Even Dr. Reynolds, who looked at everything through a scientific eye, remained at the table. Sylvia continued, "Who here tonight knew the departed? Shasta, you told me earlier you knew them mainly only through young memories, photographs, and old stories. Jagi, did you know either lady?" He shook his head. So did Doc Reynolds, who knew Linda Gail but was not willing to participate. "Looks like you're the only two left," Sylvia said as she looked to Percy and Molly. "I need you to lightly put your fingers on the heart. Don't try to move it. Just let it float."

Sylvia closed her eyes and seemed to go into a trance. She then said, "If there are any spirits wishing to make contact with anyone in this room, please come forward now." Molly closed her eyes, fearful the Devil might come out and bite her hand. Percy never took his eyes off Shasta. Their hands began to move slowly at first and then jerked suddenly to the word *hello*. Sylvia spoke softly. "We have a visitor. Can you please tell us your name?"

Molly slowly opened her eyes to make sure she was still on Earth. "It looks like the first letter tonight is *W*," Sylvia said as she looked directly at Shasta. "Did either of the women's names begin with *W*?" Shasta, who did not want to speak out loud, shook her head. The indicator moved to the letter *E*, then to a blank spot, back to the letter *E*, to the letter *D*, back to the letter *E*, and then stopped on the letter *N*. Sylvia spoke again. "Spirits, I want to make sure we have this correct. You have spelled 'Weeden.' Is that correct?" The heart moved across the board and indicated *yes*.

Only then did Percy remove his locked eyes from his daughter, Shasta. "Holy crap," he said. "The Weeden house on Gates Avenue is where my mama and Linda Gail met up with other ladies to play this parlor game. It was only a week before my mother died, and Linda Gail said that she was feeling fine, but for some reason neither of them ever spoke of that night. Sylvia, you said something about a priest cleansing this house. Father Patrick was here and gave Linda Gail her last rites. Does this mean we need to go to the Weeden home to finish the séance?"

The room became quite cool, and the candlelight flickered. "Whoever was here is gone now," Sylvia said. "The room is empty. Do you know anyone at this Weeden house so that we can continue? Is it nearby?"

In unison, four of them said, "Yes!" Molly's face answered for her. She was clueless.

Shasta and Jagi stood up. Jagi turned on the electrical lights as Shasta blew out the candles. "Let's go," Shasta said. "We can walk. It's just at the end of the street on Gates Avenue." She didn't even look back to see if anyone else was following. Jagi stayed between Doc and Percy. He was scared to death. Chase had just arrived home next door and decided to join the group.

A short time later all of them, with Percy in the lead, were knocking on the Weeden house's front door. A tiny woman in her eighties opened the door with a welcoming smile to Percy. It was Kate. She welcomed them and said, "I knew you would come one day, Percy. I just didn't know it would take you this long. Please, you and your guests must come in. Would anyone like some tea?" Sugar refused to come inside, and Percy decided to go in without her.

They all traveled past a beautifully carved, curved wooden staircase. "Percy, I know you didn't know I was still alive. Most people don't know," Kate said.

"Miss Weeden," Percy said. "I knew you and my mother were friends. What did you mean when you said you knew I would come one day? Oh, I'm sorry, Miss Weeden, I seem to have lost my manners. Let me introduce you. This is my daughter, Shasta, and her husband, Jagi, who traveled all the way from Poland; my wife, Molly; Chase, my brother; my good friend Doc Reynolds; and my new friend, Sylvia. For lack of a better way to put it, we had a séance tonight with the Ouija board, and your name was spelled out on it. I know you, my mother, my first wife, Linda Gail, and some of the other ladies played these parlor board games. Shasta keeps having nightmares of her mother screaming. Is there anything you can tell me about that?"

Miss Weeden had them follow her past the grand circular staircase, through the parlor to the right of the entrance foyer, past a grand piano with large legs, and through the thick entrance wall-opening to the dining room so that they could all sit together at the table. The window was open, and they could smell the fragrant roses outside. "You must be the one the spirits will channel through," Kate said, looking at Sylvia as if she had been expecting her for some time. "This house is filled with spirits, and I cannot hear as well as I used to, so they get my attention by moving things around."

Kate looked around at everyone and turned to Percy. "Percy, in 1905, the week before your mother died, we had a mystic reading tarot cards for us. Your mother first drew the Fool card, followed by the Death card." An audible gasp was heard in the room. "Linda Gail's cards weren't any better. She drew the Devil and the Hanged Man. My sister, Howard, drew the Death card. None of us really understood these cards so we went back to the Ouija board for fun." She opened a secret panel on the bottom of the cabinet, pulled out the very Ouija board they had used that night, and continued. "Laura Ann and Linda Gail went first. The word *death* was spelled out. We all got spooked, and everyone went home. One week later your mother died. My sister, Howard, died the day after that. She went to the post office in the morning and came home, got in bed, and, the doctor said, finally succumbed to her tuberculosis. Only a month after that, Linda Gail died. They are not the spirits who rattle around here trying to tell me something. Maybe Sylvia can contact the ladies and my spirit intruder for us tonight."

Only the flames of the nearby candles illuminated the room. Everyone held hands as Sylvia instructed. Sylvia slowly entered a trance and spoke. "Close your mind to all outside influences. Let your thoughts be still. Open your hearts to only those spirits that are true and good. Let no spirit with evil intent enter here tonight. It is universal law that if we ask a spirit to leave, they must do so immediately." All eight people sat quietly around the table, holding hands, with their eyes closed. Except Doc Reynolds. He was involved solely as a witness for scientific and medical reasons. Sylvia continued, "We are here this evening to talk to the spirits of Linda Gail and Laura Ann Taylor, mother and grand-mother of Shasta."

The doctor watched all the participants and noticed Jagi's posture begin to change. He sat up more erect, and his shoulders seemed to relax as he began to speak in a very southern accent with no Polish accent, as though he were scolding someone. "You said you would never move my rocking chair. Now it's gone. It used to be on the back porch. Who moves it upstairs all the time? The jar of nickels in the rocker is gone too. And now all my cigars are missing out of the humidor in the east parlor. Harrison Brothers got in a new shipment of tobaccos and cigars. Grace from church was kind enough to fill it up with them for me when I was too sick to get out. Now it's empty."

Sylvia spoke to the spirit talking through Jagi. "Sir, we're here to speak to two ladies, Linda Gail and Laura Ann. I promise we'll fill up the humidor and find your rocking chair. Please let the women speak first. It's very important." The room was silent for what seemed like an eternity to the people around the table, until suddenly Sylvia said in a frantic woman's voice, "The woman with hair like a bush on fire and her husband who wears steel. She killed us. Don't let her get away. She has hurt everyone at the table, or will if you let her. She uses poison, and her son, he uses poison and fire. Don't let them hurt my grandchild." The voice faded. Hot air blew down from the back staircase in the corner of the room. The flaming wood in the fireplace across the room sud-denly grew brighter. Everyone was startled by Sugar barking and whin-ing at the back door. She scratched so hard that she left claw marks in the wood. No one had ever seen Sugar act like she'd seen a ghost. She wanted to be with her human. The séance was over when Sugar flew in through an open window someone forgot to close after building a fire in the fireplace.

They decided to go back to Percy and Molly's house on Williams. No one knew of anyone dying in it or of any ghosts at that house. Shasta held Jagi back from the others and whispered in his ear, "I know everyone thinks that was my grandmother coming through. It wasn't. That was my mother...I'm pregnant."

He stopped with a shocked look and said, "Shasta, that is wonderful. I am so happy about it. I'll soon be a father!" He held her close. "But if that was your mother, how did she know?"

They shared the news with everyone when they arrived at the house. Percy was also elated and tried not to show too much concern about what had been said at the Weeden house. He was already planning to hire off-duty police officers to watch the entire family.

"Percy," Sylvia said, "another voice came through me tonight as Sugar came through the window. It was that of a scientist. It didn't make a bit of sense to me, but maybe it will mean something to you. The voice said, 'Soak clean cotton with Palm of Christy. Place over the lead for thirty days. The lead will come out naturally. No use for powder medicine.'"

Shasta stared at Percy and Molly. "How did she know about your war wound? That happened twenty years ago. We're going to get some of that oil. Maybe then you can stop taking cocaine."

As they all stood outside, Sylvia filled everyone in on her grand-children, Oliver and Opal, who were attending Howard University. She was drained from the night's experience and asked to retire for the evening for a good night's sleep before her early morning trip home. Percy had already discreetly slipped her some money in appreciation for her services. Then she said her good-byes. She reminded them to fill the humidor and get a rocking chair for the Weeden house. She also told them to remember to get a jar of nickels so the old woman would be left alone.

Before Sylvia could leave, everyone heard an automobile horn honk-ing. They stepped back out of the way from a swerving, out-of-control driver. Percy shouted, "He's yelling something out the window!"

The driver slammed on the brakes, barely missing the group. Bruce, who had never learned to drive, jumped out screaming, "It's Pierre! He's stuck at the McCormick Mansion, and I think that place is making him crazy. Please, Molly, help!"

Percy put his hands on Bruce's shoulders, trying to calm him, and said, "Slow down, catch your breath, and start at the beginning."

"We don't have time. I'll explain on the way," Bruce replied.

Molly took the lead and got behind the wheel. They all followed her and somehow managed to cram into the car with Sugar in the front seat, and sped away. Bruce explained, "Pierre has been doing all this work for that filthy-rich crazy woman, remodeling room after room. I have noticed lately after he's been there all day that he comes back to the hotel nervous, he startles real easy, and he hears things that just aren't there. He called me from there a few minutes ago and asked me to look out the window and see if the house was on fire. As you know, it is the only thing built out in that direction, and of course you can see that big house from the top floors at the hotel. It was not on fire. Every light in the house appeared to be turned on, but they would all go off at the same time. Then they would all come back on again. While we were on the phone, he told me that people were screaming at him to help them get out of the fire, but he couldn't find people anywhere in the house."

Molly drove the car up the long drive. Jagi realized he had been to the house once and announced, "This was the Kildare house before McCormick bought it. It is haunted. I am not ashamed to say I will not be going inside. I don't think any of us should."

Sylvia spoke up and said, "I have a feeling we all need to stay together." Now everyone was spooked, including Doc. The only light on was at the front door. They all held hands and bravely went inside the enormous house to look for Pierre. Sugar stayed between Percy and Molly. They found Pierre curled up like a baby under the dining room table. Sylvia stood frozen in one spot with her eyes closed. They all remained silent until she spoke. Sylvia opened her eyes and said, "We all need to take Pierre and get out of here, now!"

Nobody said a word on the ride back. They stood together on the front lawn of Percy and Molly's house, and Sylvia told them, "Never go back to that house. There was a terrible fire in the house that was there before the current one was built. The man was insane. He set his slaves free, but he made them watch as he set his own house afire with his wife and their children locked inside. The slaves were horrified and tried to break down the door to rescue the family they still loved. The man poured kerosene on the rescuers and set them on fire as well. Fate was not on his side. Sparks from the inferno landed on the man's kerosene-soaked trousers. The insanity seems to have been passed to those who inhabit the property now."

Without changing her tone, Sylvia looked at Doc. "If I had beat her here, you would be mine. She is your soul mate. Marry her soon." Doc looked surprised. She then turned to Molly and said, "Through all the events tonight a beautiful blond woman's spirit remained in the background. She had nothing to communicate, but she showered you with love." Molly looked at her, confused, not knowing what to say.

Before retiring to the guest house for the evening, Sylvia looked up at the moon and commented, "That's the second time tonight I thought I saw a man on the moon." She took the first train to Memphis the next morning, where she was to meet up with a riverboat captain. They would travel down the Mississippi River trying to make contact with his deceased daughter. He was Captain Palmer Graham, Molly's old friend.

Doc married Della the next day at the courthouse with Percy and Molly as their witnesses.

FORTY SEVEN

LADIES' LUNCHEON

Bruce and Pierre were finishing up flower arrangements in the foyer when Molly came through the front door. As usual lots of hugs and kisses ensued. "Molly," Bruce said, "you are just going to die when you hear this about Suzette's husband, Dick. I dressed Pierre up real pretty last night to go visit our friends across the river. We do that about once a month...have a beauty contest. You remember we took you to a drag party out in San Francisco once.

"Anyway, in walks the detective in full woman's garb. The entire room breaks out in laughter. He was so rough looking with his hairy man hands...*Ugly* may be the word for it. He must have done his own makeup, because he looked like one of those rodeo clowns. He tried to pretend he was someone different, but we all knew it was him.

"Can you believe he tries to push us around and bully us on the streets, and then shows up at our party? If he'd behaved differently, we may have tried to accept him. We thought Danny, the country boy, ran out to console him. Boy, were we ever wrong when we saw that yard broom bouncing off the back of Dick's head. He is not welcome at any of our parties. I bet he never tries to bother us again."

Molly was stunned. "Such a hypocrite, and that gay hag wife of his is no better. She's due to arrive any minute now. I will fill you guys in when

I get back to the hotel this afternoon. Wish us luck!" The two men left and blew air kisses to Molly as they walked across the lawn.

Suzette had a habit, developed over many years, of pushing her way into groups that did not want her. Her relentless approach usually paid off for her. Today, Shasta was hosting a ladies' luncheon. Percy was at Shasta's home for moral support for Shasta and Molly and greeted the ladies, charmed most of them, and then politely exited.

Today was a setup for Suzette. All of the invited ladies were in on it, except Suzette, of course. Truth serum has no taste, no smell, and no color. It loosens the tongue, and the person has no memory of the truth talk. Scopolamine mixed with morphine not only produces a "twilight sleep" but also can lead to amnesia around the events experienced during the temporary sedation. Shasta knew that she and everyone must not give Suzette any reason to suspect that anything out of the ordinary was happening. If the recipient suspected she was drugged, she could possibly resist the effect. Physicians used the serum as a mild anesthesia during childbirth. It depressed the central nervous system and moderated judgment and higher cognitive functions.

Shasta had gotten her truth serum powder from Carlos, who had picked it up for her during the last trip he'd made to Brazil. He had warned her to be cautious while using it and not to inhale any of it herself. His gypsy sister lived in Bogota, Colombia, where the truth powder is derived from the flower of the borrachero tree. She and two other women sometimes preyed on men by smearing the drug on their breasts and then luring the men to take a lick. Their willpower gone, the victims freely gave away their wealth and secrets to the "breast bandits."

This luncheon group had organized themselves into the Women's Christian Coalition, although their agenda was different from the usual groups with that sort of name. Janice Johnston was instrumental in including Suzette and giving the group credibility. She knew God's power worked in strange ways, and this was one of them. The other way God worked through Janice was at her hothouse flower shop, where she also sold spirits for medicinal purposes and gave the proceeds to her church.

Suzette couldn't believe her good luck at being included in the group's initial meeting. Shasta's plan was to drug Suzette with the truth serum, casually ask her about what her husband, Dick, knew about the bootlegging that the Taylor family was involved in, and then lead the conversation to the mystery surrounding the deaths of her mother and her grandmother. Anything extra would be a bonus that could be used against her later. Maybe, if they were lucky, Suzette could help them understand some details from the séance.

Shasta and the other ladies had no idea what was really about to hit them. Suzette entered and was appalled that Molly Teal Taylor was in the same room, much less a part of the group, and as much as said so. Molly said simply, "I am a woman, a Christian, and the group's founder and principal donor." This set Suzette off. Lily stepped in and kindly poured a specifically selected cup of tea for Suzette. The serum had already been placed in the bottom of the pretty little fine-china cup. Within a few minutes, Suzette interrupted Janice during her opening prayer. She started spouting off things about Molly's past without even being asked.

Molly took the cue from Shasta to quietly leave the room. Suzette looked around in disgust and lit a cigarette, blowing a plume of smoke into the group. She was only five years older than Molly, but the smoking made her look fifty because of all the wrinkles. Shasta wanted Suzette to be perfectly comfortable and trusting of the other ladies. Suzette felt perfectly at ease in telling everyone how much she had always hated Molly Teal, even when they were children. The ladies in the room had been instructed ahead of time to let Shasta do all the questioning. Shasta had rehearsed her methods of remaining calm for herself and for Suzette, and had vowed not to probe to the extent that would alert Suzette that she was being set up.

Suzette continued talking freely. "Everyone thought Molly was such a beautiful child. It just made me sick, all the attention Molly received." As a teenager, Suzette had helped her aunt and uncle sort the mail because they ran the downtown post office. She knew all the addresses, and was very good at her job. Suzette told the ladies, "A few months after Molly arrived in Huntsville, I started seeing letters from an Annie Teal addressed to her from Bryce Hospital every week. Of course that piqued my young curiosity, so I kept the letters and read them, privately. When I was finished, I would write on the envelope, 'Return to Sender.'

Dozens of letters revealed that Molly's mother was in Bryce and claimed that her evil brother, David Overton, had had her committed and then took away her daughter." Suzette gloated. "Molly was not an orphan after all. She had a mother in a crazy hospital, against her will."

Suzette said that the letters revealed that Molly's mother had always loved her child unconditionally and that her mother had pleaded for Molly not to give up on her. Her mother vowed that one day she would get out and rescue Molly. "Never give up," Molly's mother had written. "Can you believe that?" Suzette said.

Molly was listening from the butler's closet off the dining room. Of course, she knew the details of her mother's letters. She had had them in her possession since she'd recovered them from Bryce Hospital. She had read them dozens of times over the intervening years. Molly now knew about the missing piece of the puzzle: who had sent the letters back. She'd never understood why her uncle hadn't just thrown them away, if he had been the one to intercept the letters. Actually, she had blamed her cruel aunt Loretta as the most likely perpetrator, knowing that Loretta wanted to hurt her husband's sister.

Molly's blood was beginning to boil just listening to Suzette's voice. She slid down the wall as her eyes watered up and leaked down her face, but she remained quiet so as not to interrupt Suzette. Suzette continued boasting of this great accomplishment. "Then Molly turned into a whore, which we all know...even at twelve years old. That's what she was and is...a whore!" None of the ladies said a word. They only listened.

"I kept some of the letters—matter of fact, I still have them. Molly comes by it naturally. Her real mother was a whore right here in this town a long time ago...nothing but trash."

Molly turned and walked into the kitchen to keep from causing a scene. This last information stunned her. She was so young when kidnapped that her mother had never had a chance to tell her the family history. Molly needed those letters.

Shasta calmly asked Suzette to tell them how she had met Michael, Chip's father. Shasta's aunt Kelly was especially interested in this tale. Michael was her favorite nephew, and she had never fully understood how Michael had fallen into Suzette's trap. "Well," Suzette said, "that was an easy one. I wanted to live in Twickenham, the exclusive part of downtown Huntsville. My parents worked at the Dallas Mill and lived in a shitty little house in the Dallas Mill village. I wanted more. So I began to follow Michael. I knew his every move…what he ate and drank. I even went to his Catholic church," Suzette said proudly, boasting of this clever endeavor. She went on to tell them about the night she tricked Michael into bed with her. "I was so smart. I knew exactly which drug to give him. I'd planned that night for a long time. I knew my cycle and which day would be optimal for me to conceive."

The ladies were still silent, as instructed, although stunned at Suzette's conniving capabilities. But they hadn't really heard anything yet. Suzette continued, "The pregnancy didn't work as I planned. So I went to New Market to meet with 'Red the Giant.' I stayed with him and took care of all his motherless children until I knew for certain I was pregnant. All the rest of my plans fell right into place: marriage to Michael, a house downtown, and a new baby on the way. Then there was the night that stupid Michael had to get himself hit by a train. He ruined everything for me then."

Aunt Kelly was digging her fingernails into the wood of the chair's arm where she was sitting. Suzette had forgotten under the influence of the drugs that Shasta and Kelly were Michael's relatives. She went on to say, "I was so angry at Michael for getting himself killed. I was stuck with his ugly bastard baby. And for a whole year I had to fake being in mourning to get everyone's sympathy."

The only sounds in the room were a few birds chirping outside on the windowsills. Suzette loved being center stage for the first time in her life, divulging secrets that nobody else knew just to impress the ladies with how much she had been involved in events of the area. Shasta calmly asked her about Dick, her husband, and her son, Chip. "Well, my marriage and my husband are two separate things," Suzette replied. "Dick isn't a 'dick.'" She laughed loudly at her own words. "I wanted a father for Chip, and Dick wanted a wife to cover up his secret sexual lifestyle." She looked around, waiting for someone to ask something. Nobody said a word. She told them anyway. "Big ol' Dick is a homosexual, and he doesn't want anyone at the police department to know, so he goes to some odd birds across the river in Laceys Spring. I'm not exactly sure what homosexuals do with each other, but he doesn't do anything with *me* in *my* bed.

"At first I was okay with the cover-up. But as the years went by, I got lonely. I spent a lot of my time with Chip and working at the post office. Y'all remember Chip disappeared, don't you? Anyway, bless his heart… I was so proud of him. Especially when he burned down that whore-house over off Fifth Avenue. He was sure proud of himself. All the other strange stuff he's up to, I don't completely agree with…like the hotel fire and the circus animal fire that killed the horses and that woman he beat and raped on a train in Taylorsville, then blamed the jigaboo for it. That Negro got lynched, you know, and he had nothing to do with it. The last night I saw Chip. He smelled like smoke and gasoline … said he was on his way to Taylorsville for some unfinished business."

Shasta's teeth were grinding and her jaw was clenched. She remembered Chip's rampage in every detail because she had lost part of her family forever. "Did any of you know that hobo woman?" Suzette asked. "She was seen a year or so later and had a baby that looked just like Chip. She was a train hobo and up to no good anyways. That's why I never claimed my only grandchild.

"Shasta, bless your heart, you couldn't help it who your mother was. She was just a no-good bitch from Fayetteville. Your father deserved better. I would've made a good mother to you if he had just listened to me. But no, you had to grow up without a mother because he was so busy grieving over her and wouldn't pay me any attention."

By now Suzette was only rambling. "Actually, Percy Taylor was rude to me after he became a judge again. He came into the post office and accused me of opening official courthouse mail. My aunt almost fired me over that."

Suzette continued under the drug's influence, "I tell you, Shasta, I never intended to hurt your grandmother Laura Ann. She was always nice to me."

Shasta had to use all the self-control she could muster and chose to sit on her clenched fists. Nobody knew how much longer Suzette would go rattling on. This was certainly not what the ladies of the first meeting of the Christian Women's Coalition had expected.

"I hated that Laura Ann died the way she did," Suzette mumbled. "I thought I gave her only enough opium powder in her tea to slow her down, so she would need me more often, just like David and Loretta told me to do. That way I could find out the comings and goings of Percy and Linda Gail. I am so glad the coroner said she died of natural causes. I never meant to kill her with it. I gave the remaining opium to that prissy Miss Howard Weeden, Kate's sister, the next day when she came to the post office. Now, she really needed it."

"I was told my grandmother really liked and trusted you," Shasta said, with no emotion.

That comment just fueled Suzette to keep on talking about how good a friend she really had been to Laura Ann. "All I wanted was to be a part of the great Taylor family. I knew if I could break up Percy and Linda Gail, my dreams could all happen. I tried repeatedly to console Percy after I accidentally poisoned his mother. That's when we, you know Loretta and me, came up with a plan to drug him. I took off all his clothes and was naked in the bed with him when Linda Gail arrived home. I was hopeful Linda Gail would be so upset and unforgiving that she would leave Percy and Huntsville for good.

"Everything was going quite well. I was rather enjoying lying in bed with Percy, with our bodies touching. Linda Gail came into the bedroom. Instead of her leaving, as I thought she would, she whipped the sheets off us two lovebirds. Then she began trying to shake Percy awake. Over and over again, she begged him to wake up. Linda Gail shook Percy so hard, I was afraid she was going to hurt him out of anger. I tried to stop her from slapping his face.

"I don't know what her problem was," Suzette said as she continued. "She turned her violence on me! Used anything she could get her hands on to strike at me. I tried to explain to Linda Gail that Percy and I were lovers and she needed to go back to Tennessee—let Percy and me live our life out together. I told her I would raise Shasta as my own, with Chip.

"We fought," Suzette continued. "Linda Gail was real strong for her size, I guess from all that farm work. She fought me, screaming like a banshee. I was finally able to get on top when we wrestled on the floor. I grabbed the pitcher of sweet tea with the drugs I had given to Percy off the nightstand. Instead of banging the pitcher over Linda Gail's head, I poured the tea into her mouth. She tried to spit it out, but I wouldn't let her.

"I tell you, ladies, that woman had no manners, trying to spit on me. Little by little, I kept pouring it in. She must've swallowed some of it, because eventually she quit struggling and clawing at me. Just to make sure she didn't recover her strength, I poured the rest of the tea into her mouth and rubbed her throat to make it go down."

Suzette was probably the perfect subject for truth serum. Although groggy, she couldn't shut up. "Well, you can imagine how worn out I was by that time," she said as the women in the room nodded to her, disgusted, as if they understood. "I had to stand up to catch my breath. Then I caught a glimpse of myself in that beautifully framed mirror. You know the one in their bedroom? Anyway, I looked horrible...just horrible. Blood was coming from my scalp where she hit me with something hard, and welts and red scratch marks were all over my arms, chest, and face.

"*That bitch did this to me,* I said to myself. I had to think fast. So, I got dressed. I dressed Percy, although I hated doing that because he had such a handsome body. He looked so good naked. Anyway, I noticed little spots of blood all over Linda Gail's dress. So I changed her too. She had so many beautiful clothes in her wardrobe. I picked out a pretty red one. I tossed the dirty dress into the clothes hamper. I then dragged Percy over to Linda Gail's body on the floor. He was still breathing hard. Must have been all that cocaine power he used that kept him alive, but Linda Gail was not breathing. I don't take the blame for that. She should've just left town instead of beating up on me. I didn't kill her. I came up with a plan to wreck my car somewhere I could easily be found—you know, to explain the injuries that bitch did to me."

Then without changing her tone or skipping a beat, proud of everything that was coming out of her own mouth, she went on to explain that Candice Pleasants was the source for her drugs. She further explained that Candice had given Loretta drugs for Judge Lawler before David Overton killed him. This shed light on the fact that although Lawler was much bigger and stronger than Overton, Lawler apparently could not fight him off.

Suzette perked up and said, "Candice also drugged Sheriff Phillips and her husband, the assistant district attorney, before they killed themselves. Candice used my car and never returned it, and then somehow it ended up in that big shootout in Birmingham. Candice gave me an envelope to deliver to Brooks the day he got hit by a train. Loretta never once mentioned poisoning Molly's mother to me, but I know she did... Yes, she did it," she said as her voice trailed off.

This political murder and suicides had stayed in the headlines nationwide for months. Grace couldn't help herself and let out a huge sigh of relief that she had not been the cause of the men's deaths, but now, Grace was to be Suzette's target of attention. Suzette raised her chin and, staring at Grace, said, "Little Miss Religious Grace, married to a preacher and sister of Percy Taylor, is no saint. I have good word from Candice Pleasants that you, missy, were at the scene of the murder of Judge Lawler." This shocked the ladies as much as anything they had heard so far. Some of their mouths dropped open in stunned silence.

Before Suzette had a chance to continue, Shasta stood up and asked her to follow her to the carriage house behind the main house. Suzette eagerly followed when Shasta said, "There's something out there of my grandmother's that I'd like for you to have," knowing she could not be seen from the street. She led Suzette to the trunk of her car, opened it, shoved Suzette in, and slammed the trunk closed. Then she began screaming, "That's for my grandmother, my mother and father, Molly, and the O'Kennedy family, you pathetic bitch! You'll never see the light of day again, so help me God."

Shasta fell to the ground and began to wail into her hands. For years, her father hadn't been able to get past his grief for Linda Gail. Percy had been ashamed that they had found him next to Linda Gail's body, giving the impression that he was a weak man and had passed out at the sight of his dead wife. Now the truth was out. Thanks to the serum, it was now known that he had been placed next to her body while drugged into unconsciousness. He had been right about the dress she was wearing that day too. He had never been able to understand why she'd been wearing the red honeymoon dress that was so special to her.

Suzette was desperately banging from the inside of the trunk. "Let me out of here! Just think, Shasta, I kept Chip from murdering you on the night of the hanging. He stole the truck instead and went on a burning spree. What a mistake!"

Suzette's demands and screams went unanswered. "Listen, Suzette," Shasta commanded. "Your pathetic son's knees were broken, and he was tarred and tied to a post in a train after my daddy caught him poisoning Sugar. He was headed off to Canada in a car full of bananas with creepy, poisonous spiders crawling all over him. If he survived the spiders, maybe the frozen north took him. Daddy said he didn't want the murder of even an evil child on his conscience. He did put a note above him on a pole that read, 'This is the devil that provided false witness to hang a man, and he poisoned my dog. Help him at your own peril.'

"He has been gone a long time now, Suzette, and he is not coming back. I hope this causes you great pain. You are the Devil, and you spawned a Devil's son. I hope he died slowly and miserably." Shasta slid down the side of the car to the ground after she had finished shouting.

Molly came to the carriage house and pulled Shasta off the floor. They were both trembling. The monster who had so altered both of their lives was just inches away. Molly picked the keys up off the ground and tried each one to open the trunk. When it opened, she grabbed Suzette by the hair on the back of her head and with the other hand slapped her face several times. "What did you mean saying 'my real mother' was a whore? What do you know bitch? Where are those letters?" Molly screamed! Molly realized this did not make her feel any better or her pain go away. Suzette was out of it anyway. She pushed Suzette's head down again and slammed the lid. The two women closed the door to the carriage house.

Aunt Kelly had gone to Suzette's house when Shasta took Suzette outside, and returned carrying a wooden crate. The crate contained hundreds of opened letters addressed to various people. She gave the crate to Molly, and together they went back into the living room of the main house. Shasta had picked up a couple of bottles of wine as they passed through the pantry. Lily was behind her with an opener and glasses. As they walked in, the room went silent. Shasta poured a glass for everyone. She spoke softly, still in shock, just as everyone else was. "We came here to find the truth. We took an oath to one another not to speak of what we were up to today. I plan to keep that oath. Does everyone else?" All heads nodded in affirmation as the last woman said, "I swear." The glasses clinked in a toast.

They enjoyed a rare bottle of Rothschild wine. Janice spoke up. "God truly works in mysterious ways. I call this meeting to an end. Amen."

"Amen," they said in unison.

Della, fresh from her sudden honeymoon, said, "Damn, whoever said the South was boring has never been to this town!" as she held up the wine bottle to take notice of the year.

One by one they all went home, except Molly. She and Shasta took the glasses into the kitchen, where Shasta noticed a little bit of unused truth serum. She dumped it into the unfinished second bottle of wine, took a fountain pen and in big bold letters wrote "SPECIAL" on it, and then carried the bottle with her to the car.

Shasta told Molly of her plans as they drove to Taylorsville. They were both still in shock and enraged as they bumped down the road. All the while Suzette was screaming from the trunk. "Killing her would be letting her off too easy," Shasta said. "I had planned to put her in the basement of Grandpa C. C.'s house at the farm. No one goes there much anymore. I'm certainly not going to turn her over to the police so her fake husband can get her off the hook. She would just love to be in a courtroom trial and command everyone's attention. Suzette, you're just too good at lying!" Shasta shouted to the rear of the car.

"I just can't take that chance," she continued. "The rat is going into a rat hole. I'd like to take her out in a field and use her for target practice. Maybe set her on fire." Shasta ranted on and on in an uncontrollable rage about the punishment she wanted to inflict on the woman who had brought so much evil and harm to her family and others.

"God, Shasta, I can't believe she did that to Percy. Then killed Linda Gail...and your grandmother," Molly said.

Shasta added, "And if it weren't for her, you might have saved your mother. You might never have left Huntsville."

"Shasta, stop before we get to the bridge at Ditto's Landing," Molly said. "Let's get out. I have a funny story to tell you about your mother at this very bridge many years ago. She was so great to me. As a cherry on the top, this is also where Overton killed Judge Lawler." Molly proceeded to tell Shasta the story about being terrified of the bridge on her first trip to Taylorsville and Shasta's mother, Linda Gail, having to drive her across.

As the two women stood outside the car looking at the steel bridge, both had time to calm down some. Finally, it was Molly who said, "I don't want to go to prison for killing Suzette. I want to think about it for a sweet thought, maybe, but not get myself hanged. She's not worth losing Percy, you, or anyone else in my life now." They sat on the hood of the car as a gentle breeze came in off the river. In spite of all that had happened, it was a pretty day.

FORTY EIGHT

MR. DANIELS COMES FOR A VISIT

Percy had every right to know about Suzette, the truths behind her lies, and the murder of his wife and mother. Shasta didn't really feel like she was breaking her promise to the other ladies. She assumed they understood she would tell him.

Percy's face was emotionless after Shasta finished talking. "I'm going for a walk," he said, and out the door he went with Sugar by his side. Percy went to his favorite big, old oak tree near the riverbank at the arena. Lily was sitting on the other side of the tree, waiting for him. Her feet felt good in the cool grass looking toward the river. She knew he would come to this spot after Shasta told him everything.

Percy noticed Lily was at the tree as he approached it. He started to keep on walking, but before he could turn away, Lily jumped up and came to him. Percy said, "Not today, Lily. I don't want doughnuts or any good advice. Today is not a good day for Percy Taylor."

Lily already knew that. She had been there when Suzette confessed. She pulled a bottle out of the cloth sack she was carrying. "Only one doing any talking today, Percy, is my friend Jack," she said, holding up a bottle of rare, hard-to-find Jack Daniels whiskey.

Percy looked at her. "How did you get that? Tennessee has been dry since 1909. Jack Daniels is hard to get anymore."

"My nephew sharecrops some of Mr. Motlow's land up in Lynchburg," Lily explained. "Mr. Motlow can't make it or sell it legally since Prohibition, but he can give it away for medicinal reasons. He gave it to my nephew to give to me. He loves my doughnuts too!

"Percy," Lily went on, "I loved your mama and your wife. They treated me real decent. They always called me by my name, Mrs. Lily King. Never ever called me 'nigger' like so many white folks do. Taylorsville stopped living in the year those two women died."

He said to her, "Lily, those people who called you that are one stick short of a load of book learning and are just plain ignorant. I say ignorant, not stupid. They are dumbasses in that they don't know any better."

Lily looked at Percy sternly. "Now Percy, using a bad name for another who uses a bad name doesn't help it go away."

"Okay, you're right," he said as he kicked the red dirt near him. "My wife and mother were murdered by a crazy woman," he shouted as he reached for the Jack Daniels. Sugar's reaction was to bark very loudly at him as though she was scolding, and then she snorted at the strong smell of the whiskey. He and Lily took turns taking swigs out of the bottle as they sat on the ground, their backs against the tree.

As the liquor began to take its effect on Percy, he pointed up. "I reckon it's still up there." His eyes watered up. "The first time I met Linda Gail, I climbed this old tree and carved '*Percy loves Linda Gail*' at the very top. I knew that day I loved her, and it was very difficult for me to love anybody after her until now with Molly."

Lily wasn't really drinking, only pretending to as she put the bottle to her lips occasionally. Drinking alcohol just wasn't her thing. Besides, she didn't want white folks to think she was acting all important if someone should come by. It wouldn't be proper for anyone to think that she was drinking with a white man alone, even her close friend Percy.

Both Sugar and Percy had their heads resting in Lily's lap as he told stories of when he and Linda Gail first met, their travels, and when Shasta was born. Lily talked about how she and Linda Gail would walk to the garden and pick a mess of vegetables for dinner and about the two of them puttin' up vegetables in mason jars for winter. "Percy, you do love somebody. You love Miss Molly," Lily said.

A big smile stretched across his face as he said, "I do. I do indeed."

Lily was always such a good listener. Today they took turns listening and talking. Sugar moved positions. She now lay between them on her back, paws up, in the perfect position for a good belly rubbing. The humans complied as her feet danced in the air.

"Lily, do you want me to cut this tree down? Does it remind you of Earl?"

"No, Percy—the same answer I give you every time you ask. Nature will take it when it's time. Only then. Besides, this old tree is kind of special. It has become the center of my world in Taylorsville, as it was for you and Linda Gail and others. As for the lynching, it makes Earl into a hero in my heart because he saved young Oliver. Don't get me wrong. The living Earl was a bad, bad man. Sort of odd: the only kind act he ever did was after he stopped breathing, and not by his choice.

"I always felt bad for Jagi having to live with this after he saw Herman lynched too."

They both sat there quietly for a moment. Then Percy said, "He has never said a word to other people about being there. I guess he will take that to his grave, to protect everyone."

"You're the first person I ever told. Jagi and I never spoke of it after that night. He is the real hero. Him and Doc are both heroes," Lily said.

Lily began laughing and could not stop. "Okay, what is it?" Percy asked. "What are you laughing at, Lily?"

Lily continued laughing. She could not control herself. "Doughnuts," Lily finally got out amid laughter.

"Doughnuts?" Percy inquired.

"Percy, when I look up, all I can see is this old tree with doughnuts hanging from it...like fruit," she said, and started laughing again. Lily's laughter was contagious, and Percy started laughing, too, although he was not sure why. A tree with doughnuts hanging from it did seem amusing.

Lily finally got control of herself. "Percy, think about how many doughnuts have been eaten under this tree...You and Linda Gail, Jagi, Molly, me, and so many others. If it weren't for this tree, Earl, and you, I would not have my own doughnut shops with King Crispy Doughnuts," she said, and she started laughing uncontrollably again.

Percy had to admit it was funny. "Lily, I guess we have a real doughnut tree in Taylorsville," he said, and he started laughing with her again. They continued laughing together as they lay there under the old red oak…the Doughnut Tree.

FORTY NINE

SUZETTE GOES TO DALLAS

The basement at the farm was as good a place as any for now. Only after three long days did Suzette's husband come to the house on Adams looking for her. "Mr. Dick O'Neal is here to see you, Miss Shasta," announced Big Mama Ruth.

Shasta was ready and prepared for the visit. "Good to see you, Mr. O'Neal. I bet you're here to fetch your wife's car. Frankly, I can't believe she hasn't come to get it before now. It's been blocking part of my circle drive in the front yard for days."

"My wife hasn't been home for days. Do you know where she might be?" Detective O'Neal asked, forcing a look of concern onto his face.

Shasta looked him in the eye and said, "She was behaving very strangely the other day. I don't really care to see her again."

"How was she acting strange? What did she do? What did she say?" grilled the detective.

"Well," sighed Shasta, "I don't know where to begin. Suzette acted like she had taken some kind of medicine, and wouldn't stop talking crazy things. This was my first Women's Christian Coalition luncheon meeting, and she ruined it by talking about Chip's real daddy not being Michael. She went on to describe your sexual desires or lack of them for women. Why did she say you were a homosexual? Everyone knows you hate homosexuals and that's why you go beat them up all the time.

"I worked hard on that luncheon, and she just stole all the attention. I don't know if I'll ever forgive her. Suzette just had to keep everyone upset by talking about the Overton and Pleasants widows. She said they liked putting drugs into people's beverages without their knowing. Suzette didn't make any sense. You just tell her to stay away from my family and me. She's trouble."

Mr. Dick O'Neal couldn't slink out the door any faster. He didn't want to hear anything else that that bitch wife of his might have said about his good character. She could pick up her own damn car. He knew he needed to leave town for a while, until this blew over...maybe with someone across the river.

Shasta closed the front door behind him. She started laughing out loud as Big Mama came into the parlor to join her. "He won't be looking for his dear wife anymore after this visit," Shasta said. She couldn't wait to share her performance with Molly.

Percy decided that seven days was long enough for Shasta to have gotten revenge on Suzette. Shasta reminded Suzette daily of all the horrible things she had admitted to at the luncheon and that she was the one who had gotten drugged for a change. Suzette was still somewhat in the dark and couldn't remember what all she had told the ladies. Shasta had no regrets about the kidnapping and wanted Suzette to suffer.

Percy went to the basement, where the smell of human waste was nauseating. He went back outside for a hose and turned the water on from the electric pump at the well. "Stand up, you murdering bitch. You're about to get a bath." Suzette screamed and yelled obscenities and threats about Shasta. At that point Percy turned the high-powered hose onto her face. He had to repeat this several times before she learned to shut her mouth.

At his request, her automobile had been removed from the house downtown and brought to the farm. It was waiting outside the cellar door. Suzette had to shade her eyes from the sun when the cellar door was opened. She noticed the driver's side door was open, thought to herself she was being set free, and let a smile come across her face. Percy took her arm and forced her head down as he pushed her into the passenger seat. A backup automobile followed him as he drove to the nearby ferry at Ditto's Landing.

As they neared Ditto's Landing, Percy stopped on the steel bridge. "This is where they beat and shot Judge Lawler. Then they threw his body right over here and straight down into the water below. Suzette, do you ever wonder what the bottom of the river looks like from down there where they found his body stuck in the mud?"

She shook her head and said, "No."

"Well, one day you might just have to go down there and see it first-hand if you're not careful. By *careful*, I mean you are going to take this ferry across the river. You will keep going and never look back. You will never come back to Taylorsville or Huntsville ever again. I should kill you here and now, but I don't want it on my conscience that I killed a woman. I don't want my daughter or Molly to feel guilty the rest of their lives either.

"Let me just say, Suzette, that if I hear anything about your comin' back, I'll hunt you down and kill you with my bare hands. Easy defense: you killed my wife Linda Gail and my mother, and then blabbed your disgusting mouth about it in front of a room full of witnesses. Some might say let the law handle it and then watch you hang. Well, I think that's letting you off too easy. I'd rather you live on the run, always look-ing over your shoulder, never knowing when you'll get your next meal or where you're going to sleep at night.

"I'm doing this for Molly. She wants you dead and wants to do it her-self. Molly said she saw a woman burn to death in San Francisco when she first got there. That's how she wants you to die for taking away her childhood and keeping her from her mother.

"So, Suzette, here's ten dollars. You have a full tank of gasoline. Go as far away from here as you can. Not many people get a second chance. Don't blow it." Percy pulled up to the loading ferry, got out, and climbed into the other automobile, where Hugh and Sugar were waiting.

The ferry pulled up to the other side of the river in Lacey's Spring. The locals called that area Gasoline Alley because Morgan County had no gasoline tax, which made it much cheaper than Madison County and worth the ferry trip across the river.

Suzette pulled into the parking lot of the first filling station. "Who the hell do they think they are, locking me in the basement chained to a wall, then trying to run me out of town? My husband will be looking for me. I'm going back and coming up with a plan to get the Taylor family. I know: I'll go after Shasta. I'll get her first," she promised out loud, smiling as she drove back toward the ferry to Huntsville. She noticed the car that had followed her to take Percy back passed her going in the opposite direction.

The ferry operator loaded Suzette first, just as he had been instructed and for which someone had paid him twenty dollars. He told her to pull up as close as she could to the left rail's front spot. She was delighted that she'd be the first one off. She was right in more ways than she knew.

There were many loud sounds as the ferry was loaded with other cars and wagons full of livestock beside and behind her. She didn't notice that someone had slipped into her backseat until a gun was pushed up against her temple. "I know from a little birdie that you are not supposed to go back to Huntsville," a voice said as liquid was poured down the front of Suzette's clothes. "Your only chance of living is to drive through the front rail and into the water."

A match was struck, and the backseat door slammed shut. Suzette screamed and tried to get out through the driver's door, but it was too close to the ferry's side wall to open. She reached across to the passenger door, but it was too close to the other vehicles parked beside hers. Flames were around her face, and her hair was on fire as she managed to get the car into gear and ram it into the rail in front of her. She went crashing through the rail, and the car tumbled over into the river.

Smoke poured out of the windows for the short time that the car floated. The swift current quickly pulled it downstream, away from the ferry. The automobile was three hundred yards away before the top disappeared underwater. Local legend was that Suzette went to Dallas, but she was not missed by anyone in Huntsville.

Who hated her that much? Detective Dick O'Neal was hiding out in the same area. Molly wanted to see her burn. Chip had been gone a long time, but he had a real fascination with fires. Shasta knew the ferryboat operator. Percy had a car that followed her to the ferry, where many witnesses saw her in her own car. Everybody wanted her to be in hell. The sun shone directly in your eyes if you looked west from the ferry at that time of day, so nobody noticed the smoking coffin going over the side or sinking into the river. The ferry operator was busy at the other end and apparently didn't see anything either.

A few hours later, two women were fishing from the bank near Triana. "Holy shit, Mable!" said one woman.

"Why are you talking that way, Betty? Using profanity will take you straight to the doorways of hell...Says so in the Bible." Mable looked up and saw the body of a burned woman floating toward them. Both of their mouths hung wide open, covered by their fingers, but neither of them screamed.

Betty started picking up the fishing gear and said to Mable, "You know that story about a woman picking up a frozen snake? She takes the snake home to care for and nurtures it back to good health. The snake gets better and bites her. What that says is 'She knew it was a snake before she took it in'! I'm not pulling her in to find out she's a snake. Let her float on by."

"You're right, Betty. If she's dead, we may get the blame, and if she's living, someone may blame us for saving her. We've heard of other bodies floating by here from Huntsville and Cloud's Cove before, and nobody ever did anything about them." The two women walked back up the path on their way to the parking lot of the River Club Bar and passed some teenagers going fishing with a nun in full habit...an odd scene for the area. "Don't look back," Mable said.

FIFTY

VICTOR, TRUTH SERUM, AND FAKE SNAKES

A few weeks after the ladies' luncheon, Percy and his good buddy Victor, president of the bank, got together to talk privately. Percy needed Victor to join him in fighting the KKK from taking root in the area. Victor was strongly prejudiced himself. He hated Negroes. To his very core he hated them. Percy wanted to understand why.

He asked Victor if he could show him something very few people had ever seen. They drove from Taylorsville to Phillip's Pass. The pass connected Ditto's Landing, Whitesburg, and Taylorsville area to New Hope by dry land during heavy rains in the flood season. At the bottom of the pass, when it was dry, was a generally unknown cave. It was bigger than the well-known Shelta Cave that isn't far from Huntsville. Shelta Cave is known for large, fancy balls. It has electrical power and a dance floor. Phillip's Pass Cave was larger, with no power or dance floor. It usually was under water in the lake that was formed during the wet season. Huntsville's nickname, Cave City, is no accident. There is even a large cave under the courthouse. That one reaches to the Big Spring, Huntsville's first water source.

As far as Percy knew, his father had discovered Phillip's Pass Cave and rarely shared its location. Percy wasn't much on sharing its location either. In a few minutes Victor would find out why. It had been a special place for Percy and Linda Gail. After she died, he had had a dozen or so strong men roll a huge bolder in front of the entrance. He told them it wasn't safe in there. Percy and his father still had another, more secret, entrance that was camouflaged with trees and undergrowth.

Percy didn't tell Victor about the fake snakes he had gotten from his friends in the circus. Victor almost crapped in his pants when he walked right into the snake pit. Snakes were lying on the ground and positioned in the rocks. Percy felt safe, because he had feral cats and hogs all over the place to keep the real snakes away. He finally picked up a fake snake to show Victor that they were not real, only rubber. There for a minute, he had worried that Victor might have a heart attack. Percy poured out a bucket of fish, and the cats began to show up. Victor looked at Percy and said, "You're a weird son of a bitch, Percy."

"You just now noticing that, Victor?" Percy chuckled as he beckoned for Victor to come over and help remove a large stone from behind the bushes. "We don't want to remove all the rocks. We'll have to put them back when we're finished here."

They broke quite a sweat during the thirty minutes it took to complete the task. They climbed over the remaining rocks and into the cave. Sugar easily climbed into the cave behind them. Percy was carrying a large, heavy canvas bag. He reached into the bag and pulled out matches to light an oil lantern attached to the wall. He continued lighting other lanterns stationed around the room. "What in the name of Sam are we doing in this old cave?" snorted Victor. Their eyes continued to adjust to the dim lighting. Percy reached down and grabbed a chain that ran into a large body of water in the cave. He pulled out a sealed container, opened it, and pulled out a bottle of rum and a bottle of Coca-Cola.

The sound of Sugar lapping water echoed through the cave. "You brought me into this snake hole to get drunk?" Victor complained, his face contorted.

"I know you don't like the hard stuff, so look in my bag over there. Shasta left a bottle of her fancy wine in the car. I brought it in for ya. She even wrote 'SPECIAL' on it. Must be good. I didn't bring you a crystal glass though. You'll just have to swig it out of the bottle."

"Rothschild: that is special," Victor said as he pulled out the cork. "Good thing Shasta got her mother's good taste and not yours."

"You're probably right about that, Victor," Percy said. "Don't drink too much just yet. We have to climb those big boulders and slide in behind them so I can show you why I brought you in here." Victor was still hot and took another big swig. Then he put the bottle down next to the bag. Percy took the torch with them as they went down into another room, where Percy lit more torches on the wall.

Victor looked around, still confused. There were locked trunks everywhere. Percy went over, unlocked one, opened it, and turned to look at the expression on Victor's face. The trunk was filled with old gold coins. "Holy crap, Percy!" Victor exclaimed. "Where did all this come from? Why is it here?"

"Banana money," Percy said, smiling. "Victor, you're one of my best buddies ever. I trust you to not tell anyone. After the Civil War my daddy's family lost almost everything. The paper money he had was worthless. He started collecting gold instead of paper money. I pay some boys from Cloud's Cove to guard the place. They think I've got a moonshine still in here. They understand about keeping people out. Don't ever try to come here without me. They will kill you...no questions asked.

"My daddy fought for the Confederacy because he believed in states' rights. He, like a lot of other Southerners, did not fight for slavery. He fought side by side with his brothers and neighbors. After the war he never held it against the Negroes. He loved them for who they were in their hearts, not the color of their packaging. Remember his funeral? Half the folks who came were Negroes. They came because they loved him for being a kind and decent man. Victor, some of the most important people in my life are not white. So...Victor, please tell me why you have such a problem with black people."

To Percy's surprise, Victor seemed to be willing to speak the truth. "When I was seventeen years old, I started seeing the most beautiful girl in all of Louisiana, but she was not white. We were completely in love with each other. We only met in secret. One day my pappy caught us. We told him about our love for each other. He beat me so hard, I could see out of only one eye. Then two of the farmhands held me down while two others raped and beat her. Pappy made me watch while he beat her with a whip until she died.

"They loaded me into a wagon and laid her broken body inches away from me. I didn't touch her. I hurt too bad to move, so I just stared at her until the wagon finally stopped. Every part of my body was in pain. I knew by the smell that we were in the swamp. Only swamps hold the smell of musk, mildew, and mold rolled into one with other smells of rotting and dying. My body was propped up so I would be forced to watch the next horrifying act. My head fell to the side, so Pappy took both hands and held my head up straight, so I had to witness the next move with one eye.

"One man threw a stick or something into the water. As it hit, alligators started jumping into the water, ready to eat. Next, the men took Merissa's body...Merissa was her name. They dragged her beaten body like it was a slaughtered farm animal. They tossed her in the direction of the gators. Only half her body went into the water. Instantly, three or four gators were tearing her apart in different directions. My love killed this seventeen-year-old girl, and I have lived with the guilt my whole life.

"My pappy blamed the Negroes for the Civil War and his losses from that war. His pappy, my grandpappy, and two of my great-uncles were killed at the Battle of Vicksburg. As a child at Lake St. Joseph my pappy saw Union soldiers enthusiastically pillaging the plantation. Then they burned the plantation house and the surrounding buildings to the ground. They left only one small home standing. It was a reminder of all that was lost. Hell, the Union army had as many slave owners as the Confederate army.

"Pappy's hatred went to the surviving Negroes in the area. Never once did he put himself in their shoes. The Negroes didn't ask for any of that war. Most were kept illiterate and had no understanding. Many of the freed slaves stayed in the area, only to be subjected to even worse treatment than when they were enslaved. They still didn't have any rights.

"I was devastated by Merissa's murder. I knew I could not get close to any Negro again, to protect them from mean sons of bitches like my pappy. Percy, I don't know what happened to me. Maybe I started believing my pappy, and somehow I thought I had lost Merissa because it was her kind's fault. I don't know. I'm so confused right now. I don't know why I hate niggers. Maybe I don't. I know I'm not as bad as my pappy, but…I'm confused, Percy. I've never loved anyone ever again, except maybe you, Percy…in a different way. You're like a real good brother to me."

Victor stared out at one of the lanterns. He was regaining some of his composure. "Don't know where that came from. Now, why do you have all this gold in a cave?" he asked.

Percy's face looked shocked at Victor's honesty. He had never heard him be so emotional and truthful before. "Oh, the gold…the government. In 1893, Daddy started saving gold when there was a run on gold in the US Treasury. As you well know, in 1913, the politicians pushed through the Sixteenth Amendment to 'soak the rich.' Only the problem was that the super-rich, like John D. Rockefeller, the Standard Oil man; J. P. Morgan, the financier-banker; Andrew Carnegie, the captain of the steel industry; and a few others owned these politicians. They made sure the new tax bill contained a provision to exempt religious, charitable, scientific, or educational purposes. These multimillionaires had these kinds of foundations set up long before this new income tax was in place. President Wilson was just their most recent patsy.

"So, Victor, I'm afraid that this tax will grow and grow. Income tax is awful and has stolen the right to privacy and property rights, which were given to us in the Bill of Rights, Article Four. Anytime Congress wants, it can take a hundred percent of our income. All they have to do is use the Internal Revenue Service as the police force over us.

"My daddy said, 'Son, get paid in gold anytime you can,' and I have followed that advice. During the Great War, I gave more than half my gold to fund our nation's efforts. I bought up hundreds of acres of swampland over in Muscle Shoals to contribute the nitrates for ammunition and explosives. I thought I would be stuck with it.

"A few weeks back, Henry Ford and Thomas Edison came to look at the unfinished Wilson Dam with a vision of transforming the Shoals into a metropolis. Ford said, 'I will employ one million workers and build a city seventy-five miles long at Muscle Shoals.' The very next day I got a long-distance telephone call from a fancy know-it-all Wall Street fellow. He offered me one hundred times what I paid for it. Won't that smarty-pants New Yorker feel stupid if Ford's deal is turned down by Congress. I got paid in gold for it yesterday."

As Percy poured the gold coins out of the heavy canvas bag into a trunk, he added, "I had to pay the government seven percent on that gold." Percy turned and pointed to other trunks. "I made all this gold before 1913, when the Sixteenth Amendment was enacted.

"All of the trunks you see here are full of old rare gold coins and gold artifacts. I don't completely trust politicians or you fancy bankers to not screw up our paper money. You could say I'm a holdover from all of my daddy's stories about Confederate money being worthless. I guess the acorn does not fall that far from the tree. That war was just sixty or so years ago. Now we have this Federal Reserve bunch, and I don't trust them with my money either."

Percy turned and stopped right in front of Victor. "You better swear to me right here and now that you'll never speak of this gold or location to anyone."

Victor immediately replied, "I swear."

"It all goes to my beautiful Molly and Shasta if something were to happen to me anyway. Those two love it in here," Percy added with a loving smile on his face. Then he said, "Victor, how long have you been wanting to tell me about Merissa?"

"Hell, I never wanted to tell anybody about her. For the life of me, Percy, I have no idea why I told you," Victor said honestly.

Percy thought for a minute about Shasta and her plan to use truth serum on Suzette. "Victor, what is your personal bank account number?"

"That's easy. It's 8171871, Merissa's birth date...I had almost forgotten why I used that number," Victor said as his voice trailed off.

"Stop, stop, and stop. I didn't really want to know. You're just being truthful. You can't drink any more of that wine marked 'SPECIAL,' okay?"

"It was really good wine, Percy," Victor said.

"I'll get you another bottle, Victor. Just don't drink any more of *that* bottle. You're coming home with me. I can't let you around anyone else for the rest of the day. Molly will be glad to see you. Maybe you can cook something special for us. I'm always telling her you cook better than any woman I know."

"Well, let's go then. We still have to put all those rocks and snakes back where they belong, don't we?" Victor said, looking here and there as if in a daze, which he was.

FIFTY ONE

BIG DREAMS OF TAYLORSVILLE, THE HARBOR TOWN

Percy and his brother, Chase, often shared time poring over papers and maps on the large dining room table at their parents' old house in Taylorsville. This particular evening, Percy was entertaining a few close friends, including Doc; Victor, the banker; Jagi, his son-in-law; and Hugh, his best friend and Huntsville's wealthiest Negro. Hugh preferred to keep a low profile. He let people assume he was just a chauffeur and butler for Percy. Of course, everyone already knew they had been best friends since childhood. They had been inseparable even back then.

Usually if Percy made money at something...so did Hugh. Hugh was a lot like Percy. He was a very generous man, giving large donations to the Mount Olive Baptist Church for Negroes. He was forever contributing to the Rosenwald School when it needed improvements or supplies for the children. One of his more passionate projects was fund raising for the Councill High School for Negroes on St. Clair Avenue. His ambition was to have an all-brick building as Huntsville's first public high school for Negroes. It was named after the founder of Alabama A & M University, William Hooper Councill, who had himself been born into slavery.

"I have all of you here tonight to keep you up to date on the big dream called 'The Harbor Town of Taylorsville,'" Percy said as he unrolled the master plan Chase had drawn up. It was an architectural rendering of the future town. "I know some of you think this is a far-fetched idea, but I'll borrow a quote from our great president, Calvin Coolidge: 'Doubters do not achieve; skeptics do not contribute; cynics do not create.'" Percy observed those around the table and looked at Victor. "Are there any doubters here today?" Then he and Chase went on to explain each area in great detail.

"I want this town to be a port city," Percy said. "We have the river for large boats and ships, and with the coming Tennessee Valley Authority dam system, we can accommodate even larger boats. We already have the railroad coming right up to our front door. We've known for years how dangerous the fast currents are down at Ditto's Landing, especially at Burdine Shoals. There's always the possibility of cargo or people falling into the water over there. I want to dig out this cotton field right here." As he pointed to the area on the map, he continued, "We can dig it deep enough to accommodate the *Delta Queen* so it can dock and safely unload her passengers. It is not due to be finished until 1927, so we have time. From what I'm told, she'll be able to accommodate a hundred and seventy-six passengers. Once she's built, at her beam, she'll be fifty-eight feet wide and two hundred and eighty-five feet long, and her draft will be right under twelve feet."

Victor asked, "What is a *Delta Queen?*"

Chase spoke up. "She's a paddle steamer they're building in Scotland. Basically she'll be a floating hotel. Taylorsville can be a destination for travelers on the Tennessee River."

Chase continued to describe their ideas for the future harbor town, pointing out details on the drawing. "Over here we will build shops for the travelers, and here we can have a big church in the town center. Next to it, we'll build a school. On this waterfront we can build a hotel, more shops, and some restaurants. In this area we can build a neighborhood of large houses on larger lots, and as we approach the town center… here…we can build smaller houses closer together.

"Everyone will be able to work, shop, and attend church and school without getting into a car or coach or riding a train. You can walk to your favorite saloon or restaurant. Maybe we could build some movie theaters, since they are becoming popular. We'll build the town center up so it can never flood, by using the dirt we dig out of the marina."

Percy jumped back into the conversation. "Ships can tie up right over here next to the railroad tracks. We can develop a system to unload the ships onto the trains more efficiently and vice versa. Jagi has experience and friends in the shipyard business. As Chase mentioned, this is a perfect location to build a hotel at the point. Can you imagine the view down the river from the upper floors?

"I've know that someday soon people will purchase smaller boats just for pleasure. Last week I ordered a Chris Craft from Smith and Sons Boat Company for Molly. Hugh and I are already looking into securing a dealership. We would put the smaller boats over here next to Banana Joe's Saloon. I'd love to get a one-eyed pirate as a bartender, and maybe one of those big talking birds to greet folks when they come in the door. I bet Carlos could get us one from Brazil. He said there are lots of them in the jungles down there. I'd love to have a working lighthouse on the point opposite from the hotel."

Percy continued, "I know you must think it would be impossible to dig a hole this big with just manpower, but let me tell you this new idea I've heard about: dynamite. We used it in the world war to blow up bridges. Jagi knows something about it too. I think we could use it to blow up large areas of dirt and rock.

"Another new thing that I've had the opportunity to invest in involves a couple of farmers from Kansas. They want to call what they have come up with a 'bulldozer.' Basically, they are trying to attach a big blade to the front of a big tractor. It would push the dirt around that the dynamite loosens up, and we could do the work of ten men in a lot less time. The Kansas men haven't gotten a patent on it yet. We're working out a deal with them to come here and experiment until they get it right. I want to be their first customer as well as an investor for their start-up capital funding.

"Steam shovels will load the dirt onto trucks, and it'll be built up over here for the town center. What we will do is dig a dry lake. Weather permitting, we would keep a dirt dam between the dry lake and the river. We will build a creek over here for the water to return to the river and keep it moving constantly, to prevent stagnation and mosquitoes. Once everything is in place and the lake is dug deep enough, we'll blow up the dirt dam with dynamite. The river will then rush in to fill the lake, and we'll have ourselves a marina."

Percy's presentation was finished. He stopped talking and finally took a much-needed deep breath. He and Chase looked around for a reaction. His friends overwhelmingly approved, although Victor still thought Percy was merely a dreamer. Their support and confidence meant the world to Percy.

The big dream was shared that night with several others as the men returned to their homes. Ground breaking began thirty days later. The group that night had realized that a project of this magnitude would take years to complete.

FIFTY TWO

BOOTLEGGER RACE, 1924

After two years of delays caused by unusually rainy summers, the access roads for the power lines were completed on Wallace Mountain. Percy owned the land. The hundred-year lease to the power company would not begin for a few more years. The roads were completed earlier than the power company executives had expected because of Percy's ingenious idea of paying bootlegger convicts as laborers. Everybody won. Men got to stay out of jail and get paid by Percy or other contributors. The city didn't have to house or feed any of the convicted bootleggers.

The power company had cleared wide paths across the mountaintop and, most important to Percy, he had an unheard-of type of mountaintop racetrack. Rules had to be established for the race he proposed. Prize money had to be set. A date needed to be decided.

"Daddy, I've checked the farmer's almanac, and September should still be the driest month this year," Shasta said. "The corn should be harvested, so we'll have open fields for campers and plenty of parking for cars and wagons. We should move the livestock early so there will be lots of room for the vendors. I suggest the semifinal be Friday, September twelfth and the finals Saturday, September thirteenth. That gives us eight months to spread the word.

"I've come up with a flier with the dates and rules. Let's open the walk-up registration on Saturday, September sixth. We can have runoffs all during the week for the early birds. I want to make sure we have the details correct. You did say a five-thousand-dollar first prize, a five-hundred-dollar second prize, and a two-hundred-and-fifty-dollar third prize, right? Each entrant will pay fifty dollars. Only American-made automobiles."

Percy thought a minute and replied, "Shasta, all that sounds good. We should make enough money off the vendors to cover the difference in paying the prize money. We have to hope we will attract enough participants to make the race successful. I plan to post announcements at all the train stations throughout the country. When the fliers are ready, we can circulate them on the train cars that come through here every day. The big moneymaker during the event will be the gambling tent. The house always has the advantage, and I'll pull money from that for the grand prize, if it's needed."

A week before the event, the hotel rooms in Huntsville and the surrounding area started to fill up. The two fields designated for parking and camping areas were also beginning to get crowded. Some vendors were already set up. Additional off-duty police officers from Birmingham were called in for security at Taylorsville. The Huntsville police were all working overtime. Nobody had imagined that the event would be so successful before it even got started. The mayor of Huntsville opened the fairgrounds downtown for the overflow, in case it was needed.

Chase moved the cattle to the spare goat fields and had workers preparing and cleaning the fields. Dozens of ten-hole outhouses were scattered throughout the property. People bathed in the river. Percy had received more than a hundred race registration forms by mail. A head-count for those who registered in person was even better than expected. Qualifying races were to start one week before the race.

The vendors were set up in a circle around Taylorsville. Percy walked around and enjoyed seeing the newcomers and regulars alike. The air smelled of every imaginable food mixed together, including, of course, the usual cotton candy, popcorn, fried chicken, corn dogs, ears of corn on a stick, shrimp, and new potatoes with Cajun spices. Gibson, the barbecue man, had two tents with hogs roasting in a pit. Even Sam, the moon-pie man from a Chattanooga bakery, had a tent on food row. There was more than one medicine man's tent for selling tonics and magical elixirs. The Hunsucker Comedy Show had a crowd gathered around their stage. Cal Breed was blowing hot glass into colorful pitchers, bowls, and vases by using fire and human breath. Carmen Preston of Birmingham was making candles. Barkley Shreve had come all the way from Mobile with fancy cheese wafers. The Heaton farm had brought pecans from Clanton.

Not surprising to anyone who lived in the area, Lily's tent had the longest lines. Percy had to poke his head in around the back entrance to say hello to his dear Lily. She looked up as he came through the canvas doorway. "Percy, Percy, I can't thank you enough for sending your friend Dykes from the restaurant supply company. He had one of his men customize these huge deep fryers over here so that I can cook dozens of doughnuts at a time, but I still go to bed late and get up early to make the dough—in more ways than one. The more doughnuts I make, the more of them people want to buy.

"Look here: I want to show you how Mr. Monroe took plain paper sacks and put my name on the side. They cost me a bit more, but it gives me some advertising," Lily said as she handed one to Percy. "See here: 'King Crispy Doughnuts.' The man from New Orleans that I met at your wedding is here. He is still trying to buy my recipe. I told him making biscuit dough with yeast and sugar is all I do. After they rise, I poke a hole in the middle with my finger. I cook them in the hot oil for two and a half minutes, no longer, then pour glaze made from confectioners' sugar over the top while they're hot.

"That's all I do. He wants to pay me money for the recipe. I told it to him for free! Can you believe that? I don't know what else to tell him." Percy suspected Lily was leaving out a couple of ingredients or steps that she had not even thought to mention. They tasted too good to be that simple, but he didn't say anything.

She continued, "Look at all these women I have working for me. They have good jobs. No white women will work for a Negro. Did you know that? I suppose they had rather have their children go hungry."

All the time she was talking, Percy was nodding his head and eating the sweet delights. "See how much he's willing to pay," he said. "Sell to him and retire. Lily, you've worked hard all your life. I'm thinking about retiring myself—selling my entire operation. You can come with me and see the world. I've just about got Molly talked into it. I've been talking to a fancy rum-runner from up north. He wants to expand his operation. The feds have been on me hard these past couple of years. Let's get past this week, and we'll talk some more. You, Big Mama, and Hugh are my family as much as Shasta and Molly. Don't you ever forget that." Lily was wearing a big smile as Percy departed.

Even with a five-dollar cover charge, the gambling tent stayed full, as did the adult entertainment tent next door. Molly had brought in extra prostitutes from San Francisco. Money and booze flowed in all week long. Streetwalkers were banded and arrested if caught. Molly always said that the *pro* in *prostitute* stood for "professional." She believed that a woman needed to work at an establishment, versus being a hooker on the street, for her own safety. The women were paid well, had free health care, and were provided birth control, legal assistance, housing, and meals. The best dressmakers were brought in to keep the women stylish, and child care was provided for any with children. Molly's women were considered affluent in most circles because they owned property, held bank accounts, and could afford the finer things in life—all without being married. Most people were unaware that they also paid taxes.

The city had more visitors than residents that week. For the first time in years all the politicians on both sides were happy. The tax coffers were filling up. At one point during the week, five hot air balloons landed, a major attraction because of the fact that they were an oddity to the people of the area. Familiar to the locals, a small red-and-white aircraft was flown over the site by Mike and Donna from their small private landing strip up the river, followed by Jarod, the first local treetop flyer, in a big yellow bush plane.

Race day arrived. The semifinal races had been held the day before, and the entrants had been narrowed to fewer than forty finalists. Although disappointed, those who didn't qualify as finalists were still pleased to be a part of this first-of-its-kind race, and the crowds had loved the semifinals. Everyone was looking forward to the final race with excitement and great anticipation. The out-of-town visitors thoroughly enjoyed the southern hospitality and the ambience of the event.

The most talked-about event of the week was a prank played on the cheaters. Some of the men who worked on the track held a "private race" not affiliated with the official Bootlegger Race. The cheaters were told of a shortcut that would give them an advantage. The pranksters paid some of Molly's girls to run naked along the "shortcut" and distract the cheaters. This rather extreme distraction caused them to think from the wrong end. As naked women jumped out of the woods, the cheaters would follow a pair of breasts to their own doom. Lured from the real track, they sped over a small hill at the bottom of Wallace Mountain, which led them steeply down a ramp and then turned them high into the air over the train tracks below and finally into the river at high speed.

The crowd roared with laughter and never tired of watching the angry drivers swim away from their sinking automobiles. Of course, it worked for a while before the word spread around to other drivers.

Percy tried his best to get Molly to watch the semifinals from up high in a balloon tethered by a rope to the ground. She refused. So did Sugar. Shasta gave little Alfy the okay based on Percy's promise to tie his grandchild to his back. Big Mama was having none of that. Even though she was getting old, she toted that baby around and was not about to let him go with his crazy grandfather's whims of rising into the sky with the birds. Alfy cried to go with Grandpapa, but Big Mama acted like she didn't hear a sound from the wailing baby.

Jagi delivered the list of finalists to Percy from the registration desk and told him, "Percy, the man in the gold Rolls-Royce told me he worked it out with you to enter the race."

"Yes, Jagi, a 'big moneybags from Boston paid a thousand dollars just to be in the race. Said he just wanted to be a part of the action and enjoy the thrill of the experience, with no claim to a prize. He has no intention of winning. I agreed, even though his car is from England. Joe is his name. He's in the rum business too. Apparently he makes a whole lot more money at it than I do. Now, let's look at the list."

"The finalists are…These are listed in order they registered?" Percy asked.

"That's the way Shasta organized them, and the order in which they start," Jagi replied. "After they complete the course, they'll finish in front of the stands at the horse track, making five final circles around the track. The officials will wave the flags to signal the last lap and announce the winners."

"Thanks, Jagi. Now let's go over the list…Blue 1921 Bour-Davis, seven passengers touring, red 1921 Hatfield coupe, cream 1921 Daniels Speedster, and a burgundy 1921 Heine-Velox limousine?"

Jag said, "I know…Who would have guessed? On the steep parts of the hills all the passengers got out and pushed. There are no rules against it, as long as the driver and one passenger stay in the car. It was hilarious watching the fancy ladies pushing that big car. When they reached the top, they all piled back inside and went on about the race. After they won that round, they walked around here in their high heels and wore lipstick like Molly's women. They told everyone who would listen that it was the most exciting thing they had ever done in their entire lives!"

"Were they all women?" Percy asked.

"Yes," Jagi said, laughing. "Including the driver. They were all, how do you say, 'drunk as—what is it you say?—'Cooter Brown.'"

"Okay, let's finish," Percy said, going back to the list. "Black 1922 Pierce Arrow coupe, burgundy 1922 Willis St. Claire A-68, red 1922 overland Sportster, bright red 1922 Mercer coupe, red-and-white 1922 Durant Model A-22, black 1922 Lincoln sedan, black 1922 Nash coupe, white-and-black Hanover Cycle Car Roadster with no year that I can see, red-and-black 1922 Marmon convertible coupe, green 1922 Handley-Knight sedan, red 1923 McFarlan, yellow-and-black 1923 Stutz-Bearcat coupe, green-and-checkered 1923 Checker Cab, black 1923 Essex Coach, yellow 1923 Kissel Gold Bug, red-and-black 1923 Jewett Roadster, light blue 1923 Cole Sportster sedan, black 1924 Sayers hearse…

"What the hell is that doing in this race—a hearse?"

Jagi laughed so hard, he had to take a minute to catch his breath. "The young driver said he's been practicing for months. Told me, 'The passengers never say a word'!" Jagi broke out in belly laughter again.

"Okay," Percy agreed. "We did say all makes and models and that they just needed to be American, didn't we? That makes twenty-two. How many more are there?"

"Just eight more for a total of thirty," Jagi said, still tickled about the hearse driver. "I wonder if he has a body in the back. We didn't make it clear if the passenger needs to be breathing."

Percy rolled his eyes. "Let's hope he has a live one with him if he wins. Let's see now…Black 1924 Chrysler sedan, green 1924 Chevrolet Superior, orange 1917 Brockway E-3000 pickup, gray 1920 Dodge Sedan, black 1922 Pierce Arrow, burgundy 1923 V8 Dual-Cowl sport sedan, gold 1924 Rolls-Royce, green 1923 Fargo truck. That sure is a variety of colors. I don't think I've ever seen an orange truck before. I wish Ford had not backed out on entering a coupe prototype they were thinking about…It had eight cylinders. They thought it might hurt their Model T sales."

Percy looked up from his list. "Is Molly still on the fence about entering? She thinks she's a better driver than any of them. You know my daddy taught her how to drive like a wild woman when she was just fourteen years old. She has never let me forget it either."

Jagi looked confused. "When did Molly know Grandpa Taylor? I thought she was from California."

"No, Jagi, she's from right here," Percy mused. "She was a lot like you and ran away from home when she was very young. I was lucky to get her back here to Alabama after many years away."

"Did she know Herman Deeley?" Jagi asked.

Percy reflected for a minute and said, "Yes, I think she did, but she may not remember him. Herman played his music at her fourteenth birthday party many years ago. He was the music man around here for a long time." Percy was staring into space, but shook it off and said, "Let's go find our lovely ladies before things get too busy around here."

Percy had to say his howdy-do's to all those he passed on the way. He reached Molly and Shasta and took it all in—how they both were so beautiful to him. "Percy, I've decided not to enter the race," Molly said. "I don't think there's a man here whose pride could take it if a woman were to beat him. Anyway, I think I do want to go up in the balloon and watch the final heat from a bird's-eye view tomorrow.

"Paul Tate, that motion picture photographer, arrived earlier today from Atlanta. He showed me where he wants to set up his equipment on the top row of seats on the new wooden stands you built. He brought a still photographer with him and wants him to be up high in the announcer's box. The newspaper journalists all have special access to the center of the track. Our entire event will be recorded, written about, and talked about for many years to come."

That evening, the final ten racers were paraded through the makeshift city on a float with Huntsville's mayor, Fraser Adams. To no one's surprise, like many other politicians, he was campaigning and taking credit for the success of the event.

Percy was indifferent to this sideshow of the parade, because word had gotten to him that the KKK was meeting at R. Craft's house only a short way down the road. Some attendees and participants were getting spooked. Percy was absolutely resolved that the race would not be a productive recruitment opportunity for the Klan. The next morning the chatter was about the race, not the explosion or the smoldering remains of a house down the road. As far as most were concerned, it should have happened many years earlier. Not a sign of the Craft family or any of the sheet-wearing organizers was ever again seen in the area.

Percy was met by a stranger that morning...a city slicker in a suit. The man stood out from the crowd, and Sugar growled at him and his assistant. Percy took notice of her behavior. Activities of every imaginable type were occurring all around them. Percy was walking toward the hot air balloon team in the southeast corner field when he was poked in his side with cold iron. "Get in, 'the Ron.' Don't ask any questions," the stranger said. Percy climbed aboard the basket of the rainbow-colored hot air balloon. The pilot was a bit startled at the sudden appearance of passengers. At the same time he noticed the gun pointed at Percy's head. "Take this bucket up high above the cotton for a ride," commanded the gun-toting mobster. "Don't take it over the water. I can't swim." The pilot complied with the demands, but he shook and prayed all the while. Nobody said a word as the balloon lifted away from Taylorsville.

Meanwhile, Sugar found Molly and pounced on her back from behind, behavior that was unusual for her. Molly immediately recognized

Sugar's distress and sensed danger. She went straight to the house and alerted Shasta and Jagi. Then she noticed the balloon lifting away. Jagi was looking through some new binoculars and saw Percy in the basket with a stranger holding a gun to his temple. "He's going to kill Percy!" he yelled to Molly. Frantic, Molly ran into the house, with Sugar close behind.

The pilot by then had the balloon about five hundred feet over the Taylor home. The stranger had cut the tether, and the balloon was slowly drifting toward the fields and the river. The stranger again pointed the gun at the pilot and said, "I told you, not the river."

The pilot, scared, said, "Sir, I have no way to steer the balloon... It floats where the wind blows. It will drift back over land just above Ditto's Landing."

"Okay, Benny can pick me up there," he said, standing as far from the two as possible with the hammer back. Percy knew it would be hard to get a jump on the man as he looked at the Taylor home below. Just moments before Percy started to make his move, there was a *swish* followed by a thump and Percy heard the report of his Remington far below. The stranger slumped to the bottom of the basket.

The balloon pilot followed Percy's lead and both men lifted the body over the basket edge, dropping it into the middle of the river. "Say hello to our friends in Dallas!" Percy said, laughing.

As the body fell through the air, Molly said to Jagi, "Who says pigs can't fly?"

Percy knew before they landed who had once again saved his life: Molly and his Remington. He thought maybe he should just give her that gun.

The pilot took the balloon down, and they headed back to the staging area, not sure what to expect next. Where was the goon's partner? Percy realized that he needed to hold a quick meeting with the fellows from Cloud's Cove to increase security and pay extra attention to cars with Illinois license plates. He also needed to speak with "the Cousin."

When they met with the police after landing, Percy and the pilot told the same story. The crazy man had obviously been suicidal as he held them at gunpoint, they said. Neither of them knew who he was or what he wanted, other than that he had shot himself and his body had fallen into the river. Percy and the pilot were visibly shaken, splattered with the crazy man's blood. One of the police officers asked them if they had also heard a gunshot from the ground, but both men claimed not to know anything about that.

Percy had Shasta call the telephone number of "the Cousin" at the bar in Brooklyn. She spoke with a French accent and was informed by someone at the other end, "Alfred wouldn't squeal to 'the Fox,' so he was taken out back. No one saw him…that is, until his body was found floating in the East River a couple of days ago."

Shasta told Percy and Jagi, and they were both shocked. "He was going to come to Taylorsville with me, from the beginning," Jagi said. "Things went so wrong for him. Why did everything turn out so wonderfully for me?" Jagi had been trying hard lately to get Alfred to move south. He wanted little Alfy to know his uncle.

Percy told Jagi, "We'll leave first thing Monday to go get Alfred's body and bring him to Taylorsville. We'll bury him next to my parents. My daddy helped Shasta send the letter you two found in Poland. I bet he will be delighted to have Alfred by his side for all eternity."

Percy felt awful and responsible. He should have gotten out of the business long ago. He had made all the money he could ever need. He knew exactly who to sell to now. Was this a coincidence or divine intervention?

Later in the afternoon, the racers were lined across a field waiting for the starting gun. When the race started, the cars moved in a wavy line at first, each driver trying to gain the lead position before the course narrowed and started up the mountain. The hearse took off first up the steep incline, with the red McFarlan close behind.

Percy and Molly were in the air. They had a radio to listen to the master of ceremonies on the ground, but the extension cord was not long enough. Fortunately the PA system was loud enough to hear most of the minute-by-minute updates. Other balloons were nearby with other onlookers. The weather was perfect, and the wind stayed calm for the duration of the race. The balloons were stable and anchored by long tethers high enough to see most of the four-hour race with binoculars.

Watching the cars from up high gave a completely different perspective. It was hard to tell just how steep parts of the track really were as the cars slowly zigzagged up and then began to go faster on the downhill slopes.

Crowds of people in the nearby woods waited and watched as the cars sped past. One group of people were barely missed when the beautiful red-and-black 1923 Jewett Roadster took one curve too many, going far too fast for the track, and slammed head-on into a tree. The driver and passenger got out with only their pride hurt. Percy understood how upset the driver must have been as he kicked the back tire and stomped on his hat.

It was a good thing they were out of the car: another out-of-control driver in a black 1924 Chrysler sedan smashed into the side, followed by the green 1923 Fargo truck. From up above, all drivers and passengers appeared to be out and walking around. Other cars zoomed on past the wreckage. No one was sure who struck first, but a fistfight broke out among some of the occupants of the wrecked vehicles. Emotions were high, knowing they were out of the prize money.

The Heine-Velox limousine and the Rolls-Royce seemed to be tied for last place. The women in the limo stopped a couple of times and got out, wearing skimpy swimsuits with matching hats. They posed as sightseers took photographs. The Rolls-Royce stopped and enjoyed a moment with the ladies. Then they suddenly all jumped back into their vehicles and got back into the race.

At the front end, the red McFarlan, the cream 1921 Daniels Speedster, and the light blue 1923 Cole Sportster sedan remained in the lead. The hearse never took the lead again. As the first three cars broke out of the woods, the crowds in the stands took to their feet, and the cheering began. They remained standing; the roar became louder as the McFarlan entered the track first. The red car stayed in the lead and pulled farther and farther away from the others. The announcer was screaming into the microphone. The hearse joined the group on the track after the others were on their second lap. Eventually, the last two showboats came rolling onto the track as the McFarlan was being flagged for the last lap.

Percy and Molly both could feel their hearts beating with excitement as they watched the flagmen wave the checkered flag to the winning

McFarlan. One car seemed to have run out gasoline as it came through the woods on the last hill. Total finishers...six!

To absolutely all the spectators' surprise, the winning driver stopped the car, pulled off his hat and goggles, and let down her long hair. "Yes, that is a woman!" came over the loudspeakers. No one could believe what they were seeing. A woman driver and her son got out of the car. The crowd went crazy and poured onto the track in celebration and disbelief.

"See there, Percy," Molly shouted above the noise of the crowd as she elbowed him in the side. "Women can be fast drivers and win races!"

Later in the afternoon, before the ceremony began, Percy's family met the three final winners. Everyone was eager to meet the woman driver and her small passenger. Percy introduced himself and his family. She said, "It's nice to meet you, Mr. Taylor. Thank you for sponsoring the race. My name is Dixie Bondurant, and this is my boy. We're from Bedford County, Virginia. My husband was robbed, shot, and killed while defending us on our way here to Taylorsville. In his last breath, Lee, my husband, told me, 'You can do it. Win the race without me, Dixie!' So my boy here and I did exactly what he told us. We won."

Molly wrapped her arms around Dixie and held her for a long, heartfelt hug. Then she asked, "How did you do it? How were you able to go on after such tragedy?"

"I'm not sure," Dixie said. "I felt his presence in the car as I drove. Jace was unusually silent. I could almost hear Lee's voice in my ear, telling me when to change gears, when to slow around curves, and when to put the pedal to the floor. Our dream was to move to the coast. Now we have the money to start over." She put her hands on the head of her son, Jace, and turned around. "Where is that hearse driver? I have the money to bury Lee now."

Clouds of dust arrived before the 1921 Daniels Speedster stopped just at Percy and Molly's feet. Teenager Mary Margie jumped out, almost spitting nails, she was so mad. "Percy, I did everything in my power to make it on time. Those brothers of mine just had to go and use dynamite somewhere here in Taylorsville last night. Just as I was paying up to bail them out of jail, that old bird of a sheriff arrived, trying to write me a ticket from a week ago. So we jumped back into the Speedster, took off, and left the grandpa sheriff just standing there. He took off after us and chased us all the way out to Madison. He finally quit chasing us when his tank went dry. I was kind, like my mama taught me, so we went back and took him some gasoline. Right when he finished lecturing me, I jumped back in and we sped away. He didn't chase us, so I reversed just to tempt him to chase me again. He yelled at me, waved his hands in the air, and said to 'Go on,' that he had better things to do.

"Sorry I missed your race, Uncle Percy. I really could have used the money," she said.

Percy wrapped his big arms around his rowdy niece. "Mary Margie, sweetheart, I told Linda Gail's family I would take care of you. Maybe you should slow that Speedster down a bit around the sheriff."

She shot Percy a pouting look. "Why would I want to take away all the fun?"

They both started laughing and headed over to the refreshment tent. Percy said, "You're definitely kinfolk of my daddy, with all that crazy driving. Are you sure he didn't teach you how to drive before he died?"

"Not unless he taught a six-year old baby," she said.

"Your daddy, Officer Lanier, was a great policeman," Percy said. "We were so sad to hear he died in the line of duty. Huntsville's loss."

"Percy, before he was shot, he told me our family was very special, that we were related to President George Washington," Mary said, giving him that "You better tell me the real truth" look.

"Yes, he was correct. You are kin to the first First Family," Percy said.

FIFTY THREE

NATIONAL FOOTBALL CHAMPIONSHIP, 1926

Percy and Molly had spent the better part of the year traveling to see all of Percy's old rum and banana distributors to ensure they would stay with the new owner. They had made a fortune off selling their businesses to Joe in Boston, which included their ships that had been working the Cuba and British Honduras imports for some time.

After the success of the Bootlegger Race, Percy turned over the operations of future races to the city, a move that kept the feds out of town, out of the adult tent, and, most important, out of the alcohol-filled gambling tent. He found out later that the goon from Chicago had been sent by "the Fox," who was setting up a gambling city in the Nevada desert. He apparently had thought Percy was cutting in on his action, information that was pressed out of the goon's partner left on the ground. Cloud's Cove security was able to work wonders out of the squealer...appears there was also a reward for him back in Chicago. They turned him over to Brad 'Dog' Salvage and his wife, Patti, up from Birmingham to see the race. "Yeah, I'll carry the sumbitch to Chicago for the bounty," Dog said.

In memory of Alfred, his young widowed bride, Josephina and their two children, Percy chose to sell everything to Boston Joe. Someone mentioned that a similar car race had been tried in Massachusetts, but it never came close to the success of the Taylorsville race.

"Molly," Percy said, "let's talk about planning a trip to Pasadena to see our Alabama football boys play for the national championship. Game date is January first...four weeks from today. The train trip takes five days. I hope we can show all the naysayers across the country that Alabama can compete as well as any team in college football. The snobs of football think our team players are nothing but a bunch of farmers in uniforms. We can compete! I just know it. I'd like to get a lot of people on the same train as the players to show our support. Alabama is my alma mater. How many people do you think we can get to go with us? We'll be gone over Christmas. If the players can sacrifice the holidays, so can we."

Percy's battle cry for his team was met with overwhelming support. So many people from Huntsville agreed to participate in the train convoy that extra trains were added for that day. Many had to go ahead of the team's train, during the days before. Alabama's presence would definitely be noticed in Pasadena at the 1926 Rose Bowl.

While waiting for passengers to board the trains in Tuscaloosa, Percy noticed that Molly seemed unusually distracted and was looking off into empty space. It suddenly occurred to Percy that Molly's mother, Annie Teal, was probably buried next to Bryce Hospital in that area of the state. He got off the train to make some phone calls and nearly missed getting back on before it departed. While he was gone, his college roommate, Bo David Carter, and his wife, Jeannie, joined the group for the trip. Strange thing Percy noticed...Victor gave up his seat for the Carters and was now seated next to Olivia.

After departing Tuscaloosa, Coach Wallace Wade had the players get out at every stop and do sprints to get ready for the game. Watching the beefy players at each stop, Molly's girls decided to go to the game after all. Originally they had planned to go on to San Francisco after dropping off passengers in Pasadena. Molly warned, "Do not tempt any of these young men before the game. We want to win, and don't want the players worn out from extra activities. Not even for free. Leave them alone. Let's not have the rest of the country label our players as losers and a bunch of hicks."

Begrudgingly, they agreed. Martha, one of the cutest of Molly's girls, said, "How about on the way back? Do you care? I have my eye on one of those boys. At the last stop, he noticed me too!"

Molly laughed and said, "We don't care how anyone celebrates our victory. You go catch one if you can, Martha."

"Mazel tov!" said Charlotte the decorator. She noticed that people's faces looked puzzled. "Good luck, Martha!" Then they got it and laughed.

Molly asked Roseanne to close the Lady Luck Inn on game day so many of her customers and working girls, wanting to make the trip down from San Francisco, could attend the Alabama versus Washington game. "We need as many fans at the stadium on our side as we can get!" she told Percy. Percy was surprised at how much football spirit Molly had acquired since the trip began.

Charles Paddock, former Olympian and sportswriter, was at the microphone. The game was making its radio broadcast debut. "Ladies and gentlemen, happy New Year! Welcome to the twelfth Rose Bowl game here in sunny Pasadena, California, and its first-ever radio broadcast. We have the ten-zero-one national champs, the unbelievable Washington Huskies. We'd like to thank the Rose Bowl committee for extending an invitation to the nine-and-zero undefeated Alabama Crimson Tide in their first bowl game." Charles had to wait until the cheers from the Alabama side quieted down so he could continue. "To all my radio listeners out there, we have fifty-five thousand fans in the stadium today. You don't know what you're missing. I don't think I've ever in my life seen so many beautiful women as there are here from Alabama. Wow, what a great turnout. No offense, Washington ladies, but these women from the South have taken the breath away from all of us here in the broadcasting booth today.

"Now let's get on with football. Our Huskies are predicted to win today by several touchdowns. Starting for the Huskies…Now on to the Alabama starters…"

At the end of the game, a recap was told as many were still absorbing the upset of the century. "Ladies and gentlemen, we are still shaking our heads here in the booth, as are the fans on the Washington side of the stadium. It was said earlier this week that the Huskies were taking practice pretty lightly, and the Crimson Tide gave it everything they had today. Scoring all their points in the third quarter, Alabama is walking away today victorious with a score of twenty to nineteen. This may be the game that changes the South."

On the train ride home one of the women took a shot at one of Alabama's star players only to be told, "Ma'am, you sure are pretty but I have a girlfriend. We're getting married in June." That young man later became a Hollywood star.

Martha met her admirer, and somewhere on the train ride home they were married. She never went back to the business or to Huntsville ever again. Two of Molly's other girls got off the train in Tuscaloosa to enroll in school. Molly was happy for all of them. She planned to make the announcement when they arrived back in Huntsville that she was selling the hotel and going straight.

Meanwhile, Percy met the coroner at the freight car near the rear of the train. Molly was overwhelmed when Percy arranged for a graveside memorial and burial of her mother at Maple Hill Cemetery. It was just the two of them and a Catholic priest. Later that day she hired one of the historians of the county, Tom Rankin, to assist her in her family history search for information about a woman whose name was spelled Mollie Teal, who was also buried in Maple Hill Cemetery. Molly gave Mr. Rankin the box of letters she had received from Aunt Kelly at the ladies luncheon implying her real mother may have been the notorious madam in Huntsville in the late 1800's. It had taken a very long time, but Molly was ready to move forward.

A couple of weeks later, Percy said, "Molly, I have a surprise for you! While you were out, Tom Rankin stopped by to deliver the report you requested. Let's go to the farm and meet the other Mollie Teal at the Doughnut Tree. I have finished the new tree house and can't wait for you to see it."

"Percy, you are so funny—the only person I know to name a tree. Let's hurry up and go. I can hardly wait to see the tree house you have been working so hard on. Did you know that the morning we left the farm to go find my mother I climbed up into your old tree house? It was beautiful. When I climbed down the ladder, Lily was there and gave me doughnuts. That was the first time she and I met. So, in many ways you've given the tree the perfect name."

Molly about cried when they arrived and she saw how Percy in the simplest ways had the biggest heart. Instead of a ladder, a series of ramps were built from the ground so Sugar could join them. Sugar was getting older, and Percy wanted to spend every moment she had left comforting and spoiling her. The three climbed up, and next to the front door Percy had carved above two rocking chairs, in the tree, "Percy loves Molly." Molly was radiant and happy as she threw her arms around Percy's neck.

The view was incredible from so high up. Finally Percy said, "I've been building tree houses in this same spot since I was a child, and this is the best one so far. Come in; let me show you the inside. Pierre and Charlotte did all the fancy decorating. I really hope you like it." It was more than Molly could have imagined.

"Percy, before we look into my family history, there are a couple things that I always meant to tell you...I know a little late now, but for some reason I think you should know. As a joke I sent letters to Lawler blackmailing him and others. It was just a joke. I was only seventeen. I didn't mean for them the kill each other. And then there was Heaven's Gate Hunting Club..." Percy interrupted by gently putting his fingers on her lips saying, "You can talk all you want if you need to, but I hope you don't expect me to confess all the crap I've done. I sure don't want to run you off and besides...it would take too long." Percy and Molly looked at one another and smiled. They had an understanding.

Percy poured two glasses of wine and said, "Let's sit in the rocking chairs outside and read the report." The cover read, "Mollie Teal 1852–1899." The first page inside said, "Mollie Teal History." The first pages were a summary. Mollie was born near Nashville, Tennessee. Her father died when Mollie was four years old, and her mother fell into financial hardship. With no means to support herself and a small child, she began to operate a house of ill repute out of their home. This became a way of life to the young Mollie.

At fifteen years old Mollie Teal moved to Huntsville to be joined later by her mother. Although very young, she was able to purchase a house immediately. Her business of running a brothel became very prosperous because of the fact that Huntsville was running over with Union soldiers who remained behind after the war for the reconstruction of the South. Included in the file were real estate, tax, and probate records, personal interviews, personal letters, and photographs of a beautiful young girl at different ages.

In 1891 Mollie gave birth to a baby girl and named her Molly. The father could have been the judge, the mayor, a police officer, the sheriff, or a riverboat captain—none of whom Mollie thought would make a good father. Percy looked at the photographs of young Molly with her beautiful mother, Mollie, and said, "Your mother looks familiar to me. I can't put my finger on where I would've met her. Maybe she looks familiar because you two look so much alike."

Determined not to have a third-generation prostitute in the family, Mollie sacrificed her only child, giving her to a cousin in New Hope and arranging for him and his wife to leave Huntsville and move to Nashville.

Her cousin Ivan and his new wife, Annie, the former Annie Overton, were thrilled with the new baby and vowed to love and care for her. As directed, Ivan and his wife never disclosed the identity of Molly's biological mother to anyone, including Molly. Mollie compensated them with monthly cash payments and tuition for college. Ivan died suddenly in 1898, leaving his wife and young Molly in hard times. Before Annie could contact Molly's biological mother, her evil brother David Overton came from Huntsville to Nashville, which resulted in a nightmare for the mother and child.

In failing health, angry, and unable to see her daughter, Mollie thought her cousin Ivan had double-crossed her and was withholding information when he did not show up for his monthly visit to bring pictures of young Molly and pick up money. Mollie Teal, a very wealthy woman, vowed that none of her relatives would ever inherit any of her money or other property. Some believed Mollie Teal died of a broken heart. She left her Victorian mansion to the city of Huntsville to be used as a hospital.

When she was only eight years old, Molly's uncle David Overton had kidnapped her and had his sister institutionalized.

The report continued and was very thorough. After Molly and Percy finished reading it, Molly put down the papers very gently, as though they were fragile and would break. "Percy, I simply cannot believe this report, the timing of everything. This needs to be in a book! If this is all true, we were just at the cemetery where my blood mother and grand-mother are buried side by side, not too far from where we just buried the only mother I ever knew and still love as my mother, one I know loved me. But who would read a book about generations of madams?

"I want to go to the Huntsville Infirmary and find out more. Maybe they still have some of her things. I need to go before the new hospital is opened and they throw away important things in the move.

"Percy, I've really never wanted children because I was afraid if I did have a child and someone did to them what happened to me, I'd kill them...in cold blood...I'd kill them. Now, after reading this report, I'm even more sure I don't want any children. I am as happy as I can be with your grandchild and all of Grace's kids too."

Percy looked at her sadly and said, "Molly, I'll do whatever you want, but I do think you would make beautiful babies. I also think you would make a great mother. I give you my word as a gentleman that if you ever change your mind, I will lay down my life to protect our children." Percy picked up the report. "What I get out of this is that you were loved by two mothers, and so was I."

FIFTY FOUR

MIAMI HURRICANE, 1926

Percy got word from South Florida about a hurricane that had gone through, leaving great devastation and a gruesome aftermath. The storm was bearing down on the Alabama coast, and forecasters feared an outbreak of tornadoes throughout the southeastern states.

Percy and Chase were preparing the farm for what could be disastrous tornadoes spun off from the hurricane that was now almost certain to hit south Alabama. Their fear was that the storms would arrive during the night that they were planning a really big get-together at the farm. Percy thought, *What the heck*. It was a celebration of family and friends. If there was a tornado, he had a storm and wine shelter that would protect all his guests. He would have someone listening to the radio and watching the evening sky. He decided to not cancel the party.

Luckily, the guest list that afternoon and evening included his family: Molly; Shasta; Jagi; little Alfy; Alfred's widow, Josephina and her two children; Big Mama; and Lily with her new husband, Charles, the chef from New Orleans. Chase, who had finally made Heather his wife, was now living at the farm. Hugh, his wife, and all their children were invited. Doc Reynolds had married Della Downes, the ballerina. They were already at the farm, having arrived the night before.

Victor, the banker, brought Olivia. They pretended she was helping him with a health issue and in writing his memoirs...but a few trusted friends such as Percy knew the truth. Most of the farmhands and workers from the construction site of the harbor town arrived last.

Percy was worried sick about Grace and Preacher Travis. They had taken all their children, and many in their church, to the cabins in Gulf Shores. Grace hated water and was afraid of drowning. Percy did something he wasn't that familiar with: he prayed for his sister and her family's safety while they were in the houses on stilts along the coast.

Percy and Chase had excused themselves and gone out on the top deck of the farmhouse. Together, they leaned on the rail and a porch column and looked out over their beloved farm at Taylorsville. The cattle had been herded to a field without trees and were all lying down. The other livestock were in barns close to the foot of the mountain. At the construction site, all the equipment and supplies had been gathered together and covered.

Chase was looking out at the horizon with Percy's binoculars. "Did you hear about Craft?" he asked.

"Last time I heard about him, he was working for the revenuers," Percy replied.

"He was assassinated driving in from Gurley to Huntsville," Chase said.

Percy turned and stared at Chase. As he turned back to look at the approaching storm, he mumbled in a low voice, "I should have done it myself."

Chase yelled out, "Percy, I see one! It's coming over Lacey's Spring. I'll go get everyone into the wine cellar." He handed the binoculars over to Percy as he turned and quickly left to go warn the guests.

Percy looked out over the construction site in the direction of the coming twister. "Son of a bitch! I know Chase wanted me to see the twister coming from the west, but I swear I see that little turd Chip down at the construction site. He's back. Unfinished business bites me in the ass every time. He's walking around the dynamite building."

Percy put the binoculars down. Time to head for shelter. The storm was starting to sound like the roar of a fast-moving freight train. Everyone else was in the shelter by now. Percy, with Sugar by his side, walked down into the cellar.

As he passed the last window, he stared at the old oak tree across the field. He believed in the Doughnut Tree...not Herman Deeley's hundred-year curse on the area. He looked at the old oak standing strong in the face of the coming storm, waving her branches as if she were trying to shoo it away. He wished he could reach out and comfort the old tree. *I pray she makes it*, he thought.

Some of the other trees began falling as he closed the door to the cellar. Percy had a smile on his face and chuckled softly. He couldn't wait to tell Lily what he imagined he had seen.

THE END

AUTHOR BIOGRAPHY

Catherine L. Knowles considers herself an unlikely author. As a child she often skipped school, preferring adventure to the classroom. She discovered early on that you cannot pirate a Tennessee River dock and use it to float to the beach.

The inspiration for Knowles's ideas come from watching the waters of the Tennessee flow past her home in Huntsville, Alabama, where she and her architect husband live with Sugar, their spoiled-rotten rescued dog.

Caught up in her husband's quest to rebuild the small abandoned town of Taylorsville a half-mile from their home, Knowles found herself deep in the library archives researching the region's history from 1900 to 1926. A woman who once skipped history class became hooked on the past, and her imagination of what it was like to live in this remarkable period of Alabama's history...a passion that led to *The Doughnut Tree*.

www.thedoughnuttree.net

This web site contains photos, links and other information on this colorful period in Alabama's history.

Made in the USA
Columbia, SC
04 February 2020

87500521R00200